The Forgotten Daughter

The Forgotten Daughter

RENITA D'SILVA

bookouture

Published by Bookouture

An imprint of StoryFire Ltd.
23 Sussex Road, Ickenham, UB10 8PN
United Kingdom

www.bookouture.com

ISBN: 978-1-909490-27-7

ACKNOWLEDGEMENTS

A huge thank you to Bookouture for your continued belief in me, to Oliver Rhodes and Lorella Belli for all your help, advice and tireless efforts in making my books reach a wider audience. I am so grateful to Oliver Rhodes for another beautiful cover – once again, it surpassed everything I had imagined and hoped for, and also for the idea that the whole book hinged on. This book would not have been possible without my wonderful editor, Jenny Hutton, who managed to look beyond the first and subsequent drafts to what the book could become. Thank you.

Also, a big thank you to my family – my children who kept tabs on word count, cheering when I reached my quota for the day and nagging when I didn't, and who did not complain when it was pasta, yet again, for dinner; and my husband who took over all the chores so I could write and put up with a wife who was spending more time with her characters than with him.

And thank you, reader, for buying this book. Happy reading.

To my grandmother, Mary Rodrigues,
Ba – the best cook in the world.

And to Loy – you make it all possible.

With Love.

Chapter 1

UK

Nisha

The Incompetent Messiness of Tears

My mother:

1) She bit her lower lip when she was thinking.

2) A dimple danced in her left cheek when she smiled. She was annoyed by it and would complain: 'Why only my left cheek—why not both?'

3) She wore her hair in a bun at the nape of her neck. On the rare occasions she set it free, it tumbled down her back in a velvet cascade of curls.

4) She walked with a slight limp, a legacy of an accident when she was younger, which is why she never drove.

5) She hated cooking.

6) She loved crime novels.

7) She bought suits six at a time from M&S and wore them to the office, alternating between each. At weekends she lived in T-shirts and jeans. She never wore dresses or skirts. For funerals, weddings and other celebrations, she wore her suits.

8) She rarely laughed but when she did, it was a loud guffaw bursting out of her chest in a snort.

My father:

1) He was six foot six, tall for an Indian, and in my eyes a giant who could do no wrong.

2) He was a reserved man. But when I was little, he would carry me on his shoulders and from that vantage point, I imagined I could see the whole world. This is my only recollection of him physically interacting with me.

3) Whilst on his shoulders, I also had a bird's-eye view of the ever-widening bald spot on the centre of his head, and he would ask me to tabulate the rate at which it was growing. We created a chart, drew a graph of the results. 'So, how is the world looking today, Nish?' he would ask every morning. 'Fine, thank you,' I would reply politely, snug on the throne of his shoulders, queen of all I surveyed. 'And how is the bald spot?' 'Growing, Daddy.' 'Not good, is it, eh?' he would sigh. 'Well

you know what to do,' and he would pass me the tape. I still have the tabulated results with me.

4) He had Type 2 Diabetes and was not allowed sweets but would sneak them into the house and eat them when my mum was not looking. He was caught once or twice and tried blaming me, but that didn't fool my mum any.

5) His favourite sweets were the Haribo eggs. I would suck out all the gummy yolk and put the creamy whites back into the pack to torment him.

6) He was a quiet, soft-spoken man, except for his snores. Booming bursts like the cannonball that fired once when I went to a castle on a field trip with my class. I was the only one who didn't flinch. My mother slept with earplugs in.

7) He had a mole at the centre of his chin, in lieu of a chin dimple he always said, with a couple of hairs growing out of it. I chopped them off with scissors once when he was sleeping and watched with wonder as every day they grew back a little at a time until they were longer than they had been before.

8) He was always reading, never without a book. He loved nothing better than locking himself in the toilet with a tome on whatever subject he was into right then. He tended to lose track of time in there. My mother would bang on the door and yell for

him to come out, wondering why the smell didn't bother him; was something wrong with his nose?

Note to Self:

1) Thank-you cards—list of attendees in top drawer of desk in study.
2) Cancel Mum and Dad's credit and debit cards.
3) Research the science of dreams—specifically significance of jasmine scents.
4) Review the paper on statistical analysis of risk in a volatile climate and make notes.
5) Pull yourself together—you are back at work in three days.

Nisha is unravelling. She is the errant thread poking out the edge of a splendid tapestry, tempting, tantalising. One yank creates an angry slash across the multi-hued drapery. A few more and the tapestry folds into itself, disintegrates into a chaotic jumble of yarn.

Two urns in her bedroom—all that's left of her parents.

Her mother, crisp in her business suit, turning to wave goodbye, her features in silhouette, sharp, defined. Her mother's rare, warm smile, a gift bestowed, her eyes crinkling upwards at the corners like lines radiating from the sun in a child's painting. Nisha recalls the way a wayward wisp of hair escaped her mother's bun and painted a question mark on her forehead when she got home from work, the suit just a bit crumpled, the shirt hanging out. Her smell: perfume intermingling with sweat, sharp and sweet and musty. Uniquely Lekha.

Her father, the way he combed his sparse hair carefully over his balding head, the way he threw his head back and laughed. The way his laughter started somewhere deep in his stomach, reverberating through his body in infectious waves that always started her off.

She shakes her head to chase them away, these images that sting her eyes, which threaten to combust into tears. This is not like her. She is competent, practical. She shies away from sentiment—the silliness, the luxury of mawkishness. And yet in the last week, she has been a mess of emotions. 'Losing both your parents in one fell swoop would do that to you,' her boyfriend, Matt has said. 'Let go, Nisha, Give in. It's fine, it's okay,' he has urged.

But she can't. Not completely. She regards it as weakness. She doesn't like the loss of control that giving in to tears would bring, doesn't know how to deal with it. She doesn't know herself when she is like this and it scares her. She wants the certainty of knowing herself in this uncertain, unexpectedly bereft world she finds herself in.

And this is what she knows (as is her wont, she makes a list. It gives her something to do, calms her down):

1) I am a statistical consultant. I love my job.

Her parents always told Nisha that their profession defined who they were and she feels the same. The thought of her job brings with it a measure of peace. At the funeral, when things got too much for her, when she was in danger of breaking down, she did mathematical calculations in her head and that saved her. Psychologists would have a field day analysing her, she knows. *To each his own,* she thinks. Some people have alcohol, tobacco, drugs. She has the soothing solitude of sums.

2) I have organised the funeral and it went according to plan. The crematorium was full to bursting. My parents would have been proud.

The stinging feeling at the back of her eyes again. *Three days to go,* she thinks. She will go through their effects and then she will go back to work, lose herself in the indulgence, the calming order of numbers, away from this mess of emotion. She is fine during the day; she soldiers on. What she cannot seem to control are the nights. She is awake for a long time and then she falls asleep and dreams, vivid dreams that she cannot quite remember, that stay just out of her grasp: elusive, enticing. She wakes with the smell of jasmine in her nose, overwhelming her, engulfing her with nostalgia and yearning—for something she cannot name. She knows it is the smell of jasmine, sweet and haunting, and yet she cannot remember ever having seen the flower. She has googled 'jasmine' and the images look vaguely familiar: pale creamy white like the essence of a dream you cannot quite capture. She googles 'dreams, significance of jasmine' and one site tells her it denotes 'love, beauty, protection, happiness'. What a load of nonsense. Researchers disagree on the function of dreams; some say they serve no purpose at all, others that they help deal with trauma. She will read up on Freud, see why she is riddled by these particular dreams. Up until she lost her parents, she has always slept well, has never had a nightmare, her life proceeding on an even keel just as she had planned it in her many notes and lists. Which reminds her of one last thing she has to do.

❄ ❄ ❄

The solicitor is short, squat and balding. She towers over him. He fiddles with his tie as if it is strangling him as he sits down behind the polished walnut desk and ushers her into the seat opposite. Sitting down, they are the same height and she wonders whether his chair is higher or if perhaps he is perching on a cushion or two and then mentally chides herself for entertaining an inconsequential thought at such a time.

He clears his throat, his watery blue gaze flitting this way and that like a startled fox picked out by headlights before settling on her. 'Thanks for calling back and coming to see me,' he says.

He had called the day of the funeral but she hadn't had the inclination to return his call then. After the funeral, she had gone to the flat she shared with Matt and sat up in bed reading papers from work, the rows of figures, the precise array of mathematical calculations reassuring in their order.

He pulls at his tie again and she is impatient. *For God's sake, remove the bloody tie if it's strangling you,* she thinks, surprising herself. She is not normally like this. Is she—could she be nervous?

'Your parents left everything to you—the house and its contents. All their assets and possessions.'

She nods.

'And they also left you this.' An envelope, the pale pink of the inside of a rose petal, taken no doubt from the top of the pile that always sat on her mother's dresser: a sheaf of multicoloured envelopes in muted colours.

Her hand trembles just a bit as she takes the letter from the solicitor and she despises herself for this weakness. 'Nisha Kamath', penned in her mother's slightly sloping handwriting, neat like her mother had been.

'Thank you, Andrew.' Her voice is brisk with the effort it takes not to tear open the envelope right there and devour its contents. What is happening to her? Who is this person who has taken over the cool, poised Nisha she knows? 'Is that all?'

'Yes.'

She leans across, shakes his hand, wet, slippery as a dream just beyond grasp. 'Thank you.'

He smiles, a gash punctuating his plump face, looking relieved. 'If there's... um... anything you'd like to ask me...' He pulls at his throat again.

'Goodbye.'

The house reeks of the wilting flowers that dot the rooms in their multitudes, the orchids that her mother so loved: the purple of stormy seas clashing with the scarlet fury of a summer evening; the pale white and soothing yellow of sedate lilies, their heads bowed like nuns in prayer. The cloying smell she will always associate from here on with death.

The letter is a damning presence in her coat pocket, clamouring for attention. Her parents didn't know they were going to die—she only fifty five, he fifty nine. Her mother was planning a big do for her dad's sixtieth. They hadn't foreseen that they would go together, in a car crash. What was it they had to tell her that was so important that they had penned a letter and left it with their will, just in case?

She pulls it out. She has made herself wait until now, until she got back to her parents' house, driving with hands that shook as they clutched the steering wheel to punish herself for her uncharacteristic responses at the solicitor's office. This is what her parents would have done. They would approve.

She remembers the time her mother bought her a toy, a doll she hankered after, with sapphire eyes that miraculously closed when the doll lay down and opened when she sat up. Her parents had promised it to her if she performed well in her exams. She had aced all her subjects and her mother had taken her to the toy shop and bought the doll for her. Nisha had been on tenterhooks all the way to the till, but once she'd paid for it, her mother had not given her the precious doll. Nisha had begged and begged until finally her mother had said, 'You can hold it, but only open it when we get home, mind.' Nisha would have promised her mother the moon right at that moment just so she could hold the doll she had coveted for so long in her arms. She sat obediently on the bench in the grocery store, waiting for her mother to finish shopping, cradling the box with the doll she had christened Lucy in her arms. Her mother was taking *ages*. Nisha waited and waited, trying to ignore Lucy's urging: 'Please open me. I am trapped here.' 'I have to wait for my mum, Lucy,' she whispered. 'Pretty please,' said Lucy, winking, those gorgeous blue eyes smiling at her. By the time her mother called to her, Lucy was in her arms, the packaging discarded and forlorn on the bench. Her mother had not said a word, just held her hand out. Nisha had cried all the way home, silently—her parents did not believe in loud, messy sobbing—the tears snaking down her cheeks and staining her mauve top the inky purple of night. She had been convinced that the little girl who had been fortunate enough to walk past and be handed the doll by Nisha's mother was, right at this moment, pulling out Lucy's silky yellow hair, hitting her, hurting her. Nisha was convinced she could hear Lucy calling out for her.

'There is a time and place for everything, Nisha,' her mother had said softly that night as she tucked her into bed. 'Good things come to people who wait.'

I waited and waited for Lucy, she had thought.

Her mother had read her mind. 'You could have waited just a bit more, couldn't you? If you had, Lucy would be right here next to you now,' she had said, pulling up the duvet tight around Nisha's chin, bending down to peck her nose. Nisha had waited until the door closed behind her mother before smothering the hiccupping sobs that arrived in unappeased waves with her pillow.

When she did well in her next set of exams, she did not ask for a reward. And yet a doll appeared, identical to Lucy, nestling by her pillow still in its packaging, there when she came up to her room to change after school. She had removed the packaging carefully, kissed it, rocked it, spent hours playing with it. But she did not name it, half afraid it would disappear. It was still there somewhere in the loft, her Lucy replacement.

The envelope is thick, stuffed full of paper. She runs her fingers over the writing, picturing her mother's hand scripting her name with that precision she afforded everything, pulling back, scrutinising it critically, eyes scrunched, the way Nisha had watched her do a thousand times, blowing on it so the ink would dry. She strokes her name, knowing that this is the closest she will ever get to touching her mother again. Her parents left her a letter—that's good, isn't it? Then why is she so reluctant to open it, read what they have to say?

Because they were not the kind of parents given to sentiment, to elaborate avowals of love. She does not remember either of them ever saying 'I love you' to her, which is why she finds it so hard to say it to Matt, even though he tells her he loves her often and would like to hear it back at least once, she knows. Does she love him? She doesn't know. What is love anyway? Is it the warm feeling she gets in her chest when she is with him, the ache to see him, talk to him when he isn't around?

It eats away at her, this not knowing. She knows she loves her parents, irrevocably—that is a fact, unshakeable, solid. But romantic love? Why doesn't romantic love come with a set of ten theorems, say, that you can prove or disprove and, based on the outcome, decide whether you are in love or not? What she feels for Matt is special, that much she knows. She certainly hasn't experienced that depth of feeling for the boyfriends that came before. But does that mean she loves him? And when she is this doubtful, how can she tell him she loves him? And how does he know he loves her; how can he tell her that every day, even sometimes minutes after they've had a fight? How can she believe him?

She doesn't remember cuddles as a child. Whatever is in the letter, it is not a declaration of love; that much she knows. 'Emotions are a waste of time better spent working,' was one of her parents' favourite axioms. There aren't any pictures of her as a baby but there are several framed photos of her winning awards. Her parents paid for private schooling for her all the way through, always making sure she was aware of what they expected in return. 'We want nothing less than the best from you, Nisha. We know you can do it.'

She slits open the envelope. Several sheets of paper, the pale lilac of an expectant sky hankering for a thunderstorm. Her mother's handwriting, her father's signature. A knock at the door. *Oh, go away, leave me be.* A series of staccato knocks, persistent, increasing in tempo.

She stuffs the sheets back into the envelope, tucks it under the cushion and goes to answer the door. The florist, face camouflaged by a profusion of cream lilies pale as dawn's delicate brushstrokes lightening the drowsy night sky: delivery from a distant relative in Australia. She thanks the florist, shuts the door and leans against it for a brief minute, the wood cool at the back of her head like wet grass on a hot summer's day.

She walks purposefully to the sofa and scrabbles behind the cushion. Nothing. No letter. Confusion, unease, grief. And then she realises it is the wrong side, the wrong cushion. She retrieves the letter, telling herself to get a grip and, with a deep breath, opens it, starts to read.

'Dearest Nisha,' the words swim before her eyes. She blinks hot tears away. 'If you are reading this, darling, then that means we did not get around to telling you.'

Her stomach roils, the cereal she had for breakfast threatening swift exit. She presses a hand to her stomach, willing it to settle. *Telling me what?*

'You are adopted.'

What? The words sway before her eyes. There must be some mistake. She squints at them again. There they are, solid as the wall up ahead, which is, unfortunately for her, oscillating dangerously, swimming, drowning. She closes her eyes, clutching the cushion to her stomach, which recoils in protest. She runs to the bathroom, makes the sink just in time, is sick, loudly, messily. *Get a grip, Nisha.*

She rinses her mouth, welcoming the stinging feeling of the mouthwash. Everywhere else is numb. She stares at herself in the mirror above the sink. Her hair stands in messy clumps about her face, most of it having escaped the clip fastening it up at the back. Purple circles frame huge eyes that dot a face bleached of colour, the complexion sickly beige.

Who am I?

She runs her fingers down the ridged skin above her upper lip, a relic of her cleft palate, drawing reassurance from the one thing that hasn't changed.

She remembers asking her mother once, as she dressed for work, her hair in a bun at the nape of her neck, the syrupy smell of flowery deodorant, 'Is this hereditary?' fingering her scar.

Her mother had paused for a brief moment in the act of patting her hair in place. Her gaze, reflected from the mirror, had met Nisha's. There was something in that look, something Nisha couldn't quite understand at the time. Then her mother had turned away, busied herself with smoothing her trousers. 'No. No, it isn't.' Her mother who had taught her the importance of looking right at people when talking to them, holding their gaze.

'You are adopted.' She whispers the words to the girl in the mirror and she stares back, shocked, her lips moving in a ghastly echo.

The mirror steams. She is aware of her naked feet freezing as the cold seeps in through the tiles. *Perhaps this is my parents' idea of a joke*, she thinks, and her ghostly reflection, silhouetted in steam, perks up. Except, they didn't joke. Ever. Her parents had no sense of humour whatsoever. *Perhaps it is a forgery.* Her reflection attempts a smile. She watches the edges of uneven lips, one slightly higher than the other thanks to the cleft scar, try and curl upwards. They don't make it. Instead, they droop back down, defeated.

She hobbles to the sofa, circulation slowly returning to numb feet as they make contact with warm carpet, and picks up the letter.

Her mother's handwriting. Not a forgery.

How could she not have known? How could she not have had a clue?

She will not believe it. Where is the proof? She is someone who will not accept anything without proof. Her parents would approve, having drilled this axiom into her from childhood. *No baby pictures,* the voice in her head whispers. *There's your proof. There is a reason for that,* she thinks, indignant. Her parents are not sentimental. *Were,* she corrects herself, '*were* not sentimental.' And anyway, she remembers her mother saying something about a fire.

Let's assume for a moment that what is written here is true, the practical side of her blessedly takes charge. *All this time, why didn't my parents tell me? Why keep it quiet? They were scientists; they dealt in facts, numbers, the unshakeable proven truth. Then why didn't they tell me?*

The letter, words she cannot erase: 'We could not have children. My limp: a legacy of that accident I had. Well, my uterus had to be removed then. We were resigned to the fact. And then, during a trip to India…'

India? Her parents went to India? Her Westernised parents who lived Western lives and had never been to

India, at least not with her in tow? *She* has never been. And now, she's finding out that *they* have.

She remembers coming back from school when she was seven, 'Mum, am I from India?'

Her mother, tight-lipped, 'We are of Indian origin, yes.'

'Why don't we go to India?'

'Why do you ask?'

'There's this girl at school who is from India and she goes all the time.'

'Well, we don't have any family there, no ties.' Her mother had then proceeded to lecture her on roots and migration and they had spent the afternoon learning about immigration and the reasons for it.

As a family, they went to the US, to Canada, they toured Europe. But they never went to India on vacation. She has never thought of herself as Indian or even as someone of Indian origin. Yes, she has brown skin, but as far as she is concerned, she is English. British. She never fills those forms that ask her for her Ethnic origin. She feels she will be lying if she ticks the 'British Indian' box. She is not anything Indian. She is British and that's that.

She did learn to read and write Kannada, though, along with Russian and Chinese. Her parents had insisted she learn these languages alongside the French, German and Spanish she was doing at school, painstakingly coaching her in their spare time, being of the opinion that mastering languages opened the mind, boosted brain development. 'Why Kannada?' she had asked, curious, having never heard of the language until her parents decided she learn it. And her mother, her face suffusing with colour, her voice brisk, discouraging further questions, had replied, 'It's our mother tongue, your father's and mine.'

Nisha's eyes drag back to the sheet of paper in front of her. '...we found you.'

What do you mean, 'found me'? Found me where?

Facts. She wanted facts. Here they are in front of her. In black and white. She is adopted. A fact. Like any other. *My parents are dead. A car crash. A lorry driver asleep at the wheel.*

I am adopted.

'We might as well tell you—we were involved in a project at the time, Nurture versus Nature. And we were in India doing research. And then we found you...'

I was a project to you? Is that all I was?

A project specimen like the rats in their lab, the rats they called by fancy names: Harry, Henry, Hubert.

She cannot believe it. She is reeling, she is lost.

The letter, the words written in her mother's hand, swimming before her eyes: 'Yes, you are adopted. But you are precious, Nisha. You are loved.'

She runs a finger across those words. The closest her parents have ever got to declaring their love. Here it is. Proof. Of their love. Or is it?

'You are loved.' *You say that, Mum, in the same couple of sentences that also state I was one of your projects. So, how did you love me? Like you loved the rats who provided the proof for your theories? Or in my own right? For who I am?*

What a fantastic lab rat I proved to be, eh? What a brilliant argument for nurture trumping over nature!

From the moment she started school, her parents had made it clear what they wanted of her: she was to be high achieving, to do well in everything she tried her hand at. Dancing, drama, debating, music, academics. She never questioned it—she assumed it was their Indian roots. She had done a little research of her own, read somewhere that Indian parents are 'pushy'. The article said that because they had come out of hardship and poverty via education, they wanted the same for their children, if not more. The other Indian girls in her class moaned about their parents all the time. 'Whatever we do, it is never enough,' they huffed. 'They are always comparing us to the rest of you, and if that is not enough, to cousins in India. They are always wanting more from us than we can give.' Nisha had assumed that, even though her parents did not acknowledge their Indian roots, there was that ingrained fear of sinking back into bone-wrenching poverty, the worry of where their next meal was coming from (reasons gleaned from the article). In her more fanciful moments, which became few and far between as she grew older, she imagined it was because of this that they shunned their roots, because they did not want to be reminded of what they had been through to get where they were. They had got past it, they had survived. What was the point of ruminating? It made absolute sense for her no-nonsense, forward-looking parents.

There are a few more sentences: 'You were adopted from the Sacred Heart Convent, Dhonikatte, India.'

She stops. She cannot read further. Not until she has processed this information.

India. I was adopted from there. Why don't I feel any connection? Why can't I remember anything at all?

There are pictures of her flashing her broken-mouthed grin (the operations to repair her cleft palate were still ongoing then), looking starched and stiff in her uniform—she remembers the crisp new smell of it—on her very first day of school. She had just turned five. Her birthday is in May, so… Or is it? Did her parents know her birthday at all? Or did they just make it up? Surely they wouldn't? But if they had collaborated in such a big lie, kept this huge truth from her all this while, what else had they been hiding?

Her head aches. Her heart aches. She doesn't know how to deal with this. She is rubbish with emotions. Why did she call the solicitor? Why? What wouldn't she give to go back to when she knew for certain who she was, who her parents were.

She leafs through the notebook she always carries around with her, looks at the last entry, the list she made just that morning to calm herself down. The facts about herself: I am this, my parents are this…

I am not who I always assumed I was.

Matt. She wants to talk to him. He will ground her, he will talk her through the facts, he will sort this out. But he is at work, lecturing his class right at this moment, his phone switched off. Together he and his students will be working on a mathematical puzzle that at the beginning is just a muddle of numbers. Step by step, the numbers will be ordered, they will be multiplied and divided, added and subtracted and suddenly, the puzzle will make sense, the solution obvious. Matt will turn to his class and beam, 'See, I told you so. Every problem, however complicated, has a solution.'

'What is the solution to this, this mess I find myself in, Matt?' she will ask.

'Nothing. There is no mess. Let's approach this logically,' he will say. 'What has changed, Nisha?'

'Everything.'

'Everything?' He will smile, the left side of his face lifting upward in that lopsided grin she loves so much. 'Really? You are still you: brilliant, stunning, perfect.'

And he will hold her close and she will rest her head against his chest, the bulk of him reassuring in its solidity. She will breathe in his smell, musk and soap, and she will feel safe, the turmoil inside her easing a little.

Thinking of Matt calms her; her heartbeat decelerates, resumes its normal rhythm.

I was adopted from India sometime before I started school, before the age of five. A human being starts retaining memories at the age of three. Why don't I remember anything? Has my subconscious repressed all those memories? Why?

When she and Matt first started going out, he'd said, 'Nish, shall we go travelling round the world? We could start with India. I cannot believe you've never been there.' She had been adamant. 'Why should I go there? Just because I am of Indian origin? I do not feel Indian, I am not Indian. I am as British as you are.' She has felt no connection, no pull to the place. Never wanted to visit. And now, knowing what she does, she wonders, why not? *Why didn't I feel anything?* And where is Dhonikatte anyway? She needs to check, find out. Or does she?

She reads the sentence again. 'You were adopted from the Sacred Heart Convent, Dhonikatte, India.'

Sacred Heart. A picture of a benevolent Jesus, his clothes parted at the chest to reveal a heart pierced by arrows, red drops dripping onto white cloth, that she had seen somewhere once. *Does that mean I am Christian? Rubbish, Nisha, you know who you are. You do not believe in organised religion. Your religion is Mathematics; you worship at the altar of numbers, proven facts, solvable theorems. A piece of paper does not change anything.*

An echo of the dream that has dogged her these past few days: the smell of wet pews and sweat, camphor incense tinged with jasmine; the whisper of hymn books; the plaintive voices of nuns rising in song.

Why does she suddenly remember more of the dream? Is it a dream or her subconscious memory manifesting itself? Or is it her imagination, skewed and distraught by trauma and revelation? *What's happening to you, Nisha? How did the cool, practical woman come to be hijacked by this fanciful creature?*

'The phone number for the convent is 08202367867. In case you want to find out. Research your roots.'

Research. That word. *I am the living proof of the research project of two scientists.*

She flings the letter. It doesn't land far, collapsing with a soft sigh on the carpet. The oppressive smell of wilting flowers nudges in, engulfing her nose, making her want to gag.

A memory: coming to in hospital after one of the many operations she had to endure to fix her cleft palate. Groggy with pain, the faces of her parents swimming before her eyes. Worried, pale facsimiles of their usual brisk selves. 'Mum,' she says. And her mother beams. Absolutely glows. She bends down and kisses Nisha, and Nisha breathes in her mother's smell, that tart, sweet smell that is pure Lekha. Are those tears shining in her mother's eyes?

They loved me, they did.

My parents. The man and woman who gave me life. Who are they? She fingers the ridged skin above her upper lip. *Did you give me away because of this?*

'I am adopted.' She rolls the words around in her mouth, the fat syllables reverberating with shock, her murmur loud in the empty room, ricocheting off mourning walls dotted with drooping flowers.

Stop this nonsense, Nisha. This changes nothing. You are still you. And then, another part of her, '*Are my birth parents still alive? Why was I adopted from the convent? How did I end up there?*'

She pictures an alternate life, growing up in India, the India she has seen on television—bustling, colourful, noisy. A snort of startled, slightly hysterical laughter escapes her as she pictures herself in a sari, tall and willowy, waist peeking out of the red-and-gold folds draping her body, hair bunched back in a silky plait. *I am going mad.*

She pictures herself telling Matt, 'I am afraid I am finally giving in to whimsy.'

She throws her head back among the nest of cushions and laughs, and somehow the laugh morphs into a sob and Nisha, unflappable, unruffled Nisha who did not cry at her parents' funeral, who has kept herself together until now, gives in to the sobs which rend her slender body, reverberating through her like waves building into a tsunami. She is not a machine anymore; she is human, torn apart by feeling, by the fear creeping up her spine, destroying the certainty that has always been with her, the knowledge of who she is, as she gives in to the chaos, the incompetent messiness of tears.

Chapter 2

India

Devi

Cod Liver Oil

Ma,

It starts with a phone call—as these things do. A number is dialled, a number known by heart. A familiar voice is expected to pick up at the other end after which cheery hellos, how are yous and confidences will be exchanged, news will be bartered and gossip swapped. Instead, the number rings and rings, each subsequent ring more ominous than the first. Weight is shifted from foot to foot as slivers of unease worm their way up the spine. And then there is a sound at the other end, the thunk of the receiver being lifted, positioned in that snug space between one's ear and shoulder. The blur of static. A heartbeat of silence, a crackly hiss, then… a breathless voice mouthing hello, not familiar at all. 'Come home at once. Your mother is sick.'

At first, I do not believe the woman on the phone. I think this is just another of your ruses, Ma. Then, in a sudden flash of recognition, it dawns on me that I know those long drawn-out vowels, the way she says 'Deeeeviiii'. Shali the fisherwoman. She tells me she came up to the house to check if you were okay when you did not turn up at the market for a week. She saw the dog whining, his head cowering in a defeated pose by the front door, guarding something, a dark shape—was that a head? She squinted, moved closer and spied you, a slip of a woman lying unmoving on a worn mat by the open door—an invitation for the stainless-steel-utensil burglar who's been causing havoc in the village. She thought you were dead. She ran all the way up the mud path to the road, down the road to the rickshaw stand and begged one of the drivers lounging there smoking beedis to take you to the hospital. The rickshaw driver carried you, carefully navigating the slippery mud dislodging in clumps off the rain-drenched path, your body so hot it felt like he was handling lightning. Shali tells me that she came back to get some things for you to use in hospital and picked up the phone that kept on ringing and ringing. A petulant note creeps into her voice and I bite back the urge to apologise. Why should I? You are my mother; I will call you a hundred times if need be. The accusation implicit in Shali's tone is 'Bad Daughter.' *Pah,* I think, *what does she know?*

We've come full circle, haven't we, Ma? Back to where it all began. Back to it being just you and me.

I look at you, lying unconscious, strapped to machines that breathe for you, and I struggle to discern the woman who conjures up in me a burden of emotions—

guilt plaited with hurt and anger and, struggling under there somewhere, trying to swim out from beneath this avalanche, *love*.

I want to reach across and shake you, want to say, 'Wake up, Ma, wake up. I have news that will make you happy. Wake up so I can tell you, so I can see your tired face that folds itself into lines of worry relax in a smile.' But you lie there, eyes closed, lost to the world, lost to me.

I try telling you my news, Ma, but I cannot. Everything that has happened between us comes in the way: recriminations and regrets and deflated hopes, like the sagging bellies of middle-aged women. And guilt arrives, familiar as a childhood friend, one I've grown up with, casually slinging his heavy arm around me, weighing me down. And with the guilt comes a dark anger that makes me want to reach out and jolt you awake. How can you not be there for me now, when I need you the most?

The anger engulfs me, it takes me over. It is hot, it is real and it is liberating. 'My girl loves being angry. I don't know how the feisty little thing came out of my belly,' I overheard you say to a relative once and there was a hint of pride in your voice. True. The emotion that I evoke the most, that makes me feel the most alive, is anger. Remember the time I talked back to the teacher when she made the boys line up ahead of us? I refused to line up behind them and you had to be called in. 'Why?' I asked. 'Why can't the girls line up first?' It chafed me, the injustice that occurred casually on a daily basis, which was accepted without contest—a way of life. I ached to change it, I refused to accept it. I was always fighting for my rights. A feminist even before I understood the concept of feminism.

Remember that time in Rao's shop; I must have been what, nine? We waited and waited to be served, me hopping from one foot to another. I was barefoot, had ignored your admonishments to wear chappals and the sun-baked ground was beginning to cook the soles of my feet. I skipped to avoid laying my feet on the hot earth for more than a few seconds at a time, holding on to you, the vinegary smell of oil and raw rice and asafoetida assaulting my nostrils and making me sneeze, particles of flour swirling white in the sunlight dancing a tango with the fuchsia-tinged dust motes. At long last it was our turn, but just as Rao spun towards us, Lalu from down the road walked up, saying, 'Give me a bushel of rice and a litre of oil,' and Rao turned to serve him instead.

I erupted. 'Hey!' I yelled. 'We were here first.'

Rao looked at me over the tops of his spectacles, the round, rimless frames and the shiny bald head crowning a wiry body making him look like how I imagined Gandhi to be. 'Did you say something, girl?' His voice was harsh, his eyes flinty.

Your hand was covering my mouth, 'Shush, Devi,' but I pushed you away, stood up straight on both legs, even though the scorched earth seared the naked undersides of my feet, and stared right back. 'I said,' I enunciated clearly, 'that we were here first and we have been waiting patiently for a very long time while you have been serving everyone else. Now it is our turn. He can't just barge in and you cannot serve him.' I pointed an angry finger right in Lalu's face. It hovered somewhere in the region of his nose.

Lalu perused me, his hands on his hips, a smile playing on his lips.

You said, 'Shush, Devi,' once more, your face flushed with embarrassment. People milling around the market gossiping stopped what they were doing to look. Women hefting shopping baskets on their hips lowered them onto the sweltering ground, wiped their sweaty faces with their pallus and watched the show. Men nattering by the sugar-cane stall, their mouths ringed with foamy froth, hitched up their lungis and inched closer.

'This is my shop. I will serve whomever I want,' Rao said.

I mustered all the disdain I could and injected it into my voice, 'I always thought you looked like Gandhi, Rao-anna, but you are nothing like him. Nothing at all.' My voice, so steady all this while, shook as I uttered the last sentence. 'Come, Ma, let's go.'

You did not know what to say, where to look, your skin dark as blood rushed to your face. 'We need the rice, Devi,' you murmured, fiddling with the pallu of your sari, staring at the ground as if the pebbles scattered by your feet were of the greatest interest.

One of the women came forward, 'The child is right, you know. Shame on you,' she spat at the ground in disgust. 'I watched them wait there for the last fifteen minutes. Look, she is barefoot, her feet are blistering. Can't you give them their groceries first?'

'Yes,' other women joined in, 'go on.'

'I can wait,' said Lalu, smiling down at me as if he was doing us a great favour, Ma, 'Serve them first.'

I looked away from him, refusing to smile back, even though you nudged the small of my back to stop me being so rude.

Afterwards, after the money and rice and oil exchanged hands, you thanking Lalu and Rao effusively, me deigning not to look at either of them, we walked back through the fields, me sucking on that frozen badam-milk-filled tube that I so adored, and you said, between puffs—those bags were heavy—'You should have said thank you, Devi.'

I snorted and ran off, to get away from you of course, but also to soak my burning legs in the stream up ahead, '*You* should be the one to thank *me*,' I yelled. I turned back from a safe distance to look at you. You were smiling, that rare carefree grin that lit up your whole face, the grin I so loved.

Did I ever tell you that, Ma? No, I don't think so. But I am telling you now. I do. I love your smile. Smile for me, Ma, go on. Just the one.

The doctors say you are not in a coma per se, just unconscious, but that if the unconsciousness continues—and they assure me that they will do all they can to ensure it won't—it will morph into a coma. They say I should talk to you, that there is a possibility that you might hear me. But I sit, Ma, in the room that houses you: a slight figure lost in a vast bed under a scaffolding of discordant machines, in that room infused with the bitter medicine smell of fear and disease and death, and words fail me. I sit there in a silence punctuated by the delirious shouts, the pain-filled screams drifting in from other rooms, watching your chest rising and falling with each rasping, aided breath. I look at those hands that held me, that oiled and massaged my hair, that fed me, and words fail me. They fail me completely.

How, Ma, how did it get like this, that you lie there unable to speak, and yet I cannot find the words to break the ice, to bridge the gulf that separates us?

I have decided that I am going to write to you, write out all the emotion that is clogging up my throat, robbing my tongue of words, rendering me mute when I am with you. I write sitting in the house in the dark as the crickets chirp and dusk envelops me in a soothing curtain, as the mosquitoes bite and the candle flickers and wax stings my hand, Bobby beside me, a comforting warmth, twitching every so often in his sleep. I write so I will be able to read this to you tomorrow, when words betray me. I write so I will have something to say, so I can fill the thick, ailment-infused air between us with words, not regrets. I write hoping that it is not too late. I write hoping it will be enough.

Remember you loved to ask me, 'Devi, what are you thinking? What is going on in that pretty head of yours?' And it would irritate me, this affectation of yours, this wanting to know every last thing about me so I had no privacy even in my thoughts. Your trying-to-please voice annoyed me; so did that face, tender, all mushy when you looked at me. 'Nothing,' I would say shortly and your face would fall and you would turn away, busy yourself with cooking, and that would rile me as well. There you were slogging after your ungrateful daughter who refused to grace your simple question with an honest answer—that's what your slumped shoulders suggested didn't they, Ma?

So, now that you are not able to interrupt, now that your facial expressions give nothing away, the many grooves that crisscross your face, that narrate their own story, ironed out in repose, *now* I can tell you. I will read them to you tomorrow, my thoughts, and you will not interject; you will not say, 'That is not what happened—this is.' You will not sigh in that maddening way you have, exasperating me, and I will not drop what I have written, a sheaf of paper, my words carpeting the dirty yellow tiles of your depressing hospital room, and leave in a huff.

I have thought long and hard about everything that's happened and I think I can now pinpoint just when it all started to change. Like a wave building, gentle at first, then gradually gathering force. For me, I think, it all started the day I went swimming...

This is *my* version of events, Ma.

I am drowning, gasping for breath, my sari bunched around my face, the weight of water pulling me down. As if from a distance, I hear a voice, 'Kick, Devi, kick. Use your legs.' I try, but the water is too strong and it pulls me down however hard I push against it. Strong arms around me, supporting me, hoisting me up. I break the surface and breathe in air in huge strangled gulps. He laughs. I catch a brief glimpse of my reflection in the water: Hair bunched in clumps around my face, having escaped the bun; my yellow sari now dirty brown and dripping water. I am trembling, unable to stop. 'You will learn to swim yet,' he says, diving in gracefully and swimming across, neatly splitting the emerald water in two, his honey-gold muscles rippling, sun-kissed droplets gleaming on coffee-coloured skin like foil on chocolate.

I sprawl by the side of the lake in the shade of the banyan tree, heaving great big swigs of air, trying desperately to get my breath back, velvet moss soft as a quilted bedspread beneath me. I will the sun to dry my sari and watch Rohan, his strong hands parting the water effortlessly, his head bobbing up and down. The air smells green, of grass and budding life and of the lake, slimy and wet. *Never again*, I think, *and especially not wearing a sari.* It almost strangled me, and if not for Rohan's arms pulling me up, where would I be now? And then what would you do, Ma?

Thoughts of you bring with them waves of guilt at what I am doing. And the familiar anger, settling bitter in my throat, like that cod liver oil you make sure I drink every morning, your voice weighted with martyrdom, 'Do you know how much this costs? Drink it up, it's good for you.' Like I am a baby still. Sometimes, I keep the cod liver oil in my mouth, despite the fishy taste making me nauseous, and then spit it outside amongst the hibiscus bushes, rushing to the bathroom and gargling furiously, rinsing my mouth after and chewing on a neem leaf to get rid of the fishy tang. As I spit, knowing you work so hard to get me the medicine, knowing how much it costs, knowing it is good for me, guilt stabs, searing like the first bite of raw chilli. And yet... there's the part of me that *has* to do it: I breathe easier after, Ma, savouring the hint of neem, hugging close the secret of not having followed your will.

You think I am with Sharda revising. I shouldn't be here, in Dainagar, at the lake, learning to swim with a *boy*. This is going a step too far—even for me, the girl who consorts with boys.

'No one will see you,' Rohan had said earnestly that morning when he was persuading me to join him at the lake. 'None of the people from your village come to Dainagar anyway. And in the afternoon, the lake and its vicinity are completely deserted.'

And he is right. Not a soul has passed by on the path above the slope which leads down to the lake.

If we are caught, my reputation, which is already substantially tarnished, will be well and truly ruined. '*So what?*' I think, a thrilled shiver running up my spine.

Ma, I don't give two hoots about my reputation. But you do. Sometimes I think you care more about my reputation than you do about me. If word of this got out, you would be devastated. So I have taken care to hide under the banyan tree. No passer-by can see me here. You see, I am protecting you, Ma.

On my first day at college, Rohan came up to me in the canteen at lunch and asked, 'Is the seat next to you taken?'

I took one look at this tall, handsome boy and fell head over heels in love. All your decrees—'*Don't talk to boys; remember, for a girl, reputation is of paramount importance*'—forgotten. Not that I had been planning to heed them anyway. I sidled up and he sat next to me, so close I could feel his warm, spiced breath on my face, spy the black hairs curling invitingly on his fair hands. We shared upma and chattambades and cardamom tea. Afterwards, he said, 'So, care to be my friend, Ms Devi?'

'Depends,' I replied, wondering as I did so if I was ruining my chances with this man. *Well, tough*, I thought, *at least I'll get his measure sooner rather than later.*

He looked at me, eyebrows creased, lips curling upwards in an amused grin. 'On what?'

'On what you want from a friend. If you want demure, a "yes woman", you can pass me by. I am not demure.' I replied.

He had thrown back his head and laughed. All the bodies in the canteen had swivelled our way. *There goes my reputation.*

He had bent close, his breath tickling my ear. 'Just so you know, demure bores me.'

And from then on, we were inseparable.

Lying there in the shade of the trees, I revel in the music of the water. The breeze drifting from the lake, smelling of promise, whispers endearments in my ears, tickling my wet skin.

There is a loud splash and I watch as Rohan walks out of the water, his shorts clinging to his legs. My arm is slung across my eyes to shield them from the sun but from beneath it I can see everything. I know I look pretty lying there, among the moss and the reeds, under the canopy of banyan tree branches, in my yellow sari which clings to my curves as it dries.

Rohan walks up to me saying, 'Aren't you going to try one more time then?' I don't reply, pretending to be asleep. I watch as he comes to a stop near my feet, as his gaze travels up my body, as it comes to rest on my breasts. I feel hot everywhere, a heat that has nothing to do with the sun that is beating down on my head, and I feel something warm and liquid stir deep inside. I want something I cannot name. I want.

I watch his expression change, his eyes darken. He squats beside me and moves in close, so close that I can feel his warm breath smelling of lake on my face. 'Devi?' I don't move, don't respond. My heart thuds loud, hard. What is he going to do? He bends over, so his lips brush my cheek and the liquid feeling spreads everywhere from that secret part of me. I want to pull him down on top of me, want him to caress my body like my wet sari is doing. I stir, sigh.

His hand is on my arm, the touch igniting something. He has touched me so many times before, but it has never felt like this. 'Devi.' His voice thick.

I pull my arm away from my eyes and squint up at him, his face in shadow, wet hair haloed by sunlight, hoping my expression gives nothing away. 'What?' I ask faking a yawn.

His hand travels down my arm, his fingertips barely touching sun-caressed skin, raising goosebumps. I want him to hold me close so I can feel his heart beating beneath mine. I want him to kiss me. *This is wrong,* one part, the sensible part of me, thinks while the other asks, impertinently, *Why is it wrong?* I sit up, abruptly, hoping that will chase the liquid feeling away. It lingers, pulsing, wanting, aching.

'Devi,' Rohan says again.

My name on his lips, soft, a poem of longing.

'Yes?' My voice is shaking, I cannot think straight, talk straight. He looks up, directly at me then, and in his narrowed eyes, in the way his mouth is open just slightly, I recognise the desire I feel. And then he is moving closer, his face so close I can see the tiny mole under his left eye, I can feel his warm breath stroke my face.

There is a harsh clang from somewhere behind us, vulgarly loud, shattering the heady quiet of the drowsy afternoon, and we jerk apart. Someone swears. A bullock cart trundles past on the road above, laden with stainless-steel pots and pans, the bullocks looking peaceful, their blue bodies smeared brown with dried mud, their horns curving gracefully, the bells that hang from their necks tinkling in tune to their marching feet, the man screaming obscenities as he urges them to go faster.

I pull my sari close and slink backward, folding into the trunk of the banyan tree. 'We shouldn't be here,' I say, not looking at him.

The bullock cart turns the corner and is gone. My heart thuds loudly in my chest. As if on cue, I hear your voice in my head: 'Lucky escape. If you were caught, what would happen then? Devi, you are a girl, you have a reputation to uphold. Remember the boy always goes scot-free. Remember that.' *You win*, I think bitterly, *you always win. I cannot do anything I want without feeling guilty, without your voice echoing in my head.*

I look at Rohan's bent head and have a sudden urge to stroke that profusion of hair that is always a bit too long, encroaching on his face, obscuring his twinkling eyes. *I love him*, I think. *I love him.* So then, why is what we are doing so wrong? 'You are not married.' Your voice again, from where it has taken permanent residence in my brain. Other people have a conscience. I have your voice. 'And he is Catholic. Do you want to marry him? Perhaps. Will he marry you? He might want to. Will his parents let him? You can bet one lakh rupees they won't. You are a Hindu, a Kshatriya at that—not even a Brahmin—plus, a poor girl. You know how proud Catholics are.' News of my escapades always reaches you via the village gossip network, travelling faster than the hurricanes besieging the Arabian Sea. This was part of your latest lecture, part of your quest to dissuade me from 'cavorting', as you put it, with Rohan. I hadn't realised how deeply your words, the very words I pooh-poohed, had embedded themselves in my psyche.

The thing is I like Rohan. Very much. More than I have ever liked anybody before. I don't want to be cheap in his eyes; like you have warned that girls will be once they have gone the whole way.

And so, I brush my hair off my face with fingers that tremble. 'I need to go home,' I say. *For all my bravado,* I think, *I am still a meek mummy's girl.*

'Okay,' he yanks a reed from beside him and sticks it in his mouth, sucking deeply.

He stands and gives me his hand to pull me up. I do not take it. I hold on to the banyan tree for support and heave myself up on unsteady legs, dust my sari, which is thankfully dry now. His hand drops to his side and I keep my gaze fixed on it as he turns and starts walking up the slope to the road, as I slowly follow.

When I rush home, an hour later than I said I would—common practice for me, you know to expect it —frenziedly trying to iron out my crumpled sari and dislodge the clumps of mud adhering to the skirt, you are waiting, your eyes wild, an expression in them I cannot name. You do not say anything, anything at all, just allow me to talk myself out. And still that expression, that strange glint in your eye. The first sliver of foreboding slithers down my spine. I have never seen you like this. Usually you are shouting, you are yelling, you are smacking your head, you are sobbing. You are never silent.

Still not saying a word, you retrieve the cane from its hiding place behind the kitchen door. You've only ever used it to scare the crows that dare to steal grains meant for the chickens. You come towards me and only then, far too late, I comprehend what you mean to do. I make to run but you are already there. You do not heed my pleas, my entreaties, my explanations. You ignore Bobby the puppy's whines as he cowers beneath the aboli bushes howling mournfully, his paws covering his ears. And you whip me for the first time in my life although I've given you plenty of cause to whip me before. I am too stunned to protest, too shocked to fight back. You whip me frenziedly, desperately, the fragranced breeze lifting my sari and helpfully exposing tender flesh. You whip me, unmindful of the tears streaming down your face and soaking your sari blouse. You whip me until Jalajakka comes back from the market and yanks you off, her face blanched of colour, her basket of shopping scattered all over the courtyard, bitter gourds bursting in a spectacular green-and-white mess, a marrow regurgitating creamy gooey fluff; and the chickens have free rein, pecking at the seeds of the watermelon which lies broken and ruined, a green-backed book with red pages, bleeding pink water onto dry red mud, tinting it the dirty orange of sadhus' robes, leaving me sunken on the ground, weeping red welts rising on my back and arms.

Dusk descends; the sky a warm golden pink. Crickets sing. Bobby comes up to me, tail between legs, and licks the tears off my face. The air reeks of rotting watermelon and decomposing vegetables, a rich organic smell. Lights come on in the houses among the fields and on the far side of the hill a flickering light jumps, playing hide and seek with the shadows. The first of the glow-worms arrive, a series of pearly illuminations which turn on and off, on and off, tantalising. Dancing to a tune only they know.

After a bit, you come outside, your face and eyes swollen from crying.

Why are you crying, I think, *when I am the one you have hurt?*

You gather me in your arms and carry me inside, and I am too tired and in too much pain to protest, though my mind rebels. You apply salves to my wounds and bandage them, the smell of mint making me want to retch, the agony making me feel faint. Your hands are deft, your touch gentle. You feed me rice and fish like you used to when I was a child, fashioning a ball of rice with fish in the middle just the way I like it, and I force it down past the lump in my throat and all I taste are tears. Salty with an aftertaste of rage, hurt and a residue of the guilt that is ever present. Afterwards, we sleep side by side, you and I, sharing a mattress as is our wont, and still you have not said a word and neither have I, although I know you are not asleep—your breath too even, too controlled. I am unable to sleep because of the aching, throbbing pain in every part of my body and the anger that bubbles up inside, threatening to burst out of me in scorching waves.

Ma, wet splotches dot this sheet of paper and I realise that I am crying, tears of rage. I look at it all written down here and I can taste the pain, touch the anger bursting out of me. The hurt is as raw now as it was that evening. I cannot write anymore. Not today. I think there is enough here to keep us both occupied at the hospital tomorrow, to fill the silence.

Oh, I almost forgot. Ma, just as I was leaving your bedside this afternoon, the nurse came to me, holding out something, 'Here, this was lying beside your mother. That woman, Shali, brought it in.'

A tattered, worn notebook, like the ones I had at school. I opened it—could you fault me? A diary. Yours. The first entry written when you were just a child, your handwriting neater than mine ever was. I have started reading it—I cannot help it, Ma. I am giving you the gift of my thoughts; isn't it but fair that I get a glimpse into yours?

Yours,

Devi.

Chapter 3
Shilpa

Plantain Podi

Plantain Podi (Serves 4):

Ingredients:

Vegetable oil–3 cups
Two green plantains, sliced thinly into rounds
Gram flour–2 cups
1 teaspoon chilli powder
Water as required
Salt to taste

Method:

Place gram flour in a mixing bowl along with chilli powder. Add water and mix to a gloopy paste, not too watery, mind. Add the plantains and mix until each piece is fully covered.

Heat the oil in a deep-bottomed frying pan. When the oil is very hot, drop the plantain pieces in, one by one, standing back so the oil doesn't splatter you. When the pieces turn the deep orange of the sky at dusk, take them out using a porous ladle. Serve hot with coconut chutney (recipe to follow).

❄ ❄ ❄

Dear Diary,

My name is Shilpa and I am thirteen and three quarters years old. Today I got my period. To celebrate the occasion, my mother presented me with you, dear Diary. You are the first gift I have ever received and are the only notebook I have that is brand new. My school notebooks (I go to the local government school which is free), are all hand-me-downs, sewn together from loose, empty sheets torn from other books. My mother must have been saving for a very long time to be able to afford you, dear Diary. As it is, we hardly have enough money to buy rice and dhal and oil from the ration shop.

I went to bed last night with a pain in my stomach and lower back and when I woke this morning, the old sari we use as a mattress was stained. My mother pulled water from the well (usually my job but I was in pain all over and couldn't do it) for my wash, and then we cleaned the mattress together, she scrubbing and I rinsing. Then she sat me down in the shade of the banana and coconut trees, the crows cackling and the frogs croaking as the wind hissed among the trees, the fragrant air tasting of rain, her hands smelling of the soap used to scrub the mattress, and she told me the story of my birth.

I have heard this story a million times before and yet I never tire of it. We are poor now, but when my mother first came to this village as a new bride, she and my father were poorer still. On their wedding day, my father made it clear to my mother that her job was to produce healthy strapping boys to help out with the farming. While she waited to get pregnant, my mother worked as a servant except for three months of the year during the monsoons when all the women in the village were incorporated into sowing paddy saplings. 'Our duty as women,' my mother intoned in her musical voice as she plaited my hair, 'is to get married, have children.'

'But Ma,' I said, 'I want to study, work in an office.'

'Aiyyo, don't tell your father that,' she grumbled. 'You are only going to school because it is free and because nobody will take you on as a servant. You are too scrawny they say.' She sighed deeply. 'Wish we had enough money to buy some meat so I could fatten you up,' her voice took on that melancholy tinge I hated. Any minute now she would commence sobbing, hitting herself with her fists, lamenting the fact of her birth, my birth, our sorry circumstances.

'Tell me the story,' I said, desperate to stop her tears.

A year went by, then two, my mother said, her hands gently working warm coconut oil into my hair, her touch comforting as a soft pillow at the end of a long day. People started to talk, calling my mother barren, urging my father to leave her and marry a fertile woman instead. And then, just when she was despairing, my mother got pregnant. She prayed and my father prayed for it to be a boy. Her belly grew bigger and bigger and she grew more and more tired, but she had to work. And then one stormy afternoon, as the clouds held court and thunder reigned supreme, as the intermittent bursts of lightning picked out rows of women, their backs bent, singing to ease the mind-numbing rigour of sowing paddy saplings, their voices carrying over the drumming rain, the mud squelching beneath their bare feet, my mother felt this bolt of pain in her belly, like nothing she had ever experienced before. Her thighs were soaked as a burst of water ran down between her legs, nothing to do with the raindrops pelting down from up above, the gods crying, bemoaning their fate for being stuck amongst angry clouds. The air tasted of earth gorging on rainwater; a pregnant, sated smell. The pain assaulted my mother again and then again until, with a thump and a plop, I dropped down into the mud with a high-pitched squeal to rival the groan of thunder and the screech of my mother's agony. A squirming raging bundle, christened in mud. A girl.

'I did not have any more children after you. I could not.' My mother sighed. 'But your father did not leave me.' This is the bit I like best. I think it is so romantic.

'Why, Ma? Why didn't he leave you if he wanted sons so?' I asked, knowing that any minute now…

My mother blushed, colour flooding into her face, making her honeyed complexion glow. 'He likes my cooking,' she mumbled.

'Anyway, enough said.' Her voice was brisk as she tied my plait up neatly with a strip of old housecoat masquerading as ribbon and turned me round to face her. 'You are a woman now. You know what this means, don't you?' Her eyes were serious.

A butterfly, brilliant yellow wings tinged with emerald, landed on a hibiscus flower. The sky was a bright blue, cloudless. 'Yes, Ma.'

'Your duty as a woman is to make a good marriage. Your husband may not be as forgiving as mine, Shilpa.' Her voice soft as a ripe cashew. 'So remember this.' My mother cupped my face in her hands. This close, her eyes were tawny, like the muddy water collecting in pools in the holes in the road during the monsoons, and flecked with gold. 'Please your husband. He is your God. Keep him happy. Give him children. Throw away all these fancy ideas of studying and working in offices. You are going to stop school as soon as you get a job in one of the houses where I work. Come,' she said.

My mother is permanently tired, always grumpy. She is either yelling or crying. Today she was neither. My coming of age had surprised a rare good mood out of her.

'To celebrate your becoming a woman,' she said, 'we will make plantain podis today, with the plantain Mrs. D'Sa gave me. You make them. I will watch. From now on, you do all the cooking. I know you can cook, but that is not enough. You have to cook *well.* The most important skill you can learn is how to make something out of nothing, feed the brood. There will be times when all you have in the house is half a potato, a sliver of onion, no chillies, a smidgen of tomato and no money to buy any more. Yet you will be expected to cook and feed a dozen people. We might as well start now. I will tell you all my secrets.'

She walked up to where the bedding was piled haphazardly and picked something from underneath the pillow. 'I got you this,' she said and there was a strange expression on her face. I realised with some shock that she was shy. My mother. 'I was waiting for you to become a woman to give it to you. Since you like your learning so much…' Something flat and rectangular. I took it from her, my heart fluttering like a trapped bird. A book. Shiny and new and imbued with the fresh smell of promise. You, dear Diary. I hugged you close, held you next to my burgeoning chest. At that moment I would have done anything my mother asked, even if she had ordered me to wed the sun.

'You can write your recipes in this,' she said. 'The ones I teach you. I have them all in here,' she tapped her forehead. 'But you like writing things down, I know.'

And so I have compromised. I have written the recipe on one side and my thoughts on the other. You are so beautiful, your pages so pristine, unsoiled, untouched by grimy hands before mine that I almost didn't want to sully you with writing. Soon your pages will be thumbed, your edges will become worn, but I promise you this: I will keep you always.

The green plantain podis I made today were the best I have ever tasted. I thought it was just me, my pride in my cooking, but my mother's smile, her nod of acceptance, her, 'Not bad,' when she bit into one, my father's gulping them down with gusto, mumbling, 'These don't even need chutney, they are so good. You will make some man very happy one day,' between hasty mouthfuls—these were reward enough.

Afterwards, as I went about doing the myriad chores that define my day—drawing water from the well, watering the plants, feeding the chickens, sweeping the floor, grinding masala into paste, my back aching and my stomach hurting, I thought of the family I would one day have: the handsome husband, the brood of children—who would all take pleasure in my cooking. My husband would beam at me and say, 'I am so lucky to be married to the best cook in the village.' My children would cluster round me, like the hens were doing as I scattered grain for them. They would tug at my sari, wrap their twig arms around my sari skirt: 'You are the best Ma in the world.'

When I was little, some minister or other from the local government visited our school. It was a big event. We all had to line up and salute as he arrived. We had to walk up to him and shake hands while pictures were clicked. My best friend at the time, Anisa, was scared by the flashing camera and burst into tears. The minister had sat us down in a circle and asked each of us what we wanted to be when we grew up. Most boys said 'farmer', some girls said 'secretary', Duma's son said his dream was to be a watchman. When it was my turn, I said, very loudly and clearly, 'I want to be a minister like you.' The minister had laughed then. 'Come here,' he had said. I had walked up to him and watched my hand being swallowed up by his huge one. It was wet and slimy like the frog that took refuge in our kitchen once, hiding from the rat snake that had made our courtyard its home. 'And why do you want to be a minister?'

I had turned round and looked at the snapping camera, the dozens of adoring, admiring eyes facing me, Anisa's scared, tear-stained face. 'Just looks like something fun to do,' I had said and the minister had burst out laughing, and that was the picture in the newspaper the next day, the minister's face, mouth wide open and displaying yawning gums like a python's the moment before it gobbles up its unsuspecting victim, and me standing next to him, looking poised, my hand disappearing in his clammy one.

I was the heroine of the school for the ensuing two days, revelling in all the attention from teachers as well as students. I discarded Anisa's friendship as casually as throwing away a mango pip and chose friends from the many offers that were forthcoming. I was rude to my mother, not caring when she said I was getting ideas above my station and whipped me. I asked my teachers if they knew how one became a minister. Not one of them had a convincing answer.

But now—today when I served my father the podis I had made, when my mother bit into one, I saw the same admiration, basked in the same feeling I had enjoyed that day when I stood holding the minister's hand. Pleasure, that was it, pleasure and a sense of accomplishment.

So, if someone asked me now what I want to be when I grow up, this is what I would reply: I would like a house to call my own with a kitchen where I will concoct delicacies to feed my family—my husband, my children.

A wife and a mother. That's what I'd like to be.

Chapter 4
Nisha

Broadsheet Confetti

Questions crowd Nisha's head, demanding answers like a class of unruly children. The letter sits on the sofa, a few sheets of paper the greenish blue of Matt's eyes when he just wakes up. How can a few words have the power to uproot her, destroy her life, her belief in who she is? To calm herself, she leafs through her notebook, coming to a stop at the notes she has made about her parents. She reads through, picks up her pen and starts writing:

9. They never told me they loved me, per se, though they did sign letters, notes and emails 'Love, Mum/Dad.' No x for kiss.

10. My mum used to kiss me goodnight when I was younger. But that stopped around the time I turned twelve and started puberty.

11. My happiest memories of my parents are when they were teaching me something. They would be

so animated then, so eager to impart knowledge, so full of praise when I caught on. I wanted to learn more just to please them.

12. They never told me I was adopted. They never let on. I didn't have a clue.

Nisha rereads what she has written. Not much. She cannot think of anything else.

Twelve points describing my parents—that's twelve more than what I know about me. Who am I?

Enough of this, Nisha.

She closes her eyes, pictures the man and woman she still thinks of as her parents, who will always be her parents. Her mother, those leaf-shaped eyes that crinkled when she smiled. Her father, the way he rubbed his nose when he was thinking. Should she add that to the list? That would make it thirteen, which some people consider unlucky. Not her, she doesn't believe in such nonsense. *Do I really not believe or have I been taught not to believe? If I had been brought up in India, would I have been different?*

Nisha, what's got into you?

I have been living a lie, that's what's got into me. I am not who I thought I was all this while, the daughter of Lekha and Ravi Kamath, renowned scientists. I am the daughter of a couple in India who did not want me, who gave me to the convent from where I was adopted. Why? Why did my birth parents give me away? Was it because I was ugly, an imperfect baby with a gash for a mouth?

She had always secretly entertained the notion that her parents had no pictures of her as a baby because of the way she looked before the many rectifying operations for her cleft palate. Something in the vague way her forthright mum said, 'Oh I think they were destroyed in a fire,' not really meeting her gaze, had roused her suspicions.

Forthright? Her mother? *I have to question not only everything I know about myself but everything I thought I knew about my lying, deceiving parents.*

In a sudden fit, she tears the sheet of paper off her notebook, crumples it into a ball. Rogue tears threaten again—tears she thought she had exhausted. She is angry, so angry. She wants to shout, scream, rant, break something. Instead, she sits quietly on the sofa, the crumpled sheet in her hand the extent of her rebellion.

She remembers the time she came home, her face purple with rage, kicking and thrashing at the bin in her room until it overturned, then shredding the paper spilling from it in white-winged waves into slivers, scattering it about the room: broadsheet confetti.

'What is the matter?' her mother had asked, coming in, her eyes wide.

'The boys on the bus… they called me a dirty Paki.'

Her mother had smiled. It had made Nisha wild. 'How can you stand there and smirk?' she had yelled. 'Do you know how it feels to be made fun of, ridiculed like I am worth nothing at all?' she had yelled.

'Shh…' her mother had said, still infuriatingly calm. 'There is no need for this, this anger, this hissy fit. Anger is just a waste of your energy and time.'

'Oh, don't start, Mum,' she had yelled, surprised by her own daring, the pain inside, the humiliation she had experienced, making her lash out.

'By letting those boys' ignorant words get to you,' her mother had explained patiently without raising her voice, 'you are affording them power. What you should do is laugh at them, pity them because they don't know any better. Come, eat something and then we'll see why they were wrong, we'll read up on it.'

Her parents' answer to everything—read, study, research. Funnily enough, though, it had worked. Armed with knowledge, she had felt invincible. Words had lost their power to hurt. Those boys had plagued her again a couple of times but when they realised they couldn't dent the wall she had built around herself, they had left her alone, targeted some other gullible victim.

She is spent, exhausted. She has lost the knack for anger she had as a child. She can perform complicated calculations in her head but she cannot rant, cannot vent. She looks at the crushed page in her hand, irons it out. Then she goes hunting for glue. She loved her parents; nothing can take that away from her she thinks as she glues the page containing her memories of the beloved, fiercely intelligent couple she had the privilege of calling Mum and Dad, back into the book. *You were the parents I knew and loved. Perhaps you didn't deserve it. Perhaps your love wasn't pure. But mine was. And that is enough. It has to be.*

She fingers the number for the convent on the sheet of paper. Should she call? Why should she? *Because…* the voice in her head says. Because what? Why indulge the 'what ifs?' And anyway, the number may not be the right one; it is twenty-odd years old.

Why is she wasting time deliberating? This is not like her. She needs Matt. Almost time for him to leave work, thank goodness. It feels like years since she woke in his arms, said goodbye to him as he left for work and then came here, to her parents' home. He will be round to pick her up soon, his tie loose, his eyes lighting up, the lines around them crinkling, softening into creases, as they do when he sees her. He will swoop down for a kiss and she will anchor herself in the haven of his arms. They will stop off at Marks, buy a bottle of wine and the meals in their 'Two for Ten' offer. After dinner, they will snuggle in bed and talk and she will give him the letter and he will laugh and say, 'This had you worried?' 'Yes,' she will say and he will smile, reach out and tip her face up with his finger and gaze at her with those liquid eyes the colour of grass after a summer shower and say, 'You were not a project, Nisha, you were their child. But of course they loved you. How could they not?'

She opens her notebook to a new page. She will write about Matt; it will ease the turmoil she feels.

Things I adore about Matt:

1. When he holds me, I feel safe. I feel cared for.
2. The first time I saw him: I was invited to give a guest lecture and he met me at the university steps, his hand held out, his beard catching the

light and glowing honey gold, his eyes warm with approval as he said, 'You must be Nisha. Gosh, what a pleasant surprise. I was expecting an old fuddy-duddy who would need help up the stairs. What made you choose such a stuffy, ancient people's subject, Ms Kamath?' I was charmed. I had laughed, and he had looped his arm round mine and said, 'I will help you up the steps anyway; the pleasure is all mine.' He had bent down close, his breath warm in my ear, chocolate and peppermint, a strangely intoxicating smell. 'And after the lecture, would you care to have a drink with me and tell me why statistical analysis fascinates you?' And I had surprised myself as much as anyone when I said yes.

3. He makes me laugh.

4. When I am with him, I feel whole. (Is this love?)

5. He is neat and methodical and loves numbers as much as I do.

6. He gets me—my penchant for having facts at my fingertips, for wanting to know things and have proof to go with them; my need to compartmentalise, slot everything neatly in my brain. He accepts me for who I am, despite all my issues: my prickliness, my intense reserve, my asymmetrical face, the scar above my upper lip—a relic of the cleft palate.

7. He doesn't ask me to give more than I am willing to—as the other men I have been with have invariably tended to do.

8. I admire very much the dogged determination with which he worked at breaking the walls I had built around myself until I gradually let him in.

9. I love the way the morning sun slanting in through the window makes the hairs on his chest glow and he looks as if he is alight, on fire.

10. His intelligence, that pleasure he gains from amassing knowledge that I share.

11. The mischievous glint he gets in his eyes sometimes, that naughty side that only I am privy to.

12. The little snores that escape him when he is fast asleep, one arm slung carelessly across me.

13. I miss him when he's not around, ache for him at odd, unconnected times of day. Anything can set me off—the curve of a jaw, a glimpse of long, tapering fingers, someone saying 'Hello' with the emphasis on the 'o'. (Perhaps this *is* love.)

14. My parents approved of him.

Was Number 14 the reason that clinched it in the end? Was it?

As she waits for Matt, she rereads the letter, her legacy from her parents. And a question looms. *Was my birth mother unmarried?* In India, twenty-odd years ago, that would have caused a furore, she suspects. Perhaps that was it, the reason for Nisha's eviction to the convent, and not her cleft palate at all. Or perhaps it was a combination of both.

Her mind is like a roulette wheel coming to rest on the same few sets of questions, the same queries. *Who are my parents? Why did they give me away like an unwanted present?*

Who am I?

Chapter 5
Devi

Slimy Fingers

Ma,

So, there were no weighted silences in your room today. I hate that room, by the way: the smell of death; the determinedly cheery nurses with their high-pitched voices into which they inject optimism as they inject medicines into the few veins on your arms that have escaped, so far, being pricked by the needle (I flinch for you when they do that, you don't of course); the nuns who seem to float past in a prayer-haloed haze, their habits rustling and swishing in a clandestine dialect, their faces calm and unaffected by the suffering surrounding them; the moans dripping with pain drifting in from other rooms on a gust of bitter, medicine-scented breeze. I envy the nuns their peace—it almost makes me want to find God myself. I tell you this, hoping it will elicit a laugh, shock you out of your unconsciousness, but you are unresponsive, serene in a way you never were before.

So I sat and I held your impassive hand and I read to you. When I came to the part about you hitting me, I dropped your hand. I couldn't help it. I am angry now, just thinking about it. You whipped me, Ma, for the first time in my life. Whipped me like I was a sheet you were ridding of dust motes, or a bullock that refused to do your bidding. Ma, even after all this time my blood roils…

The morning after that fateful day, I wake to the smell of mint and eucalyptus oil, to gentle fingers working my wounds. You are applying salve once more and I am consumed by the urge to push the dish containing it off your hand, onto the floor. Instead, I pretend to be asleep. Afterwards, you plant soft kisses on my cheeks and I have to exercise all my willpower not to flinch, to scream, to pull away. You stand, knees creaking as they have taken to doing lately, and a heartbeat later, I hear the thwack as the wooden bar holding the kitchen door closed is moved and it is flung open, Bobby's joyful bark as he bounds in, the hick hick hick of your vigorous brushing, the thoo of your spitting underneath the jackfruit tree. You like to lean against its trunk, I know, and feel the morning air on your face, fresh and clean and smelling of promise, carrying a slight hint of night. You like to study the leaves, every one underlined by the crust of dew clinging to its base. Are you looking at the spot where I lay sobbing as you whipped me mercilessly, I wonder? Or do your eyes avoid it, deliberately slink away from it? I hear you hobble in, listen to you call upon Lord Ganapathy, as is your habit when you bend your knees to climb over the stoop and the joints resist, hear the hiss of the fire as you put the conjee to boil, breathe in the smell of smoke, orange tinged. I hear the clank as you wash the pans ignored in last night's ruckus and gathering flies, the sizzle as hot oil hits the frying pan, the swish of rava frying, the starchy smell of potatoes boiling and the tear-inducing spiciness of chillies squished to release their seeds.

I wear a long-sleeved salwar kameez to hide the welts, flinching as the cotton rubs against the weeping wounds. I ignore the breakfast you have set out for me—upma with peas and potatoes and plenty of green chillies, my favourite—and the plea in your eyes. I grab my satchel and bus pass and leave without a backward glance. You clutch at my arm, and I yell involuntarily at the pain. You drop it at once, your face awash with tears. 'Devi…' you begin but I storm off, unable to look at you, to stand being near you. You, who judged me without a backward glance when, for perhaps the first time in my life, I didn't deserve it. I didn't do anything even though I was tempted. I was *good.* And you didn't ask, didn't listen, just flogged me like Sumitranna does his cows. Why should I be good? Why should I do anything you ask of me when I will be deemed bad anyway? Why?

I ignore Bobby bounding up to me, circling my legs, tongue hanging out, begging for a pat, a play. I walk past the spot where I lay the previous evening as blows rained on me. I stride with my head held high, knowing that you are standing beside the tamarind tree, watching, waiting for me to turn and wave goodbye. I round the corner, climb the couple of haphazardly placed stones impersonating steps that take me to the road, past the makeshift temple beside the anthill which everyone believes houses Naga, the Snake God, and to which they feed pots of milk during the feast of Nag Panchami. I walk past the priest doing circuits of the statue of Lord Ganapathy holding a flickering lamp smelling of hot oil and incense, vermilion smeared across his forehead in horizontal gashes, rose agarbatti in his cupped hands. I walk to the bus stop and I do not look back.

Rohan is not at college. Is he ill? I desperately want to talk to someone, but I don't have any close friends apart from Rohan. There is Sharda but she is part of a giggly group and I cannot stand their shallow talk—not today.

Rohan is the only one who will understand, but I do not have his phone number. I never thought to ask him for it. I imagine dialling his number, picture his mother's shock when she answers and hears my voice at the other end: a girl, having the temerity to call Rohan, asking to speak to him! Rohan has grumbled about his parents, complaining that they are too strict, commiserating with me when I have groused about you. 'We are alike in that we are both only children. I too, feel weighted down by the burden of my parents' expectation. At least you only have your mother,' he has said. '*Only* my mother—she's enough for anyone,' I have laughed.

Did Rohan's parents find out about the previous day too? Have they banned him from seeing me? Is he so weak that he will agree, give me up so easily? If so, then I was right in not letting him do what we both wanted down by the lake…

I spend the day in agony. I am hot in the long-sleeved kameez, the sweat pooling down my back, my arms, irritating the wounds, which chafe and itch. To add to my discomfort, I am hungry. I did not have breakfast and stubbornly did not take the lunch you prepare and pack lovingly into a three-tier tiffin carrier for me every morning.

After classes finish, I go to the library, trying to ignore the smells of seera and goli baje, puri and chapatti kurma that drift from the canteen. I did not take money with me either, in my rush to leave home, escape you, this morning. I watch the rain creeping down the window pane with slimy fingers that dissolve into ghoulish patterns, making the gate outside and the students walking across the grass appear blurry, indistinct, coated in a shimmering curtain.

I miss Rohan, feel the vestige of the desire he aroused in me the previous day stir, that raw warm feeling. And then it is gone, replaced by a simmering anger that bubbles to the surface, wanting to burst out of me. Deep inside, a small part of me asserts that you were right in a way: I did lie after all, say I was with Sharda. I shush it impatiently. You could have talked to me, asked me what I had done, before hitting me like Jemma does his wife, like I am an object, a cheap possession.

The library closes at six. The librarian shoos me away. I don't know what to do, where to go from here. By rights I should have been home by now; I know you will be panicking. The thought gives me courage. Good. You deserve it.

I walk briskly to the bus stop, climb on a bus going to Mangalore, the opposite direction to home, glad that I have my bus pass if nothing else. The rain has let up a bit and the moist air whipping my face through the corroding red-tinged window bars brings with it raindrops smelling of earth, seeds sprouting and the tangy, slightly bitter smell of lime leaves with a faint undertone of rust.

I picture you waiting under the tamarind tree, your vantage spot from where you can get the first glimpse of me as I turn the bend, deciding when I don't get home at half five that I have missed the Kundapur Express and taken the Brahmavar Local which makes scheduled and unscheduled stops at every corner. As the clock drags towards six o'clock, you will reason that the driver stopped the bus to jump outside and pee in the bushes, or partake of a leisurely beedi and a steaming tumbler of tea with one of his cronies, as he has been known to do, while the passengers wait, hot and sweaty, packed like rice grains jostling in gunny sacks, so close together that they can look down each other's nostrils—not that they want to, of course. You will walk up and down, up and down, wearing the mud path thin, walking progressively faster in proportion to the size of your worry. Bobby will nip at your heels, thinking this is some sort of game and you will bend down to scratch behind his ears, 'Shh, Bobby,' you will say. 'We are waiting for Devi is all. Once she's here, I will give you your supper.'

Your face, worry lines creasing your eyes, dragging your mouth down in a frown, blooms before my eyes… I blink it away. What do I care? You say that I was your reward, achieved at great cost, your eyes iridescent with tears, each word binding me to you as surely and insidiously as the umbilical cord. When I ask what you mean by reward, what was the great cost, you don't tell me. Instead you say, eyes shining, 'You are all I have, Devi. My precious gift.' You say all these things and then you hit me, hurt me like there's no tomorrow. No, I will not come home. I will not.

The bus lurches over potholes overflowing with the evening's downpour, dirty yellow water splashing the children walking back from school, their backs, weighed down with satchels, bent like saplings in a brisk breeze. They skip away to try and avoid the muddy water, but some of them are too late, their blue uniform shirts and navy skirts autographed with buttery smudges. The road construction workers huddle in the cloth tents they have built beside the road as shelter against the elements, their lungis and saris gaping with holes and stained orange with mud, their gaunt faces peering out. Beggar children with bloodshot eyes, bare feet and naked bodies dotted with pus-oozing sores run beside the bus, bedraggled hair flying, their stomachs curved inwards, their legs like the reeds that grow in the marshes. A lorry piled high to overflowing with hay overtakes, nudging the bus onto the ditch beside the road, and the conductor lets out an ear-splitting whistle, half his body and one leg dangling out of the bus, the wind ballooning his hair and shirt, inciting the sheaf of tickets tacked to a board that sits snug under his arm into rebellion. I pull at my kameez shawl, agitated, and it tears in two. Tears sprout and I angrily brush them away.

Mangalore is dizzy with people, awash with shops, frantic with vehicles. Buses scream, music blares, autos screech, people yell. I don't know where to get off, and just sit tight until the bus pulls into the bus station and a whole load of people rush to get on, squeezing the breath out of me, loath to let me disembark. I manhandle my way through the crush, my arms like batons, breathing in the stale smell of other people's sweat, the tang of toddy, sour breath, the bruised-tobacco whiff of half-chewed paan, the smell of curry and spices clinging to women's saris. Men grope at me, a hand on my breast, squeezing hard, and I attack wildly, my arms flying like missiles. 'Ayyo, enamma,' the man beside me yells, cowering, protecting his face with his hands, those same hands that have just violated me. I land a thump on his head with my elbow for good measure. At last I am free, swallowing the gasoline-stained, blue-tinged, smoke-scented air of the bus station in frantic gulps.

Afterwards, I walk in the pink-spattered orange-red twilight, clutching my bag close, keeping my eyes down, hunger a dull throbbing in my stomach. Men leer, someone wolf-whistles, another sings a Kannada blockbuster song off tune, a group of boys smirk, 'Hey, do you want to come with us?' An auto rickshaw dawdles, 'Ma'am, I'll take you anywhere, only fifty rupees.' A man cycles past, legs working furiously, whistling while ringing his broken bell, a discordant noise that sets the hens, out of sight behind a broken, weed-infested stone wall, squawking. Washing flaps on the balconies of the flats opposite, multicoloured flags painted a uniform monochrome grey by the fast-approaching night. There is a screech and clang as shops shut for the day, weary shopkeepers pulling down the burglar-proof (they hope) aluminium shutters, working the many locks.

What am I doing? Have I gone mad? I should be home now. A picture of you, your expression soft, eyes tender, holding my face in the cup of your palms, 'Devi, you are my life.' I will it away.

I quicken my pace, ignoring the smells of cooking drifting from every side that torment me. My stomach rumbles, it gnaws, it complains. I picture a myriad dinners being cooked, women hunched over the stove, sari pallus tucked into their skirts, hair sticking to their foreheads, rolling chapattis, boiling rice, searing onions, roasting garlic. I picture siblings doing their homework, chewing their pencils until they taste lead, arguing as they wait for food, their rumbling stomachs contributing to their irritability. Men washing to rid their bodies of the day's grime, grandmothers praying, worrying the beads on their rosaries, or if they are Hindu, hands folded in front of shrines overloaded with garlands and anointed with agarbatti. Ordinary lives being lived while mine has turned upside down.

One moment, one raised hand, a stick coming crashing down, tender flesh tearing with a raging crack, the searing taste of anger, the reek of guilt, the branding of shame. And everything changes. Nothing is the same again.

Lights come on in houses. The sky fades from orange to black. Beams flash, twinkling yellow lights relieving the inky darkness redolent with night jasmine and spices and gasoline-stained smoke, as vehicles roar past, drivers rushing to get home. Crickets hum, mosquitoes buzz, frogs grumble. Flies circulate. A dog barks. A woman yells. A child giggles, a burst of delighted laughter undulating in sputtering waves.

What should I do? What will I do? It is too late to go home now; the last bus departed a half hour ago. As I walk, stones smacking the soles of my sandals, inspiration dawns. I will go to the train station. That will be open.

I turn, retrace my steps, past the bus station, now dark, closed for the night, down the alleyway, sprinting, ignoring the drunk huddled beside the road whose hand jerks out, circles my leg. I shake it off. I run faster.

The sky is clouded over. Threatening. Grey clouds tinged murky yellow stark against undulating dark black. Footsteps behind me, 'Hey, Miss.' I quicken my pace. A hand whisks out of the darkness, encircles me. I struggle, try my utmost to wriggle out from under the arm, but the grip is firm, rigid. The arm pulls me roughly and I am smack against a hard chest, the tang of vinegar and sweat. Cigarette smoke in my face. 'Hey, baby, what's a pretty girl like you doing out at this time of night?' Rank breath, smoky sour in my ear. A hand kneading my breasts hard, tweaking my nipples. The pain, the excruciating pain. Whose nightmare have I walked into? The wounds from the night before throb. The man's grasp is vicious. I lash out, hit his torso with my hands, but there is no give. He holds tight, pulls me even closer. His face is upon mine, his fecund breath on my face, rooting for my lips. I aim for the ear, bite down until I taste iron, rust, feel warm viscous liquid flood my mouth. He swears loudly, drops his hands. I run as fast as I can towards the blinking lights of the train station, past the guard house, all the time praying to Lord Ganapathy to rescue me, keeping an ear out for footsteps. None. *Thank you, Lord Ganapathy*. The man must still be reeling in shock and pain. Good. My nipples pulse in agony. My heart is a wild animal caged in the prison of my chest, clamouring for escape.

I run past the idling rickshaws which try to catch up with me, one snaking alongside. 'Where do you want to go, Ma'am? I will take you for free.' The driver bearded, yellow teeth glowing eerily. 'If you come near, I will scream,' I bite out through clenched teeth, my breath coming in pants, my mouth tasting of another man's blood. The station is not far off, I can see people milling. He holds his hands up, palms outward and the rickshaw threatens to roll down the hill. He puts them back on the steering wheel, mumbles, 'Pah, I was just being kind,' and drives off, chug sputter chug.

I run into the blinding light, the busyness of the train station, skirting between porters, luggage, commuters arguing with rickshaw drivers, loath to part with money, past the long queue snaking at the ticket counter, past clumps of tired people dozing while squatting on their luggage, their clothes rumpled, hair awry, mouths part-open and attracting flies, the mournful yellow glow of lamps dancing eerie patterns on their faces. The chaos of the railway station, the mess of weary people welcomes me with open arms like an old friend.

I go to platform 1 where I know the waiting room is, walking past the kiosk selling tea, coffee and potato vadai, the smell of Bru coffee mingling with stale oil causing my stomach to turn. The ladies waiting room is packed to overflowing, benches occupied, women and children camping on saris laid haphazardly on the floor, every inch of space taken. I climb over the carpet of bodies, babies whining, children complaining, mothers snoring open-mouthed, and try to reach the toilet. 'Hey, Miss, you have to pay to use that.' The stink is suffocating. 'Sorry, I didn't realise.' I hold my breath, walk away.

There is a family, a mother, three children squatting by the door. I squeeze in on the floor next to them. The mother is trying to soothe the baby who is crying in fitful bursts. The boy is tugging at her pallu, wanting something. The older girl says to him, 'Come here; what do you want? Don't you see Ma is busy?' The mother smiles at her older daughter, pats her head, the love in her eyes making me ache. 'Thank you, my precious one,' she says to her daughter. I sit cross-legged, put my bag on top, rest my head on it, close my eyes and try to shut out this chaotic slice of world I find myself in.

I am floating. I am dancing, my bare feet kicking up dust which swirls in red clouds around me. I am home, where I belong. I am home with you and all is well. Bobby barks in excitement, nipping at my nimble heels and you, Ma, braid jasmine while squatting on the kitchen veranda. 'Here,' you say, handing me a fragranced loop, 'for my dancing princess.' I sit between your knees as you oil and knead my hair, as you tie it in a knot and coil the jasmine around it. The breeze that drifts from the fields below and caresses my cheek carries the earthy tang of cow manure. Bobby settles next to me, his head in my lap. Crows prattle on coconut fronds and from Sumitranna's kitchen comes the angry clatter of dishes that can only mean Jalajakka has had another spat with him. I hear the sizzle of oil and breathe in the heady aroma of frying vadai. I giggle as Bobby inadvertently tickles me while twitching his nose and rubbing his head with his paw to shoo the flies away. You hum softly, a much-loved lullaby. My eyes close. I smile as I rest my head against your bosom, breathe in the warm, musty smell of you—like mangoes decaying in the sun.

Sour breath hot on my face. I jerk awake. The girl from the family next to me has fallen asleep with her head on my shoulder. I look up, meet the mother's eyes. They plead with me to let the girl be. I look away from the nakedness of the mother's gaze. The station clock blinks the time in red yawning letters: 01:33 a.m. The thought I have been trying to avoid all evening snakes in: what are you doing now, Ma? *I want my mattress, the warmth of you, Ma, next to me, your sputtering snores my lullaby.* The man's hands claiming my body, intrusive, tweaking, hurting. *You were right, Ma, in protecting me so.* The helpless, desperate feeling of being trapped. *I did not realise...* I wink the treacherous thought away; dwell instead on why Rohan didn't turn up at college. I try to summon sleep, oblivion.

When I wake, the family next to me is gone, the waiting room is half empty, but the sour-faced woman policing the toilet is still there. I stand outside the kiosk selling coffee and, with the aid of the reflection the murky glass pane affords of a girl with bloodshot eyes and drooping face, pat my hair down, pushing away thoughts of you combing it. I tidy my salwar as best I can and walk out into the early morning sunshine, tasting the nutty spiced air, towards the bus station, avoiding the alleyway which appears abandoned and harmless in the light of day. The bus station is swarming with crowds, pushing, yelling, laughing, sipping tea and gossiping. *Thank goodness for the bus pass,* I think as I board the heaving bus and, hemmed in by people, judder and bump my way back to the college.

The first person I see as I get off is you, Ma, waiting by the gates of the college, looking like you never slept, your hair awry, escaping your bun and greyer than I expected, your face needy and lined. I am tempted to hide, to walk the other way. Instead, I cross the road towards you when there is a gap in the traffic, and a bus whistles past, scarily close, the petrol-scented exhaust leading my kameez shawl in a merry, smoke-stained dance.

When you see me, your whole face lights up. 'Devi. Devi.' And then I am in your arms, kisses are being rained on my face, my hair. 'I am sorry, so sorry. I will never whip you again. Come home. Please come home. Have you eaten? Where were you?'

I notice the group of girls by the bus stop laughing at the display, the gaggle of boys who usually lounge by the coffee hut opposite pointing.

I disentangle myself from the prison of your arms. 'Go back,' I say. 'I want to go to college.'

'Please come home.' Your scrawny wrist is digging into my palm. Your nose is running, your eyes are streaming.

Despite everything I've been through, I decide that this is the worst moment by far, acutely aware of the myriad gazes fixed our way, watching agog the scene being played out, classmates pointing and laughing. I wish I was anywhere but here; even in that waiting room reeking of urine and faeces and stale sweat. 'I will, this evening.' I say, the impatient tone that inevitably colours my exchanges with you creeping into my voice.

'Have you eaten?' Your palms cool on my face, caressing, stroking.

I push your hands away, not too gently. 'I will this evening,' I repeat.

'I'll wait for you here.' You press something into my hands. A tiffin box. 'Chapattis. For your lunch,' you say.

Across the road, I spot Rohan getting off the bus and my heart executes a little flip. *He's back, he's here.*

'Go home,' I shout, not wanting you to see Rohan, and more importantly, not wanting Rohan to see you like this. 'Just go home.'

'Promise me,' your hand is still circling my wrist. 'Promise me you'll come home, Devi.'

'I promise.'

Your hand drops away. Your eyes are still wild. Slowly you lift your pallu, blow your nose, wipe your face. Slowly, you turn away, your back bent, your hair unkempt. You look like an old vagabond. The thought makes my stomach turn. I want to run up to you, hold you close. From across the road, Rohan sees me, waves. I watch you take weary steps away from me. I wave back.

Ma, you never asked me what happened that night, where I went, what I did. And I didn't tell you, didn't volunteer the information. You had to make do with the fact that I looked okay, perhaps a bit the worse for wear, but unharmed. And of course you always had the madwoman's placating words.

The madwoman.

I used to get mad at you—ha, what an apt choice of word—when you used to run to her for every little thing. But now I think I understand. We all need to believe in something, need succour from something, someone. For you this took the form of the madwoman and for me, now, I have these letters. You know, I started writing them for you, but they are helping me as well. Panning out my thoughts, my memories on paper, looking objectively at the girl I once was is so therapeutic. All those emotions swirling inside of me finally have an outlet. I can understand the appeal of a diary, Ma, why you kept one. And that is the other thing I have. Your diary.

Looking forward to reading this to you tomorrow, Ma, and to reading the next entry in your diary. I am rationing myself you know, to one entry per day. Your thirteen-year-old self wanted to have many children. And yet, you had me. Only me. Why? I suppose I will find out.

I am tempted to read it all in one go… but I won't. I pretend instead that you are writing to me, like I am to you. One entry per day. Your communication with me. Of sorts.

Love,

Devi

Chapter 6
Shilpa

Lime Sherbet

Lime Sherbet:

Ingredients:

Fresh limes from the garden.

Water.

Sugar and salt to taste.

Method:

Squeeze limes into a bowl, taking care not to include any pips. Add water. You have to be careful here—I like to make the sherbet nice and strong, so I put in roughly two cups of water to one cup of lime juice. Sugar—again, I like mine very sweet, so I add a heaped tablespoon of sugar per cup of sherbet. Salt—aha, salt you say, scrunching up your face. But this is my secret ingredient. This is what gives the sherbet its zing. Add one tablespoon of salt to the bowl after you have stirred in the sugar. Mix well.

Taste. Go on.
What did I tell you?

❄ ❄ ❄

Dear Diary,

Lime Sherbet is what I serve Manoj when he comes to see me, to ask for my hand in marriage. As I hand him the cool tumbler, the condensation dotting the silvery surface glinting like jewels, I notice his hands. A farmer's hands. Wide and callused, inured to hard work. The nails, which I can see he has scrubbed until they shine, carry traces of earth at the point where they meet skin. His skin is the smooth brown of a shaved coconut. Wavy black hairs sprouting from the tops of his hands dance merrily as he lifts the tumbler to his mouth. His shirt, which is clearly new (I can just make out the creases from where it was folded), and which he must have bought especially for the occasion, is stained yellow with sweat at the collar and his feet and lungi are dusty from the walk through the fields to our house. He takes a sip of the sherbet. Beads of perspiration dotting his upper lip tremble ominously as he drinks. I suppress the urge to wipe them away with the cloth I hold in my hand. 'Ah,' he says, looking up at me and smiling, 'This is heavenly.' And in his eyes I see the admiration, the adoration I have been waiting for. In his smile, I see my future.

This is not what normally happens, dear Diary, when the very important procedure of arranging marriages is put in motion. Like the recipes I delight in, there is an order to arranging marriages, a method.

First, the parents of an eligible boy elicit the help of the village gossip. They ply the gossip with cashew liquor and potato bondas, with mutton curry and pomfret fry. As she sucks the marrow off the bone, they tell her how the price of mutton has hit the roof and no one can afford it anymore. They tell her that the pomfret is from the fishmonger in Mangalore who stocks the freshest fish even though it costs ten rupees more per kilo, watching as she carefully prises every last sliver of pomfret flesh from the bone. They do not eat of course; they let her eat first, so she gets principal choice, the best bits. They will dine on the leftovers after she has left.

Once she has eaten to her heart's content and managed to consume two laddoos and three Mysore paks after, all the while averring that she is full and couldn't eat another morsel, once she has burped enthusiastically to express satisfaction, the boy's parents, close relatives and the village gossip sit on the veranda chewing paan and eating sugar-coated saunf, for all the world looking like companionable friends, when everyone knows they are anything but. This is a business relationship, pure and simple, and the business part of it will be conducted now.

Sitting on the veranda, the air green and smelling of churned earth, the paan satisfyingly crunchy and moist in her mouth, the village gossip brings the boy's family up to date on eligible girls in the neighbouring villages. She tells them which girls' morals are not up to scratch, which one has been seen smiling at boys, talking with them. She tells them which girls come from good stock and which girls' families have disgraced themselves. She tells them which girl is dark and which one fair, which girl has a tendency towards obesity and which one is too scrawny to lift a cat let alone a baby, which one has rounded hips conducive to childbearing and which one is as flat-chested and lanky-hipped as a boy.

The boy's family note all this down, making a list of eligible girls and ticking each one off as the gossip speaks. In the end they are left with a sum total of three girls, if that. The parents of the boy then pay a visit to the houses of each of the girls still on the list, and if they like her, if she passes their scrutiny, then they go back—with their son.

I have been through the first part of this process many times. And the second, never. The parents of eligible boys don't seem to like me. They come up with myriad reasons—my nose is too large, my eyes too far apart, my smile crooked, my hair too thin…

At twenty-five, I am in danger of becoming an old maid. The bridge of lines that dances across my mother's eyes when she frowns is now a permanent fixture. Her sari pallus are in tatters from wringing them in worry. My father walks around with a thunderous scowl on his face. My parents are weary of me being rejected by one prospective suitor's parents after another. But not as much as I am. What of my dreams? My wish to be a wife and mother to a brood of adoring children? My stack of recipes is growing every day. And with each day, my hopes are diminishing.

And now, this man is here. No parents. Just him. And he is smiling at me. Good sign? I hope so. I have no wish to remain an old maid.

Manoj doesn't have any parents—hence no first stage; he's jumped right to the second. I doubt he's hired the services of the village gossip either. His parents passed away when he was just a boy, he tells us. They were struck by typhoid, taken from him, one after the other. He was brought up by an uncle who also passed away this past year, he says. He is lonely, he wants to settle down. 'I like your daughter; I would like to offer for her hand,' he declares, setting down his empty tumbler carefully.

All it takes is one tumbler of lime sherbet. This man is easily pleased.

Afterwards, as we are washing the dishes by the bimbli tree, my mother says, 'It is a good thing he doesn't have any parents. There will be no one to nag you, order you around. You get to be your own boss, run your house the way you like.'

My house. I feel a shiver of anticipation, of excitement, run up my spine. This is what I have been waiting for all these years.

And so, it is decided. Over my trademark green plantain podis, my father broaches the subject of dowry.

'I don't want any dowry, Sir, your daughter is enough,' Manoj says, surprising my father so much that he chokes on his plantain podi and has to be slapped on the back by my mother.

'But... she is our only daughter; we have to send her to you with dowry,' my mother says firmly and my father looks fit to choke again.

'How do you plan to look after her?' my father asks, sufficiently recovered but still quite red in the face.

They are discussing me like they would debate what fish to buy at the market, whether the mackerel is fresher than the sardine. Outside, the chickens cluck plaintively, a cow moos somewhere among the fields. And here, my future is being decided over plantain podis and tumblers of cardamom and ginger tea.

'I work for Sumitranna in Sompur—you know him?' Manoj looks at my father who nods. 'He has agreed to loan me a quarter of his field in which to build our house. He will take a portion off my earnings every month until I have repaid him.'

'Well then, we will give you the money we have been saving for Shilpa's dowry towards the cost of materials for building the house,' my mother says even as my father sputters a, 'But he doesn't want...'

And just like that, it is decided, the date is set and my lifelong ambition is looking to be fulfilled.

Chapter 7
Nisha

The Smell of Prayer

Nisha hunkers down among the pews, breathing in the tang of turpentine, the wood jutting against her ribs and back, soothing in its familiarity. Around her, the whisper of hymns, the sigh of prayer books being opened, the giggle of children, the hiss of parents telling them off, the familiar mothball odour of desperation, of entreaties to the Lord. She can see the prayers making their way heavenward, carried upward by the voices of the nuns raised in chorus, by the dust motes swirling in the multi-hued patterns created by the sun reflecting off the stained-glass windows, by the mosquitoes and the flies that lift them up with their wings. She can hear how hollow the prayers sound as they make their way to the very top, past the mother crows jealously guarding their young snug in the nests tucked into the beams. The prayers get stuck in the roof, quivering helplessly, looking to her for assistance. She draws air smelling of incense and a hint of jasmine into her lungs, inhaling some dust motes in the process and blows, poof, and away the prayers go, through the cricks in the mellow orange Mangalore tiles, heaven-bound. 'Thank you,' the prayers sing, their voices as precious and insubstantial as fairy dust, before they fly into the arms of God. 'Thank you.' The statues of the Mother Mary of Miracles and Jesus on the cross, St Francis of Assisi and St Paul and St Peter, all smile down at her and she feels their collective approval like a warm caress, enveloping her in its velvet arms.

There's a gnawing deep inside her. Her stomach is cavernous, a yawning tunnel that wants to be filled. It rumbles, the sound loud in the shadowy blue underneath the pews. She smothers a laugh. No one must know she is here. She sees toes, so many toes, some painted, nail varnish peeling off, others dusty, a broken nail, a weeping gash, a toe shaped like a question mark, another like a comma. She pictures God opening up the Heavens with a crack like lightning, his hand, golden and iridescent wafting through and plucking at the prayers. He smiles down at her and her hunger disappears. She is sated, happy, her stomach warm and full like when she has eaten a masala dosa with lots of sambar and a whole container of chutney.

The smell of sweat from the many bodies packed into the church envelops her along with the aroma of spicy fried fish with a faint undertone of jasmine drifting in on the breeze from Duja's compound, and a whiff of camphor incense from where the altar boys are swinging the thurible a bit too hard, earning a raised eyebrow from the priest. Then she is in the cool vestry as if by magic; she is watching the priest put on his robes, transforming from an ordinary balding person in a white cloak into someone magnificent. A Miracle, like the nuns keep going on about. A real live Miracle. He carries the golden orb containing the Sacrament, the Body of Jesus, and she watches transfixed. The altar boys whisper among themselves and the priest quiets them with a look. *Watch out, boys, he can perform Miracles; he might transform you into frogs if you're not careful.*

Her stomach rumbles again, God's benevolent munificence gone. She is hungry, so hungry. She goes to the convent in search of food. She wanders into the chapel. Empty. The dining hall, empty. The prayer room, same. The confessional. Not a soul. She is running, through every room, calling for the nuns, shouting, her voice echoing back, shrill, tinged with hysteria. Empty. Empty. Empty. Where is everyone? Where is she? She is lost. She is lost. Her stomach feels hollow. Her breath comes in gasps.

She is lost.

'Nisha, darling, wake up.' And she is in Matt's familiar embrace, breathing in his smell, faint remnants of the musky cologne he wears. Sweat. Her eyes are streaming. Her throat feels hoarse. 'It's okay, babe,' he says, rocking her in the cradle of his arms. 'It's fine.'

Slowly she comes back into the present. The gnawing in her stomach—not hunger. Loss. Hurt. Betrayal. It hits her then, the ache, and she wishes she was back in the dream again. She prefers the feeling of being lost to the feeling of being adrift, a directionless compass. Her insides are hollow, she is a shell.

'A nightmare?' Matt asks, his voice soft, as he switches on the bedside lamp.

She squints in the sudden yellow light, warm and mellow as yolk oozing out of a runny boiled egg, flooding the room. The remembered smell of jasmine and camphor inundates her nostrils. 'What is happening to me, Matt?'

He pours her a glass of water from the jug sitting handy beside him. 'Drink,' he says, 'then we'll talk.' His eyes are soft as a meadow soaking in the first golden rays of warm spring sun after a hellish winter. She wants to sink into them, stay there.

The previous evening she had showed him the letter, asked him if she should call the number for the convent.

'What do *you* think?' he had asked, stroking his beard the way he did when he was thinking, his gaze tender.

'I… I don't know.'

'Sleep on it, Nisha. Sometimes, your subconscious has a way of providing the solution.' He had smiled then, the smile that lit up his face like a beacon, like a house just visible through a blanket of blinding fog, a hazy silhouette that provides the promise of shelter to a weary traveller lost en route to wherever he was going.

She had clung to Matt, taking comfort from the steady beating of his heart, so solid, so real. She had pushed all thought away, focusing instead on calculating the value of pi to as many decimal places as she could. Matt was not sleeping, she knew; he was waiting for her to fall asleep first and for this she was inordinately grateful.

'What are you thinking?' she had whispered, her soft hiss loud in the thick silence of the darkened room.

'I'm thinking of you,' he had said, turning round, smiling down at her. 'Of how much I love you.'

She knew he wanted her to say, 'I love you too.' She wanted to say it, if just to please him, give something back, but her tongue wouldn't, couldn't push out the words. How could she, when she didn't know for sure? How could she, especially now, when she couldn't even be assured of her parents' love—the one thing she had taken for granted, accepted without proof? Neither of her parents had said those words to her, and the couple of times she had told them she loved them out loud, they had blushed, embarrassed, and swiftly changed the topic. And yet, she had always known she was loved. She, who never believed in anything without accompanying evidence, had accepted her parents' love as a given. Why hadn't she questioned it, requested evidence?

'And you?' Matt had said after a bit, 'What were you thinking?'

'I was calculating the value of pi—had reached up to ten decimal places,' she had said and he had thrown back his head and laughed, a low rumble starting in his stomach and bursting out of him in sonorous waves.

'Shh,' she'd nudged, laughing along, 'you'll wake the neighbours.' And then, 'Matt?'

'Yes,' he'd stopped long enough to squint down at her.

'You don't have any surprises up your sleeve do you? You aren't biding your time waiting to spring something on me?' She felt naked, vulnerable, asking. She could not hide the tremor in her voice.

'Oh, Nisha.' He had bent down, kissed her, his eyes boring into hers, doing the talking. And then they had made love, slowly, drawing comfort from each other. Afterwards, he had said, 'This is me. All that I am. All yours.' And she had fallen asleep, anchored in his arms, safe in the knowledge that this at least was real, the truth.

Now she shivers as she recounts the dream, still so tangible that she can smell the pews, see the prayers, touch the thurible dispensing incense, experience the palpable fear. 'This is the dream I have been having the past few days, I am sure of it,' she says. 'I used to wake with the smell of jasmine invading my nose, but I couldn't remember anything at all. And then, when I was reading the letter…' The letter, that awful, damning letter. '…fragments of it came back. Do you think this is my subconscious at work, Matt?'

He scrunches up his nose in that way she loves, strokes his beard thoughtfully, 'I don't know, sweetheart.'

'Go back to sleep,' she whispers, padding out of the bedroom in her slippers, pulling her dressing gown close around her naked body to ward off the chill, the cold air sneaking in through the vents. She doesn't like the heating on when she sleeps and she keeps the vents open. She gets the laptop, climbs back into bed. Matt is still wide awake, propped up amongst the tangle of duvet and bed sheets.

When he sees her approach, squat cross-legged on the bed and open up the computer, he smiles, shakes his head. 'You are still you,' he whispers.

She types fast, fingers flying on the keys. 'Our brain deceives us,' she says. 'Memory is surprisingly easy to trick,' she says. 'Aha, a paper on research of suppressed memories resurfacing as dreams.' She scans the article, turns to him. This is her forte. Research, talking ideas through. What she does best. 'I might be having these dreams because of trauma, my parents dying. But why would I dream of the convent? Could be because of the letter. Hmm.' An idea is beginning to form. She turns to Matt, 'Or… I was adopted at four, say, definitely before I turned five. Suppose the trauma of separation, the transition to a new country and culture, having to accept these strangers as parents was too much for me and I "lost" all my memories. Don't forget, just after I also started school, my parents making sure I knew what was expected of me from day one, so there was the added pressure of settling in, performing well. Also, I started having rectifying operations for the cleft around then too. All reasons why I could have repressed memories of my life before—they would have been too much for my brain to cope.' She ticks points off on her fingers as she speaks, holding Matt captive with her eyes, 'So now, when my parents die, the trauma serves as a trigger and then I get this letter…'

'Makes sense,' Matt says.

She takes another long gulp of water. 'Matt, if what I experienced there was a suppressed memory, then I was a very imaginative child. Where has that girl gone?' She pauses. Then...'Or it could be my subconscious messing with me, the contents of the letter playing on my brain and triggering vivid dreams. But... Matt, it felt like I was there. And the detail: the priest's robes, the brown rows of feet in fraying sandals—how could my mind have made that up? And the smells? The vivid smells which accost my nose even after I'm awake?'

'Your subconscious has definitely done its job, been working overtime,' Matt says. And then, softly, 'So... will you call the convent then?'

'I... before this letter, I knew myself, who I was. It was a certainty I took comfort in. You know I like to slot facts into compartments in my brain. It makes me feel good, feel whole. And now, all the compartments have burst open, spilling their contents. What I knew to be the truth I now find out is just an illusion. I am a puzzle and until I solve it, until I slot the pieces together, I will not feel whole again.'

'I understand,' Matt says and in that moment her affection for him overflows.

Is this love? What else could this emotion that threatens to engulf me, take me captive, be? I wish I could stop analysing every single feeling and just tell him I love him. I wish my throat wouldn't clog up every time I open my mouth to convince him, convince myself of the depth of my feeling. She reaches out and caresses his lower lip gently with her finger. He looks at her and she knows he understands. But it is not enough, not nearly enough.

That girl, the imaginative girl from the dream, would she have been able to express what she felt out loud without feeling there was a boulder stuck in her oesophagus preventing speech?

'If I called the convent, I wouldn't know where to start. I am so angry at them, my parents…' She bunches the sheets in her fists. 'All they leave me is a slip of paper telling me not nearly enough. Typical. They were never good with words of this kind. It would have been different had they been writing a scientific paper…' Her eyes fill with involuntary tears. She can picture how hard it must have been for the dry couple who shied away from emotion to sit down and write the letter: each word a struggle. How can she understand them so well when they duped her so, when they let her live a lie her whole life?

Matt reaches across and touches her face. A tear trembles on the tip of his finger, a shimmery globule, suspended, fragile.

That is exactly how I feel, like I will shatter into a thousand disjointed pieces any minute.

'There are so many questions…' she says instead. 'They buzz round my brain like a babble of wasps. I just… I need to sort them out in my head first, then I will be able to call…'

'Write them down,' Matt says softly, 'write all the questions down and then we will approach them one by one.'

He knows her so well, knows the comfort she derives from making methodical lists.

And he said 'we'. He said 'we', not 'you'.

She reaches up, and with one finger traces the outline of his face, his eyes, his lips. And as dawn's blush suffuses the drowsy sky the rosy pink of newborn skin, Matt makes love to her, erasing the imprint of the dream, writing himself into her mind instead.

Chapter 8
Devi

Hymn of Pain

Ma,

This morning as I was reading to you in that stuffy room, I thought you stirred. I paused, looked up. Nothing. You lay serene, unruffled, breathing with the aid of those machines, electronic monsters bolstering you, holding you in place. I went back to reading to you and you moaned. I looked up. This time, you moved. I rushed to the door, shouted for a nurse, a doctor. You thrashed about wildly, dislodging the drip that feeds nutrients into you. I bent close. 'What is it, Ma?' I asked.

'Baby,' I made out. 'Wise woman.' Your first words since all this happened, Ma, and guess whom you call upon! I shouldn't be surprised, really.

Was it the mention of the madwoman in the letter I was reading that triggered something, fired your synapses into action? Did the madwoman have a baby? Is that what were you trying to say, Ma? Of all the things that

I imagined you would say when you regained consciousness, this was furthest from my mind…What is going on in your head as you lie there looking so calm, Ma?

By the time the nurse arrived, you were back to your unconscious state. At least when you inhabit that state you are peaceful, not flaying about, agitated. 'It is a good sign,' the nurse said, expertly fixing your drip, noting down the readings on your various machines. 'She is trying to come back. There is no imminent danger of her slipping into a coma.'

Well then, that's fantastic, Ma, that means these letters are helping. There's more of a mention of the madwoman in this letter—I know you hate me calling her that. 'She is wise, not mad,' you have said a million times. But to me, she will always be madwoman—the raving ranting witch who had an insane hold over you to the point that even now, when you come back briefly from your unconscious state, you invoke her, not me.

Anyway, let's see how you react when I read this letter out to you.

So, I ran away from home and you spent an agonised night waiting for me by the college gates, praying that no harm would come to me. You told me later that the madwoman had said, 'Devi was singed but not burnt'—your only reference to the night, your eyes asking me a question. 'Your prayers worked, Ma,' I replied, not wanting to acknowledge the madwoman one way or another. You smiled, relieved, and never brought that night up again, preferring to forget. I was fine with that; I wanted to forget too. And anyway, the events that took place after rather eclipsed that night, didn't they?

That morning, after I have sent you on your way with promises to come home after college, the discomfort of the previous night manifesting itself in aches and pains all over my body, my roiling anger having dissipated to a dull throb, I turn to wave at Rohan. He bounds across the road towards me, his smile mesmerising as a peacock strutting its plumage. He takes my arm and once again I try not to flinch as the healing sores are bruised afresh. I watch you hobble to the bus stop, stop to catch your breath and turn around, your eyes searching for me. I turn away.

'Guess what,' Rohan says, waving a piece of paper in front of me, his eyes shining. 'I have won a place at King's College, London! To work towards a doctorate in biochemistry. They have also offered me a small stipend!'

I stare at him, blank. This is the first I've heard of it. The air smells fresh, spiced, of last night's rain and of the tamarind rice and sambar cooking in the little shop across the road. It caresses my face, soft as your best Kanjeevaram silk sari, Ma, the one you claim you wore at your wedding reception. A mynah bird sings from the bowels of the banyan tree above and my classmates chatter happily around me while my world turns upside down once more.

'I told you I was applying.' His face is glowing; he can't seem to stop smiling.

I don't need to ask the question that hovers on my lips. I already know the answer. *I cannot rely on anybody,* I think. *Everyone betrays me.* You, Ma, claim to love me more than life itself and then you hit me mercilessly for something I didn't even do. And now Rohan, whom I love, perhaps the first boy I have properly loved, is leaving. I should have let him do what he wanted, what *I* wanted that day at the lake, claimed him for a brief while. I got whipped for it, regardless. Was it only two evenings ago? It seems so far away now. Tears threaten. Lack of sleep is making me uncharacteristically maudlin. I blink them away, will a smile to grace my face. 'Good on you, Rohan,' I say and my voice sounds cheery, thank goodness. 'I wish I was going abroad, far away from here. This stupid place with its constraints on women.' That man squeezing my breasts, the feeling of being trapped, violated. 'Where men can do what they like but if a woman does, she's branded a whore.'

Rohan smiles down at me, his eyes soft, 'Society is changing, Devi.'

'In the cities perhaps. Not here. Not yet.'

'So do you want to come with me then, my feisty firecracker, to a country where you can do what you like, when you like without fear of being branded anything?'

Have I heard right? Was that a proposal couched as a joke? I stare up at him. 'You are joking, right?'

He grins at me, grabs my hand, 'Come with me.' And in the next instant, the smile is gone, his face serious, his gaze intense, eyes the honey gold of sugar syrup, boring into me. 'I cannot live without you, Devi.'

What is it you like to say, Ma? 'Beware. They will have their way with you and discard you like a used cloth.'

What is Rohan asking exactly?

'Marry me.'

Oh Lord Ganapathy. I sway on my feet. Too little sleep. I am dreaming. Aren't I? His face, grinning like the monkeys that invade the temple by the sea and snatch laddoos from unsuspecting devotees' hands, and even, oftentimes, their mouths.

'I am serious. That is why I wasn't in yesterday. Was trying to sort it out with my parents. They are still not okay with it, with me marrying a non-Catholic, but I will work on them.' And, his eyes lighting up as an idea takes root, 'Come home with me this evening, Devi. When they see you, see how much we love each other, they will have to agree.' And then, the grin disappearing, looking suddenly worried, 'You do want to marry me, don't you?'

❄ ❄ ❄

I stand in the stuffy phone booth opposite the college, which reeks of cow dung and Bru coffee wafting from the little hut doing brisk business next door. 'I love Sneha,' 'Raghu is a bastard,' 'Go to Hell,' and other obscenities are scrawled in a jumble of Kannada and English in rickety letters on the thin cardboard wall opposite where I stand, cramped in the too small space. Sweat travels down my head, and I can feel my hair getting sticky, the coconut oil used to work it into submission collecting in clumps. My salwar kameez reeks of last night, of railway station, of that man's smoky sour breath. I long to have a wash in the poky bathroom at home, the walls stained dingy black with soot from years of heating the water in the big aluminium urn, coconut fronds and twigs haphazardly adorning one wall, stored there to avoid getting drenched in the rain. The thought of pouring the scalding water smelling of earth and coconut husk from the cracked aluminium mug onto my head, my body, washing away the travails of the previous night, the blessed relief of it, is inviting, beguiling. Instead I stand here perspiring, the blisters weeping and itchy inside my kameez, dialling the number of the phone at home with moist fingers. It hardly ever rings. You will have just got home from work, cleaning other people's houses, and you will be putting the rice on to boil. You will be startled by the ring of the phone. You will worry.

I have told Rohan it is not a good idea, that I don't look my best, but he is adamant that we visit his parents today, convinced that once they see me, see how much he loves me, how much we love each other, they will give permission for the wedding.

'You are so naïve, Rohan,' I say. 'Just because *you* like me doesn't mean *they* will. In fact, I am sure they won't. I am not meek, submissive, good daughter-in-law material, you know.'

'Aargh, I don't know why they are so rigid,' he grumbles angrily. 'I don't know why they cannot say yes. I love *you*; want to marry you, not some Catholic girl they have chosen for me.' His words, the vehemence with which he says them, melt my heart—and it doesn't melt easily, you of all people know that, Ma. His words wipe away the intense tiredness that is making me sway on my feet.

'What if I lose it with them? You know what a short fuse I've got. I might just blow it.'

'We'll cross that hurdle when we come to it. Come with me. I want them to see the girl I am going to marry,' his eyes shining as he says those last few words.

How can I refuse?

And so, I am here, and the phone is ringing and ringing. *Come on, Ma,* I think. *Pick up.*

Boys cluster in twos and threes round the little hut outside sipping coffee and eyeing the girls emerging from college or waiting for the bus, catcalling and wolf-whistling, making it impossible to hear anything. The coffee hut is run by the same man who owns the booth—he came up with the brilliant idea of adding a cardboard box beside his shop, installing a phone inside and charging students the exorbitant sum of ten rupees for a local phone call. 'Free coffee,' the man said to me, eyes flashing, mouth stained scarlet with paan. 'Go on,' Rohan said, pressing the money into the man's palm, 'quick. I will wait here.' I look at Rohan silhouetted against the cloudy, graffiti-encrusted glass. He is kicking the dust in front of his feet, something he does when he is thinking deeply, when he is worried or nervous. Is he having second thoughts? Stray cows mill close by and the barking of dogs reverberates in the smoky yellow, dust-stained air.

'Hello,' I hear, as if from a distance. Your voice, laced with panic.

'Ma, it's me,' I shout, trying to be heard above the noise, the cacophony of a bad connection.

'Devi,' my name an entreaty on your lips. 'What's happened?'

'Nothing's happened,' I say. Rohan is signalling something to me from outside the window. I can hear Bobby barking, you yelling at him to shush. 'I will be a bit late coming home today, that's all.'

There is a pause, punctuated by Bobby's barks. And then, I hear you sniffing in that telltale way that signals tears, lots of them. 'I am sorry for what I did, Devi, I was worried about you, so worried. See, it is my job to protect you—my only child. You are so pretty, you are prey for all the bad people out there…'

I bristle. 'I was with Rohan. He is not a bad person.' *And he's just asked me to marry him.*

A pause, 'I thought… I thought…'

'The worst of me.' Hurt makes my voice sharper than I intend for it to be.

'Please come home,' you sob.

'I will,' I say, shortly, 'I have to do something first.'

'Wait,' you plead. 'What time will you be home?'

'Before dark,' I say and plonk the phone back in the receiver before you can say any more.

❄ ❄ ❄

Rohan's house is on the downward slope of a little hillock, next to the unlicensed arrack shop, where a long line of men mill, sucking on beedis, scratching their crotches.

They enter furtively via the back door and emerge carrying hazy glass bottles filled to the brim with snot-coloured liquid. The front of the shop displays peanuts in dirty glass jars and ten-paisa sweets: fingernail-sized balls of sugar wrapped in plastic, chikkis: yellow peanuts encased in golden sugar syrup, and chakulis: prickly rounds of yellow dough. Plastic bags of tubular buttery snacks and bananas dangle from the beams of the ceiling. There is no queue at all in the front of the shop, except for the couple of children playing hopscotch right outside, so covered in dust that only the whites of their eyes are visible, spookily milky against the orange of their bodies. Even their eyelashes are stained red. They ogle the sweets cannily, hoping to nick some when no one's looking.

Swirling dust displaced by a bullock cart, a lorry or the occasional rickshaw making its creaking way down the road above, settles on the house, so it has a permanent red haze. The windows are covered by old saris masquerading as curtains, which dance in the occasional dusty breeze, allowing neighbours of houses higher up the hillock tantalising glimpses into all the rooms. Pungent fumes assault my nostrils and one of the men waves at me from across the road, flashing toothless, black gums before turning away and lifting his lungi. A milky trickle falls into the ditch below and the murky yellow tang of urine colours the air.

'Rohan, is that you?' his mother calls as she comes out onto the veranda, wiping her hands on her cotton sari, dirty green with creamy flowers which look like splotches of runny egg yolk. 'I...' her words die on her lips as she takes me in. I can picture how I must look to her: my hair bedraggled, my blue kameez auburn thanks to the coat of dust painted on during the walk from the bus stop to the house. 'Why have you brought her here, Rohan?' Her voice is high-pitched, purple with shock.

Neighbours collect in verandas and gape shamelessly, sipping on tea, eating vadai and partaking of the teatime entertainment obligingly provided by the D'Cunha family. Rohan looks down, kicks up dust. 'Ma, shall we go in?'

'You tell me, why, after our discussion yesterday and this morning, is she here now?' Voice strident.

Silence on the busy street descending like a hawk swooping on an unsuspecting rodent, as sudden as when the drape is pulled up to signal the commencement of a play. The clink of bottles from the arrack shop stops. The line of men turns to face us. Children stop playing and walk down the hill, collect in groups, hopping over each other to get the best possible view. The woman drawing water from the well of the house up the hill stops mid-pull, the pail halfway up the well tilting, dropping water in a silvery trickle and a hollow splash.

'Ma, please,' Rohan says, still not looking at his mother.

I feel the heat rise from the base of my stomach, up my throat and suffuse my cheeks. Everywhere there are people staring at me, as if I am a monkey escaped from the zoo, an actor in the Yakashagana performance of Shoorpanakha. The air reeks of humiliation, hot, scarlet. This is the second time in one day that I have been the main character in a drama. Not to my liking, I think; I don't suppose I will ever take up acting. Why am I thinking such facetious thoughts? What else can I do? I am seeing a different, diffident side to Rohan, the most popular boy in college, the boy all the girls fancy, the boy who wants me. I look at my feet, clad in the open-toed Bata sandals you buy at great cost, while you go barefoot and are forever removing corns from your feet with the kitchen scythe. My feet are stained like sin, with a vermilion coating of dust.

'My only son, and you want to marry a Hindu. Why? Aren't there enough Catholic girls around? What does she have'—a trembling hand, plump, nails bitten to the core, pudgy fingers pointing at me—'that the Fernandes girl doesn't?'

My eyes sting. My blood roils. *Come on, Rohan, say something. Stand up for yourself, you idiot, stand up for me. If you don't, I will. I cannot take this for much longer.*

Rohan's feet draw busily in the mud. I notice that his second toe is bigger than his first.

A commotion. Rohan's father elbows his way through the rabble, a lopsided bag slung wearily across his shoulder, coming home from work to find his house the setting of a play being enacted for the benefit of his neighbours and the village drunks. People agog watching his wife screaming, her face slack and yellow with fury. Everyone still, soundless but for the crunch of chuda, the munch, the gulp, the hurried swallow of goli baje, the slurp of tea. Food and drama go hand in hand, don't they?

'What's happening here? What's the matter?' And then I feel his eyes on me. One tear breaks free, travels down my face, following the curve of my nose and slipping between my open lips. Salt. Mortification. Rage. You, Ma, whipping me, the barley-scented air tasting of brine, smelling of anger, guilt, hurt: a blue-tinged black smell. 'Don't mess with boys. They are not worth the effort.'

But I love him, Ma. He is doing this for me. It takes a certain kind of courage to brave all these people, their probing gazes, their tongues wet and salivating with the itch to spread the gossip unfolding right in front of them.

Although I would prefer it if you stood up to them a bit, Rohan. Come on; I am reining my fury in, waiting for you to speak up.

'Why is she here?' Rohan's father's voice is accusing, made harsh by weariness. He has not expected to come home, hot and bothered from a long day's work, looking forward to his cup of cardamom tea and the Maggi noodles his wife makes for him, tangy and spiced with chillies and red onions and cumin powder, to this, I know.

I am tired of waiting for Rohan to do something. I have had enough.

'Stop talking about me in the third person; I am right here.' I look right at the both of them, his parents.

A ripple rocks the crowd, a collective, 'Ooh, Aah, Aiyyo Devare.' A child cries—a plaintive sound like the whine of a distressed siren.

'I love Rohan, he loves me and we are going to marry each other.' His parents stare at me open-mouthed.

The crowd: 'Aiyyo, did you hear what she said? How dare she? Too bold she is, this one.'

Finally, his mother finds her voice, 'Rohan? Putha?'

Rohan looks up at last from his perusal of the circles he is drawing in the mud. His hand finds mine and squeezes hard. 'I love Devi, Ma. I want to marry her.'

I am mad at Rohan for bringing me here, subjecting me to this, for taking so long to stand up to his parents, and I have a good mind to push his hand away. But I see his mother's gaze riveted on our linked hands and so, I let it be.

The crowd: 'She is a minx; she has him under her thumb. What else would you expect from Hindu girls?'

I want to lash out at the crowd, but what is the point? It will not achieve anything. I wait for the message that Rohan is not going to back down, give in, sink into his parents' minds. I am aware of everyone's gaze fixed on our entwined hands.

What would you make of this display, Ma? You who have tried so hard, so against my own will, to protect my reputation.

'I am going to marry Devi, either with your approval…' A louder murmur from the crowd, sounding like an impending thunderstorm. '…or without.'

'No!' his mother screams. 'Have you gone mad? What is it about her you like—her beauty? Why, there are so many prettier, fairer Catholic girls! Why this one, putha? You are innocent, baba, but she is not. I have heard that she has had so many boyfriends. Her name is bandied about, always in association with boys.'

The heat in my body explodes onto my face. A crow cackles and a sudden gust of breeze carrying the fruity whiff of guava and cashew lashes my face. I reclaim my hand from Rohan's grip and walk up to his mother who is standing on her front step. She recoils. The crowd emits a collective, 'Aiyyo, what is she doing?'

'I have had friends who are boys, yes,' I say loudly and clearly. 'Your son knows that, don't you, Rohan?'

He nods, his face flooding with colour. 'And Rohan also has girls who are his friends. So, what is the difference, tell me?'

His mother opens and closes her mouth like a drowning man gasping for breath. Rohan's father says shortly, 'He is a boy. He does not have to explain himself.'

'And I do? Why? He can strut around town with a bevy of girls doing his every bidding, but when I have friends who are boys; I am a bad girl, is it? I cannot marry him.'

'Yes,' Rohan's mother says, having retrieved her voice from wherever she had misplaced it. 'That's right, yes.'

A collective hush, a fascinated sigh.

'Well, tough. I am marrying your son, whether you want me to or not.'

The crowd erupts, chattering noisily. 'Did you hear what she said? Did you?'

And then, his mother is in front of me, too close, hands joined as if in prayer, 'Please, don't take my only son away from me.'

Murmurs from the crowd, their faces frozen in exaggerated expressions of shock, mouths open, eyes wide: 'The bitch, making Mabel Bai plead!' 'I wouldn't let my son…' 'These Hindus, no shame, any of them!'

Rohan's mother prostrates herself on the ground in front of me, displacing a mini avalanche of red dust, unmindful of the pebbles digging into her thighs, her green sari collecting a brown gloss of mud. She holds my feet with both hands in a surprisingly strong grasp, trapping me. 'I am begging you.'

I should be home, squatting beside you, Ma, on the kitchen veranda, eating red rice and dry fish chutney, throwing Bobby the scraps. Why am I here, subjecting myself to this?

So much time has passed and yet I feel the humiliation as if it was yesterday. If you were awake, Ma, you would cringe as I read you this. You would cup your ears in your palms and ask me to stop. 'Please don't continue, Devi, I don't want to hear,' you would say. Will you stir when I read this to you tomorrow, Ma? Will this account shock you out of your unconscious state? If so, then some good would have come of the shame I endured, at long last...

The crowd is in uproar. 'Her mother should have looked after her better,' someone says. 'Fancy letting her gallivant with good Catholic men all hours of the day and night.' 'Does her mother even know where she is at this time of the evening when all the good girls are indoors?' 'Why does he want her, what does he see in her, our Rohan?' I hear.

Oh Lord, I think, trying to escape the stranglehold Rohan's mum has on my dirty feet, *this is getting tedious.* Trapped yesterday and again today. I am tempted to kick her off, but that would be going one step too far.

Rohan's father is yelling, 'Mabel, what on earth are you doing?' his voice laced with desperation.

I bend down and grasp the woman's shoulders, aiming for gentle although every instinct shouts otherwise. 'Please stop this,' I say, trying to soften my voice. 'It is not helping.' She doesn't budge. The urge to kick is getting stronger, threatening to overtake my resistance of which there is precious little.

Thankfully, Rohan comes to my rescue, or to be more precise, to his mother's rescue, reading in my eyes the impulse I am tempted to give in to.

'Ma,' he says, bending down and helping his mother up, her green sari tinted dusty auburn, yellow splotches no longer visible, the roll of wobbly pink flesh visible between sari blouse and skirt dotted with pebbles, 'She hasn't taken me away from you. I am still yours.' His voice is tender. His mother leans against him, spent, and all of a sudden she looks very old.

'Then why are you behaving like this, putha? First you tell us you want to go far away to study. What is wrong with Indian universities, tell me? Anyway, we agree to that and then you say you will take this... this Hindu girl with you.' Her voice blue with pain. 'And not just any Hindu girl either. This one, whose reputation precedes her by a mile.'

I should have kicked her, the old hag.

'Ma, what does it matter, Catholic, Hindu? But if you care so much, Devi will convert to Catholicism, won't you, Devi?'

It is on the tip of my tongue to say, 'Why should I?' But Rohan is looking at me with that expression on his face, the one that entreats, 'Please, go along with this, Devi.' I stare down at the ground, watching a line of red ants hoist crumbs of obscene yellow laddoo proudly on their backs.

I escaped yesterday's nightmare—I determinedly shrug away memories of that man's sour breath hot on my face, his hand on my nipples, the boom boom of my heart loud in my ears, the iron taste of alien blood in my mouth—only to find myself embroiled in this one. I do not want to go along with it, I don't. I am annoyed with Rohan for being such a patsy initially, though he did come through in the end. And now he is spouting this Catholic nonsense. He is too soft where his parents are concerned, but then he is like that with all the people he cares for; he is the same with me. That is what I love about him. I give him a look that says, *I am doing this for you,* and mutter, 'Yes, I will.'

The crowd, which has been leaning forward, ears flapping, settles. 'Ah,' I hear, 'at least that's something.'

What will you have to say to this? *'Ma, I am getting married to Rohan, becoming a Catholic.' 'But, Devi, you were Lord Ganapathy's special blessing…'* How many times have I heard you say those words? Words binding me to you and to a God I am not even sure I believe in, a God I call upon only when I am in the kind of scrape I cannot see a way out of.

'Won't you change your mind putha?' Rohan's mother begs of him, tears crowding her eyes.

'Ma, please... Devi will become a Catholic; we will have a Catholic wedding.'

What? We have not discussed any of this. What is he promising? What does it matter?

'Will you?' they ask of me, both his parents as one, his mother squinting at me suspiciously.

'Yes,' I murmur, not looking up.

The crowd erupts. His parents look at each other. I catch Rohan's eye. *You owe me big,* I mouth. I see the corner of his lip lift up as he tries not to give in to the smile blooming in his chest. *I love this man,* I think.

'I have to go now. My mother will be waiting,' I say to Rohan's parents.

'Tell her we will come and see her next week, to arrange all the details of the wedding,' Rohan's mother says. And just like that, it is over.

Rohan comes up to me, squeezes my hand, his face radiant. The crowd, at the point of dispersing, oohs again. He grins and leans close, his spiced breath warm in my ear, 'We are getting married.' The crowd leans in, trying to catch the whisper. 'We are going to England. You can wear miniskirts; even frolic naked if you so wish, although I'd rather you didn't.'

'Look at what he is doing,' someone says. 'Hey, you are not married yet; spare us the display,' shouts another.

'Rohan,' his mother calls, establishing hierarchy.

I deliberately lean into Rohan, knowing it is petty but not caring. She deserves it for all the horrible things she's said about me. 'I will wear what I want to wear and don't you go telling me what you'd rather I did or didn't,' I say, and he arches an eyebrow and smiles.

'Rohan,' his mother calls, sounding testier than before.

'You will have plenty of time for that after marriage,' someone leers.

'Yes, we will,' I retort.

The man who spoke recoils as if stung. 'God, she has a tongue on her, Rohan, watch out. I wouldn't marry her if I was you,' he says, heading to the arrack shop for sustenance.

I walk up to the man and lean close. He grins from ear to ear, tickled by the fact that I am singling him out.

The crowd, which was on the point of dispersing, angles in so as not to miss a thing.

'No one would want to marry you, you creep,' I say loud enough for the crowd to overhear and his face turns first yellow and then a purplish blue, 'You need someone with balls to marry a girl like me and I'm afraid you haven't got any.' His face loses colour and he slumps down.

'She's destroyed him,' the crowd yells. Someone mimics firing a pistol with their hand, 'Dishum, just like that.'

Rohan, his face red with the effort it is costing to hold in his grin, mouths, 'Go, before my parents change their minds.'

'Will that stop you?' I ask, my words a challenge.

His smile as he looks down at me is fond. 'No, but I'd rather they gave me their blessing. I don't want to leave them and go to England on a bad note.'

This is precisely the quality I admire in him so, Ma. He doesn't like his parents' interference but he is able to feel affection for them, treat them well. Unlike me. Somehow, when I am with you, Ma, anger hijacks affection, resentment usurps any kindness I might feel towards you.

The crowd disperses, busy embellishing the story in their heads, adding little details as they go, so that by the time the story reaches old Pedru Ab by the lake, only the main protagonists are the same, everything else has changed.

'Shall I walk you to the bus stop?' Rohan asks.

Twilight has fallen while the drama has been taking place. The sky is all the shades of pink, from pale peach to rich cerise. A light breeze smelling of fish, arrack and jack-fruit caresses my cheek. Flies buzz and mosquitoes feast. The drunks have all congregated outside the shop and are humming tunelessly while the crickets and frogs join in the chorus. They squat in a cosy circle in the middle of the road, waving their bottles, lost in song as the warm rose-tinged evening fades to black.

'Yes,' I want to say, 'yes please.' Truth is, after last night's disastrous experience, I am a little scared. But I do not want to display this weakness, even to Rohan. 'I will be fine,' I say.

Glow-worms are twinkling in the fields below as I walk down the familiar path from the road, past the stream, my feet taking me unerringly home, even though it's hard to see anything. The power's out. I squint to try and look out for snakes hiding in cover of darkness, waiting to strike. Sumitranna will be making his way down the hill in the distance around now, only the flicker of a candle bobbing up and down among the glow-worms giving him away. And you will be standing somewhere in the darkness, wondering where I am and why I am not home yet, waiting for me to emerge out of the gloom, worry warring with hope, the lines in your face travelling downwards like the map of a busy road. After what feels like an age, you will spot me and you will smile and start to speak but I will shush you, 'I have something important to say, Ma.'

Your face will fall, just like that, the glow on it at the sight of me replaced by anxiety, and I will tell you that I am getting married and that I am becoming a Catholic and that I am going away to England and you will keen, your words a hymn of pain.

My hand aches, Ma, my eyes hurt from squinting in the droopy yellow light of the candle. I will stop now and read the next entry in your diary that I have been saving up like a treat. It was a gift to read about Da in your previous entry, Ma. You've always been so reluctant to talk about him, my queries meeting with monosyllabic replies, that look entering your eyes, taking up residence, a ghost haunting.

Da as an earnest young farmer. You as a young woman who desperately wants to get married. It is such an unexpected reward, this diary of yours, and any guilt I felt when I started reading your private words is displaced by the pleasure of getting to know the woman you were before you became my ma and the man I never met. My father.

Love,

Devi

Chapter 9
Shilpa

Coconut Barfis

Coconut Barfis:

Ingredients:

Freshly grated coconut–2 cups.
Sugar–2 cups.
Cardamom–4 pods–seeds crushed to a paste.
Ghee–2 tablespoons.
Cashew nuts roasted in ghee and chopped–to serve.

Method:

1. Mix grated coconut with the sugar and crushed cardamom seeds.
2. Pour ghee in a hot pan.
3. Add the mixture and keep stirring to avoid burning.
4. Grease a serving dish with butter or ghee. Pour the cooked mixture onto the dish.

5. Cut square pieces after the dish has cooled down a bit. Sprinkle chopped cashew nuts and serve.

❄ ❄ ❄

Dear Diary,

For me, food doesn't just taste sweet, sour, spicy, what have you—it tastes of feelings, it invokes memories.

Conjee tastes of childhood. When I slurp conjee, I am transported back to the house I grew up in. The gloopy smell of conjee bubbling on the hearth, the lime tree in the garden, its piquant, slightly bitter scent. The chatter of birds, the tang of cow dung used to sweep the compound.

I bite into an onion bhaji and I taste comfort. When I eat onion bhajis, I remember huddling with my ma by the front door, watching the trees dance in the storm, pineapple-scented drops lashing our faces, the dank smell of wet hay dripping from the roof, the mad rave of droplets on mud, onion bhajis warm in our stomachs and cardamom tea by our sides.

Every food has a feeling, a memory. Every important milestone in my life has a food associated with it. That is why this diary couldn't just be for recipes. That is why I am narrating the story of my life via food.

Coconut barfis are served at our wedding. The cost of the wedding is shared by both parties, half paid for by my father and half by Manoj.

I have had the pleasure of making coconut barfis once before, when my mother was gifted ten coconuts—a fortune—

by Mrs. Mendonca on the occasion of the feast of Nativity. The kadai had hissed and crackled as I cooked and the house smacked of roasted coconut and caramelised sugar with a subtle undertone of cardamom for days. After, rows and rows of golden barfis, dotted with plump tan cashew nuts and browned coconut shreds, had lined the kitchen floor, honey yellow, oozing syrup, begging to be eaten.

At my wedding, I bit into a barfi. The crunch of the coconut, the treacly sweetness of the syrup, the nuttiness of the cashew—and I tasted hope, anticipation, the realisation of dreams. What I had yearned for, for so long, was coming true. I was a married woman now. We would have four children at least, I decided. Three boys and a girl. As if he could read my mind, the man sitting by me —my husband! —turned to me and smiled. I smiled back.

So, I am a married woman now. One tick in the box of my ambitions. And as for my other two ambitions, the house and the children, we are working hard on both!

The plot of land we have to build our house on is small, and the house will practically sit on top of Sumitranna's. When he first drew up the plans, Manoj went up to Sumitranna, showed them to him, pointed out that our houses would be back to back and asked if he would mind. 'Go ahead. Deters the burglars,' was Sumitranna's answer. Like Manoj, he's a man of few words. A nice man, a kind landlord, unlike some others. He told me with what approximated to a blush that he was getting married, that I would have some company soon. That would be nice, though I must say, I do like cooking for both the men in the makeshift hut Manoj and I are living in while the house is being built, basking in their oohs and aahs of delight as they gulp down the food I've prepared and ask for seconds.

'Shilpa, you work magic in the kitchen,' Manoj tells me, beaming, after his third helping of curd rice.

'Manoj, you are a lucky man,' says Sumitranna after he's devoured my fish fry. 'When I tasted your cooking, I realised what I was missing, Shilpa—a woman to look after me.' Sumitranna looks at me admiringly, 'That is why I am getting married.'

What a compliment. My cup of joy is almost full.

❄ ❄ ❄

Dear Diary,

Sorry to have neglected you for so long. Being a married woman, managing a home, doesn't leave you with much time on your hands to write. But I will more than make up for it now—I have so much to tell you.

So, our house is built. I absolutely love it. It has two rooms: a longish front room which doubles up as bedroom, and of course my kitchen. I adore the kitchen; it's small, but it is *mine.* There is a veranda outside the kitchen which links to the small bathroom adjoining, which houses an urn where we heat up water with kindling for our wash. We also have a well and a tiny courtyard in front, where I've planted aboli and jasmine and have inveigled a vegetable plot too.

It is the most wonderful feeling in the world, to have a house to call your own. The only thing that could top this feeling is if I got pregnant.

In other news, Sumitranna got married, came home with a wife—a slip of a girl, barely sixteen and afraid of her own shadow. Sumitranna brought her to me, snivelling and wiping her tears with her pallu.

'Please could you take Jalaja in hand and teach her how to manage a house?' he begged. 'Her parents said she could cook like an angel, that she was a whizz at cleaning and that she kept house and looked after her eleven siblings all on her own. Since she got here, all she's done is cry.' His voice sounded harassed and impatient. Jalaja flinched. 'I have no time for histrionics; I work very hard and when I get home I expect a cooked meal at the very least.' He turned tail and walked off in a huff and the girl dissolved in a mess of tears.

Turns out she is desperately homesick. She is the oldest of twelve and there was always noise and laughter and comings and goings at her house and here it is quiet and nobody around except her grumpy husband who doesn't tell her what he wants and then gets angry when she doesn't do it. 'How can I be expected to read his mind?' she cries, wiping the tears which just keep on coming with her pallu which resembles a sodden rag.

I have my work cut out here, I think. But I do relish a challenge and it is nice to feel appreciated. I have to admit I was worried when Sumitranna announced he was getting married as to the nature of the competition. But this girl, she looks up at me like I am her saviour, her huge eyes lighting up when I show her what Sumitranna wants done, as I guide her through the recipes Sumitranna loves, as I instruct her on how to clean and keep house to Sumitranna's satisfaction. And I must admit, it is nice to have company when the men are at work. Once our chores are done and the rice is bubbling merrily on the hearth, we sit on the veranda and share a paan.

'It hurts,' she tells me, her face red as a hibiscus flower, red as the paan staining her lips. She is looking straight ahead. 'Does it hurt for you too, or is it just me?'

I debate whether to pretend I don't understand what she's talking about. The air is yellow, sullen. It reeks of sweat and parched fields and the sickly sweet odour of overripe fruit. The monsoons are late as ever.

'Oh, you just have to grin and bear it. It will get better with time,' I say finally.

She sighs. 'I hope so,' she says. 'I hope I get pregnant soon, then he'll have to stop for a while at least.'

I look up at the sky. It is pale blue, almost white, like the inside of an egg shell. Frisky clouds, light and fluffy and definitely not laden with moisture, dot it in places. The boiling rice rattles the lid that covers the mouth of the pot like a visitor demanding entry. Dragonflies hum as they alight on aboli flowers, shimmering rainbows dotting the sedate orange petals. A cluster of chillies the dark green of envy hug the branches of the chilli plant and a prickly yellow pineapple ripens slowly in the mid-afternoon haze.

A baby, gap-toothed, smiling, gummy eyes following my every move. *That is what I want too; that is what I am waiting for,* I think, my words a wish, a prayer.

Chapter 10
Nisha

The Stranger in the Mirror

Lounging amongst the pillows, she watches Matt dress for work, admiring the care he takes working the knot on his tie, how he hastily runs a comb through his wayward hair, committing to memory all these little quirks while faint echoes of the dream plaintively reverberate from the night before. It is uncharacteristic for her to lie here doing nothing. Normally she would be up before Matt, would have had a shower by now and be dressed ready to go to work—or, as she has been doing these past few days, to her parents' house to sort out their effects. She certainly wouldn't be languishing in bed after seven in the morning. The adage that lying in equates to wasted time has been drummed into her from childhood. When she was little, her mother said that brains worked best in the mornings, so after a quick breakfast of porridge, Nisha would sit down and tackle homework, even at the weekends. She never stayed in bed past six. If she did, her mother would be sure to be along. Three brisk knocks. 'Wake up, sleepyhead, the day's waiting for you.'

Matt comes over and kisses the tip of her nose. Lemony smell of aftershave. Beard tickling her cheek. 'Will you be okay, babe?'

She nods, already weary thinking about the day ahead. Was it just yesterday that she saw the solicitor, that the letter exploded like a bomb in her face? It feels like aeons ago. It feels like just now.

His face is so close she can see the small shaving nick on his chin sprouting a tiny bubble of dried blood. She touches a finger to the bubble.

'Make your list. Then call me,' he says.

She nods. 'I will.'

He places a kiss on her lips like a gift and is gone, a whiff of citrusy musk all that remains of him.

She lies back, pulls Matt's pillow over her face, breathes in the salty night smell of him, stretches, claims the bed, luxuriating in the space for a brief minute. Then she flings the sheets away, goes to the bathroom and stares at her face, trying to solve the puzzle lurking there.

When she was little and just beginning to understand the logistics of genes, she would peruse her face for hours on end, musing whether she got her huge wide-set eyes from her mother, whether her nose was her father's. 'Look at you, a copy of your mother,' people would say and she would stand up straighter, the better to mimic her mother's regal stance. Or, 'You definitely take after your dad, don't you?' they'd say. Only once, a woman at a wedding

(Nisha realises, in retrospect that she must have been drunk), had weaved her way to their table and squinted at Nisha with glazed eyes that had fascinated her, 'So you're the black sheep, then,' she had said, waving a sharp finger so close to Nisha's nose that she was afraid the woman's pointy nail would poke her eye. Her mother had held Nisha close and said to the woman in a voice that reminded Nisha of the icebergs she had been learning about in geography, 'I think you should leave now.'

I am; I was the black sheep, she thinks now, scrutinising her reflection. *How could I have thought I looked like either of my parents? My mother's eyes were nothing like mine, and my father's nose was squat while mine is long, curving slightly at the end.*

Tears sting her eyes and she blinks them away furiously.

Would I be different if I had grown up in India? She asks and, just like that, she is her childhood self again, balancing on the stool on tiptoe, wiping the steam off the mirror and studying the stranger staring solemnly back at her. *More emotional perhaps? Able to cry and shout and rant and vent. Not so much in love with numbers. Free with hugs and kisses. Not standoffish and reserved. How much of my personality is taught? How much of it is part of my upbringing? I have questions enough to conduct a research project of my own.* She watches the reflection in the mirror, familiar and yet inscrutable, lift the corners of her lips up in a wry, lopsided smile. *In that dream, if those were my memories… I was so inventive, thinking prayers were making their way to God, fancying God was talking to me. If I had grown up in India, would I believe in God? Walk more gracefully? Laugh easily? Cook all those exotic dishes? Why, I don't think I even like Indian food. How could I be Indian, then?*

She shakes her head, decides that she will go for a walk to clear it. Within minutes she is clattering down the stairs, into the brisk freshness of a morning at the straggly end of winter, revelling in the feel of icy air caressing her cheeks, the smell of frying bacon wafting from the café, past the school where cars snake in an endless barely moving line, mothers struggling to park and drop their children off.

A woman wielding a walking stick hobbles to the bus stop, asks the teenage girl sprawled on the bench, taking up the whole seat, to move up. The girl pulls earplugs out of her ears and squints up at the woman. 'Can I sit here, please?' the woman asks. The girl nods, pushing the earpiece back in and moving her head to the tinny thump thump which reverberates out of the headphones. The older woman shakes her head, smiling. 'Funny weather we're having,' she says. 'Reckon it will brighten up later?' Nisha realises with a start that, lost in thought, she has been staring right at the woman and that she is talking to *her*. She blushes, embarrassed. She is not one for small talk. Most people don't get her—she has been told she is too reserved, too abrupt. She's never had any close friends with the exception of Matt and her boss at work, Ross. No girlfriends. The few girls she invited back to the house when she went through the brief phase of trying to fit in at the start of her teenage years came because they adored her parents, the way they treated them as equals, the way they didn't talk down to them. It made Nisha proud and, once in a rare while, when her period was due and she was achy and hormonal, it made her mad. Sometimes, just sometimes, she would have loved to have been treated as a child: given a cuddle and the false reassurance of saying everything was going to be okay—something her parents never did. They said it would be lying. Ha.

The woman is looking at her expectantly, waiting for an answer. Nisha has always found discussion of the weather pointless. Why not leave it to the weathermen? There is a whole science to it. What is the point of discussing it when you don't have a clue? 'Let's hope so,' she manages, pleased that her voice comes out sounding fine. She cannot believe she is having such an ordinary discussion when her world has tilted, making her lose her bearings.

A mother and child brush past, the mother cajoling the child along, 'Come on now, you like school really. You'll have fun with Reece and Ethan, won't you, and play that pirate game you told me about?' The child stops, refuses to move. His eyes overflow, silvery rivulets pooling onto his cheeks, sparkling in the desultory morning light. 'I don't want to.' His mother squats right there on the pavement, folds the child into her arms. He buries his head in the curve of her shoulder, his little body snug in the shelter of her body while around them people rush past, on their way to work, to the shops, all in a hurry.

When she was little, Nisha had ached to be held. She would watch other mothers lift their children, twirl them around, pull them close, kiss them for no reason at all, say,

'I love you' with abandon. And every night before sleeping, she would wish that when she woke up, her mother would transform into one of those mums who cuddled their children, who cooked muffins and cakes, took them to the park and pushed them on the swings, not used the equipment for the purpose of a science lesson on pendulum effect and gravity. As soon as the reprobate thought dared flit into her brain, guilt would chase it away, and when her mother came to tuck her in, Nisha would hold her close, a moment too long. Her mother would gently release herself, put off the light and leave the room.

Her mother had never picked Nisha up from school; a childminder had until Nisha was old enough to walk home on her own—except the once, when her mother finished a project early. When Nisha came out of the gates and saw her mother standing slightly apart from the other mums looking desperately lost, she had rushed up to her and enveloped her in a hug. Her mother had blushed to the roots of her hair and gently disentangled Nisha. The slightly bitter tang of disappointment was forgotten when her mother had walked her home the long way, pointing out different land forms, picking up rocks and pebbles and explaining the striations in them. Other children had looked on curiously and disappointment had ballooned into pride. No, she had decided then, she would take her scientist mother over a mum who baked and cosseted any day.

Next to Nisha on the busy pavement, the mother picks up her boy, hefting his precious weight in her arms along with his schoolbag and lunchbox and makes her careful way to the school.

Would her birth mother have been free with hugs and kisses? Nisha wonders and just as quickly blinks the rogue thought away. *Your birth mother gave you away to the convent.*

No. Her mum will always be the tall, besuited woman who took great pleasure in imparting knowledge, whose eyes would soften when they looked at Nisha sometimes. She needs to hold on to all those memories before they disappear into ether.

Why are you thinking about what might have been? Since when did you start asking pointless questions, wasting time like this?

She realises she has come to a stop in front of a familiar building. For the first time in what feels like forever, she smiles. Her feet, of their own accord, have conveyed her to her office. She is not due back for two days yet, but now that she is here, she is tempted to go in, lose herself in work, forget the tumult playing havoc within her for a brief while. There are decisions to be made, she knows. The letter, the phone number for the convent, the dream all vie for attention. But the pull of numbers, the ache for the soothing order of figures convinces her to push the revolving door open, nod at the doorman and make her way to the lift.

'Nisha,' her colleagues smile as she approaches her cubicle, 'You are back.' They do not meet her eye, worried that she might expect from them the comfort they are powerless to impart and for this she is grateful. They do not say, 'You are two days early.' They understand.

They are like her: more at home in the world of figures than in the real one. Give them a complicated mathematical problem and they will solve it in minutes, but in the face of messy emotions, they are lost. At sea.

There is a card waiting at her desk. Signed by every one of her colleagues. 'We are sorry for your loss.' They knew and respected her parents. They had been round to her parents' house a few times. Her eyes swim. *My parents.*

A memory: She is ill, burning up with fever, hot all over. There is an incessant pounding in her head. She wakes. The room is dark and someone, something startles in the corner. She yelps in fright, but the yelp comes out as a distressed whisper. The thing comes closer and it is her dad. He had been camping on the chair beside her bed. He touches her forehead, then leaves the room. *Don't go,* she wants to shout. *Don't leave me alone.* But her throat is hoarse and she seems to have lost her voice. He comes in a minute later followed by her mother whose eyes are sunken in her head. She is still in her suit, uncharacteristic for her. She bundles Nisha up, holds her close and they drive to the hospital in the night. She is in the hospital two days and they spend it by her side, not going to the lab, sponging her forehead with cool cloths, feeding her sips of sweetened water with a spoon.

If that is not love, she thinks now, *what is?*

Her boss, who has over the years morphed into one of the few friends she has, sticks his head round the cubicle door. 'Nice to have you back, Nisha.' His benevolent brown gaze holds hers. 'You okay?'

'Yes,' she croaks, managing to squeeze the word out past the frog in her throat. 'Thanks for this.' She holds up the card.

He waves his hand in the air, colour flooding his face. Nisha absently notes that this is the first time she has seen Dr Ross Cunnett—PhD, twenty five years of experience, unfazed by any work-related problem no matter how complex—blush.

'They were amazing people.' He manages at last, clearly lost for words.

And amazing liars.

'Meeting in five minutes, board room,' he says, and just like that they are back on normal footing, both equally relieved.

A discussion on a project to do with prime numbers. Prime numbers are solitary, she thinks, lonely. For the first time ever that she can recall, her mind drifts away from the comfortable camaraderie of the meeting, the place where she feels most at home. She remembers returning from school one evening, the question that had been burning in her throat all day bursting out of her as she stepped in the door: 'Mum, why do I not have a brother or sister?' Her mother had been chopping beetroot for salad, she remembers now. And the reason she remembers is because her mother's face had flushed as red as that beetroot. 'What is the matter, Mum?' She had asked, 'Are you ill?' Her mother had turned to face her, her hands tinted pink, knife waving in the air. 'Nothing, I'm fine.' Now, in retrospect she understands. She had forgotten her question in the novelty of watching her mother turn a strange colour, worried that she might be poorly.

She has always secretly yearned for a sibling, has watched siblings curiously, the way they bond, the chemistry between them. How novel it must be to share the same genes with someone else, the same history, the same memories…

At least now I know why I never had any siblings. That piece of puzzle is in place, she thinks, and she puts it in a compartment in her brain and closes the door. The rest of her brain is in chaos but that little bit is in order and it makes her feel good.

'Nisha?' Ross's voice intrudes, 'What do you think?' and her mind snaps back into the present, the snag the project is facing. She looks at the papers spread out in front of her, her mind working quickly, rearranging the numbers into workable columns. And, just like that, it is there, the solution, staring her in the eye. 'If we do this and then this…' she begins and realises as she explains the solution to her rapt colleagues that just now, she knows exactly who she is. It doesn't matter that she doesn't know who her real parents are, that she was given away like an item surplus to requirement. Mathematics, numbers, anchor her, define her. *This* is who she is.

'We missed you, Nisha,' Ross says warmly as her colleagues disperse to their respective cubicles and she smiles. 'I missed work too.'

At 1:00 p.m., Ross sticks his head round the door. 'Going downstairs for a sandwich. Want one?' Soft butterscotch eyes crinkling.

She has been so absorbed in reading up on the project that she has lost track of time. She is aware, all of a sudden, of her stomach rumbling, aware that she did not have breakfast, and with that awareness comes the reminder of things she'd rather forget, things that need to be dealt with. 'Ross, I… I just found out I am adopted.' Somehow, the words are out before she can stop them, before she realises she has spoken out loud.

Ross's head disappears and then reappears along with the rest of his body. The greying wise head, the kind face that is now looking at her with such tenderness. It is too much for her. Tears sting her eyes, threaten to overflow onto the landscape of her face. What has got into her? She is known for her famous reserve, the walls she's built around herself. But since the letter, she's been crumbling, disintegrating into a thousand pieces inside, barely holding herself together. And just now, when she saw this benevolent man who's always reminded her of her dad, it just burst out of her.

'Oh, Nisha, I am so sorry,' he says, and in his eyes she sees such compassion, such understanding.

Now that she has started to talk, she finds she cannot stop. 'I was adopted from India… I… I don't remember, Ross. I don't feel any connection at all to the place.' Outside, someone laughs, the merry sound obscene in the angry quiet of the cubicle populated by her hurt, her grief.

Ross pulls up a chair beside her. 'May I?'

She manages a nod. 'I didn't have a clue. I have been wondering if perhaps there were obvious signs that I missed along the way? If there were, they passed me by completely.' She folds her hands on her desk, rests her head on the pillow of her arms. Hot tears inveigle out of her eyes, wet the thin fabric of the sleeves of her top.

'It must feel like such a betrayal, especially after the shock of their loss...' Ross's voice is soft.

'Why didn't they tell me, Ross?'

'I... I don't know.'

I do. Because I would have stopped being an acquiescing lab rat; I would have asked questions, rebelled, perhaps even asked to go back.

'I have had an upbringing where love was held at a remove. Would it have been different if I had been their biological child? That is one of the questions doing circuits in my head,' she says softly.

A rhetorical question. 'This is one which you will never be able to prove, so why ask it?' her parents had said when she asked them something pointless without thinking once. 'It is a waste of your time and ours. Remember, you will never get back this moment in time. Remember that.' She learnt to think before she spoke, preferring sometimes not to speak at all instead of talking for the sake of it. *This is one of the reasons I don't get on with people; they say talking to me is like drawing water out of a stone.* 'I never know what you are thinking,' a date said to her once. 'I am working out puzzles in my head most of the time,' she'd replied, the truth bursting out of her in an unguarded moment. She never saw the date again.

Her head on the desk, so heavy she cannot seem to summon the energy to lift it. The bitter, inky smell of words, of paper, soothing, comforting, mixing with the salty tang of tears.

Ross's voice, 'They loved you, Nisha. I know that. I saw it shining out of their eyes when I visited. They were highly intellectual people who did not know how to show love; the physical manifestation of it embarrassed them. I know because I am the same. My wife is always complaining that I do not show her any affection, even though, if something happened to her, I… I couldn't function.'

Ross is right. My parents weren't even affectionate towards each other. They never hugged or kissed or cuddled; there was always this distance, this barrier, even though anybody could see they cared for each other—or at least I could.

Her parents were not comfortable with words unless they were of the scientific kind, and neither is she. When her first ever boyfriend left her the day after sleeping with her, she had not been able to confide in her mother. She had not confided in anyone. She had gone to work and buried herself in numbers. (Yes, it had taken her that long to find a man she had liked enough to sleep with.)

Her head aches, it hurts, she wants it to stop. She is seized by the sudden impulse to make that list she's promised herself and Matt, to put down in words all that information flitting around in her head, crowding it. She has been procrastinating—something she didn't think she was capable of, a trait her parents always frowned upon. And now she realises she is just like everybody else. When something has the capacity to hurt, to pull the ground out from beneath her, she will put it off, will try and ignore it. She is human after all, she thinks, fallible—and that is not a bad thing, even though, had her parents been here, they would have convinced her otherwise.

They were fallible too; they lied, they deceived, they died and left her with this… this mess.

She wipes her eyes surreptitiously on her sleeves, lifts her head, manages a smile that hurts her cheeks. 'Thanks for this, Ross. Go on, get that sandwich. I am fine.'

She will order the information swirling around her head into neat piles, classify it into 'important' and 'not important', compartmentalise it.

'You sure?' Ross's caramel eyes probe hers.

Without that she cannot function, she feels she is floating somewhere where she cannot find herself.

'Yes, thank you.' She manages to hold his gaze and he walks to the door.

'I will get you your usual, shall I? Tuna salad baguette?'

And armed with this list, she will call the convent, find out why she was given away, discover the truth behind her parentage.

'Yes, please.'

He leaves, snippets of conversations of colleagues lunching at their desks, the aroma of coffee, the tinny tang of tuna drifting in briefly as the door opens and shuts behind him.

She whips out the little book that is her faithful companion, starts to write.

Project Who Am I

1) The dreams—more vivid, more colourful than my life has been up until now. Real events that occurred before I came here? Memories manifesting themselves? Death of parents, letter could have been triggers?

Proposed Solution: Call a psychologist, talk it through.

Truth is, I am afraid to do this. I have long suspected I might be somewhere in the autistic spectrum; what if they find that out? So what? I have already found out the life I was living was a lie. What difference will the knowledge that I am autistic make?

Or… since my dreams centre on the convent, I could call the convent.

Which brings me to the next question…

2) Why do all the memories (if they are such) take place at the convent? Was I given away at a very young age, so young that I have no recollection of my birth parents? Was I born at the convent?

Again, call the convent. I would like to know the precise age at which I was adopted—my penchant for facts coming through. 'Nothing wrong with that,' my parents would say. It pays to be thorough. Memory is imperfect, facts are not.

Her head feels a bit less crowded already, now that the first few questions have been sorted, out of the way. *This is so not like me,* she thinks, *this deliberating, this fabricating reasons out of thin air. Was this Nisha hiding inside all along waiting to be released? Is this the real Nisha?*

3) Why was I adopted? Why me? Why not someone else?

For this I might have an answer—perhaps it was because of my cleft palate. Since I was disfigured, my parents might have thought it would stop me focusing on my looks and that I would concentrate on books instead. A horrible reason, doesn't bear thinking about, but then what they did, adopting me for purposes of research, doesn't bear thinking about either. Which brings me to the next question…

4) Did my parents adopt me only as a project or because they loved me?

This is the question that bugs me the most, hurts me the most if I am being completely honest, the one I cannot turn away from. Perhaps the nuns at the convent would know? What if they don't/can't remember? After all, it is so far in the past. Perhaps I will never know… Or perhaps… Aha… I'm sure there is a research paper somewhere with details of Project 'Nurture VS Nature'. Was it ever submitted?

This is my forte. I will research all the publications my parents submitted to, speak to their colleagues. Oh Lord, did their colleagues know? Those dry people I met once a year at Christmas parties, the colourful paper hats at odds with their starched navy suits, talking rats at the table as they munched on turkey, trying to smile at the jokes from the crackers, their mouths stretched in a parody of a grin. But then, my parents were not expecting to pass on so soon. So perhaps it was never submitted. If so, it must be somewhere in their house…

Nisha is invigorated, full of energy. Writing things down makes her notice things her mind is trying to process, see connections that were obscured by unnecessary facts. She is charged with purpose for the first time since the policemen turned up at work, their faces sombre, and told her about her parents. Her head feels free for the first time since she opened the letter. Blessedly organised. Not rushed and buzzing and threatening to implode. She calls Matt; he is in class, the phone switched off. She leaves a message, knowing he will pick it up when he's finished. Then she leaves a note on Ross's desk and drives to her parents' house. She will begin with the study and work her way from there…

Chapter 11
Devi

Bruise-Red Effigy

Ma,

Today, once more, you stirred. 'Wise woman,' you breathed. 'Child,' you whispered. 'Gave away.'

'Did the wise woman give her child away, Ma?' I asked.

You gripped my hand hard. 'Gave away,' you said, your voice as empty as the well during the drought, your eyes closed, eyelids fluttering like a butterfly trapped in a jar.

Did the madwoman, who did not have a husband as far as I know, have a baby? Did she give it away because of the disgrace? Is that why she became mad? Or, as you termed it, *wise*, Ma? If so, why are you thinking of that now? Why is it at the forefront of your mind? What is going on in your head as you lie there, peaceful as the Virgin Mary whose statue graces the entrance to the hospital? And yet, when you come to, briefly, you are so agitated, your pupils struggling like a captured animal under closed lids. Why? What is upsetting you? Why is the ghost of the madwoman causing havoc even now, after all this time? What hold does she still have on you? Why are you so upset that she gave her baby away—if that is what you are trying to say? Because you wanted children so desperately? Perhaps.

Ma, I think it is time to tell you my news. Somehow, writing all this down, reading your diary, getting a glimpse into the girl you were once, has loosened something inside of me. I am able to find the words to tell you, although I wish it didn't have to be like this. Reading in your diary your desire for a child… I am pregnant, Ma. I am going to have a baby. My body is changing, housing a new life and it is a fabulous feeling, this. More amazing than anything I have experienced thus far.

In your diary, you say you want lots of children. I think I am beginning to see why, when there was just me, you loved me like you did.

I am already so defensive of this little being, at present no more than a collection of rapidly multiplying cells, that graces my womb, Ma. I shy away from tea and coffee, I drink only boiled water, eat plenty of fruit. I understand now why you were so protective of me, the protectiveness that suffocated and chafed, that felt like shackles I yearned to be free of…

When I walk home that evening after that dreadful trial with Rohan's parents, you are waiting in the shade of the tamarind tree, as I expected, pretending to shell coconuts, when really you are watching out for me, any fool can see that, as there is not enough light to shell coconuts by.

Glow-worms twinkle and crickets sing. You squat above the little wooden stool which has a scythe attached to the front with which to shell the coconuts, not concentrating, your eyes wide and peeled as if that will help pierce the darkness. Bobby dances beside you, tail wagging, once in a while snapping at a fly that buzzes too close. The air smells yellow, of bruised mangoes and crushed tamarind.

Your face lights up when you see me, your teeth glowing turmeric in the darkness. I walk up to you and, without pausing to catch my breath, say, 'Rohan has asked me to marry him.' Your hand on the scythe stills, too suddenly, and you cut yourself, bright red blood gushing out from between brown wrinkled skin. Bobby barks, makes to lick it. I rush inside, tear a piece off an old nightie and deftly bind your hand to stem the bleed. 'And before you ask, his parents have agreed.' I brush aside the humiliation stinging my eyes —the insults bandied, the accusations levelled at me —with a rough swipe of my elbow, my hands busy wrapping the bandage. 'They are coming here next week, to discuss the details of the wedding. See, not all boys are bad, like you said.' The gloating does not provide the satisfaction, the thrill I had expected. Perhaps because of what had happened at Rohan's house. Perhaps because I had been terrified on the walk home on my own, twilight tinting the sky the dusky pink of the inside of an unripe guava, memories of the night before making my breasts throb in remembered agony. Each whispering footstep beside me, behind me, had been a predator, every man a monster. I hadn't realised the previous night's scrape had affected me so. *Why didn't I accept Rohan's offer to walk me home? Stupid, stupid pride.*

You do not say anything. You are whimpering quietly, sounding a lot like Bobby does when he is told off for stealing Sumitranna's dog's food. I suspect it is not the cut as much as the hurt I am inflicting. Familiar guilt makes an appearance at my shoulder, whispering taunts couched as sweet caresses: *Look what you are doing to your ma. Look at the pain you are inflicting.* The rebellious part of me is having none of it: *Why should Ma be upset? A good marriage for me is what she's always wanted.* You are fond of declaring that, until I am married, you will worry about me. After, you will entrust that responsibility to my husband. 'I am not some pet, in need of looking after, whose responsibility needs to be foisted from person to person,' I have yelled many times, this speech of yours always making me wild. 'I am more than capable of looking after myself.'

'I am going to become Catholic,' I say while briskly tying the knot holding your bandage in place. 'He is going to study in England. He is taking me with him.'

You close your eyes, rock on your feet, whether from the blood still gushing out of your wound and staining the pink nightie the bright red of kumkum or from my words I cannot tell. 'So far away?' you say, your voice soft, your face ashen, defeated. 'What will I do without you, eh, Devi? How will I live?' Emotional blackmail, you are a deft hand at that, Ma. Irritation instantly bubbles up inside me. *Steady on, Devi,* I tell myself. *You are going to marry Rohan, go away. You can afford to rein in your temper, be kind for a few weeks.*

A week later, I sit bedecked in all my jewellery, perspiring heavily, battling the urge to itch my nose right where the nose-ring pierces it, weighing it down —you insisted I wear it and I gave in, deciding that some battles were just not worth the effort.

Believe it or not, I have been feeling sorry for you since my announcement. You are so deflated, not your usual self at all. The thought of me going away seems to have sucked all the puff out of you. And what is worse, you've lost the madwoman. She died, but not before telling you to go ahead with my marriage. *Thank you, madwoman; you've done us all a favour.* 'I would have married Rohan anyway, Ma, madwoman's blessing or not,' I said gently when you told me and you exploded in a paroxysm of tears. 'What will I do without her? And she's a wise woman, she's not mad. Was. Aiyyo.' You started hitting your forehead with your palm in lament. 'How can I live, not knowing the future?' 'Like you have lived up until now,' I replied. 'Why does everyone have to abandon me? First you say you are leaving and then she goes, just like that,' you sobbed, sounding bewildered, 'Why, Lord Ganapathy? Why?' There was no point in continuing the conversation. I left you to it, Bobby licking your tears, Jalajakka comforting you much better than I could.

My hands clink loudly every time I move my palm to shoo away the mosquitoes, the gold bangles twinkling in the syrupy sunlight that pours in through the window bars. The room smells of the sweetmeats you have spent the afternoon preparing despite my protests to just serve them lime sherbet and shop-bought chakulis and laddoos. You've prepared vadai and chutney, upma and seera, kheer and masala dosa. In a two-room house comprising of living room and kitchen with the bathroom and toilet outside, linked by the veranda, there is not much space for smells to circulate. Nowhere really for them to go.

You are in the courtyard with Sumitranna, Jalajakka, and their son, anxiously awaiting Rohan and his parents. I am aware of sweat staining my sari blouse and beading above my upper lip. I close my eyes and imagine I'm in my light cotton salwar kameez dancing among the fields, the ears of paddy kissing my feet.

'Is it really necessary for your parents to meet my mother, for all this formality?' I had enquired of Rohan. 'Isn't it all decided already?'

'My parents want to talk to your ma about a special dispensation we need to obtain from the bishop on account of you being non-Catholic, so you and I can get married in the church,' Rohan had smiled. The plans for my grand conversion to Catholicism were on hold due to the lack of time available for me to master all the prayers requisite for my baptism and for this I was grateful. 'Let's humour them, Devi. After all, we are escaping them soon; why not give in to a few of their requests, keep them happy?' Rohan had pleaded.

He is so sensible, so unlike me. I have taken his advice to heart, tried being patient with you. But, oh, it is hard, Ma, especially when you begin your, 'I will be all alone, discarded like a used cloth' spiel. What am I supposed to do?

Take you with me? Stay with you forever, each of us getting on the other's nerves?

Outside, Bobby barks sharply, a series of staccato barks signalling intruders. Sumitranna's voice, excited, a pitch higher than his normal gruff tone. 'Shush, Bobby. Shush.' Rustle of saris. Your ingratiating laugh. The face of the Sumitranna's son appears in my window, framed by bars. 'They're here.'

I do not want to see that woman, Rohan's mother, again. I do not want to be in the vicinity of her thinly veiled contempt, the anger coming off her in waves levelled at me—the wanton vixen who has stolen her oh so innocent son. I have enough trauma coping with one wronged woman—you, Ma—I do not need another in my life.

'She is fine, really,' Rohan has assured me, 'She doesn't hate you. It's just that she is a bit possessive as I am her only son.' *A bit possessive?* I think but say nothing. How can this charming, intelligent man be so deluded when it comes to his mother? 'And anyway, my parents are funding us, Devi, they are paying for our travel, the initial rent and expenses we will incur until the stipend kicks in, out of their savings.' His eyes plead with me to understand. I know he desperately wants the two women in his life to get along and this is his way of asking me not to judge his mother too harshly. But that is the worst of it—the undeniable fact that I am beholden to his parents. I have rebelled against feeling beholden to you all my life, Ma, against your daily spiel: 'Devi, I gave up so much for you. I work so hard to ensure you are well fed,' uttered in that mournful, whiny voice that is your speciality, your lips dragging downward in a pitiful frown. 'We'll only be living with them for two weeks, just until I get the documents sorted and then we're off,' Rohan has added, squeezing my hand.

Two weeks. My heart sinks. Two weeks in that claustrophobic house, being peered at on all sides, fumes of alcohol drifting in, drenched in dust. Two weeks with all those people who took part in the scene that day whispering whenever I pass by. 'Only two weeks,' Rohan has nudged, 'and then...we can have our honeymoon in England, far away from everyone.' Asking me with his imploring eyes to acquiesce, to maintain the fragile peace he has tried so hard to instigate.

Fourteen days. I will take them one at a time. I will not antagonise his parents, I will not talk back. I will ignore them. When anger threatens, when a retort blooms on my lips, I will think of escape, that soon I will be away from all this. My in-laws' disapproval. You.

And now, here you are, holding my hand, pulling me forward.

I walk into the courtyard beside you, the air fragranced with jasmine and cashew. I look up, see Rohan, dashing in a navy suit and yellow striped tie, his eyes widening in delight at the sight of me, bedecked and bejewelled. *Don't, Rohan,* I mouth, knowing he'll tease me mercilessly later. He knows how much I hate this display; I have moaned countless times to him, to you: 'Why do I have to wear this sari and blouse and underskirt in this heat?

Why can't I wear shorts?' 'Because men will leer, they will get feelings they are not supposed to,' you have yelled. 'That's *their* problem,' I have countered. 'Why am I being punished for it?' 'Lord Ganapathy, why did you give me this trial to carry?' you have groaned, smacking your forehead. What sort of an answer is that?

As I watch, Rohan winks very slightly and I swallow down the laughter bubbling in my throat. I picture myself in England, wearing nothing but a vest and shorts, not even a bra, no itchy bra straps, no sweat pooling under the cups, no underwire digging into my flesh. I imagine the freedom of it and that allows me to look at his parents—at his father, sweaty and uncomfortable in shirt and tie, and his mother, stern, resigned, folds of tamarind-hued flesh bursting out of her red-gold sari —and smile sweetly, brilliantly at them, shocking his mother into returning a smile of her own, a reluctant lifting of her heavy lips for a minuscule moment.

You go forward, hands folded. In apology? In prayer? Why do you have to do that, Ma? We are not inferior to them in any way.

'My Devi,' you say, voice unsteady. 'My precious, only child. She will be an asset to your family—she has a voice to rival a mynah bird. She is very good with her hands; she has won every prize for craft at school. And just look at her, she has a naturally fair complexion. Doesn't get tanned in the sun. Has never applied Fair and Lovely or any sort of makeup in her life.' You are desperately listing all the points in my favour, while both Rohan and I cringe.

Please stop, Ma. I am not a commodity they are looking to buy. 'Look at her hips. Perfect for childbearing. She will not put on weight after marriage or childbirth. Runs in the family. I lost weight barely weeks after Devi was born.'

Oh Lord Ganapathy, please make her stop.

You take a step forward and then you are surrounded. You are a black cloud, angry, buzzing.

No! What's happening? Oh, dear Lord, what the hell's happening?

Someone screams. Loud. Spiked with pain. Then a flurry of sounds. People talking all at once, tones frantic. Bobby cowering and whining. You are a black dot running up and down the fields. Rohan's face frozen in shock. Sumitranna sprinting after you.

Did I cause this somehow, Lord, by asking you to make Ma stop?

And suddenly, there you are again, in your best blue sari. Except it is not you but an effigy of you, a ballooning, bruise-red effigy. You are standing and then you are swaying, in Jalajakka's arms, on the ground, sweating profusely, the mud around you staining orange.

Please, Lord, make her okay. Please. I do not want this. I did not mean for this to happen.

'Someone get a rickshaw,' Jalajakka yells, voice wobbly, straining at the edges. 'We need to take her to the hospital.'

And that is how my betrothal to Rohan is sealed, in your sweat and my guilt-infested tears, as you are rushed, bloating rapidly, in Rohan's parents' hired car to the hospital.

Ma, this is helping me so much, this writing down of everything that's happened. I am jotting it as much for me as for you, I can see that now. And, yes, it does not take away all that hurt, those arguments, that history between us. But when I read out loud to you, some of the anger melts away and there is an acceptance in its stead.

Yes, it happened, but we have moved on. Now, I want you to be there when my baby comes. I want you to know this. I hope it is not too late.

Love,

Devi

Chapter 12
Shilpa

Fish Fry

Fish fry:

Ingredients:

Fresh fish of your choice (this recipe works for two large fish).
Bafat powder–Two tbsp.
Chilli powder–Two tbsp.
Turmeric powder–One tsp.
Ginger paste–One tsp.
Garlic paste–One tsp.
Vinegar–Three tbsp.
Salt and pepper to taste.
Coconut oil for frying.

Method:

1) Clean, gut and scale the fish.

2) Make slits in the flesh, rub with salt and set aside.

3) Meanwhile, mix all the ingredients to make a paste.

4) Rub this onto the body of the fish, so that both sides are nicely coated. Leave to marinate for at least an hour. Keep a close eye on the fish, shooing away any cats—yours or your neighbours'—who might try to get at it.

5) Pour coconut oil in the frying pan so as to lightly cover the base and when hot, add the fish. Once the fish is cooked on one side, turn it over with a spatula, taking care not to split the fish. Once both sides have fried to perfection, serve with fat red rice and fish curry (recipe to follow).

Note: Some people coat the marinated fish in rava just before frying—it gives the fried fish a nice crunch. Not me. I prefer mine spicy and unsullied by rava.

❄ ❄ ❄

Dear Diary,

It's been a long time. So much has happened; I don't know where to start.

I will begin, as I do, with the recipe. I asked Manoj to get me the freshest pomfrets all the way from Udupi, risking Shali the fisherwoman's sulks ('What's wrong with my fish, tell me?') and fried them the way I have described in the recipe. I kept one for Manoj and none for me even though my mouth watered at the smell, at the crispy golden sight of the perfectly fried fish wrapped in banana leaves to give to the madwoman along with vangi bhath and mutton curry, even though mutton costs the earth and some more these days. I would have cooked the moon in a delicious curry and given that to her if it was possible, believe me.

'Who is this madwoman?' you may ask, dear Diary.

She appeared under the peepal tree one day as if, instead of adventitious roots, the peepal tree had sprouted a real live, ranting, raving madwoman. I asked Shali, who squats by the bus stop next to the tree hawking supposedly fresh fish caught that morning, discreetly, where the madwoman had come from. 'God only knows; she was there when I arrived,' Shali said, her whisper loud as the horns of those screeching buses that race past Sompur, displacing an avalanche of dust in their wake. If the madwoman heard—and how could she not? —she didn't give any indication.

'Why are you giving food you cannot afford to a madwoman?' you might query, dear Diary.

Ah, well, since you asked…

Six years it's been since my wedding, since I came here as a not-so-young bride. I wanted a husband and a house. I got both. I wanted children. I didn't get that. I didn't.

My parents passed away, one after the other, imploring me, even on their deathbeds, for a grandchild. I did not get to revel in the joyous sight of my children cavorting on their knees.

Jalaja got pregnant, went to her village for her delivery, came back with a strapping boy. I cooked for Sumitranna while she was away like I had done when I first came here, when he was still unmarried. That long ago time I used to have a spring to my step. Not anymore. I did not have the four kids I had always wanted; all I had instead were a string of miscarriages. And time was running out. At this rate, I would be lucky if I had one child. When Jalaja came back, little boy in tow, I seriously considered snatching him and running away. But where would I go? How would I look after him without the shelter of the roof Manoj had provided over my head and the food he put on the table?

It has been torture watching Jalaja with her child, watching him totter after her, she the centre of his little universe. How I want that! He loves me, I am like his second mother, but of course Jalaja is the one who takes him to her breast. She is the one he will always turn to first when he needs something.

Jalaja knows how much it hurts me to watch her with her child. After all, she is the one who has nursed me back to health after each miscarriage.

So many miscarriages, my babies seeping from me as easily as the tears that track my face in earmarked grooves. Tongues are wagging nonstop. Whispers follow me wherever I go, some loud, others not so, every single one intended to be heard: 'There goes the cursed woman, the barren one. Pretty as a picture but what's the use? Womb is not welcoming. Must have done something in her past life.' I have learned to walk with my head held high, however hard it wants to droop, to pretend not to hear what is being said, even as every word assaults me, rapes me and leaves me gagging. 'Just goes to show that one shouldn't always fall for a sweet face,' they say. 'Poor Manoj,' they sigh. 'He doesn't deserve it.' Jalaja, that slip of a girl who was afraid of her own shadow when she first came here, comes to my rescue. 'Shut up,' she yells at the malingerers, 'or I will tie your tongues in knots.' 'Poor Sumitranna,' they say, 'to have to wake up next to that shrew every morning.' 'Thank merciful God I don't have to wake up next to you,' she retorts.

This is not the kind of attention I yearned for, growing up.

I prayed, cajoled and bargained with Lord Ganapathy. 'For Manoj's sake, Lord. He's a good man, one of your biggest devotees,' I entreated. 'Just one child, Lord. Just the one.' I performed countless pujas and penances. I fasted on Fridays and feast days. I circumnavigated every temple I visited on my knees and have the scabs to show for it, praying prostrate at each shrine I passed.

I got pregnant. Hope flared, reflected in Manoj's eyes, in the way he insisted I rest, in the way he hired a girl he could ill afford to help me out so I wouldn't have to exert myself. 'Rest,' he said. 'Rest,' the matrons of the village advised. And I did, for the most part. Then, ten weeks into my pregnancy, the familiar, excruciating pain in my stomach as I bent to pick up the mangoes which Nagappa's son had climbed the tree and shaken free; lying under the mango tree, looking up at the honeyed sunlight filtering in through the canopy of leaves, tinting them gold, the air smelling sharp and tangy, with a hint of rust, an undercurrent of pain; Jalaja, fanning me with the pallu of her sari as yet another baby trickled out of me in agonising bursts.

Manoj took me to see a doctor in Manipal, even though we could ill afford the cost. The doctor did a million tests and in the end he called us both in. One look at his eyes was all it took. My tears were already collecting under my chin, soaking my sari blouse when he told Manoj what I already knew.

And then one sun-dappled afternoon, as I trudged back home after buying fresh mackerel for that evening's supper, I locked eyes with the madwoman who'd set up camp under the peepal tree. And everything changed.

It was a sweltering hot day. The earth smelled yellow and overcooked like leftover conjee boiling in a pot. I shifted the basket from my left hip to my right. The fish was starting to smell in the heat, even though Shali had generously given me some of the ice it had been packed in, which was now melting and dripping onto my sari. Across the road a little girl skipped along barefoot, humming to herself, her churidar bottoms torn, hair escaping the plaits tied up securely with red ribbons in bows behind her ears. The bus pulled up, the girl's mother got in and both she and the conductor started yelling at the girl to hurry. The girl took her time, skipping and singing, head down, lost in her own world. The mother slapped her forehead with her palm, bemoaning her fate for all to hear, 'Oh Shiva, what am I going to do with this one?'

I turned and found the madwoman, who was strangely quiet, no histrionics, no wildly shaking head, staring directly at me. 'You want one, don't you?' I thought I heard her say, in a gravelly voice so unlike the high-pitched keening she usually indulged in. 'Huh?' was all I could manage once I got over the shock of seeing the woman actually making conversation. 'Your hostile womb will let you carry one pregnancy to term, if you so wish,' the woman said clearly, still holding my gaze, 'Only one.' I noticed that her eyes were a curious colour—the same shade of steel grey as the bushy clouds of hair obscuring her face—even as the import of what she was saying sank slowly in. 'But…' she continued and I leaned forward, the better to catch every word, 'you will be stealing from fate. It will cost you dearly.' The madwoman's clear gaze bored into me—the smoky grey of a stormy sky, of ashes in the hearth, of monsoon clouds pregnant with the promise of rain. 'Are you prepared to pay the price?'

A baby… I did not hesitate. 'Yes.'

'Go to Manil and pray to Lord Ganapathy.' And before I could say anything more, she resumed shaking her head and muttering to herself, the activities that had earned her the sobriquet of madwoman.

And so Manoj and I donned our best clothes, packed neer dosa, upma, vadai, coconut chutney and dry fish chutney in two three- tier tiffin boxes and endured the two-and-a-half-hour journey to Manil, via four buses and a bullock cart. We joined the long line of people snaking to get a glimpse of Lord Ganapathy, eating our lunch while we waited.

The river gurgled on one side and the sea roared on the other, crashing against the rocks. Temple bells sang and bhajans roared from the loudspeakers of vans of those people rich enough to have arrived in them rather than the bullock carts; as the temple was at the confluence of river and sea, there was no proper road leading to it, hence no bus service. Bullocks were washed by their owners before they made the journey back to the bus stop and they mooed gently in protest as the cold water splashed their haunches, as their owners rhythmically rubbed sudsy sponges on their muddy hide and shooed away the crows which persisted on using their broad grey backs as landing pads. The cloying heady scent of rose agarbatti mingled with the salty, musty smell of sea.

Devotees who had finished puja and darshan bathed in the sea, the men in dripping white dhotis, wearing beatific expressions beneath red slashes of vermillion. The women, their pallus flapping like multi-hued kites, lifted their saris above their ankles as they bravely waded into waist high water, their eyes closing as it enveloped them in an intimate caress. Children danced among bubbly waves while simultaneously trying to stuff cricket-ball-sized prasadam laddoos into too small mouths. A few brave souls tried to jump between the rocks dotting the water —black beacons mapping a frothy, azure landscape. They missed and fell into the sea with a squelch and a scream, to the accompaniment of laughter. Squawking seagulls descended fearlessly, snatching scraps of prasadam from the children's hands and the children screeched and flapped brackish water everywhere in protest.

Hawkers walked past selling Lord Ganesh figurines which they claimed had been blessed by the high priest.

Little carts on wheels dotted the indistinct path between river and sea, the better to zoom away when the weather turned, a storm threatened or the sea, on a whim, decided to claim the strip of land for its own. The carts did busy business: one sold puri bhajis, dosas, goli baje and all things fried. Another declared 'Chineese food, Verry Testy, Gobi Manchuri,' in bold red letters on a white cloth banner which strained in the wind, not taking kindly to being tethered to the cart. A couple of the letters had bled into the white—the sign must have been put up without the words having properly dried first. It looked like a poster displaying a ghoulish horror movie—almost as bloody as the gloopy mixture which the vendor was stirring with relish on a huge wok right under the sign with the longest ladle I had ever seen.

A feisty breeze wafted rich, spicy smells from the carts right up to us queuing shuffling devotees. I wearily shifted my weight from one aching foot to the other and wondered if setting out on a pilgrimage on the behest of a madwoman made me just as mad and then quickly quelled the thought in case Lord Ganapathy decided to punish me for my disbelief.

That night, after the myriad pujas, after I had done a circuit of the temple on my knees, praying as I went, after we had partaken of the rasam, sambar, curd rice, jalebi and payasam—the prasadam meal provided by the temple for all the devotees—after we had washed in the sea and marvelled at the multi-hued sunset, we slept in the long narrow room provided by the temple for the devotees who didn't have the resources to hire vans and had come by public transport. There were no bullock carts available after six in the evening and for most of the people who had spent the day queuing for a darshan with Lord Ganesh, no means of returning home that day. And so we queued up again, and were pointed to the corner of a room, stuffed to bursting with people, the two of us pressed up against the wall, using my spare sari as a mattress. And, surrounded by snores on all sides as people slept after a busy day of prayers, as children mumbled in their sleep and somewhere close by someone assaulted by a nightmare screamed and across the room a woman giggled, as saris rustled and dhotis swished and mosquitoes feasted, Manoj pulled me on top of him and entered me urgently. And in that prayer-infused room redolent of musky sweat and salty sea, the air pregnant with the dreams of a thousand devotees, with Lord Ganesh keeping watch and the sea gurgling outside, the child the madwoman had prophesied was conceived.

Six weeks later, I went to the madwoman with the food I had prepared: mutton curry, fish fry and vangi bhath. 'Thank you,' I said, placing the food in front of the woman. The madwoman ignored me, muttering steadily to herself, but as I turned to go, she grabbed my hand, startling me. 'This pregnancy,' she said, her grey eyes never leaving mine, 'will cost you. Dearly.' I nodded, one hand guarding my stomach, awed, afraid. 'Protect the precious cargo within. It is your duty as a mother.' My hand on my stomach tightened. 'Even if you have to give up one you hold dear.' This was said in a whisper. What did she mean? Oh, Lord Ganapathy, what on earth did she mean?

Dear Diary, my hand aches as I read back on what I have written but I do not want to stop. I want to record every single detail, lest I forget. I did what the madwoman said and I am pregnant. My baby thrives inside of me. I know I will carry this pregnancy to term, I am sure of it. But for this privilege I will pay, I will lose something. That is what the madwoman has predicted. I am worried what form the cost will take, of course I am. But mostly I am happy. Manoj is always watching, asking me to rest, worried about the possibility of miscarriage. I am not. I am going to have this child, this much I know. And I will do anything for him, anything at all. I have waited for him for so long, have endured so much. So many lost babies. So much pain.

I had a dream growing up and it is about to be fulfilled. The madwoman—I will call her wise woman from now on—said I have to protect this child at all costs. I will. Fiercely. With my life.

What did I do before the wise woman came into my life? How did I manage? I think she turned up just to help me, guide me in the right direction. She can predict my destiny, see into my future. What a gift! I revere her.

Chapter 13
Nisha

Wood Polish and Beeswax

She finds the document in her mother's section of the study, in the sturdy wardrobe the orange-red colour of autumn that has always been there, in the third drawer from the bottom. It is locked, but she finds the key in the fob that hangs off the peg by the front door. So easy. But then her mother had known she would never think to look. Nisha was not that kind of person: snoopy, suspicious.

The smell of wood polish and beeswax takes her back to the memory of hiding here once, under the table. She had performed abysmally in her exams, and she knew the school had sent the report, she had seen the slim envelope waiting to be opened when she came home. She had sat under the table, her thighs wet and slippery with sweat, the air heavy with anticipation, tasting of fear. She had heard her mother calling and she had not replied. She heard her gentle footfall disappear up the stairs, heard the soft swish as the door to her room was opened, heard her mother make her way down again, heard the study door open. She had wet herself, she couldn't help it. Her mother's eyes, peering under the table, meeting her own. Holding out her hand to help her up. Fear reeked of urine, tasted of humiliation, looked like a wet orange patch on beige carpet. 'I am disappointed in you,' her mother had said, quietly, her gaze unwavering. 'We both are—your dad and I. You could do so much better.' Her mother had handed her bleach and carpet cleaner to scrub the area where she had wet herself. The chemical, sickly sweet smell of artificial flowers not quite masking the faint tang of ammonia is what she associates to this day with nausea, fear at the pit of her stomach, her mother's disappointment.

She had been unable to meet her parents' eyes that evening at dinner. Unable to meet their eyes until the next report, and the next. All of them good. She never did badly again. Once was enough.

It is a wide, comfortable room and it looks out onto the garden: a glorious early spring afternoon. The sun, having recharged its batteries all winter, is showing off. Golden rays, deliciously warm, snake in, making the top of the bookcase, which desperately needs dusting, shimmer and glow. Her father used to sit here, in that armchair beside the bookcase, his nose buried in a book while her mother worked with her, joining in their discussion every so often. When she was little, she had tried climbing up the ladder of his legs, slipping onto his lap, dislodging his book, 'Whoops, daddy.'

Outside, the grass, which desperately needs mowing, glitters, still wet from the mid-morning's surprise shower, and the fat droplets that cling tenaciously to the blades sparkle. Yolk-yellow daffodils bow gracefully in the mild breeze. Crocuses the pale purple of a bruise wink in the dappled sunlight. There is a carpet of pink snow under the cherry blossom tree, which is in early bloom, pink buds bursting in glorious colour. A gust of breeze displaces them and they swirl in the air, an ethereal rosy cloud. Birds twitter and a magpie lands hopefully in the garden, fooled by the glittering raindrops. The air that snakes into the room smells of new life, of buds bursting and trees eager to flower. It tastes of hope, the exact opposite of what she is feeling.

Spring has sprung, she thinks, without her noticing.

She is putting off the moment, putting off opening the file labelled 'Nature VS Nurture' — a surprisingly slim one. She has seen some of her parents' files on other projects. All of them thick, full to bursting. Why didn't they submit this one? The project was a success; she is proof. So, why didn't they publish the findings, keep this file in the lab with all their other completed projects?

Proof. It is just as she thought: she was a project. She wishes otherwise, but here it is in black and white. Here it is and it is time to face the facts.

Her mother's handwriting, with her father's notations in the margin. She notes the date of the first entry, makes a quick calculation. If her birth date is right, they started the project two years before she was born. She opens the file, flicks through the entries, each one meticulously dated until, aha, Case Study 24: Mangalore, India. 'Trip to India planned to research the roots of subject C, an accountant of Indian origin who was adopted by a British couple in 1960.' Did this give them the idea to do the same, she wonders? She glances at the date. When they travelled to India, she would have just turned three and a half.

Couple more entries and then, 'In Mangalore. Have heard of a curious case of twins, identical in every way except that one of them has a cleft palate. Find out if the twins could be part of our study?'

Wait a minute, she thinks, *wait a minute. Am I reading this right? Are they talking about me here? I am a twin? A twin? I have a sister? A sister who looks like me? A sister in India? My doppelganger?*

The next entry—the last: 'We are going to take a break from this project and work in general—we are going to be parents!' Exclamation marks in a project file—the equivalent of a string of jubilant swear words for her dry, officious parents.

It was me, wasn't it? It was. She runs to the bathroom, makes it just in time. She is sick over and over. She wobbles back on jelly legs, picks up the file, fingers trembling. Reads the last couple of entries again. Typical of her parents to not say much, as always so economical with words. She wants to know more, she wants to know if it was her they were talking about. But who else can it be? Dhonikatte is a village in Mangalore she knows, thanks to her research. How many children with cleft palates could there have been in Mangalore at the time her parents adopted her? And for the entry about them becoming parents to come just after the one about the twins… that cannot be a coincidence. So that means… she is a twin? But how? How can she not remember such a crucial part of her? How can she have blocked out the memories of the person she shared nine months in the womb with so completely? *Proof. I want proof. I cannot just believe everything that is written here. If I was a twin, an identical one at that, I would have felt something; I would have had an inkling, wouldn't I?*

She flicks through the pages of the rest of the file urgently, heart clamouring within the prison of her chest, her fingers shaking. Nothing. She is distraught, filled with a blinding rage. She flings the file. It collapses on the carpet, spine upwards, translucent innards sprawled messily, an orange pyramid spewing vomit-hued paper stained inky blue with her parents' writing. But something is not quite right with the picture. An anomaly. She bends down, leans closer. A black card with grey edging peeking out of one of the sleeves of the file.

She plucks it out. A photograph. Baby girls. Chubby arms and legs waving in the air. Identical chocolate eyes. Eyes she recognises. Eyes that stare back at her from the mirror every morning when she brushes her teeth, dresses for work. Identical high foreheads, identical wispy, coffee-coloured hair. Identical pointy chins. But the mouths, ah, the mouths: one with a grotesque laceration; the other perfect, sporting a toothless smile for the camera.

There's my proof.

No baby pictures, her mother had lied. None.

Emotions, twenty-odd years of repressed emotions, bombarding her. Nisha runs her finger over the image of the other girl. *My sister. My sister. I have a twin sister.* She slumps down onto the carpet, tastes grief, salty, swallows it down past the bitter lump of regret and guilt sitting heavy in her throat. *Why don't I remember you? Why do I have no recollection of you at all? We started life together from the same fertilised egg; we shared nine months in the womb and, judging from this picture, some months outside the womb together. How could I have forgotten you, lived all these years without knowing, sensing that a part of me was missing?*

Anger, raw, burning like a fire eating away at her innards. Why didn't her parents leave this picture with the letter? Perhaps they forgot it existed. That would be like them, to completely block out things they didn't want a reminder of, like they did their past, their Indian roots. But surely when they were writing the letter, they would have recalled the photograph? Perhaps they couldn't find it and thought it was lost. After all, Nisha only found it when she flung the file and the picture dislodged from its hiding place amongst the sleeves at the back. But then why didn't they tell her about her twin in the letter? Why?

A memory. She is twelve years old, learning about genes and heredity. She comes home buzzing with questions, hounds her parents. Unlike other times, when her questions have been a source of joy, this time they are strangely reluctant, answering in monosyllables, trying to put a stop to her questions, changing the topic. It had seemed strange at the time, she recalls, and very unlike her parents…

A picture begins to form. They must have written the letter to ease their consciences that summer when she kept asking question after question. They would have given it to the solicitor for safekeeping with their will, never considering the possibility that one day she might be reading it. They would have always meant to tell her in person and when they did, they would have shown her the file, told her about her twin and the photographic proof they had sadly misplaced. They would never for a moment have assumed that she would be finding out like this. That is why the letter was so lacking—they never really expected her to read it.

Another possibility: Her parents did not mention her twin in the letter because there was no accompanying proof—they thought they'd lost the only piece of evidence they had. And so they gave her the number of the convent they had adopted her from and hoped, no, assumed that she'd find the rest, knowing her penchant for solving puzzles, finding solutions.

A burst of scorching rage. *This is my life, not some mathematical riddle.*

How can she know these people, the workings of their minds, so well when she doesn't even remember her sister, her own flesh and blood, someone who looks exactly like her except for the cleft palate?

And now she understands why she was given away. A couple are blessed with twins, identical in every way except for their mouths. So they keep one, no points for guessing which one, and give away the other. White hot, scalding fury directed at the couple who gave her life. *I know I was damaged, ugly. Perhaps you couldn't bear to look at me, at my devastated face.* She rubs a hand over her scar, a reflex. *But you were my parents. You were supposed to love me, unconditionally, no matter how I looked… If my child was born with a cleft palate, I would cherish her, not discard her like used wrapping paper. If I hadn't been adopted by people who cared for me, loved me—yes, they did—what hope would I have had?*

Or did you give her away too? My sister… Supposing you did, where is she? She could be anywhere, with anyone. Tenderly, she caresses her sister's face. *Were you at the convent with me? If so, why do I not remember, if these dreams I have been having are really repressed memories?* Guilt. Hot, searing, ripping her insides to shreds.

How could I forget my sister? How?

Why didn't my parents tell me? When were they planning to, if at all? What right did they have to keep this from me? All these years I have ached for siblings, lived a solitary life, numbers my only real companions—until I met Matt. She is angry now. Raging. The fire consumes her, makes her open her mouth, produce a mad keening. So loud she surprises even herself. What else have they hidden from her? How many more lies will she discover?

I want to find my sister, I want to meet her.

We could have grown up together.

I look at her picture and yet, I cannot remember her. Why not? She has my eyes, my nose, my forehead, my hair. If not for the cleft, she could be me.

Slowly, she picks up the file again. Slowly she opens it. Then she flicks through the pages, then she is shaking them, even as she is shaking with sobs, softly at first then hard. She wants more pictures, she wants a different life, one with her sister in it. She shakes and sobs and screams and cries. She hits the table, the wardrobe. She sends the bowl of potpourri—the only concession to aesthetics in the room—flying, purple, magenta, violet and red flakes spraying like confetti, smelling like grief, tasting of salt. She shakes it long and hard, wanting to know what she was missing, wanting to know her sister, wanting the lost years back, wanting.

And then, all of a sudden she is spent. She slumps back down. The last entry was when they wrote, 'We are going to be parents.' A misunderstanding; that is all it was. She pulls out the letter they left her, reads it again: 'We might as well tell you—we were involved in a project at the time, Nurture versus Nature. And we were in India doing research. And then we found you…' They had found her *while on* the project. She wasn't part of the project, even though they had initially visited with that intention. They must have seen her and fallen in love with her. Despite her cleft palate. Despite it. They took a break from the project when they adopted her, a break that lasted their entire lifetimes. That is why this file was not in the lab with their other completed projects, lounging instead in the study at home, a slim dossier of the one time they chose personal gratification over professional gain.

They loved her. They did. That is enough. It has to be. Why didn't they tell her? Why?

And sitting there on the same carpet where she wet herself all those years ago, now littered with multi-hued potpourri flakes smelling of loss, a salty flowery smell, beside the ghosts of her father in his armchair, her mother on her desk, spectacles sliding down her nose, squinting at something, with the sun holding court outside to an audience of twittering birds on the glittering lawn, a picture begins to form. Lekha and Ravi, renowned scientists, are blindsided by emotion when they see a little girl with a cleft palate waving her gooey arms at them. Love with all its messy accoutrements snakes in, demands residence. They take the little girl back to England with them. They are amazed by the ease with which she takes to an alien country and culture, calls them Mum and Dad, starts school, allows herself to be subjected to the many operations to repair her cleft. They mean to tell her the truth, of course they do. But she's forgotten her past, erased her memories, completely. How can they without sending this girl who has been through so much into turmoil? She is their daughter, she has accepted it—isn't it better to let it be?

I was not wanted by my birth parents. They didn't want to tell me, hurt me. They were protecting me. Perhaps that is why they never visited India again, never took me there. But how could they keep the knowledge of my sister from me, whatever their reasons? They did not have the right to make that decision for me. They did not.

A rogue thought insinuates: *Where is all this coming from? I am becoming just the sort of person my parents scoffed at, a fanciful person giving in to whimsy, my head in the clouds.*

And, *Good. Good on you, Nisha.*

She fingers the picture in her hand, feels the tug of loss, the tsunami of tears threatening again. *Who is she, this sister of mine? What has she become? What has she made of her life?* She caresses her sister's face again. *I hope you are happy, wherever you are. I hope you have had a good life so far.*

She clutches the file to her chest and then, being the person that she is, she cleans the study, chucks the potpourri in the bin, hoovers the carpet. And then, she searches the house, top to bottom, every nook and corner. Nothing more. So this was it.

She watched a man being struck by a car once. He was walking across the road in front of her and this car came out of nowhere. The man was tossed into the air and in that moment of tossing, as he flipped like a coin, an acrobat, his eyes met hers. They were wide open, there was fear dawning and also surprise. Mostly surprise. That is what she feels. The man had escaped unhurt except for a few scratches. What about her? How will she be when all this is over? Is it finished? How much more to come? How many more secrets to uncover? How many more lies?

She sits down and peruses the photo again, drinking her sister in. Then she opens her notebook and writes.

This is what I know:

1) My parents loved me. I was never a project. They loved me.

2) I have a sister, a twin. Does she know about me?

3) If I was to meet her, I would ask: Who are you? What is your name? How has your life been until now? Do you like maths and numbers as much as I do? Do you find difficulty experiencing emotions? Are you as hung up on facts as I am? Do you pull your left earlobe when you are nervous like I do? Now that I know of you, I miss you. I miss the shared past that we could have had, all the memories that we could have created together.

She has to see her sister, the one other person who is blameless in all of this. She calls Matt, leaves him a message. It feels like ages since she left him the last one telling him she was going to search the house, see if there was a file. And then she collapses on the sofa, the very same sofa where she opened the letter that started everything, and closes her eyes.

She is running, running as fast as her little legs can carry her, looking in all the rooms. Nothing. No one. The smell of burning candles, vast empty space, fear. She runs into the chapel. Empty. The slap of her bare legs hitting the stone floors, echoing eerily in the limitless silence. She crawls under the pews and from her vantage point, she looks to the altar, the statue of Jesus on the cross, blood dripping from his many wounds, the crown of thorns piercing his head like the stick piercing the foaming profusion of cotton candy she's had at the parish feast. *Where are they? Please, Jesus, Lord, let me find them.* The Lord smiles down at her, his suffering face relaxing for a brief while.

That gives her courage. She climbs out gingerly on legs that refuse to do her bidding, tired as they are with all that running. The soles of her feet are bruised and blistering. She has misplaced her chappals somewhere, in her mad rush to find everybody.

She limps from the dark chapel into an abundance of frothy golden light that hits her pupils, makes her blink rapidly as her eyes adjust. The courtyard, with its lime tree and jasmine bush, the air fragranced with jasmine and a hint of lime—tangy, slightly bitter. Deserted. Where have they gone? Where is Sister Priya who always sits here, at all times of day except when she is at mass, threading jasmine flowers into garlands? The sun beats down mercilessly, a punishing yellow ball. Sweat beads down her face, soaks her dress.

A movement by the gates to the convent. She looks up. Nothing. But she thought she saw… something, someone familiar. A fleeting glimpse. Perhaps Sister Priya is locked outside? She runs to the gates. Peers out from between the bars. The iron smell of rust. She moves to the wall beside the gate, flattens herself against the velvet moss cushion and looks out sideways. A bulbous coffee eye raining tears like sparkly jewels. And another. Straggly hair, black as the soot collecting in the hearth after the conjee has been cooked of a morning. A face broken, compartmentalised by bars. A face awash, shimmering, crumpling. A face she knows… She opens her mouth to call out but just as suddenly as it appeared, the face is gone. As if she had summoned it into fleeting existence and then wished it away again. She runs to the gate once more. Nothing. She flattens herself against the wall on the other side of the gate and peers out. The mud road outside the convent gates is deserted, dust swirling in a sooty cloud in the lethargic mid-morning haze, no face framed in it. A queer feeling—part bewilderment, part upset, part fear—beating hard against her rib cage, manifesting in gasping sobs tearing out of her.

She runs away from the rusting bars, away from the heat, the hurt; she runs as fast as her blistered weeping legs can carry her into the convent, runs straight into the arms of Sister Priya. 'Baba, what's the matter? Where were you? We were looking all over for you. You missed the Stations of the Cross up at Marybai's house. Never mind.' She buries her head in the crook of Sister Priya's neck, where stray hairs escape her wimple, curly commas waving. Sister Priya smells of candle wax, of vanilla incense, of musk, of prayer. A familiar, soothing scent. Her thudding heart slowly resumes its regular beat, her sobs sputter, then die away completely. *Silly me*, she thinks. She forgot all about the Stations of the Cross. Her stomach rumbles. Sister Priya lets her hold on, carries her inside, 'Time for lunch. Your favourite: fish curry and brinjal fry.' She holds on tight, her legs crossed around Sister Priya's back, her hands arched around her neck, revelling in the bounce, bounce as she is carried in Sister Priya's arms, the thump, thump of Sister Priya's heart, the wiggle of her footfall rocking her body, her warm breath coming in gasps of exertion tickling Nisha's cheek. She is safe, not lost anymore.

She does not look back.

Nisha sits up, disorientated, her nostrils suffused with the bittersweet scent of jasmine and lime. She is in her parents' house; the clock blinks 16:10 in orange letters that pound in her head, mellow honey-gold rays of setting sun slant in through chinks in the curtains, shadow puppets cavort on cream cushions. She is bathed in perspiration. She reeks of sweat, fear, worry. Who was that person? Big eyes, wispy hair, framed in the bars of the gate? Woman? Yes. Familiar somehow, arousing something in her, a ghost of a feeling… Nisha had almost recognised her, made to call out… but the woman had disappeared, morphed into a cloud of dust. She can still experience the ache of loss she had felt then, sitting hard as a ball in the base of her stomach. So very real. Who was this apparition—a dream within a dream —who had aroused these feelings in her?

And a name, plucked from the dregs of the dream: Sister Priya.

I loved this Sister Priya, whoever she is, and she loved me. I felt safe with her, her arms my harbour. I need to call the convent, find out how much of these vivid memories, more tangible than this sofa I am sitting on, are real, how much my imagination. The crinkle of paper in her hand, the file the burnt-orange colour of leaves swirling in early autumn sunshine, the precious picture. *I need to find myself, who I really am. I want to find my sister. I want to know why my birth parents gave me away and if it was only me they didn't want or the both of us. I need to know.* She looks again at her twin sister, drinks her in. *If my dreams are memories, then how come my sister is not in them? Why can't I remember her? Why?*

What are you doing now, twin sister? Do you remember me? Miss me? Feel like a part of you is lost? I will find you, I will, she mouths softly into the quiet room.

'Oh, Nisha,' Matt says, when he comes in, bringing the crisp smell of outdoors with him. 'I wish I had been here for you when you found out.'

She relaxes into the solid reassurance of him as she wordlessly hands over the photograph. She watches the expressions flitting across his face. Surprise, wonder, awe.

'She looks just like you,' he whispers. And then, his eyes softening in that way of his when he looks at her, 'How did you feel? What did you do? I wish you hadn't found this alone; I wish I had been there…'

'I screamed, I raved, ranted. Threw things. Broke the bowl of potpourri.'

He smiles, that smile that lights up his face, and if possible the wonder on his face is even more pronounced. 'You did that? Wow!' He bends close, breath warm in her ear. 'Good on you.' He rubs his hands together. 'This is a cause for celebration. Knowing you have a twin sister of course and this. This is the beginning, Nisha.'

How on earth did she manage to snag this wonderful man? He gets her, knows how big a deal it is for her to lose her cool, to give in to impulse.

'The next time I will celebrate is when you start hitting me and ranting at me during a fight instead of withdrawing into yourself.'

She smiles.

'And, when you can tell me you love me.' His voice soft.

'Matt, I...'

'I know,' he says.

A thought. She doesn't want to ask and yet she is itching to know. After what's happened, what she's found out, she needs to know. 'Matt. Suppose. Suppose you had to choose between me and my sister...' She fingers her scar. 'I mean, I am not putting this properly... This is what my parents would have said was a rhetorical question... Would you have chosen her? The better one, no blemish marring her face?'

His eyes shine and there is such tenderness in his gaze that she is awed. 'Oh, Nisha, I wish you could see what I do when I look at you. You are the most intelligent woman I have met, and the most guileless. You do not care about clothes and yet you are always effortlessly chic. You are so strong and yet so vulnerable when it comes to emotions. And you are beautiful.' He is so close. His words touch her nose and eyes, his minty breath hugging her. 'I love you. You. I meant to do this properly, at a more romantic setting, but...' He drops down on one knee, holds her hand, his eyes never leaving her, 'Will you marry me?'

She is shocked, she is overwhelmed. She is frightened. 'Matt, I... I cannot do this right now, commit myself to someone else when I don't even know who I am...'

His eyes cloud over. He stands up, nods once in her direction and walks into the kitchen. 'I'm going to have a glass of wine. Want one?' Not a question, just a statement recited in a flat voice so unlike his exuberant tones of earlier.

The tears she has been trying to keep at bay overflow, pushing past the bridge of her eyelids, stumbling over the slide of her eyelashes, suffusing her cheeks. 'Matt, I'm sorry,' she says, following him into the kitchen.

'Bad timing. I understand.' He speaks to the open fridge, not looking at her, his voice cold. An icy blast on her face. The stale smell of old food, compressed air.

'Matt, I… I wish I was different, I wish I found this easier... I… care for you, a lot. But I… I have been lied to by my parents. I have just found out I have a twin sister whom I cannot remember at all… I… need to find myself. I… I am not capable of giving love when I don't know what to feel. I am exploding inside.'

He shuts the fridge, looks at her, his eyes glistening, the colour of the roiling sea in the midst of a winter storm. 'I am sorry too.' He lowers his head into the cradle of his hands. 'It gets tiring after a while, Nisha, the one sidedness of it all… When I asked you to marry me just now, you looked scared, like you wanted to bolt… I do not want to have that effect on you. I love you so much, have done since the moment I met you. It hurts that you don't feel the same way…' He rests a hand against the cool white of the fridge, and she looks at it, pink skin framed by creamy white, so she doesn't have to see the pain in his eyes, his eyelashes fringed with shimmering drops. 'I have been so patient, but sometimes… I just…'

She takes a step closer towards him. She aches to hold him, be held by him. Will he let her? And in that moment she understands how it is for him, to never be sure of her love. He has always taken her on her terms, held her when she's needed it and let her be when she has craved solitude. And he has always, without question, been there for her. She cannot remember a time when he has pushed her away, said, 'No, I don't feel like it. I want space.'

She longs to tell him she loves him, but how can she when she has been hurt so badly by the lies of the people closest to her? Isn't it better to say nothing at all until she is sure? She cannot do to him what has been done to her, she owes him that much. She opens her mouth, but he leans forward, puts a finger on her lips.

She takes another step forward, his finger still on her lips and then, he opens his arms and she folds herself into them. She nestles in the solid haven of his embrace, rests her head against his heart, is soothed by its rhythm. And she wishes she could stay here forever; she wishes she could give herself completely to this man, say what he wants to hear. She wonders for the umpteenth time if, had she grown up in India, would she have been different. She wonders if the sister she has just discovered finds it just as difficult to process emotions. Her tears soak his shirt and his soak her hair as they stand there, and in that moment, there is just him and her, their hearts beating in sync. And for now, that has to be enough.

Chapter 14
Devi

Coconut Shell Spittoons

Ma,

I can see now why you believed in the madwoman. I would, too, if I had to endure but a fraction of the agony you suffered.

After I read your entry, Ma, I went to see the gynaecologist. I asked if miscarriage is genetic, if it runs in the family. 'No,' she said, 'but miscarriages are very common.' She smiled softly at me. 'Rest,' she advised. 'Try not to lift anything heavy. And I know it is hard in your situation, what with your mother... but try not to be too stressed.'

Afterwards, I went to the temple for the first time in years. I prayed to Lord Ganapathy even though I wasn't sure I believed in Him. And today, as I entered the hospital, I paused in front of the statue of the Virgin Mary. If I wasn't sure about Lord Ganapathy, the God I grew up with, I believed in the Virgin Mary even less. And yet, I prayed to the both of them. I prayed that my baby would be healthy, safe. And I prayed for you, Ma.

I ridiculed your belief in the madwoman, Ma. How little I knew! How naïve I was! We all need faith, I realise that now. Perhaps faith is blind but it is better than nothing. Sometimes, blind belief is all we have.

Ma, in your diary you mention that your parents yearned for grandchildren just as much as you yearned for a child. You regretted that they died without seeing me—their only grandchild. Please come back to me, Ma. I do not want to harbour the same regret.

Ma, did you know that while you were in this very hospital recovering after walking into the hive of bees the day Rohan and his parents came to our house, a contingency of village matrons paid me a visit, trying to dissuade me from marrying Rohan?

The conclave of village matrons, led by Durgakka, are squatting on Jalajakka's veranda chewing paan while they wait for me to return from visiting with you, Ma, their mouths stained red with betel juice, their spittoons, fashioned from coconut shells, within easy reach, the brown of the inside masked quickly by a viscous crimson, replete with bubbles and swarming with flies. As soon as I near the tamarind tree, they congregate in the courtyard, cornering me. Sweat drips down their grave visages, creating runnels in the mask of talcum powder caked onto their faces in an effort to lighten their wrinkly russet skin, staining their saris, suitably sombre in deference to your condition, Ma: greys and browns and muted golds.

Their oiled gleaming hair is pulled back in identical severe buns that etch deep grooves onto their faces. They look like a posse of ducks, their plump bodies straining against the constraint of their saris.

It is too late to turn back; they have seen me see them.

'We are here because we care, dear.' Durgakka, their designated spokesperson, takes a step forward, her face ballooned with the import of what she is saying. 'What with your poor ma in hospital, we are taking on the mantle of guardianship on her behalf. After everything she has done for you, all the sacrifices she has made, she does not deserve this. Lord Ganapathy has spoken.'

'What has he said then?' I ask, smirking.

The ladies take a step backward, as if slapped. Their mouths open in a collective O of shock, displaying reddish-yellow paan in all its half-chewed glory.

Durgakka sighs sternly and launches right in. 'Your mother walking straight into a swarm of bees, puffing like a puri in hot oil, was a bad omen, child. It is Lord Ganapathy's way of warning you that a union between families of different religions is wrong, even though Rohan seems a nice enough boy, even though his family came from good stock.' The other ladies' heads bob up and down in unison. 'It is not done to ignore the signs. And anyway, that boy's family are only accepting you on *their* terms. You are to have a Catholic wedding, no puja, nothing, just some pish pish in a church and those hymns like somebody crying out in pain, like tears at a funeral, like river water gushing, frogs farting—no rhythm, no raga, nothing.

No soul,' Durgakka's face scrunches in an expression of disdain. 'Not like bhajans.'

I am impressed by Durgakka's oratory. Has she prepared this speech in advance, perfecting similes over time, or has she just made it up? The ladies' heads are moving so fast, I worry they will fall off any minute.

'And not only that,' Durgakka continues, her voice increasing in tempo, 'you have to convert to Catholicism, turning your back on the very Lord Ganapathy who blessed your mother with you, after five miscarriages. Five.' Durgakka's eyes are large as laddoos. 'Now, after all that, marrying a Catholic, becoming one, would be the worst kind of betrayal. Lord Ganapathy wouldn't be best pleased. Aiyyo, he is already showing his wrath—why else the bees?'

'Thank you very much for your concern, but I am going to marry Rohan, omens or not,' I say, trying not to smile at the identical expressions of disbelief on their faces.

As I write this, Ma, I think that perhaps those bees *were* an omen. Perhaps they foretold what was to come, that some years later, you would be lying unconscious in the same hospital that managed to cure you of the bee stings even though the doctor did say then that you had had a lucky escape, that if there had been a delay of a few minutes, the poison would have infiltrated your bloodstream and it would have been too late. Is it too late now, Ma? I desperately hope not.

The evening before my wedding, I sit on the dew-stained veranda, listening to the music of crickets. Twilight paints the sky in navy-tinged pink strokes.

Droning flies venture valiantly to the lone lamp flickering with the ever-changing voltage. Mosquitoes buzz. Night jasmine infuses the air with its heady scent. Snatches of voices raised in argument echo in the charged silence of impending night—they are fighting again in Murli's household. Soorya stumbles home through the fields, singing drunkenly. Your voice, high-pitched with strain, drifts from inside. You are telephoning the caterers with last-minute changes: Aunt Mini has suddenly decided she doesn't like onions in her food. After that you will call the band, 'Mangalore Disco', to confirm that they will be playing a mixture of Tulu and Konkani hits to cater to both Hindu and Catholic tastes. Later, you will telephone the relatives who need to be personally invited as invitations by post just won't do, Aunt Amita being top of the list. And then, of course, you will have to appease and cajole all those relatives who have refused to come because they maintain you are committing a terrible, irrevocable blunder by marrying me off to a Catholic when there are a hundred, no, a thousand, very suitable Hindu boys, some even in England, if that's what you and I are after. Next, you will go to the kitchen in search of the lime sherbet you made earlier in order to ease your throat, sore from all the shouting—Aunt Amita in particular is partially deaf. In between soothing gulps, you will get the saris, the gold ready.

You had transported the gold, gleaned through years of scrounging and saving, from the bank the previous day in a pouch tucked beneath your sari blouse and kissing your flesh, and kept it locked in Sumitranna's Godrej safe for the night. (Sumitranna had stayed guard the entire night, sleeping sitting up on the chair by the front door, holding the old plough in one hand and the heaviest idli steamer in the other, just in case the burglar who had been stealing his chickens and coconuts got wind of the gold and decided to visit.) You had laid out all the gold on the dining-room table and it had winked up at us in vibrant shades of turmeric. 'As part of your dowry,' you said, looking at me fondly, the look that always made my hackles rise.

'But Ma, Rohan has said his family do not want any dowry.'

'Yes, but I cannot send you into their family with nothing. You are not a beggar,' you said firmly. 'Here —two pairs of bangles, three pairs of earrings, two rings, three bracelets and three necklaces.'

This wedding is wiping you out, I know. You have borrowed money from Sumitranna and taken a loan from the bank. 'My only daughter will be married in style,' you say to anyone who will listen. 'I don't want Rohan's family to look down on our family just because we are poor, live in a two-room cottage.' It makes me grit my teeth, this affectation of yours. 'We *are* poor. Everyone knows it. There is no need to make yourself poorer just for this one wedding. His family have offered to pay for the wedding; why don't you let them?' I have shouted, more than once. 'It is not just any wedding—it is *your* wedding. I have been preparing for it all your life. I will give you away properly,' you replied, speaking like a heroine from a Kannada blockbuster.

And then, softly, 'I do not want to be beholden to them. As it is, they are paying for your ticket.' Why do you have to remind me of that, Ma? 'When I get to England, I will find some work, any work, and pay them back, don't you worry,' I yell, and watch your face fall at the mention of England. You know I am going, Ma, then why not accept it, get on with it instead of flinching away from every mention, your face like a punished child's? I cannot wait, Ma. I cannot. Much as you are savouring these last days with me, I am willing them away. 'You don't want to owe Rohan's parents, but you don't mind being beholden to Canara Bank and Sumitranna then?' I scream before storming outside to sit on the veranda. Truth is I don't like the thought of you having to work harder than ever to repay the loan, especially as I won't be nearby to keep an eye on you. It annoys me that you couldn't just have accepted Rohan's parents' offer. So you suffer a small blow to your pride, so what? *I have*, I think, as hot-red memories of that cringe-inducing evening outside Rohan's house inveigle in, the bitter taste of shame assaulting my mouth.

From the kitchen drift spicy aromas: fish frying, rice boiling and sambar bubbling, enough to feed all the guests who have arrived early and camped in our too small house. Rathi, the girl you have hired to help with the wedding, is in the bathroom heating the big urn of water which will have to bathe all of us. Rathi feeds the fire coconut husks, which even I know not to do, and clouds of thick pungent smoke invade the house sending everyone into coughing fits. Jalajakka, who is helping with preparations of course, storms into the bathroom yelling, 'Have you gone completely mad? Now I have burnt the fish.'

Uh-oh! Aunt Mini won't be pleased, I think. Aunt Mini came to stay three days ago, four bags in tow, lugged by the rickshaw driver who wouldn't budge until you paid him thirty rupees from the wedding fund. 'Her luggage punctured the tyres,' he had yelled, shooting dirty looks in Aunt Mini's general direction. Aunt Mini had arrived early, ostensibly to help with the wedding. In actual fact, she camps in the kitchen offering advice on how everything is done, ordering food to be made especially for her as per her stringent requirements and getting on everyone's nerves.

'Stop daydreaming about that useless Magesh and do at least one thing properly,' Jalaja yells at Rathi, taking out all the bottled-up frustration she feels at being ordered around by Aunt Mini on the poor girl.

Magesh, the village postman, is Rathi's betrothed. At Jalajakka's admonishment, Rathi bursts into tears. Jalajakka storms out of the bathroom and into the kitchen from where loud shouts ensue, rapidly escalating to enraged shrieks. I recognise Aunt Mini's high-pitched whine and of course Jalajakka's booming bass.

This is what the stress of organising a wedding does to a household, I think. I look up at the sky. The stars are out in their millions, winking down at me. And I think, *these very same stars will be in England too.*

My wedding day. When I wake and see you next to me on the lumpy mattress, your housecoat bunched around your knees, your mouth slightly open and little snores escaping it, Brrr…. Brrr… sounding like the bore well pump that we use to get our water when the well dries up in the height of summer, I know it's early. You are normally up by five, when the deep grey outside is stained cerise by dawn's flush, and these last few days you have been waking up even earlier, preparing for the wedding.

A mild breeze floats in through the open window, fragranced with night jasmine and aboli, and it dawns on me gradually that this is my last morning at home, waking up next to you, Ma, feeling your familiar warmth next to mine. Now that I know what I know, I can see that that was the last time everything was normal in my world, everything as it should be. You and I at loggerheads, bound by a love that brought out the worst in both of us. Now that I know what I know, I want to preserve that moment, to reach back in time and whisper in the ears of the girl that I was, 'Go slow. Don't wish it all away. Savour this moment, do.'

As if I have heard the caution from my older, wiser self, I bend down, plant a feather-soft kiss on your forehead. You twitch and continue to snore. Your bindi's gone awry, curling at the edges, the gum peeling off, and I gently push it back into the centre of your forehead and press it down. I love you best when you're asleep, Ma, when I don't have to see the naked love in your pleading eyes, when your mouth is not working overtime administering endearments and admonishments in equal measure.

What irony, that now I have my wish and you are asleep all the time, I want you to wake up, to yell, to rant, do anything at all except lie there, unresponsive, lost to me…

My eyes slowly get used to the dark and I make out the many bodies squeezed into the room. The chairs have been pushed to the corners and cane mats have been placed haphazardly wherever there's an inch of space, and all the relatives who have arrived early for the wedding snore happily side by side even though when they are awake none of them get along. The air hangs heavy in the centre of the room—a dense, humid cloud, weighted down by a night's accumulation of sweat and dreams. Gingerly stepping over the bodies, I make my way to the loo.

Afterwards I go to the kitchen. Rathi is already awake, her mat rolled into a cylinder and tucked away in the hollow space between the rotting beams chomped on by woodlice and the roof, which also houses coconut husks, mats woven from coconut tree fronds and other sundries. She squats on the floor, grating coconuts. The paste of rice and lentils she ground the previous day has already risen and bubbles out over the muslin cloth tied to the top of the pot—effervescent white foam licking the sides of the mud-coloured earthen urn sitting on the soot-stained hearth, looking for all the world like a wizard's cauldron.

Jalaja arrives, shushing Bobby's low growl, bringing the smell of night and the bluster of dawn breeze with her. She squats on the floor and starts pounding rice into the paste required to fry koilolis for breakfast, rubbing sleep out of her eyes with the pallu of her sari, the squishy roll of flesh visible between her sari blouse and skirt jiggling in time to the beat.

I squat down on the cement floor of the kitchen, sipping the hot, sweet tea flavoured with elaichi and ginger that Rathi has just placed in my hands, watching her and Jalaja grind and slice and pound and squeeze, watching the smoke rising from the hearth to add another coat of soot to the beams of the ceiling and the blackened walls. *At last,* I think, a thrill caressing my spine. *I am escaping these walls, this poky cramped house, you.* And almost immediately, guilt lashes out: *What is wrong with you, Devi? Shouldn't you be sad, upset at leaving home, this house that has been your security all your life, your mother who has loved you more than life, as she is fond of saying? Shame on you.*

I deliberately cast the heavy mantle of guilt aside and think instead of England. A cold country with limited sunshine, I've heard. I cannot imagine not having sun. Even now at the crack of dawn, the rising sun's mellow rays snake in to where I sit by the doorway to the kitchen, deliciously warm on my bare arms. 'Posh Mrs. Josephine's daughter lives in London; you make sure to meet her after you've settled in, okay?' you have said. I will run a million miles before contacting anyone who has even the remotest connection to this village. I do not want my escapades fed back via the gossip network. I want to be free, free to find myself without constraints, without frequent reminders of what I should be doing and how I have failed to meet expectations.

I sip the tea and eat the hot idlis, soft as buttermilk, dipped in steaming sambar that is not too sweet nor too spicy, dotted with cumin and dry red chillies, mint and coriander chutney on the side, tangy with tamarind. You enter the kitchen just as I am finishing breakfast, your hair awry, your eyes bloodshot with dark shadows under them. 'Oh, Lord Ganapathy, help me, I overslept, today of all days,' you say. Your eyes soften when you see me, 'Good, you've eaten. Now come, have a shower and then you should start getting ready. We need to be at the church in a little over two hours.' Your eyes dart this way and that as you speak, no doubt making a list in your head of all that needs to be done. 'Now, what time did Shami say she was delivering the flowers?'

After that, it is rush, rush, no time to think. The beautician arrives just as I finish my shower, the water that Rathi has spent the previous hour heating to boiling point scalding my flesh pink. I change into my white sari and don the matching silver jewellery, fawning sunlight pouring through the windows like honey, dancing on the sari, illuminating me, so it looks as if I am glowing. 'Lord Ganapathy is showing he's pleased by singling you out,' Jalajakka says fondly, her eyes shining as everyone (Aunt Mini included) oohs over how exquisite I look.

There is a queue for the bathroom as all the relatives rush to wash the night off their bodies, to beautify themselves and don their best clothes. Aunt Mini complains that the water is not hot enough and orders Rathi to heat the urn again. Rathi grumbles that she has quite enough to do thank you very much. Aunt Mini carps about the cheek of the girl and moans that you give your servants too much leeway, Ma. You say quite sharply that Rathi and Jalaja have kindly offered to help and are *not servants*. Jalaja takes Rathi's side for once and says that if Aunt Mini had not complained about the idlis being too soft and the chutney being too bitter and the sambar being too sweet and asked for upma instead, Rathi would be free now to heat the water instead of rushing around washing all the extra dishes soiled because of making a whole other breakfast today of all days.

Aunt Emmi asks if there are any safety pins in this house, and you insist that you bought ten packs, you knew they would be needed to pin up all the saris. Where are they? A mad hunt ensues and the safety pins are found underneath the sari Aunt Mini is going to wear to the wedding neatly folded and waiting while she has her shower. 'What are they doing here?' Aunt Emmi asks and Rathi smirks knowingly. 'Has anyone seen the hair pins?' asks the beautician. 'I need them for Devi's hair-style and for the flowers to loop over her bun —a garland of jasmine and another of aboli, is that right, Shilpakka?' You nod, your mouth full of safety pins, your hands busy working the pleats of Aunt Emmi's emerald sari. 'Have you looked under Aunt Mini's sari blouse?' Jalaja asks and they all check that Aunt Mini is still in the bathroom hav-ing a shower in the 'lukewarm water' before they burst out laughing, shushing each other conspiratorially—you laughing so hard (and a tad hysterically) that the safety pins burst out of your mouth in a silver shower. 'Thank the Lord Ganapathy that they were not open; they could have pricked someone and I would be mopping up blood right now—not a good omen on a wedding day,' Rathi says, squatting to pick them up. 'Don't speak about bad omens, girl,' Aunt Emmi chides and I am reminded with a pang of the bees, the picture of you swelling like a blow-up doll floating before my eyes. 'Ow, you stepped on my hand,' Rathi complains of Jalaja. 'Well, you shouldn't be scrabbling under my feet then, should you,' Jalaja retorts, serenely plaiting Aunt Kushala's hair.

The room smells of talcum powder and sandalwood perfume, as the ladies get dressed, giggling as they affix the silk saris firmly to skirts with safety pins so they will be able to dance at the wedding without fear of the saris tumbling in a silky heap around them. Once in a while a rumble of deep-throated laughter floats in from the kitchen where the men are getting ready and the women yell at them to stop laughing and get on with it. 'What's this?' they yell back. 'You take longest. We will be waiting for you for hours after we have finished.'

I listen to all this banter, the business of a house preparing for a wedding, as the beautician works my face, her hands gentle as they slap sweet-smelling lotions on my cheeks, massage my eyebrows, knead my chin. *I will miss this*, I muse. *I will, much as I long to escape*. I try not to think—just feel, hear, take it all in. I will store this away in a corner of my heart, this memory of my last few hours at home to take out and cherish later. *I am not a monster after all,* I think, relieved. I have feelings, though they are so mixed so much of the time.

Afterwards we pack into the three cars that you have hired to take us to the church. 'Our first Catholic wedding, eh?' the relatives laugh, a tad nervously. The women walk gingerly up the mud path between the fields to the cars waiting on the dusty road, lifting their saris high so the ends don't get muddy, trying not to get their new shoes grimy and dirt-stained. Sumitranna and two of my uncles hoist me up and carry me through the fields, to the accompaniment of loud cheers. Aunt Mini pushes everyone aside and tries to get into the car, but Jalaja yells, 'Let the bride go first.'

I get in, followed by you, Ma and Aunt Mini who has somehow nudged into the bridal car. You tip my face up with one finger and look at me, eyes shimmering like the silk of your sari, 'I wish your father could have been here to see you now.' Your voice is wobbly. 'But he is watching along with Lord Ganapathy from up there.' For once, I don't pull away. My eyes sting and in that moment, I miss desperately the father I have never known. You wipe your eyes with the new handkerchief that Rathi pressed into your hands as you were setting out, bought especially for the occasion—'You cannot afford to dirty the pallu of your sari; the mother of the bride has to look her best.'

Once the cars fill up, the remaining relatives take the autos that are waiting in a patient line behind the cars, the drivers lounging by the ramshackle bridge which mans the stream beside the road, sharing beedis and gossiping as they wait, curls of grey smoke sullying the cloudless azure expanse of sky.

The church is on the banks of the river Ganvi, and I watch the water glitter and swirl as I climb up the steps to the doorway where the priest and my betrothed wait. Rohan smiles at me and the mixed emotions I have been feeling, the pang at leaving you, ma and our house—the only house I've known all my life—disappear, to be replaced by the excitement, the sense of exhilaration I have felt ever since Rohan asked me to marry him. The ceremony starts, Rohan chants prayers that are alien to me, the altar looks remote, a bleeding Jesus on the cross stern and a tad scary, and it is as if I am far away, removed from this situation, an outsider observing it. Saris rustle behind me, whispers are shushed, babies quieted. A little boy's voice, petulant, 'I want…' the rest of the sentence drowned as the mother leaves the church.

And then, the priest asks if I, Devi, will take Rohan as my lawfully wedded husband. And I look up at Rohan, at the familiar contours of his face and I say, 'Yes, I do.' From the corner of my eyes, I see you wiping the tears streaming down your face with your pallu, disregarding the handkerchief, and then the priest is asking Rohan if he will take me as his wife and Rohan is saying yes and we are wedded.

The feast begins in the hall adjacent to the church—the eating and drinking, the dancing and merriment, the ogling and flirting, the arranging of marriages for the next lot of eligible girls, the comparing—who's sporting the most gold, the costliest sari, the heaviest makeup, and the note-taking—is a Catholic wedding better than a Hindu wedding, is the hall decorated grandly enough, is the food tasty enough, is the crowd big enough, is the venue posh enough, is the wedding as impressive as the Mangalore Shetty extravaganza, the Kemmannu D'Souza Dhamakha?

Afterwards, we stand on the steps leading up to the church and one by one, the guests wish us a long and happy married life, many strapping children. And then, it is done and everyone is leaving but you. You cling to me and you sob. 'Oh, Devi,' you say, 'what will I do? Oh, what will I do?' And I feel the familiar irritation bubble up as you won't let go, as we stand on the steps, you sobbing, me biting my lips to hold in the hurtful words that ache to smash out of me, my sari slowly getting soaked with your tears, as the twilight air caresses my face, briny with an undertone of rose incense wafting from the church, as the setting sun stains the beige sky a glossy pink and the river red, like blood. We stand there, as the blackout blinds of night kiss the scarlet water and shut out the russet curtain of sky. And the moment that I have been waiting for, my first evening as a married woman, is ruined, coloured by my irritation, my barely suppressed anger, flooded by your tears.

After what feels like an age, I push you away, not too gently. 'I have to go now,' I bite out.

And yet you hold on. You have to be peeled off me, and my joy in being married is marred by the sight of you, lying in a crumpled, broken heap in Jalajakka's arms, a sorry picture which forever tints memories of my wedding day.

And as I leave with Rohan to the hotel he has booked for us to celebrate our wedding night, as the car speeds up, taking me away from you, Ma, I finally breathe freely without worrying about you hovering, wanting to spend every remaining minute with me, your face the picture of misery.

It is done. It is over. A chapter ends. A new one begins.

Ma, if I could turn back time, relive those days before my marriage again, I would be kinder, I like to think, more patient. I was selfish, Ma, I realise now. I wanted so much and I felt so inhibited, so bogged down. I wanted to fly but I was lucky if I was allowed to limp. With the brash disregard of youth, I did not put myself in your shoes, in anyone's shoes but mine—and they didn't fit, they were much too small for me. I was a caterpillar who knew she would be a beautiful butterfly if only she could escape, the ugly duckling who would be a swan if she left, the snake who could only grow if she shrugged off her mother like an unwanted skin. I am sorry. Forgive me, Ma.

Ma, this afternoon you thrashed about and lashed out once more, dislodging the drip, setting the machines to beeping frantically. You gripped my hand with a wiry strength I did not know you possessed. 'Jalaja,' you whispered. 'Jalaja.'

'Shh, Ma, I am here. Devi,' I said, hurt blossoming in my chest, manifesting in a lump in my throat. It hurt that you called upon Jalaja and the madwoman before that but not me. Why? While I was deliberating whether to call the nurses, you opened your eyes for the first time and looked right at me. There was a glazed, wild look in them. You were far away, looking at me but right through me, fixated by something only you could see.

'Jalaja,' you called. 'Twins,' you whispered. And then you closed your eyes and retreated into that strange world you inhabit, wherein you look so peaceful and yet when you claw your way out of it, you are disturbed, you are fighting something, you are not at peace. Is that world that much better than this one, Ma? Are you scared to come back? What is it here that upsets you so? What are you struggling against—because you certainly give that impression?

Ma, did Jalaja have twins? If so, what happened to them? Where are they? Did you have something to do with their disappearance? Is that what is plaguing you? And what about the madwoman's baby that you mentioned?

Why are children so much on your mind? I know you ached for children once, but that was ages ago… Is that where your mind is now? In the past? With all those babies you lost? But I am here, Ma, the baby you didn't lose… I am here. I have come back to you.

Look at me, Ma. Talk to me.

I miss you. I even miss our fights. What I wouldn't give to have a nice fiery fight with you!

Love,

Devi

Chapter 15
Shilpa

Curd Rice

Curd Rice:

Ingredients:

2 cups cooked rice
3 cups curd (yogurt)
1 tbsp coconut oil
1 tsp mustard seeds
1 tsp cumin seeds
2 green chillies slit in half lengthwise
Curry leaves–a handful
Coriander, handful, chopped for garnish
Salt to taste

Method:

1. Combine the rice and curd together in a bowl and keep aside.

2. Heat the oil in a vessel and add the mustard seeds.
3. When the seeds crackle, add the cumin seeds, green chillies, curry leaves and cook on a medium flame for a minute while stirring continuously.
4. Add the rice-curd mixture and salt. Mix well and cook for another minute. Serve hot garnished with coriander.

❄ ❄ ❄

Dear Diary,

The matrons have ordered me to eat only white foods during my pregnancy. It will guarantee a fair baby, they say. And curd rice is my absolute favourite. I have been eating it in spades.

Food cravings—I've had some. To bite into a pomegranate and have the burgundy seeds explode in my mouth in a profusion of liquid sweetness. To sink my teeth into the watery coolness of a perfectly ripe watermelon on days when the sun is waging war on us, the juice dribbling down my chin and collecting in the folds of my neck. I yearn for the mackerel masala and the sardine curry my mother used to make. Whatever I wish for, Manoj brings, Jalaja cooks. I am blessed in my husband and in my neighbours and in the wise woman who can see into my future and knows who my baby will be even though I am the one growing it.

The day after I told the wise woman I was pregnant and thanked her with food, the day after she whispered,

'Your pregnancy will cost you dearly.' I was walking back from the tailor, where I had gone to get my sari blouses and skirts loosened in anticipation of my changing figure, when I saw something shiny sitting in my line of vision under the peepal tree. Getting closer, I saw a pile of gleaming aluminium dishes, *my* dishes, reflecting the light filtering through the leaves, twinkling like posh Mrs. Josephine's pearls, washed better than I ever would using coconut husks and that washing powder that smelled like mud. The wise woman was nowhere in sight. She did not return for a week, and when she did, I took red rice, mango chutney and my special egg curry to her (my secret ingredient is the coconut shavings I add to the curry when it is simmering on the fire—gives it an additional sweetness and crunch). Once more, she did not acknowledge me, except to leave the cleaned dishes by the tree again the following day.

Manoj began setting aside money for dowry, just in case the child turned out to be a girl. The money set aside during my previous aborted pregnancies had been used up long since on various emergencies: the cow shed burning down; the well which was the source of all our drinking water being infested with hundreds of baby adders when a snake decided to use it as a birthing pit; the milking goat dying of a cobra bite while it was grazing in the fields.

Village matrons turned up with offerings of curd rice and sago payasam and made sure I ate in front of them. They shrugged off all my excuses of having just eaten and of being full—'You are eating for two,' they said.

They sat and watched as I made a ball of rice with my fingers and stuffed it into my mouth. They admonished when I chewed slowly, saying I should eat quicker and tutted when I gulped it down, asking why I was in such a hurry, did I want to choke the baby? They brought pictures of fair, beautiful babies, mostly white, torn from newspapers—the Johnson and Johnson baby, the Rentokil cough medicine baby and the Boroline baby —and asked Jalaja to put them up on the walls pronto—'Shilpa cannot risk climbing on wobbly stools to put pictures up,' they said—and they told Jalaja off for sporting a sour face when doing so. 'Don't you know your neighbour should be shielded from all bad things, especially long faces?' they admonished. 'Smile, girl, for God's sake.' Manoj and I did not quite succeed in providing a satisfactory reply to Sumitranna's son's query as to why our house looked like Doctor Kumar's waiting room, filled to bursting with smiling, blond-haired, blue-eyed babies.

The matrons begged Manoj to stop his subscription to the *Udayavani*, at least for the duration of the pregnancy. 'Don't you know that these papers nowadays are full of horrors?' they said. 'Killing here, fighting there. Shilpa should be shielded from this. If she is happy, the baby will be happy. Remember the miscarriages,' they said. Manoj didn't want to be reminded of the miscarriages so he duly cancelled the subscription.

'Think good thoughts,' they implored of me, promising that this would guarantee a beautiful child. 'See how the bump is low and spread about?' they said. 'That is definitely a girl in there.'

I was four and a half months pregnant and out in the orchard picking ambade for pickle when the pains began. Pains shooting right down my abdomen fit to slice it in two. I hobbled to the lean-to toilet behind the house and when I saw the spotting, I fainted. When I came to, I found myself on the veranda outside the kitchen bathed in sweat, the sun a scalding insinuating presence upon my drooping eyelids, mosquitoes feasting on the bare flesh of my arms. Jalaja was fanning me vigorously with the peacock feather fan she was inordinately proud of, that I had always thought was more for show than anything else—countless multi-hued eyes mocking me as they moved up and down, close and far: *swish, swish, bad mother, bad mother, why were you bending down when you were so tired, why weren't you resting, swish, swish, bad mother*. The pains had stopped. I looked down, trepidation warring with the need to know. The bump was still there. *You don't deserve that baby, swish, swish, that baby doesn't deserve you.* I asked for water, gulped it down and, ignoring Jalaja's cries, ran barefoot in the blistering heat, through the fields and past Beerakka's tumbling down cottage, past the church, the Catholic school and Master's shop, to where the wise woman sat ranting under the peepal tree. I grabbed her hand much like she had grabbed mine once before. 'Please. Tell me. Will I have this baby?' I bit out between gasps. Steel-grey eyes met mine. The wise woman gently disentangled her hand from my grip and rested it on the curve of my belly. She smiled, the smile transforming her face. That was enough. And there, in the mud and dust under the peepal tree, the air permeated with the smell of rotting fish from the market, as a small crowd gathered around us, I prostrated myself at the wise woman's feet, not caring about the grime, the stones pressing into my arms, my thighs. 'Thank you.'

'What are you looking at?' the wise woman asked of the crowd, 'Shoo.' And they dispersed, buzzing busily, gossip already spreading into the next village and beyond.

Before I left, as I stood and brushed off the dirt and twigs sticking to my sari, I asked of the wise woman, 'What is your name?'

The wise woman's eyes—the colour of the sky just before it disgorged rain—softened as she smiled once more. 'Devi,' she said.

'It means Goddess,' I smiled at the woman: fading sari, dishevelled appearance, arresting face. Great people always came in humble guises. Jesus was born in a stable. Buddha had started his religion from under a Bodhi tree. 'Fitting,' I said.

I was the talk of the village for a few days. 'She's become like that madwoman she's befriended. This pregnancy is driving her crazy,' people muttered in not-so-quiet whispers behind my back. I smiled happily at the whisperers and they stopped, shocked. They had meant for me to hear of course but they hadn't expected this reaction. 'See, what did I tell you?' they said, drawing concentric circles in the air near their forehead with their index fingers as

I turned and walked away, shoulders pushed back, head held high, basket containing food for the wise woman tucked snug under my arm, my heart singing, 'My baby is safe. My baby is safe.'

Two weeks later when I felt the first fluster in my stomach, my baby waving hello from inside the womb, I went to the wise woman. I sat down next to her on the disintegrating cane mat under the peepal tree. It was a sweltering day, the kind just before the monsoons, when there is a shimmer to the air, everything is still and a hush descends, heavy, weighted down with anticipation. Sweat collected under my armpits and in runnels down my back. The peepal branches afforded some shade but not much. The stray cows and dogs that usually roamed the streets lay down exhausted, the dogs' tongues hanging out, the cows mooing weakly, their tails twitching busily to frighten away the flies that dared settle on their backs. I squatted as comfortably as I could, which was not very much, what with the bump and the heat, and waited. A flutter. Another. I took the wise woman's hand and put it on my stomach and my baby obediently performed another little flurry, waved hello. And at that moment the heat broke, the clouds opened and the monsoons announced their arrival with a majestic clap of thunder and the exuberant whipping of coconut trees into turmoil. The cows stood up, mooing urgently, the dogs barked and they started their usual beat, walking up and down, a motley crowd laying claim to the mud-drenched, rain-scented streets of the village. Under the peepal tree, sheltered from the rain, fat drops clinging to the leaves and alighting on our heads like blessings, the air fragrant with the scent of sated earth, beneath the wise woman's touch, my baby danced. The wise woman smiled and in her smile was reflected the joy, the contentment that I felt.

My baby grows and my delight grows with it. Everyone says how wonderful I look, how this child is going to be good-looking judging from the way its mother is blooming.

And I eat curd rice and mashed banana, boiled eggs and curries cooked with coconut milk as I wait to be acquainted with my beautiful child, as I wait for my dream, my lifelong ambition, to finally be realised.

Chapter 16
Nisha

Ruby-Tinged White Orb

Her hands trembling uncontrollably, Nisha picks up the phone. Just a few days ago, she would have despised herself for this weakness, this display of fear, of emotion. Not anymore. *Is this my true self coming through?*

Fingers shaking as she dials. The photograph is in front of her, and she breathes her sister's face in, awed every time she looks at it.

She drops the phone. Picks it up. Redials. A pause. A beep. Then a high-pitched whine indicating a wrong number. She is not prepared for the disappointment she feels. It is almost physical, crushing down on her like a weight pinning down her chest. She looks at the numbers she has punched; cross checks them against the numbers on the sheet her parents have bequeathed her. Bequeathed, why did that grand word inveigle its way into her mind just then? 'Here, I bequeath you your history—a set of numbers that do not work.' And then it hits her, all of a sudden.

What she is missing. She needs to add a country code, as it is an international phone call. She looks up the country code for India, her hands trembling. 0091. She punches in the numbers again. A beep. Static. Then a ring, two, three. Her heart beats like a prisoner behind bars, raving and ranting, wanting out. Four rings, five. This number must be out of date, she thinks. But knowing her parents, they would have done their research carefully, made sure to include the most recent number—it all depends on when they wrote her the letter of course.

She is used to solving things, hunting for answers, not resting until she gets them. But she is beginning to realise that all the rules change when the puzzle is you. How can she wait? How can she not? She will do what it takes to find her sister, unearth her roots, discover who she is. Even if it means travelling to India, to the ends of the world to track her sister, her birth parents down. She wants answers. She wants to know why she was given away like a surplus kitten from a litter. She owes it to herself and to Matt.

On the ninth ring, someone picks up. 'Hello?' a benevolent voice, older, heavy Indian accent, emphasis on the 'llo', tilting in a question at the end.

She cannot speak. The words she has so carefully prepared are lost somewhere in her chest. Her eyes blur.

'Hello, *Kon ulaytha*?' The soft words of a language. Not Kannada, she would have recognised that. The words unintelligible and yet somehow vaguely familiar, shifting something inside. Some ghost of a memory. She pictures flowers blooming, bursting in a riot of colour out of the nun's mouth. That's how the sound of this foreign language makes her feel.

Somehow, hearing the soft voice say something incomprehensible galvanises Nisha. 'I am looking for Sister Priya?' she blurts, her voice high, squeaky. Where did that come from? That wasn't the question she had been planning to ask first, if at all. There might not be a Sister Priya and this soft-voiced nun might dismiss her as some crank. And yet…

A heartbeat of static. Hiss. Splutter. Then, 'Sister Priya is ill, my child,' the woman says, in English, her voice apologetic. 'Who is this?' The nun's speech is like caramel, smooth and honeyed, the accent lilting, soothing, the words slipping out of her mouth like precious stones, prized gifts bestowed to the listener.

So there is a Sister Priya. *It may not be the Sister Priya from your dream. There can be more than one Sister Priya, you know.* Her inner voice, chiding.

'I… I am calling from England. My parents died a few days ago in a car accident. They left me a letter.' Her voice trembles, tilts alarmingly. She swallows.

The nun waits, somehow sensing Nisha has more to say, and her measured breathing, in between sputters of static like a car engine struggling to start in the dead of winter, calms Nisha somewhat. 'I was adopted around twenty years ago from your convent. I must have been about four?'

'I am sorry for your loss, child.' The nun's chocolate voice is her undoing. She watches her tears splat onto the letter, the list she has made and the laptop on which she googled country codes.

'I would like to find out about my roots, who I am.' Saying the words out loud gives them meaning, weight. 'I… I have so many questions.'

'I am sure you do, child. You were adopted twenty years ago, you say?'

'About then, yes.' And, 'Were you there at the time?' Perhaps she knew this woman.

'No, child.' The nun's voice rueful. 'I wish I had been for then we could have sorted this out here and now. I joined this convent four years ago. They move us about now, see, every five years. Change in policy. The nun who has been here longest is Sister Priya. She refused to move. The Mother respected that, did not press her. She has been here, what, fifty years? Her whole adult life. Joined as a novitiate.'

Her heart does a little jiggle. So it *is* her Sister Priya. It is. Her dreams are suppressed memories after all. What a fantastic machine the brain is. These memories must have been some of her very first. She remembers her joy from the dream, the relief she felt when she saw Sister Priya, how she had rushed up to her and hugged her. She tries to picture her face but it just doesn't form. How can it? After all those years of suppressed memories, she can't just expect perfectly formed pictures of long ago loved ones to fall into her head. 'Do you still give children up for adoption from your convent?' She had tried looking up information on the convent but there was precious little on the Web, even in this day and age.

'No, child, we don't and I don't think we used to back then either, not regularly. But I will check.'

She likes the heartfelt way the nun calls her 'child'; the word is like a hug, enveloping her in its warm depths. Cocooning her, shielding her like a womb.

'What is your name, child?'

'Nisha. Nisha Kamath.' *Was Nisha the name my birth parents gave me, or did they not bother to name me at all?*

'Your parents' names?'

'Lekha and Ravi Kamath.'

'I will see if I can dig out your records.'

She takes a deep breath, thinking, *in for a penny, in for a pound*, 'I would like to know who my parents were, how old I was when I was adopted from the convent, how my adoptive parents found me. Also when I arrived at the convent. And… if there was another little girl with me. My twin.' Saying it out loud overwhelms her. *My sister. My twin.*

'Please could you repeat what you just said, child? I am not getting any younger, my memory is not like it used to be,' the nun's voice apologetic. 'Go slow. I will note everything down.'

She repeats her questions. Then, 'Thank you.'

'Take care, child, God bless.' A pause.

The nun is waiting for her to say her goodbyes. And then, the words slip out, as if of their own accord, 'I just… Is there a courtyard in your convent, with a jasmine bush and a lime tree?' The sharp, slightly acidic smell of limes ripening in the sun. Sister Priya plaiting the jasmine in neat orderly rows into wraiths that will adorn the statues of the Holy Family in the chapel. Memories flooding her, bombarding her, after a hiatus of over twenty years.

The woman peering through the bars. Straggly hair. One huge eye, raining rust-stained tears.

'The jasmine bush died after Sister Priya fell ill, no one to tend to it, see. Do you remember it all, child?'

Oh, Lord. She has never felt the need to call on a higher power before. She doesn't even believe in Him. *This is real. This is real. I actually experienced it all. That little girl hunkering among the pews, running into the courtyard, hunting for Sister Priya. Me. In another country. In another life.* Softly, 'I do now.'

'Call me tomorrow. I will find out what I can.'

Afterwards, she cradles the phone in her hand before gently replacing it in its holder. The smell of incense, wet pews and sweat reach out from the past, from a different country, and engulf her, taking her to a sun-roasted garden, surrounded by high compound walls and a tarnishing iron gate, bringing up hazy pictures of a little girl dancing, her hair flying in the aromatic breeze wafting in from outside the gate, bringing with it the smell of sugarcane and frying peanuts, while a nun plaits flowers as white as her habit into garlands. An ache of pure longing to be that little girl again, carefree, her only worry what to eat next, loved by the nuns, secure, permeates her entire being even as dulcet tones reverberate in her head. 'God bless you, child.'

❄ ❄ ❄

Nisha wakes to the feeling of warm jasmine-perfumed breeze caressing her skin, the melodious tones of long-forgotten hymns crooned in the nuns' honeyed voices loud in her ear, the taste of Eucharist bread dipped in sweetened wine in her mouth—the ruby tinged white orb melting deliciously almost as soon as it lands on her pink tongue.

She sits up, finds a note on the pillow next to her: 'Off to work. Didn't want to wake you. Looked like you were having a beautiful dream for a change. Your grin wide as a hyena's. Was it about me? ☺ See you later, Love you, Matt. xxx'

He has not changed towards her. He is still the kind, caring, understanding Matt she's always known. More than she deserves. That evening, after their fight, they had made love right there in her parents' house. And she had looked at him as he came inside of her and tried to convey via her gaze everything she felt for him, all those feelings that she couldn't find words for, that evaporated on her tongue when she tried to force them out of her mouth. And he had smiled and kissed away the tears beading her face. Tears of emotion, of exhilaration after their lovemaking. Tears of love?

She puts his pillow on her face, breathes in his smell. But her nose is infused with rose incense, the pull of the past, lost to her for so long, suddenly too strong for the present to compete with. So many memories, taking the forms of dreams, assaulting her senses and awakening in her yearnings she did not know she had, for a country and a culture she never felt an appeal for, never even knew she belonged to, had experienced first-hand.

Yellow rays of weak spring sun inveigle through gaps in the curtain and dance on crumpled sheets. She squints at the bedside clock. 08:30 a.m. God, she is becoming positively lazy, she who thinks waking after seven is sacrilege, a waste of a day. Used to. She is changing. Gradually, the rigid rituals and laws that governed her life are relaxing. She is learning to let go, learning that every hour spent not working, not doing, is not wasted. It is *lived.*

It is afternoon in India. She picks up the phone. Dials the number from memory.

The same gentle, caring voice of before, sounding breathless. 'Hello?'

'Hi, I called yesterday, about...'

'Oh it's you, child. I was in the garden drawing water from the well; sorry you had to wait a while.' The garden—the straggly overgrown aboli bushes, a favourite haunt of rat snakes curled up and sunning themselves, their dappled skin glinting in the sun as they waited for an unsuspecting frog to amble their way. The well looming near the compound wall, overgrown with moss, the rope used to haul the pail always getting stuck midway, water spilling in silvery billows down the sides…

Images, swirling from the recesses of her mind to the fore, borne on the winds of change, overwhelming her.

A pause while the nun collects her breath, 'We've tried searching for the documents…'

No, please don't say you don't know… She hates this waiting around, this lack of information. In this day and age surely everything should be available at the click of a button. But she is realising that it is not the case in India, that while the cities are advanced, the villages are yet to be swayed by the information revolution. She has, true to form, been doing research. After the phone call the previous day, while she waited for Matt to come home, she had tried looking Dhonikatte up on Google Earth but didn't come up with much: a road, a smattering of red-brick cottages, fields stretching endlessly beyond. She googled, facebooked, twittered Sacred Heart Convent. Zilch. If only she knew the name of her twin. If only…

'We did give some babies up for adoption but we did not keep any children here. You remember living here, you say?'

'I remember being woken by the bell for morning prayers…' The trek to chapel, her eyes scrunched shut, still half asleep, the sky the ethereal grey of night loath to relinquish its hold, the half-hearted twinkle of a couple of lonely stars barely relieving the darkness. The air heavy, weighed down with moisture, smelling of night, brushing her cheek, murmuring shadowy secrets. The whisper of habits in the hushed silence of the chapel, the swish of skirts as the nuns knelt down to pray, the silent moving of their lips. Walking back across the courtyard, stomach rumbling in pleasant anticipation of breakfast—seera? Upma? Puri bhaji?—under a sky glowing pink at the advent of dawn, the world awakening, noises reaching the quiet nuns from the world outside: the milkman whistling as he cycled past, the clank of the milk jugs jostling, morning joggers panting as they paused outside the compound walls to gather breath, the distinctive clip-clop march of Colonel D'Souza who sometimes came to church, regaled her with stories of the war, and lifted his flapping trouser leg to show her his stump, Nisha watching in fascinated horror, her uneven mouth forming a lopsided O…

How can I remember Colonel D'Souza and not my sister? Why is she not here in these memories?

'I remember sitting in the cramped hall with the nuns and having breakfast.' Dosas with chutney: she would painstakingly remove all the chillies and the mustard seeds flecking her green chutney brown, arrange them neatly on the sides of her plate. 'They are not for plate decorative purposes you know,' Sister Priya would laugh. Upma—she would remove the peas. Sister Priya would say, 'Eat them, child, they are the best bits.' And, 'God gave you the peas as well as the upma,' smiling.

'I tried asking Sister Priya. But she is old and ailing, child. Huge gaps in her memory. I will try and catch her in one of her lucid moments. They are few and far between now…' The nun's voice echoing down the phone, encored by static. Hiss. Crackle. Sputter.

After breakfast, going to the church, cleaning the statues of the Holy Family and all the saints until they sparkled, dusting the pews, helping Sister Priya with the all-important task of filling the chalice with Eucharist bread: 'Not blessed yet, mind.' Afterwards, dunking Marie biscuits in tea in the warm rectory kitchen suffused with the spicy aroma of fish curry bubbling on the stove, slurping down the tea and swallowing gloopy lumps of disintegrated biscuit that had collected at the bottom.

'I… we seem to have no record. The logs go back more than twenty years. Most of the papers from that time, if any, are woodlice-ridden and falling apart, difficult to read…'

The priest's room, always dark, always solemn, smelling of books and secrets, a forbidden, grave smell. His kind eyes, perusing her over the top of his spectacles. 'Now, child, have you been good?' 'Very good, father.' 'Then here's a little present for you.' Holding out something that glinted invitingly, his eyes twinkling. A pendant of Baby Jesus. 'Thank you, Father.' 'God bless you, child.' Spectacles on, giving him an owlish look, back to his books, the scratch of pen on paper.

Outside, blinking her eyes in the resplendent sunshine after the gloom of Father's room, the jackfruit-scented breeze instructing the coconut tree fronds to bow down to her and wave hello. Watching the peon water the coconut trees, the water gushing out of the pump tube gurgling joyously, a silvery-blue waterfall. The dry red mud inhabiting the little moat dug around each tree trunk becoming sloshy orange as it guzzled water. Carefully pocketing the pendant and begging the peon, 'Please can I water one?' and feeling pure joy blossom inside her as beautiful as the tiger lilies dancing in profusion from the beds in front of the grotto housing the Mother Mary of Assumption, when he handed her the pump with a monosyllabic grunt. Watering the base of the tree until the moat overflowed and bubbly orange water kissed her bare feet, cool and reassuring. The smell of wet earth and ripe mango. The feeling of contentment, of being loved by the Lord, like Father had said, for being a Good Girl.

Watching the peon chat to the coconut picker, while she watered the trees, every once in a while being told to concentrate and not douse the whole orchard in a flood of water; did she want the well to dry up, what with another drought looming; didn't she know there hadn't been so much as a rumour of the monsoon? The sun beating down on her head, plastering her hair to her scalp. Beads of perspiration trickling down her face. Spraying her legs with water when the peon was not looking—deliciously cool. Thinking that perhaps Heaven was like this. The cloying scent of rotting cashews. The coconut picker blowing a puff of smoke up into the cloudless sky, twisting a coconut to pluck it off the bunch on the tree, his dangling twig legs painting a wobbly number eleven the colour of dry tamarind against a leafy green backdrop, snatches of blue sky silhouetted among the fronds. The coconut picker shaking the coconut and putting it to his ear to hear what it sounded like inside. Saying to the peon, 'Hmm... Your crop is very good this year.' Watching fascinated as the coconut picker lit his beedi with a match, while dangling nimbly monkey-like at the very top of the coconut tree. 'Ugly girl, what are you gaping at?' 'I am not ugly; I am good, Father said so.' The coconut picker laughing as if she had cracked the world's funniest joke, his crooked yellow teeth shining bright against his sooty face. 'Well, you've got a hole for a mouth, that's for sure.'

Sister Priya calling for her, and she dropping the pump, leaving the coconut picker perched at the top of the tree, knees drawn and tongue hanging out as he tried to wrench a particularly stubborn coconut free, his face warped in concentration. Sweat glistening on his bare black torso, making it gleam like the burnished coffee-wood sculptures in Father's office. Wondering how earth he managed to keep his footing as he used both hands to pull at the coconut.

Sister Priya laughing as she scooped her up, 'Look at you, all wet, what have you been doing?' Showing her the pendant, 'Look what Father gave me.' And, 'Am I ugly? Do I have a hole for a mouth?' Sister Priya putting her down gently, kneeling beside her, 'Who told you that?' Fiddling with the pendant, not looking at Sister Priya, feeling the hot flush of shame spread through her like a gradually creeping rash: 'The coconut picker.' 'Wait here, sweetie, I'll be right back.'

Not obeying, breaking one of the Ten Commandments and trailing behind Sister Priya. Hearing her beloved Sister Priya raise her voice for the first time in her life, wagging a finger at the coconut picker who is staring open-mouthed, 'Don't you dare call her ugly! That is what you are, for calling a child that. Don't you know that Jesus said, "Unless you turn from your sins and become like little children, you will never enter the Kingdom of Heaven?" What a pity that you cannot see the beauty in little children.' Sister Priya turning and striding towards her, her body shaking, her face like the sky before a thunderstorm, the peon and the coconut picker's brown faces suffused with red.

'Child,' the dulcet tones say now, 'I will try and find out for you. It might take a week. Where do you live, did you say?'

She touches the ridge of bumpy sewed-on skin above her upper lip. 'I... I live in England.'

'So far.' A pause, then, 'Has life been good to you, child?'

Her graduation: Clutching her diploma and picking out her parents in the crowd below. Their faces lit up, beaming. Their eyes shining. Afterwards, in the crush of the pub, filled to bursting with celebrating parents and graduating children, her mother leaning close, the pungent tang of the red wine she favoured on her breath, 'We are so proud of you.' Her eyes shimmering.

Her father in hospital when he had his hernia op, squeezing her hand, 'I am glad you came.' Big coming from her reserved, taciturn dad who shied away from the simplest of emotions.

Their delight in her, how happy they had been when she told them about her job. How their eyes sparkled with appreciation when they met Matt for the first time and later, as she helped to load the dishwasher, the low voices of the men echoing from the other room, her mother, bashful, touching her wrist shyly: 'He's very nice.'

'With the exception of the last few days, life has been good to me.' And she realises as she says this that it is true.

And then, before she has a chance to take it back, 'I will come there, meet you and Sister Priya. Perhaps seeing me, she will remember something.'

'Perhaps. I will pray for you, child, and we will expect you here soon. God bless you.'

'Wait...'

But she is gone. The ring tone is loud in her ear. That woman, framed by the gates, bushy hair. It was a woman wasn't it? That had been the impression she got from the dream. The achingly familiar woman—like the wisp of a memory just out of reach—rousing something in Nisha. Who was she? Might they know? She meant to ask, but now she thinks, how would this nun know?

A letter slit open, a sheaf of pale mauve paper, deceptively harmless, lurking among legal documents. And her whole life overturns. An entire book of memories manifests itself: Boo. Memories that have been loitering all these years in the recesses of her mind.

She discovers a sister—her twin, someone with whom she shared nine months in the womb of a woman who is a stranger.

What else has she forgotten? What else has she lost? Who are her parents? Are they alive? Where are they? Why did they give her away?

How many more surprises to come?

And now, she will travel to a country she has never really given much thought to, a culture she has turned her back on, and adopt a way of life she did not know she knew intimately until recently.

Adopt. What an apt word.

Chapter 17
Devi

Butterfly Wings

Ma,

Today, I felt the first tiny flutter, like butterfly wings brushing against the lining of my stomach. I was awed. I was overcome by the miracle growing inside of me. I called Rohan, but I couldn't quite describe the feeling, though I revelled in the joy, the excitement in his voice. 'I wish I was there with you, Devi,' he said, his voice wistful.

Ma, Rohan wants to be here, with me, with you. But he is in the middle of his dissertation and he cannot leave. He calls every day, asks after you.

Ma, I wish you would wake now, put your hands on my stomach, your eyes lighting up, beaming that rare, jubilant smile that transforms you, makes you look years younger. I want you to share this joy with me, Ma…

The day after my marriage, I wake to a wide expanse of cream, silvery rays of sun, streaked ghoulish white like a phantom's fingers, snaking in through the blinds, wrapping themselves sensuously around the wardrobe, casting the room in a mellow buttery glow. No cramped mattress, no Bobby howling outside, scratching the kitchen door, wanting to be let in, no trickle of rain down the pipes by the side of the house, no cawing of crows, no air snaking in smelling of dew and morning rain and bitter mango leaf and buds in bloom and drenched earth. Instead, the smell of roses and musk and Rohan's arm slung across my naked breasts. I look at his face, the long eyelashes, curling on cheeks pinpricked with sprouting stubble. I marvel at the tiny snores escaping from between partly open lips. He opens his eyes, looks up at me and I am suddenly very aware of myself, of my naked body, his hand on my breasts, his head on my shoulder, the unfamiliar and yet not unpleasant ache between my thighs. 'Good morning, gorgeous,' he says, smiling. 'Am I dreaming or what?' I smack him lightly even as I feel the blood rush into my cheeks. He laughs, and then, suddenly serious, whispers, 'I have always wanted to wake up next to you, like this, ever since I met you.'

Afterwards, we talk, about everything and nothing. I open up to him, unsparing, telling him about the constant struggle I have with myself regarding you. 'She believes in destiny—thinks she wrested me off the arms of fate—her words not mine—and that she has to keep me close at all times, watch over me like a hawk. I just… I love her, and yet, I cannot stand her. I am not the pliant daughter she wants me to be—why can't she accept that? I feel I am permanently disappointing her by not being the daughter she wanted.' I taste salt and realise I am crying. Rohan gently kisses away my tears, one by one, his eyes tender, his touch soft as cotton candy. 'When I was younger, I so wished for a sibling, prayed for one, so the pressure would be off me. This was before I realised that you needed two people to make a child, that a father was vital.' I smile ruefully and Rohan smiles along with me.

Then, 'You miss your father?'

'I think if he'd been around, my mother would have been different, more relaxed, not so fixated about protecting me, doing the best by me. As it is just she and I, I am all the more precious.'

'You are that,' Rohan says and takes me in his arms, and after that all thought flies.

That afternoon I change into a T-Shirt and jeans, instead of the sari I know I am expected to wear. I do not don a single piece of jewellery, the hallmark of a married woman, except my wedding ring, thinking I might as well start as I mean to go along. Ma, remember when I insisted on going on my own to shop for my wedding trousseau? When I returned from my shopping spree, I did not show you my purchases, saying I had packed them already. I know you were suspicious but for once you didn't push, you let me be. I got jeans and trousers, Ma, not the saris and churidars you wanted me to buy. I wasn't planning on wearing saris or churidars in England, so what was the point of wasting good money on them?

I walk out of the bathroom after I've changed, wondering if Rohan will say anything, ready to take on the first challenge of our marriage. If he does comment, we will have our first fight sooner than I expected, but that is fine. It will be done and dusted, out of the way.

Rohan laughs, bends close for a kiss. 'What? I look funny?' I ask, pulling away so he kisses the air instead, an edge to my voice. He pulls me into an embrace, 'My feisty firecracker,' he says when I am snug in the haven of his arms. 'Trust you to spoil for a fight and our marriage not even a day old. You know my parents will complain. Try and be nice to them; they are old and we are leaving soon.' How can I be angry when he is so good-natured? When what he says makes sense? When he accepts me for who I am, loves me for it, a welcome change from you, Ma, like the contrast between lace and a burka, between chilli powder and doodh peda.

We check out of the hotel and take an auto rickshaw to his house. As the auto trundles off the tarred main road onto the dusty path which leads to the hillock housing Rohan's abode I feel my high—emphasised by the freedom of wearing jeans, no salwar kameez shawl to keep pushing up my shoulders and down over my breasts, no itchy jewellery jangling every time I move —come crashing down. Rohan senses it in the involuntary tensing of my body. He takes my hand in both of his, regardless of the rickshaw driver's eyes focused on us in the rear mirror widening so much that he looks like a bulbous frog about to pounce on an unsuspecting fly, despite him nearly driving into the bramble and dung-populated ditch by the side of the road where an unwary cow grazes, tail twitching to deter flies.

The auto judders to a halt and Rohan pays, the driver accepting his fare with a knowing wink and grin, the drone of the rickshaw slowly fading into the drowsy afternoon.

Rohan picks up my bag and starts down the hillock and I follow, my new blue sandals (I deliberately bought plain blue sandals eschewing the patterned gold ones you wished me to) acquiring a sheen of red dust with each step I take, the ends of my jeans becoming vermilion stained. The arrack shop is deserted this time of the afternoon, the man running it snoring happily, sleeping off his cashew-feni-induced stupor so he will be ready to imbibe more with his customers as the late afternoon wanes to dusk. He is framed by the snacks of yellow tubes in transparent bags dangling from the ceiling, his hand resting protectively on the glass bottles of sweets in case children walking home from school try to nick some. Small bursts of air escape from between his half-open lips, disturbing his magnificent moustache, which reverberates with each burst. A fly buzzes, incessantly, angrily and his nose twitches in response every so often. Nobody else is about. The neighbours are all inside, having their siesta. Doors stand open to let the barely there breeze circulate, the power being out as usual, and I spy the occupants of the house above Rohan's lying on mats on the veranda, the man's dome of a stomach rising above his stripy green lungi, obscuring his face, the pallu of the woman's turquoise sari slung carelessly across her face, rising into the air with each gigantic snore she produces, the folds of flesh of her stomach beaded with sweat, her feet bare and very small compared to her husband's hairy, dirt-encrusted ones, the skin cracked and sore. Cows squat beside the road, lethargically chewing cud. Hens cluck. A crow caws.

Rohan's mother appears at the door, yawning loudly. She stops mid-yawn to stare at me, eyes wide. 'What's that rubbish you're wearing?' she mocks. 'Couldn't your mother send you with proper clothes, were boys' garments all she could afford?'

The anger is red hot, all-consuming, like the time I ate ten green chillies for a dare. I will fight with you all I like, but I cannot bear for anyone else to mock you, make fun of you, Ma. An image of you flickers before my eyes, your lined face, your soft eyes: 'I will give you away in style.'

'Ma…' Rohan begins, but I cut him off. 'I will wear what I like; you have no right to comment on it and please do not insult my mother.'

'Rohan,' my mother-in-law screeches, shattering the drowsy peace of the afternoon, causing my father-in-law to come running outside in his lungi, shirtless and nervously worrying the wiry grey hairs on his chest, his spectacles awry, eyes bloodshot, his sparse hair standing on end. 'Control your wife. Tell her to watch her mouth. We have allowed you to marry her, but I will not take this… this talking back in my own house.'

Shutters creak as windows are opened and faces peer out. The grumble of gossip rumbles down the hill. 'Aiyyo, look what she's wearing the new bride. No sari, no karimani, no covering with a shawl. They are in for big trouble—what did I say?'

'Ma, shall we go inside?' Rohan says, leading his mother in.

I follow, so angry that I am trembling. Before I step inside, I turn and stare at each window in turn until the mass of crowding faces disappear and the shutters close in my face.

I lock myself in Rohan's room for the rest of the afternoon. When I hear a knock, Rohan's voice, I fling the door open, 'I will not apologise, Rohan. I hope you are not expecting me to.' He looks tired, defeated and my anger dissipates. He collapses onto the bed, 'I can understand where you are coming from,' he says wearily, rubbing a hand across his eyes. 'I do know how it must be for you. But it is going to be a long two weeks.' I lie down next to him, 'Tell me about it,' I say and he smiles, pulls me close, and for a brief while we forget the world and lose ourselves in each other.

It gets better after that. Whatever magic spell Rohan has weaved on his mother, it works. Both his parents are remote, they let me be, they do not comment on my clothes or anything else, which suits me perfectly. I like that my mother-in-law's considerable energy is focussed on her son, on what to pack for him, what to feed him, how to spoil him in the two weeks that his parents have left with him.

I endure mass with the in-laws every morning. Since they are being so accommodating, I have decided it would be churlish to refuse. Sitting in the church, listening to the monotonous drone of prayers I cannot understand, kneeling and standing up and sitting down and standing up again, the mournful sound of the hymns designed to put even someone who hasn't woken up at the crack of dawn to attend mass to sleep, trying to smother yawns, my mind wanders. I think of my future: England, that land of McDonald's and boutique stores, of parks sporting endless swathes of green, of shameless people who kiss and do whatnot in public. Just me and Rohan. No interfering in-laws spouting religion and suffocating mothers offering doses of tearful love. I can be shameless if I want, wear short skirts if I please; there will be nobody to judge me. My mother-in-law pokes me in the elbow, a sharp dig. 'Pay attention,' a harsh whisper, 'the priest is looking this way.' I put on a suitably pious expression, fold my hands, close my eyes, bow my head, and imagine biting into a burger, meaty juice running down my chin.

After church, I walk to the shop for groceries with my mother-in-law, another command couched as a request I cannot refuse: she needs help carrying the bags, she says, as Rohan and my father-in-law are not around. Everyone we meet stops for a chat. 'Oh, so this is the daughter-in-law. Quite fair for a Hindu. Can see why Rohan fell for her, especially if she was wearing these figure-hugging clothes. A bit forward, no?' I bite back the retort hovering on my lips, thinking, *one more week. You would be shocked at my restraint, Rohan,* I tell my husband in my head. *I am becoming positively demure!*

A drunk weaves past, stumbling and yelling obscenities. A woman strides behind him wielding a broomstick. She screams at the top of her voice, hitting him when he stumbles, and he cowers and yelps much like a scared dog.

'She's converting as soon as they reach England,' my mother-in-law says shortly in her staccato voice, gruff like a duck's quack, as if converting to Catholicism will automatically make me less 'forward'.

'Where's Rohan, then?' they ask, eyes narrowed in curiosity, nostrils flared to sniff out lies, casually spitting frothy red dregs of paan smelling of sick onto the dust by the side of the road, staining it a bloody maroon.

'Sorting out visas and all the other paperwork. There is so much to do when one is going abroad,' my mother-in-law sighs self-importantly.

'Greasing palms more like,' they say and guffaw, their yawning mouths the amber of tree bark.

Standing there, I count down the days until Rohan and I can get away, sweat pooling down my back and soaking my T-shirt. I can smell my armpits, the reek mixing with the pong of weeds and decay drifting from the lake. The banyan tree bends down as if to drink from the water and I wish I could be anywhere but here, stuck with my mother-in-law making insipid conversation with strangers who judge me. I cannot even summon the energy to ask the toothless old man who is staring right at my breasts if he has found what he is looking for. I am ready for England, for the cold. Anything but this.

In the evenings, as I sit on the veranda and feel myself gradually getting coated in dust, scrunching my eyes against the grimy particles swirling in the ochre-tinged breeze, trying to worm their way into my pupils, beside my strident mother-in-law who is reading the Bible out loud to me, my mind wanders and I think of you. What are you doing now? You would have come home from work, heated the water in the urn in the bathroom with kindling you picked that morning. Then you will feed Bobby scraps from last night's dinner and then you will cook something for yourself. Are you eating properly? I picture you lying on that hard mattress, lonely and missing me, and feel a pang.

Every alternate evening, as twilight chokes the oomph out of daylight, that sullen yellow time when birds call plaintively as they rush home to their nests, I telephone you, Ma. You sound determinedly cheery and that too-cheery voice grates on me. I know that you are grieving and trying to hide it. It intensifies the guilt eating away at my insides, pouncing when I least expect. Most of the villagers have chastised me at one time or another, have wondered how I can bear to treat you so badly, to insist on marrying outside my religion and going so far away, leaving you all alone. An only daughter at that. Isn't it my duty to look after you? How can I be so callous? Aren't daughters supposed to be more caring? I flinch at the hard-edged vicious incision guilt carves down my abdomen, inducing nausea, making my tone sharp with you.

'Are you happy?' you ask, the hope naked in your voice.

'Yes, Ma,' I sigh.

Outside, it has started to rain. Big drops land with a thud, displacing dust, drawing concentric circles in the mud.

Plop, plop, plop. The circles spread outward gradually, blend with others, disintegrate into slush the orange of sadhus' robes.

'I have made lime and mango pickle for you to take, and I am starting on the sambar and rasam powders now,' you say.

Children playing hopscotch in the dust dance in the squishy mud, revelling in the sudden shower, their hair bedraggled and sticking to their faces in wet tendrils, their arms open wide, twirling. I want to do that, I want to be out there.

'Not too many, Ma. There's not enough space in the suitcase.' Rain-lashed coconut trees are silhouetted briefly by a sudden flash of lightning.

'Bobby misses you.' I know that this is code for *I miss you*. Irritation. Bitter like biting into mustard seeds. Why can't you come straight out and say it? But I know that if you did, I would be annoyed at that too. I would read it as a blatant attempt on your part to hijack my happiness. *Be kind, Devi. You are going away in a few days.* I make a conscious effort to tone down my voice. 'Yes, I miss him too.'

'Okay, then,' you say. 'When will you call next?' You try and fail to mask the need, the desperation in your voice.

'Soon. This is not my phone, so I have to be careful.'

'Yes, of course,' you say. Defeated.

'I will call the day after tomorrow, Ma.'

'Okay. Bye.'

Through the open front door, a spray of rain drifts in on a gust of scented, slightly bitter breeze, smelling of mango, guava, guilt, freedom.

❄ ❄ ❄

You and the in-laws stand in a subdued line waiting to say goodbye, like children about to be chastised. I look at you, Ma, your slight stoop, the wiry grey hair escaping your bun, your familiar yellow sari, your lined face that has been the last thing I've seen before drifting off to sleep and the first when waking up for so many years, now obscured by tears. I cling to you and breathe in the smell of you, sweat and talcum powder, the smell of my childhood, the smell of comfort. Then Rohan's hand is in mine. 'Time to go,' he says softly. Gently, I extricate myself from your grasp, and it is as if I am finally letting go. Of my childhood, of the person I have been for so long: someone who is never really sure of who she is, always struggling against the constraints of what she can and cannot do, what she feels and what she *should* feel but doesn't. I plant a soft kiss on your papery cheek, 'Bye, Ma.'

'Wait.' You fumble with the pallu of your sari and I notice the knot you've made. This is where you keep your money when we go to market together. I have always admonished you about it—'What a silly place to keep your money, Ma; all the change will fall out.' Your trembling fingers finally manage to get the knot undone, just as I reach to help. Our fingers touch for a brief moment and you hand me a packet. A sheaf of lined notepaper.

I can see your busy handwriting on the pages. *This is her way of keeping a hold of you even after you are gone from her grasp. Stop this, Devi, you are all she has in the world and now you are abandoning her too.* This is what I hate, the two parts of me, constantly in conflict, especially when it comes to you, Ma. I tuck the packet into my purse. 'Bye, Ma.'

I take Rohan's hand and walk away from you, away from my old life and towards independence and a new persona—the person I have waited all my life to become.

❄ ❄ ❄

England is like everything I imagined and like nothing I imagined.

Heathrow Airport. While we queue up at Immigration, I watch the other passengers yawning, stretching, chatting, smiling, frowning. Black, brown, white, pink, gold. Fat, thin, small, big. Some so weighed down by coats and scarves, their faces are barely visible. Others wearing shorts and vests scarcely covering their bodies. I look at all of them and I think, *Where was I all this while?* In a little village in the corner of the world, hemmed in by narrow-minded people and their small opinions. *I haven't lived,* I think. *My life is just beginning.*

We inch up the line and reach the Immigration official, a glowering Sikh who studies our passports, asks Rohan a few questions and then lets us past with a nod of his navy-blue turbaned head. I squeeze Rohan's hand and he looks at me, his face etched by lines of weariness. And I kiss him right there, full on the lips, and he laughs, a burst of surprise erupting out of him, and no one exclaims. No one says, 'Arre, look at them, the shameless couple.' No one bats an eyelid. My grin extends from one side of my face to the other despite not having slept a wink during the nine-hour flight, determined as I was to enjoy every single minute, staring at the map as it took me, irrevocably, finally, farther and farther away from home, from you, Ma, and with each jump of the tiny airplane on the minuscule screen in front of me, I felt lighter, so much lighter, and somewhere over the Middle Eastern desert, I shed my load of guilt.

This is freedom, I think. *At last.*

The flat we are renting is poky, in the middle of nowhere. The cramped lift smells of urine, is autographed with graffiti. Arguments and the sounds of other peoples' televisions echo through the brittle, peeling walls. But I don't care. This is *our* house, only ours. No one telling us what we should do, how we should do it. 'Go to mass.' 'Wear something suitable.' 'Don't talk to boys.' 'Why do you not do anything I say?'

And so we settle into a new country, a new marriage, a new life.

Rohan starts his course, leaving at the crack of dawn to escape the rush-hour traffic and coming home only when the shadows lengthen, dancing patterns on the dirty yellow walls of the flat. I find a job babysitting and I am happy.

All my life, I have wanted to escape, to see the world, to live a little, to experience life, not be stuck in our little village being the fodder of gossip, dying of claustrophobia.

And now I am. And it is fantastic, it is brilliant. But… at the most unexpected times, I am struck by a wave of homesickness. I miss you, Ma. I never thought I would say this, but I do. I miss you and I miss home. Not so much that I want to go back, not so. But now that I am far enough away, I am able to remember the good times, times when I was happy. And I was, a lot of the time. And slowly I am beginning to appreciate just how much you did for me.

Some evenings you call. I picture you, squashed into that little booth, the glass cloudy with dust, the inside cramped, sweaty and reeking of blood from the butcher's shop opposite. You sound as you always do—your voice breathy, slightly hesitant. And I imagine how your touch feels, Ma—comfortable like a pillow shaped to the contours of my head and neck; how your chicken sukka tastes: spicy, with the tanginess of tomato, the sweetness, the crunch of coconut; I picture how you look when you laugh—your eyes disappearing into slits, your cheeks flushed, the lines charting the life you've lived radiating outwards and upwards like crisscrossing paths on a busy map.

And so, time passes. Filled to the brim with new experiences, spent creating new memories and… a brand-new life.

I call home to tell you the news. It's been a fortnight since I called last, a fortnight that has flown by on wings with visits to the chemist, the doctor, the joy of discovery.

You do not pick up.

Outside, a helicopter's drone, getting louder. It swoops low, its invasive beams intruding into my thoughts, drawing a curved yellow track the length of the dark wall, painting a halo on my head. Can they see me, I wonder, hunched over a telephone, in the middle of a murky room populated with lengthening shadows and the ghosts of regrets, willing you to answer the phone. The air tastes inky. The blue-grey smell of words hovers, words that are poised to spring out of me, words that will trigger a smile in your voice, words that will bloom happiness, blossom hope like the first lemon-yellow daffodils of spring evangelising the promise of sun.

Your phone rings and rings like a baby's plaintive cry gone unanswered. A worm of worry wiggles up my spine, manifests as a lump in my throat.

I try calling Jalajakka. No one picks up there either.

'Ma's not answering the phone,' I tell Rohan as soon as he comes home from work, bringing with him a nippy draft of frozen air, smelling of other people's cologne, tasting of ice and borrowed smoke—a legacy of travelling by tube at rush hour.

'Have you tried calling Jalaja?' he asks.

'She's not answering either.'

'When did you last speak to your Ma?' he queries.

'It's been two weeks,' I whisper.

'Try again now,' he says.

'But it is midnight in India.'

'All the more reason to call; if she's there she'll pick up.'

You do not pick up.

'Try Jalaja,' Rohan says, and in his eyes I see the worry that is refusing to let me breathe, swallow. Jalaja doesn't pick up either.

'That's good,' Rohan says, his hunched shoulders relaxing a little.

'How?' I ask. The glass door leading to the kitchen is chipped in two places. I concentrate on the chipped glass—one in the shape of a heart, the other a bruise.

'The phone lines must be down. It's the monsoon season, Devi.' I hug his assurance close, holding it like a gift. That must be it. That must be why you are not answering the phone. *Please, Lord Ganapathy, let her be okay,* I pray, as Rohan gathers me in his arms, as he leads me to the bedroom, as he kisses my worry away.

Afterwards, just as sleep is laying its fluttery dreamy claim on me, Rohan says, 'If she still doesn't pick up tomorrow, I will ask my parents to check on her.'

I turn and hold him close, and he smiles, his eyes closed, already half asleep.

The next day, I try once again as soon as I wake up. No answer. I come home at lunchtime and dial your familiar number with trembling fingers.

It is one in the afternoon and already shadows are slanting in through the window, dancing on the walls, staining the weak not quite white light the bleak grey of ache and longing.

Please, Ma, I whisper into the sullen quiet of the room, *please pick up.*

I calculate the time difference in my head. It is twilight in India, that hour just before dusk when you will light the kindling that you have picked during the day and heat the water in the urn. The smell of wood smoke will fragrance the evening breeze, wisps of blue fading into the musky rose sky. The sun will be setting just as you hobble out of the bathroom, and you will pause for a moment on the veranda to admire the giant golden orb, now a mellow brown suspended in a pink-tinged chocolate sky, while Bobby bounds up to you and licks your palms. After, you will sit down to dinner, alone, wishing I was there with you: fat red rice, sardines steeped in a tomato, onion and chilli sauce, mango pickle, thick curd spiced with chilli and ginger, egg curry: the eggs broken into the curry while it is bubbling, gooey white tentacles with yellow eyes laying claim to the thick brown sauce. The phone will ring and you will answer, your smile colouring your voice as you will say, 'Devi, you called just as I was sitting to eat, and I've made all your favourites. You know what they say: the people who call while you are eating are the ones who love you the most.'

The phone rings and rings at the other end. No answer. *Ma, what has happened? Where are you? Is the phone line bad?* I hang up, try Jalajakka's number. No answer. What has happened? Tentacles of worry grab me in a stranglehold. I decide to ask Rohan this evening, as soon as he comes home, to phone his parents, check if they have called on you. A haunt of a familiar melody drifts from the flat opposite. The sizzle of chips hitting hot oil, the smell of dough rising.

Something makes me try again, one last time. I dial the familiar number. Wait. Five rings. Seven. And then, a beep. 'Hello? Deeeviiiii? Your Ma is in hospital. Come home.'

Ma, today you did not move, you did not stir. After I'd finished reading to you, I took your unresponsive hand and placed it on my stomach. I wanted you to feel what I felt, the miracle of my baby calling from the womb. Your hand drooped, it faltered. I held it in place firmly, like you must have held mine once, while I was learning to walk, tottering on unsteady feet, giving me the support I needed. My baby pushed against our conjoined hands, said hello. You said nothing back at all, just lay there, placid, your hand flopping awkwardly.

Ma, I confess I had entertained the fantasy that once you heard my news you would wake up fully cured, joy brimming over in tumultuous waves of laughter, and exclaim, 'But that's what I was waiting for, Devi.'

A life grows within me and I watch another slip away from me, imperceptibly, day after day.

Ma, I ran away from you once, carelessly discarding the mantle of your love. Please do not do the same to me.

Yours,

Devi

Chapter 18
Shilpa

Idli and Dosa

Idli and Dosa:

Ingredients:

Urad dal–1 cup
Rice–2 cups
Salt to taste

Method:

Soak the dal and the rice separately in water for a minimum of three hours. Rinse, but do not throw away the water they were soaked in. Grind to a smooth paste, adding the water you saved if necessary. Add salt to taste. Leave in a warm place to ferment for at least twelve hours. The mixture will rise overnight, resembling frothy white foam. Mix well.

Grease a frying pan (I use half an onion dipped in oil for this) and place it on the hearth. When hot, ladle a spoonful on and spread the mixture outwards in concentric circles. This makes for crispy dosas.

For idlis, spoon the mixture into idli cups and steam until cooked.

Serve with coconut chutney and drumstick sambar.

❄ ❄ ❄

Dear Diary,

I have paid the price. I have. And, oh, how it hurts, how it torments me, this choice that I have had to make. And yet, even though it was presented as a choice, it wasn't one really. I always knew what I would do, even in the midst of it all, at the lowest point. It was a given. It was. But why, oh why did it have to be this way? Why did I have to choose at all? Why?

In my last entry, I said blithely that I would pay, that it wouldn't matter. Then it was clear. It was black and white. I had no idea, no inkling.

It haunts me every single day, every waking moment. And it will for the rest of my life. The choice I made. It is my cross to bear.

The wise woman, whom most call mad, she did warn me: 'You are stealing from fate. It will cost you dearly. Are you willing to pay the price?' she asked, and I said 'Yes,' without hesitation. I cannot go back even if I want to. I cannot lose my baby. If I went back to that moment knowing what I know now, what would I say? The baby jumps in the warmth, the haven of my womb. There's the answer. Yes. Yes. Yes. Despite the pain. The guilt. Yes.

After all that's happened, the matrons and elders of the village, Jalaja, even Sumitranna, all ask me why, why do I believe in that madwoman so? Why do I take her words so much to heart? I touch my growing belly, which is now so big that it is difficult to do even the smallest thing, and tell them that this is proof. And that she is a wise woman, she is not mad. 'You would have got pregnant anyway,' they say. Even Jalaja doesn't understand. I had hoped she would.

So… I take refuge in you as usual, dear Diary. At least I can still write.

This is what I want to say to them, what I've tried saying to them: Take, for example, the idli/dosa mix. It bubbles and froths and looks possessed, like an evil potion with a mind of its own. But it produces the finest idlis, the crispiest dosas. The wise woman, she is like that. She looks mad, and yet she divines the future, she is a saint in a madwoman's guise. And she is just a conduit. She cannot change my fate. It was written in my stars long before her, before anyone, when the Lord Ganapathy decided to create me. I think her arrival in the village just before she predicted my pregnancy was not a coincidence. She was an answer to my prayers, sent by Lord Ganapathy to warn me and bless me. She is His messenger, that's all. You don't know what happened that day, any of you. You weren't there.

Dear Diary, I think reading the future is like cooking: discordant ingredients are mixed together to form a murky mixture which gradually clears to become something absolutely, breathtakingly delicious. This must be how it is for the wise woman. She looks at me and she sees my past, my present, my future, all haphazardly jumbled together. She has to sort through it, see what's coming and divine what it is that the Lord Ganapathy wants me to know.

I am sitting in the front room, my back bolstered by the wall, my bump supporting you, dear Diary. The baby prances about happily in my stomach, unaware. Every once in a while a sliver of the rain that is leading the trees in a wild dance and is inciting the mud to rebellion blows in on a gust of wind, tasting of sorrow, laden with memories, images I'd rather not see.

A hot airless afternoon. Everything still. Waiting. I am six months pregnant. Picking kindling for the hearth in Sumitranna's orchard with Manoj. It looks like rain. Clouds collect in clumps, hanging low, dense and pregnant like my swollen belly. Threatening. The stray dogs and cows are slumped indolent amongst parched fields, tongues hanging out. Flies buzz, the air shimmers, dust motes suspended in the lethargic haze. I pick as quickly as I can, which isn't fast, my belly getting in the way. The baby somersaults within, oblivious. Manoj had suggested we go without a wash that day as it looked like rain, but hot tumultuous pails of water cascading down my head, over my engorged belly are a luxury I look forward to, so I persuaded the poor man, just back from a laborious day in the fields, to come with me. 'With your help, we'll finish before the rain comes,' I pleaded.

A flash seeping the world of colour, drawing energy onto itself, heralding the arrival of rain. Manoj's eyes meet mine, worry in them. He picks up the basket, gives me his arm. What foolhardiness possessed me to come out in this, I curse, as thunder announces the advent of the storm like drums before a Yakshagana performance. There is nobody else about. Sumitranna and Jalaja have taken their little boy to visit with grandparents. And then it is here, the rain. Heavy drops hitting my body with a fury the monsoons cannot contain.

We run as fast as we can towards the stream which leads to the hill beyond which is our house. I yearn to squat on my mat in the shelter of the veranda, watching the rain vent its rage, to fan my face and say, 'Phew, that was scary.' I want to stroke my bump and talk softly to my child as I have taken to doing lately. I want to be anywhere but here, my sari wet and hugging my body, the rain roiling the mud into slush, making it slippery so my legs sink in and I cannot find my footing, afraid I will fall despite Manoj's arm holding me up, unable to take the next step.

Crash. A roaring in my ears, like the sea reverberating inside a conch shell. A flash. Groaning branches advancing. Brown hands with green fingers waving frantically. The world is black, heaving, upside down. When I come to, I realise, panic descending like an angry hand on an unsuspecting face, that I cannot move, cannot turn. I am horizontal, in the churning mud, the bitter smell of drenched earth and crushed mango leaves overwhelming me, trapped, a weight pinning my legs down. I turn, uncomprehending. Rain lashes my face, whipping my back and arms, claiming my body like an enraged, jealous lover. My husband's eyes. The pain in them. The pain. He is still holding me, his hand in mine. The basket is overturned beside Manoj's head. I look down, see a monster where my legs should be. A brown trunk thick as the pillar in that temple in Manil where I conceived barely six months ago this child I am carrying. The bitter smell of crushed mango leaves and smoke mixed with slush and fear. We are trapped underneath the ageing mango tree that lives beside the stream. It must have been struck by lightning and collapsed, tipped over, right onto us. I can hear the stream, normally placid, throbbing as the rain drums it to frenzy. I will not think about what could have happened if the tree had fallen not on my legs but a tad higher. This is not the time to imagine that horror.

I open my mouth to scream, but nothing comes out. Or perhaps it does and is drowned out by the angry boom of the rain. *My baby.* 'Protect the precious cargo within,' the wise woman's words echo in my ear, suddenly loud. *I will not lose my baby. I will not.* My hand rushes defensively to my stomach. I stroke my baby and it doesn't respond. My usually responsive baby who kicks and twirls like a dervish inside the womb is still. *No.* I need to go to the doctor. I need someone to check on my baby. Tell me it is fine.

My husband's eyes are closing. 'Manoj,' I say, trying not to show the panic I feel in my voice. They flutter open. The tree has fallen on his stomach. If I had been on Manoj's right instead of on his left… The thought doesn't bear thinking about. As it is, my baby is not responding. And Manoj needs help. I push my legs, wriggle experimentally. The tree stays put, but there is some give in the mud beneath. 'Stay with me,' Manoj whispers. 'Please.'

'I will,' I say, even as I push against the tree with all my might. I can move my legs, I can. Slowly, inch by inch, I wiggle out from under the tree. I should try and free Manoj, but I am afraid to try and pull the tree off. It is too big a task for me to attempt single-handed. And the mud is slippery. I might fall and then I will lose the baby. The baby. It is fine. I cannot bear to think otherwise.

I bend down, kiss my husband. 'Try and wriggle out from under there, Manoj,' I urge in his ear. His breath is coming in laboured gasps. 'Can't.' he manages. 'Hurts.' His eyes are bruised, red. Bottomless pits of pain. I cannot look. 'Please, Manoj.' My face is wet and I do not know if it is the rain or my tears. I can taste the snot, briny, smacking of pain, that is looping around my lips, sneaking into my mouth.

I love this man, so very much. This man who has stood by me, miscarriage after miscarriage, not saying a word even though I knew how badly he wanted children, showing through the set of his face, the flashing of his eyes, his displeasure when people mocked me, called me barren. This man who has always been there for me: a rock-solid presence. When I met the wise woman, he humoured me, took me to the temple in Manil. He's looked after me in his own way throughout this pregnancy and all those others, getting tender coconut water, the ripest guava, the juiciest mango. He came today to pick kindling at my behest, even though he was tired, having just got home from work, even though it looked like a storm brewing, even though all he wanted to do was to eat the food I had prepared and snooze on the veranda, wallow in a few moments of hard-earned peace.

This man who has loved me completely without ever asking for anything back. 'Please try, Manoj.' My voice is desperate.

'Can't,' he gasps. Is it my imagination or are his breaths getting slower, more laboured?

I put my arms around his shoulders; try to pull him out from under the tree. He screams, a high-pitched keen. Oh, Lord Ganapathy. I stop, shuddering sobs escaping my open mouth, tasting of salt and snot and rain and fear. I squat beside him. 'Manoj, please try and wriggle free. Please.'

'Stay with me,' Manoj whispers, his eyes hazy, distant, already somewhere else.

'I can't, Manoj,' I sob. 'I have to get to the doctor.'

'Please,' he begs, this man who has never asked me for anything. 'Please.'

And then, I do it, my greatest sin, my biggest regret. I leave the man who has loved me, who has looked after me, who has accepted me for who I am, who has stood by me during my myriad miscarriages, who wouldn't have been trapped under the mango tree in the first place if I hadn't wanted hot water for my bath —I leave him to die on his own, that rain-drenched evening, the mango tree seeping the life force out of him.

I run to the hospital on borrowed breath and energy I did not know I possessed and collapse outside the doors. When I come to, I ask after the baby. Everything is fine, they tell me. *Thank you, Lord Ganapathy.* I tell them about Manoj. I know what they will find when they get there. I know.

His face haunts me every waking moment, dear Diary. Those eyes overflowing with agony. 'Stay with me, Shilpa, please stay with me.' The only thing he ever asked of me.

Afterwards, after the cremation, I went to the madwoman. Sitting under the peepal tree beside her, listening to the cows mooing, Shali the fisherwoman hawking the last of the fish; the bus conductor shooing the cows and dogs, undeterred by the honking of horns and the swear words raining on them, away from the road; the women gossiping, ignoring the bags of rice, dal and oil weighing them down; the men laughing as they smoked beedis outside Master's shop; college girls giggling and eyeing the boys grouped outside Rao's grocery coyly from under their lashes; the air smelling of rotten fish, cow dung, deep-fried vadai and spiced cardamom tea from the little hut by the bus stop and the pineapple growing wild in the grass by the auto rickshaw stand where all the auto drivers urinated, I felt my turmoil ease a tiny bit. I closed my eyes, let the sun-kissed breeze tickle my face. His face, those eyes pregnant with pain, loomed. 'I am sorry, Manoj,' I whispered. The wise woman's hand found mine, squeezed.

I am not worthy, I wanted to say. Instead I said, 'You knew.'

She sighed deeply. 'Yes.'

What comfort there was in the warmth of her hand!

'This gift I have, this curse… I tried warning you.' Her words were earmarked with ache.

'Yes,' I said. And then, despite Manoj's face, his pain-filled eyes, 'I would have done the same, had I known. I would.'

'I know,' she said.

'I have paid the price,' I said softly. 'I have paid.'

The earth gorged on rain, smelling luscious, pregnant with new life. Voluptuous drops clung insidiously to peepal tree leaves, a shimmering sheen on velvet green. The guava and banana trees plump and sated with rainwater, leered: *There goes the woman who sacrificed her husband.*

'Not completely,' she said and my heart stilled. She patted my hand and her sigh was immense. 'Not yet.'

I stroked my bump. 'Will my child be okay?'

A flicker in those grey eyes.

I prostrated myself in front of her. 'Please, please tell me my child will be fine.'

And as I said those words, I lost her. I was holding her, she had been talking to me and suddenly she was somewhere else, her face frozen in a trance, her pupils unmoving.

I chanted her name as if in prayer. 'Devi, Devi, Devi.'

No response.

A leaf travelled down lazily from the peepal tree and plopped down in front of me, displacing a sliver of dust with a sigh. *Come back*, I thought, *come back to me.*

As if she had heard me, the wise woman blinked. 'Your greatest test is yet to come. One to keep, one to lose,' she intoned in a monotone voice. A pause and then the wise woman gasped, drawing in strangled breaths of air as if she was drowning. 'But it is for the best.'

Dear Diary, those were her exact words. I have puzzled over what she meant, but I cannot make them out. I have paid a very great price for this child but, according to the wise woman, I haven't paid fully yet. My child, this baby inside of me whom I yearn to meet… it has to be fine. It has to.

Chapter 19
Nisha

Heat

The heat. Like a jealous lover who takes hold and doesn't let go, his slimy hands creeping everywhere. Nisha can feel rivulets of sweat sliding down her back inside the cotton slip of the dress she is wearing, soaked and sticking to her like a clingy child. She realises now, too late, that it has been the wrong thing to wear, aware of scores of eyes boring into her. Men gather in clumps, stopping what they are doing to stare unashamedly right at her breasts, the outline of her bra visible through the turquoise cotton stained aquamarine with sweat. Women in rainbow saris which shimmer in the sunlight look once and avert their eyes, but not before they let their disdain show. Others whisper conspiratorially to their friends, their gaze alighting on her then quickly away like a skittish butterfly.

'This is not what I normally wear,' she wants to yell. 'Believe me.' Why has she worn this particular dress which barely comes up to her ankles? Because of her research: her

Bible, her religion. She had read that it would be hot and humid. That her uniform of suits and slacks would not do. She thought she was equipping herself for the heat. She didn't take into account the difference of culture: that this was not the thing to wear in a small village in India; that she would stick out like a green bean in a basket of red peppers. She is fast learning that research alone is not enough, that it will not do in this country.

Matt had whistled when she had tried the dress on. 'Too short?' she'd asked. 'Perfect,' he'd said, leaning in for a kiss. Matt… she misses him so. She wishes he was here with her.

'So, what have you decided to do?' he had asked that evening, in the wake of her conversation with Sister Priya. They were in bed, that soft, quiet time just before sleep lay claim like a grasping landlord. Matt was bathed in a warm gold glow, dulcet like the nun's voice.

'I need to go to India, Matt. I want to know why I was given away. I want to find my roots, discover who I am. And find her. My sister.'

Matt had nodded. 'I know.'

'I will take time off work. I am owed some anyway. ' She was owed a hell of a lot of leave. She taken barely any since she had started working at the firm to which she had been recruited straight from university.

And, 'Do you want me to come?' he had asked. 'I could do the same—get the leave owed me.'

She concentrated on fiddling with the golden down on his chest so he wouldn't see the sudden tears that pricked her eyes. He had offered; that meant so much to her. She would carry that around with her: a cherished gift. She wouldn't admit it to him but as much as she was excited, she was also scared. What if her sister didn't want to know her, had known about her and had decided not to make contact? There was no point dwelling on the negatives, on these questions, these fears that lurked like burglars and pounced when she was at her most vulnerable.

She had blinked the truant tears away, looked up at him and smiled. 'I need to do this on my own.'

He had nodded, kissing the strand of her hair that he was twirling, black wings adorning pink fingers. 'I love the way your eyes shimmer with all the emotion you find so hard to express but that I know is in there,' he had said. 'Come back to me.'

'I will,' she had whispered. And, 'Matt, what if all this changes me, irrevocably?' With the letter, she had lost herself, the snug knowledge of who she was. And now, with the discovery of her sister, this journey into the past, to a different country in search of her roots… she was losing all her bearings, the constants she had taken for granted. When all this was over, would she come to terms with the person she would eventually become? Would she even *like* her?

'You are already changing, Nisha,' Matt's eyes were soft, 'in here,' lightly touching her chest where her heart nestled, buffeted by her rib cage.

Her eyes must have betrayed her worry, her fear, for he continued, 'When you remembered the dream for the first time, you told me that you couldn't believe that that imaginative girl was you. Everything that you have experienced, it is all inside you. Let it come out. Give yourself permission to change. Don't fight it. Inside it all, you are a wonderful person, a woman who is as giving and loving as she is intelligent. Find your parents, reunite with your sister and, in the process, you will find yourself. And after, come back to me.'

What had she done to deserve this wonderful man? She was blessed.

'I will do anything for you,' he had said then, suddenly, fiercely, his hand on her chin, willing her to look into his eyes, so close that she could see the tiny beads of sweat flecking the tips of blond stubble.

She squints, pushing away sudden tears that threaten, that seem to be ambushing her all the time now, like the emotions that seize her at odd moments, making up for lost time.

She is tempted to go back to the hotel and change but nothing in her wardrobe constitutes clothes that will withstand this weather and earn the respect of these women and the inattention of the men, who hitch up their lungis and open their mouths lasciviously at the sight of her. She thinks longingly of her suits; even though she would boil to death in them here, they would at least have afforded some privacy from the unabashed, intrusive stares. She needs a new wardrobe. She needs an umbrella, like most people here, as a shield against the sun. She is jet-lagged and tired and the thought of lying down in her air-conditioned hotel room, a pillow on her face, nudges in, vies for attention, tantalising. But the need to know that has ballooned into an all-consuming urge, that had made her book her flight the very evening after she called the convent for the second time and heard the soft, musical voice of the nun and was assaulted by memories spilling out of that secret corner of her mind, that same need is now propelling her to visit with Sister Priya, to go straight to the convent, see if it is as she remembers, as she recalls in her vivid dreams, as it is painted in her memories.

Once she had booked her ticket, knowing she was definitely going to India, she had slept—a blessedly dreamless, healing sleep for the first time since losing her parents. And that pull for answers, that urge to find her sister, to meet the nun who called to her from the past via her dreams, had allowed her to say goodbye to the one person who was her constant in an ephemeral world, to leave him standing at the airport, waving, to not turn back once she'd said goodbye, to resolutely walk right on and turn only once she was sure she was concealed from sight. The sight of him: his hand still up in the air, scanning the faces, waving desperately, hoping, she knew, that she would see him somehow, even if he couldn't see her, his face bereft, expression lonely like a forlorn child. She had carried it with her in the nine-hour flight, while the lady next to her fell asleep on her shoulder, while the air hostess kept bumping her legs as she walked up and down the aisle, while the toddler in front screamed relentlessly all through, except for a blessed half an hour when he fell asleep and his mother sobbed out of sheer exhaustion—throughout she carried her lover's face with her, his expression, his words whispered in her ear as he held her close before letting her go. 'I love you. Come back to me.' His lemony-musk smell, the mint on his breath. 'I will,' she had said. And, 'I need you, Nisha,' he had mouthed, lifting her face which lay on his chest, memorising the rhythm of his heartbeat, and kissing her lips, tasting of salt and sorrow and love and loss. And she had squirreled that assurance away in a corner of her heart, for use when she was lonely, as she was bound to be, in a country and place she knew only from dreams and memories which had suddenly surfaced after a hiatus of twenty-odd years.

She had reached Mangalore that morning, after a hair-raising flight in that little bumpy plane, which she was sure was going to crash on the stony hills hugging the narrow landing strip on both sides. When, in Bangalore, a jolting bus had conveyed the passengers travelling to Mangalore to the little plane, she had wanted to ask, 'You are joking, right?' It did not look big enough to carry her suitcases let alone her plus the several other passengers waiting to board. She had kept her fingers crossed the whole way. She, who believed in facts not luck. It had been a particularly jerky ride, the tiny plane buffeted by winds and rain. As it readied to land, as it swooped down over the hills, twinkling green and steep, rocks jutting out on all sides, she had closed her eyes and Catholic prayers rusty from disuse had slipped into her head and held court: old friends reuniting. And the surprising thing was that she had let them and they had calmed her, these mindless chants recited by rote. She, Nisha Kamath, for whom not two weeks ago, mathematics, the solid rigidity of numbers, had been religion.

And here she is now, with not so much as breakfast in her stomach. She had been too nauseous after the rough flight, nerves fluttering around her stomach like a bevy of hungry moths, to even think about food. She is not sure what she will find, what lies in store for her. What if the nuns cannot dig up any record of her adoption, or even, as the nun who spoke to her said, any record of her ever having stayed there? What if Sister Priya doesn't remember her even during her lucid moments, denies all knowledge of a child ever having lived in the convent? How to find her parents, her sister, in this country of over a billion people? Where to start?

And what of her memories? How to explain them—how real they feel, as if, if she reached back into the past, she could touch them: smell the fragrant jasmine tinged with bitter lime; taste Sister Shanthi's famous dahi vadai—the tanginess of the dahi, the sweetness of the tamarind chutney; hear the crows holding court among the coconut trees on a dew-sparkled morning, the air carrying a hint of the previous night's monsoon shower and a promise of more to come; feel the Eucharist bread disintegrate on her tongue while executing the sign of the cross? How to explain the fact that she knows all the Catholic prayers and litanies, recognises all the saints, remembers all the festivals and the elaborate rituals that go with them even though she hasn't set foot inside a church, not counting one school trip when she was nine, in twenty years?

Her heart does a nervous little flip. Oh, well, she's here now; she'll find out what she can and then go home. To Matt. A sigh of longing at the thought of him. Those warm blue irises flecked with yellow. The full mouth tilted upward in an inviting smile at the sight of her. His kisses, oh those kisses, as if with each he was imparting a part of himself. 'I need you, Nisha,' he had said, his eyes shining, liquid. 'Come back to me.'

I will, Matt. I will.

Buses painted all the colours of the rainbow race past, screaming and screeching, overflowing with people who spill out the two openings, one at the front of the bus and one near the back, hanging on to the pole for dear life, their clothes puffed up by the wind and their hair flying in a frizzy halo around their heads. They ogle and grin and wolf-whistle at her and she silently wills them to concentrate on holding on; she doesn't want a death on her conscience on top of everything else. The air carries a salty tang of sea and the zing of spices. People urinate by the side of the road; children walk to school, chattering happily, their backs weighed down by satchels almost as big as them; a woman prays at a roadside shrine: a figure of a deity set into a wall and obscured by garlands, her eyes closed, hands folded, oblivious to the noise and bluster around her; little huts conduct brisk business selling deep-fried snacks a suspicious bright orange in colour, tea in tiny aluminium tumblers, pyramids of tender coconuts, diminutive bananas shaped like question marks hanging in bunches from the thatched roof.

Her stomach growls ominously as it is assailed by spicy aromas, as she clutches the piece of paper with the address of the convent and wanders the streets of Dhonikatte.

Her eyes had scrunched in the dazzling sunlight that assaulted her as she stumbled out of the airport and it was like walking into a steaming oven, inducing an instant headache. She had hailed a taxi blindly from the gaggle that descended on her. The taxi driver had recognised the name of the hotel where she wanted him to stop first so she could drop off her luggage but had not understood her accent when she tried to tell him the address of the convent, even though she spoke in Kannada, the lessons drummed into her by her parents on drowsy Saturday afternoons coming of use, wondering as she did if her parents had made her learn the language in the occasion of this very eventuality. 'Slow, slow,' the taxi driver said, pronouncing it 'Slaaa, slaaa,' his eyes never leaving her lips as he tried to read the words she was trying to say. However slowly she spoke, enunciating each syllable clearly, it wasn't comprehensible to him. So she wrote the address down on a slip of paper and thrust it under his nose. He had nodded, scratched his head and then with the same hand, his crotch, giving his balls a tight squeeze, right in front of her. *I must make sure not to touch his hand when I pay him,* she had thought. She was pretty sure he was bare under that flimsy patterned fluorescent green cloth he was wearing in lieu of trousers.

He had driven her to what looked like the outskirts of town, a hair-raising, daredevil ride scarier than any rollercoaster she had ever been on. One that involved nudging other vehicles, cows wandering joylessly smack bang in the middle of the busy road, and even a bullock cart, out of the way hither and thither. They almost fell off the rickety bridge across a dun-coloured stream, the sluggish water reluctant to so much as ripple (would it splash if the car fell in, she had wondered, or sigh softly, poof as it swallowed up the car in one big gulp and continue to wear that ugly brown frown on its mud-spattered face?) all to the soundtrack of a multitude of blaring horns and yelling people. He had brought the taxi to a screaming stop in front of what looked like a pile of rubble, guarded by the skeletal remains of a building, by which time she had recited the Rosary, alien until recently, twice over in her head. One crumbling wall was all that remained upright of what had once been, she assumed from the framework, quite a tall building in this town of squat outcroppings. The lone wall had 'Vote for Congress' etched boldly in blue ink across it, under the inscription of the palm of a hand and several other indecipherable words in different scripts. It encircled a pile of rubble and disintegrating red brick, dotted with velvet moss and nodding weeds. The taxi driver had jumped out while she was still collecting her wits from where they were scattered all over the dirty floor of the Ambassador car masquerading as a taxi. He had held out his palm for his money, his tawny eyes curiously assessing her, the ghost of a smile lurking on his face as he took in her ashen demeanour, the way she had to hold on to the car as she stepped out on jelly legs.

'This, aaaadress.' He had said, pointing at the pile of rubble.

'But...' she began.

He nodded energetically, pointing to the piece of paper. 'Aaaadress. Aaaadress.'

'No, no,' she tried again.

'Yaas, Yaas,' he had said, his head moving up and down like a fulcrum so vigorously that for a moment she worried it would fall right off.

She had given up, paid him and watched him drive away.

And now she is walking up and down, up and down, in the sugarcane-scented haze looking for someone to ask about the convent. The staring men disperse when she approaches. The women disappear into houses. She has not yet managed to find someone who will stay and talk to her.

She is well and truly lost. Her mobile phone doesn't work—no reception. She did spot a little hut with a stripy yellow sign which declared in bold black letters, 'STD/ ISD/ Intrnet'. Were they aware of the spelling mistake on the board? She had walked inside, tried conversing with the proprietor who was swatting at flies, eyes glazed in that way that suggested he was trying to ward off sleep. 'No Hingleesh,' he had said, his gaze perking up at the sight of her. She had pointed to the computers, tried explaining in Kannada that she wanted to use them. As with the taxi driver, he did not understand her. 'You can speak to me in Kannada,' she had tried again, in Kannada, but she might as well have been speaking French. He had waved his hands, repeated, 'No Hingleesh,' and pointed upwards at a stationary ceiling fan, the blades encrusted with a thick coating of grime. She had scrunched up her nose in an effort to understand. He had sighed noisily, and walked up to the computers, old chunky models dating back to the early nineties. He had switched the monitors on and off. Nothing. Then she had understood. The computers were not humming. They were lifeless. There was no power.

So she cannot do research, find out where she is. And yet, strangely, she is not scared. If this had happened to her two weeks ago, she would have been terrified by the loss of control, besieged by utter helplessness brought on by the lack of devices by which to orient herself. No phone, no computer, no Wi-Fi. She would have felt bare, stripped to the core. Now, though, she is happy to wander, take this place in. When did this change take place, she wonders. Perhaps it is only fitting to find herself lost in a strange country when she feels lost inside, within herself. Or perhaps it is the languid feel to this place, the loamy red soil swirling gently in the leisurely breeze. The men dawdling with index-finger-sized tumblers of sweet-smelling steaming caramel liquid outside thatched huts with holes for entrances, no doors, the dark interior yawning, the hole so small even the shortest man has to stoop to enter. The women sitting on verandas, their legs stretched out and holding wicker baskets, paan-filled mouths and weathered hands both working nonstop. They fill herby dung-coloured powder onto tissue paper the pale pink of the inside of a fingernail and roll it busily. Close to, the spicy aroma of the powder makes her sneeze. A young man sneaks across and whips one of the rolled-up tubes, lights it with a match, breathes in deeply. The women shriek, make to smack him. He laughs and walks away, wisps of pungent smoke colouring the air around him, and Nisha realises it is a form of cigarette they are rolling.

Dhonikatte is a quaint little village, she muses as she walks. Squat buildings in various hues contrast with orange-tiled brick houses, looking like the houses in storybooks. No one seems to be in a rush except the buses which race past, stuffed to bursting. Crows chatter on telephone poles, black buttons silhouetted against a sky that is so blue as to be almost white. This country, its people clad in colourful, worn, dusty clothes, sporting huge smiles, it is something else, she thinks. Her mind, which has been in continuous turmoil since she got the letter, seems to have for a brief moment settled, found peace. And all this without doing a single calculation in her head, she thinks, and the thought elicits a smile.

She stops at a cart piled high with green coconuts, the tops shaved white and looking like ice cream cones. She watches as the man deftly cuts the top off one revealing the creamy skin and cloudy water inside. He sticks a straw in and hands it to her.

Heaven. Cool on her parched tongue, like drinking liquid jelly. Afterwards, the man shaves off a part of the outside of the coconut to make a spoon with which he scoops the creamy insides and hands to her. Soft, yet crunchy, and deliciously sweet. *I could get used to this*, she thinks. She presses twenty rupees into the man's hand and he grins wide, displaying yellow teeth with yawning gaps, gums stained scarlet. She shows the tender coconut man the address, but he shakes his head, manages to say something which sounds like, 'Don't know,' and points her to the shop opposite, which, from what she can see, sells shoes.

The shop is stacked floor to ceiling with cardboard shoeboxes and has a small triangular space in the middle which houses a worn, wooden bench, presumably for customers to sit and try on shoes. More cardboard boxes are strewn around this tatty bench, open and spilling their wares. A man stands just outside the shop and looks at her feet as she crosses the road, narrowly missing a bicycle whizzing past at breakneck speed, the rider frantically ringing his bike and yelling, 'Lo… lo…' A motorbike growls in his wake, housing not one, not two but a family of four—the little girl sitting squashed in front of her father, almost on top of the handlebars; the dad, who is driving, peering around her head of neatly oiled hair worn in two plaits behind her ears and tied with yellow ribbon, to squint at the road. His son squats behind him, straddling the seat like his father, and the wife brings up the tail, sitting demurely sideways, facing Nisha, almost on top of the exhaust, covering her mouth with the pallu of the sari to prevent choking on the fumes, the other hand clutching on to the back of the bike for dear life. The motorbike trundles over a pothole and all of them jump into the air a little before falling back onto their seats. The woman's eyes, wide and tranquil, the only part of her face visible above her patterned red sari pallu, meet Nisha's for a brief moment.

The man in front of the shoe shop is still staring pointedly at her feet as she reaches him, so she looks down as well. Her feet are covered in red dust, her beautiful silver sandals barely visible. The nail varnish she had applied before she left, the pale pink of perfectly cooked tiger prawns, is chipped and one of her nails has clipped and is hanging off the toe. As she steps into the shop, the man executes an about turn without speaking or looking at her and enters the shop ahead of her. He walks up to one of the stacks, pulls the bench towards him, stands on it on tiptoe and, reaching up as far as his hand can go, pulls one of the cardboard boxes out as if at random. The stack teeters, makes to fall. He rights it and then steps down. He lays the box down in front of her feet like an offering, kneels down right in front of her so she cannot move forward without stepping on his head, opens the box and then yanks her sandal off. She is speechless with shock. She cannot believe the cheek of the man! He has not said a word to her, or even looked at her, and now he is down on one knee in front of her, cradling her dusty foot on his lap, and as she watches, slipping on the gaudiest sandal she has ever had the misfortune of beholding onto her foot. A be-sequinned, shiny gold creation twinkles up at her from her right foot. The man looks at her for the first time and smiles, displaying rotting paan-stained teeth. An epidemic infecting Indian men, she thinks, at least the ones she's seen here. 'Perfect fit,' he says in perfectly adequate English.

She has no choice but to buy the sandals and he insists she wear them. 'Very comfortable, perfect fit,' he keeps repeating. How does he know they are comfortable? *He* is not wearing them. In actual fact, they bloody well aren't. And how he managed to pick a box containing a pair of sandals her size —well, sort of —from a pile of identical boxes, she will never know. She pays up and hands the slip of paper containing the address of the convent over to him. 'Do you know where it is?' she asks him in English, and he nods, flashing another paan-stained smile.

Afterwards, with her dust-stained silver sandals tucked under her arm (she aims to change out of the monstrosities adorning her legs—which are already pinching the back and sides of her feet —at the earliest opportunity), she walks beside the man, trying to keep pace with his long strides, retracing the way she has come. The man selling coconuts grins at her and holds out another coconut for her to try. She is tempted but the shoe seller is already way ahead. She hobbles to catch up—the sandals are really very uncomfortable—and is arrested by the sight of the family on the motorbike milling in a ditch beside the road. The woman is sitting down on a boulder fanning her face. The motorbike is sprawled ahead, on its side, and the kids and the dad are pointing at the woman and laughing.

'What happened?' she asks her companion who speaks to the family in a rapid-fire exchange in a language she later learns is Tulu.

'She fell off it seems, when the motorbike went over the stone there.' He points with a very dirty fingernail at a rock sitting innocuously in the middle of the road, beside a pot-hole the size of Wales half filled with dirty blond water. The woman looks shell-shocked. The dad can't take his eyes off Nisha's breasts. Nisha runs to catch up with the shoe seller, who has walked off again. At least all he has been transfixed by are the sandals on her feet, which twinkle up at her, reflecting the sun from their sequinned depths.

She catches up with him at the wall where the taxi driver had dropped her off. The man walks round it and, to her surprise, Nisha spies an alleyway which widens into a busy street, at the far end of which stands a building from which young people, mostly boys, mill. They wolf-whistle when they see her.

Beyond this is a high wall, green-tinged orange bricks obscured by a riot of pink and orange bougainvillea, bursting down the wall, singing in colour. Sharp slivers of broken glass dot the top of the wall, reflecting cloudy blue and amber light, defying any burglar brave enough to try and scale it. She knows this place. She *knows* this place.

She rests her hand on the wall, to try and still her wayward heart, and jade yellow moss caresses her palm. Her knees give way suddenly, as a memory, startlingly vivid, snakes in. Touching the wall, asking Sister Priya, 'Does God make all the walls velvet?' Sister Priya laughing her deep-throated guffaw, like a man's, which Nisha has always fancied sounds like God's voice, 'No child; that is moss. But yes, God created that. How clever you are.' And bending down to brush her cheek with her lips, her spiced breath hot in Nisha's ear as she whispers, a secret imparted, shared, 'You make me see the wonder in God's creation, child. I thank you.'

She could bet the inside of this wall—on the other side, the convent side—is also carpeted with moss.

Kind eyes, the deep brown of strong tea with just a dash of milk, peering at her. The shoe seller, finally looking at her face instead of her feet. 'Are you okay?'

She takes a deep breath, smiles at him. 'I am fine.' She thanks him and presses fifty rupees into his palm.

'No, no,' he says holding up his palms facing outward, a refusal.

'Yes,' she says. 'Please.'

He accepts the note with a flash of rotting teeth. 'Good shoes,' he says. 'When they wear out, you know where I am.' That grin again, displaying that cave of a mouth. He turns to go and she watches him, his gangly long-legged stride, blending with the group of boys who are still eyeing her, curious.

She walks along the wall, holding on to it, on teetering legs which are nothing to do with the new sandals. Smells, memories assaulting her... Melodious voices raised in song, reverberating up to the ceiling. The exquisite pain of candle wax searing her hand and then solidifying while Father's sermon on the caprices of sinners droned on and on. Sunday mornings yawning endlessly, as she and the rest of the children of the parish were herded into airless, sweltering classrooms for Catechism after mass, breakfast a distant memory rumbling in her stomach. The sharp hot tang of envy when she first realised she could never be an altar *boy*. The smell of sandalwood incense, prayer, sweat. The forbidden taste of communion wafer dipped in wine, sweet, melt in the mouth.

She walks along the wall and then she is at the gate. Rusting iron bars, topped with spikes. She places her face where the woman with the straggly hair must have placed hers that drowsy jasmine-scented afternoon. The smell of iron and rust and the faint tang of lime. The lime tree, the dusty courtyard around which she danced, displacing red mud which painted orange patterns on her clothes, stained her feet amber. No jasmine bush. The bench, now broken. Dilapidated. Tired looking.

The entrance to the convent up ahead, a squat little building of red brick, smaller than she remembers, the entrance which she knows will lead into an anteroom and then the corridor with rooms off either side and which culminates in the chapel. She rests her head against the cool bars. Breathes in the smell of iron and rust and tastes salt as the tears pool around her mouth.

There is no bell. The sun bakes her head, sweat pools between her thighs, making them sticky, slippery like wet gum; it collects under her arms like stagnant rainwater after a summer storm and courses down her back; but she is unaware, caught in a strange limbo, watching her childhood self. The little girl, a gaping hole for a mouth, a gash where the lips should be, hair bathed in sweet-smelling amla oil and tied in neat plaits behind her ears by eager novitiate nuns who all fight to comb it, though she prefers

Sister Latha as she is the most gentle, her touch like the comfort of a favourite pillow. Now she is the woman peeking through the gates, her hair escaping in wiry curls, her eyes raining rusty tears. The child opens her mouth and the woman disappears. Nisha shakes her head to rid herself of this vision, this peek into the past, and rattles the gate.

A nun appears from the cool darkness within, walking straight out of her dreams and into the harsh, searing afternoon —the white habit: pleated white skirt, long-sleeved blouse with black collar and black buttons down the front, cinched with a black belt at the waist, the black headdress with the white band circling the front, the rosary dangling from the neck, dancing pendulum fashion every time the nun takes a step forward: the self-same outfit that Nisha has seen countless times in the past week pirouetting beneath her closed lids. The nun's feet, clad in sensible open-toed sandals, stomp across parched earth littered with yellowing patches of grass, and the twirling girl that Nisha once was vanishes into the ether of memory. The nun is chunky and as she comes closer, Nisha catches a whiff of cat, notices the grey whiskers marring the pristine white of the nun's habit. She has thick glasses that obscure her eyes, a mushroom-shaped nose that takes up most of her face and a moustache. She smiles and Nisha is instantly comforted. It is a kind smile, a giving smile. 'How may I help you?' she asks in perfect English and Nisha recognises the dulcet voice.

'We spoke on the phone?' she says softly, willing her breaths to steady, her wayward heart to calm down.

The nun draws her eyebrows together, giving her the appearance of a strict matron.

'I...' Nisha soldiers on, 'I called about Sister Priya and the fact that I was adopted.'

The furrowed brows clear, the smile reappears. 'Oh, yes.' She untangles a bunch of keys from the belt around her waist, unlocks the gate, which whines and complains as it creaks open reluctantly like a very old person. 'Come in, child.' And then, Nisha is squashed against the nun's surprisingly soft body which seems to spill out of her habit and enfold Nisha on all sides—a warm, sheltered feeling. This close she smells musty, sour—like those mouldy onions that used to fester at the very bottom of her mother's vegetable basket. The surprise of the hug knocks the breath out of Nisha. She wishes she could stay here forever, in this moment in this woman's warm pliant embrace. She wishes she was back in England and everything was okay, no surprises sprung on her, no lies. She wishes her sister was the one holding her like this and it were this easy to be with her, the lost years folding away like a Japanese fan.

Gently, the nun disentangles herself. 'Come,' she says, 'I will take you to Sister Priya.' And then, squinting up at her, 'Have you eaten?'

'I...'

'You should eat first and while you do, I will tell you what I know.' And, entering the doorway ahead of Nisha, 'You will be surprised.'

'In what way?' she asks, but the nun is up ahead and doesn't hear.

Have you found my birth parents? Did my sister live here once, with me? Was she given up for adoption too? She wants to shout but she reins herself in. She has waited this long; she can wait a few minutes more.

She walks inside, into the dark, mildew-scented corridor, and her past welcomes her with open arms, her memories swoop, they dive, they clamour for attention. *I haven't lived here in twenty-odd years and yet this is so familiar, so right, as if I am coming home.* The rotting beams overhead, the chipped orange Mangalore tiles that she used to count when she was bored while praying the rosary. The crumbly, woodlice-ridden doorways. The cement floor, cool after the heat of the ground outside, burning through sandals that pinch and wink. The soothing, awe-inspiring hush of prayer. The smell of spices and pews, of sweat and entreaties. Familiar. Overwhelming. She closes her eyes, breathes it all in.

This is the hour the nuns are sleeping, or praying. That drowsy hour after lunch and before chapel. The hour that she used to while away lying on the naked cement floor and staring up at the ceiling, tracing the path of the prayers making their way heavenward while she waited for the nuns to fall asleep. The hour she spent exploring, hiding under the pews, opening the altar—something she was forbidden to do, stealing a communion wafer from the chalice, waiting for God to strike her down while the white wafer melted on her pink tongue. Emboldened when God didn't strike her down, deciding, *knowing* that she was special.

This was your life once, Nisha. These familiar, crumbling walls, the silence so heavy you feel that if you poked it with your finger it would explode into noise, nuns like the wimple-clad woman walking ahead of you with her swollen ankles, her gentle smile and her soothing voice, the coconut trees basking in the somnolent honey-gold haze, the fronds waving like welcoming hands opening for a hug, the mosquitoes buzzing, the air thick with dust, the smell of rain-sodden earth, of incense. This was what you knew. And you were happy. It was enough.

Memories, assaulting her, tasting of Eucharist bread dipped in wine: the sweetness tinged with guilt, spiced with sin and fear of retribution. Running barefoot down the corridors, stealing leftover vadai and idlis from the kitchen, scattering morsels to the crows. Exploring the back garden—something she was prohibited from doing on her own; spying on the rat snake lounging in the aboli bushes from a safe distance, marvelling at the sheen of its gold-green skin, the grace of its long coiled body; teasing a millipede with a twig and watching it curl up into a tight little ball; running riot amongst forget-me-nots which closed softly with a wistful sigh as she passed and opened again soon after, a map of scratches navigating sun-warmed skin punctuated here and there with coagulating drops of red, breathing in the smell of earth, grass and something minty; snacking on fat sour bimblis and raw mangoes; following the circuitous path of a colony of ants heaving grains of fat red rice twice their size on their backs all the way to their ant hill at the base of the ambade tree, confusing them by teasing them out of their way with a gentle flick of the tamarind twig in her palm and watching them stumble but set right somehow and weave their arduous way back home.

That is how I feel. Like I was veered off path by a giant hand but am now back on track.

The dining room is empty. The smell of phenyl and curry. The neat lines of tables and benches where the nuns filed in silently, bowing their heads to give thanks. Rows of black wimple-clad heads and one oiled-plaited one. She used to always sit at the end of the first bench, nearest the kitchen. She sits there now, wondering if humans leave an imprint of themselves everywhere they live, thinking that if so, her adult self is sitting on the small imprint left by her younger self.

The nun shuffles in, carrying a stainless-steel plate overflowing with rice, chapatti, sambar, potato with peas, coconut and coriander chutney, mango pickle, and followed by a very fat tabby which mewls plaintively and rubs itself against Nisha's legs. The nun places the plate in front of Nisha. The smell reminds her of Sister Shanthi slapping chapatti rounds straight onto the gas fire, flipping them over, watching them rise, the aroma of charred dough making her stomach rumble.

'Eat,' the nun says, settling herself into the bench opposite with a little sigh and a swish of her skirts. The tabby immediately jumps up onto her lap, and pinions Nisha in its cool green gaze. The nun smiles indulgently and strokes the cat's fur. 'Don't mind Kitty,' she says. The cat purrs contentedly and settles deeper into the nun's substantial lap.

Nisha breaks off a piece of chapatti, wraps it round a smidgen of potato, watches the nun watch her, her gentle eyes warm. 'Did you find the documents of my adoption?' She tries to keep the desperate hope out of her voice.

'Not really.'

Her heart dips. 'Oh.'

'Don't be disheartened, child. And eat. Do.' The nun waits until Nisha scoops some rice and sambar into her mouth. 'I didn't want you coming all this way for nothing. So I called around.'

A crinkle of paper as the nun pulls something out of her habit, smoothes it out on the table. The tabby's head pops up, whiskers twitching. It eyes the piece of paper, then settles back onto the nun's lap, deeming the paper not worth its attention, the loss of a few minutes of sleep in its human's comfortable lap.

Nisha cranes her neck, the syrupiness of rice and sambar and hope in her mouth. She spies voluptuous letters in a neat script dancing across the page. 'The list of questions you wanted answers for,' the nun says. From another pocket, the nun pulls out a pair of spectacles, one of the arms held in place by masking tape. 'Now, let me see. You wanted to know… how old you were when you were adopted from the convent, how your adoptive parents found you, when you arrived at the convent, who your parents were, where they lived. And… if there was another little girl with you.'

Nisha looks up, this time unable to hide the naked anticipation she knows is shining out of her eyes.

'Mother Rose, who used to run the convent then, passed on three years ago, but Sister Shanthi is at a parish in North India, in Shimla.'

Sister Shanthi hoisting her up, propping her on the stone kitchen counter, giving her onions to peel, potatoes to chop, calling her 'my wonderful little helper', talking through the recipes with her: 'That's hot oil, it will splash, don't come close, Nisha, stay right there. That's a good girl. Now I will scoop up some batter, like this, and throw it in and look how it firms up into the bhajis you like. Magic!' Robust, always smiling Sister Shanthi who smelled of bubbling oil, chilli powder and sweat.

'I called her and she said…'

Nisha leans forward, she cannot help it. The cat cocks open one eye, regards her coolly, a dare.

'She said that yes, the convent did allow unwed mothers refuge, that they did give up their babies for adoption… But they did not keep babies here, not ever.'

'Oh.' Disappointment bitter in her mouth.

'Except the once.'

The ball of rice and sambar sticks in her throat.

'You were not born at the convent, and not really a baby when you got here either. You were two and a half.'

My parents kept me until I was two and a half years old and then deemed me not suitable? Why? What did I do wrong? She washes the rice down with the water the nun has placed next to her. The cat emits a contented purr from within the recesses of the nun's lap. 'My sister. Was she with me?'

'No, child. No.'

Disappointment. Crushing. Warring with anger. *My parents gave me away but kept her. Because I was flawed and she was perfect?* 'You said… that I would be surprised. By what? What have you found?'

The nun's expression is as tender as Matt's when he read the letter that changed everything. Matt. She wishes he was here. 'You are a miracle child.'

She gives up all pretence of eating. 'A miracle child?'

The nun smiles. 'Yes, Sister Shanthi said that you are a living, breathing miracle. That she always knew you would come back here. That it was inevitable seeing as you owe your life to the Mother Mary of Miracles for whom the church here in Dhonikatte is named. She knew that Mother Mary would call you back, especially now that Sister Priya is ill.'

What nonsense, she thinks, but says out loud, 'What happened?'

'You were desperately ill. The parishioners, the nuns and the priest had been keeping vigil and praying for days. Your fever was not shifting, the medicines not working. You went from delirious to comatose. In the end they carried you into the church, it seems you weighed so little by then. They carried you to the church of the Mother Mary of Miracles and laid you at the altar like a sacrifice.'

That altar where she spent many happy hours helping Sister Priya with the cleaning and polishing duties, the altar where she ran amok. A picture arrives in her head perfectly formed. A slip of a girl, lying at the altar, speckled light reflecting off the stained-glass windows, painting rainbows on her unresponsive face.

'The priest prayed; he asked the Lord for his help, he asked Mother Mary to intervene. "Mother, you were the force behind Jesus Christ's first miracle in Canaan where he turned water to wine. Please intervene to our Lord Jesus on this little girl's behalf." A hushed peace descended on the church, a strange calm and then, it seems the Mother Mary smiled, she actually smiled—everybody in the church witnessed it. And then…' The nun pauses, smiles benevolently at her. The cat stirs.

'Yes?' Her voice comes out as a whisper.

'And then you blinked and sat up and said in a clear voice that you were very hungry and was there any food. And the priest went inside and gave you some un-consecrated communion bread.'

The conviction the little girl that she had once been had had that she was special. The dreams she has had of watching prayers make their way heavenward. Of God's hand opening, of God's munificence toward her. The taste of Eucharist bread in her mouth even though she was not old enough to receive communion. She blinks. *Nonsense, Nisha. What nonsense.*

'After you have seen Sister Priya, you should visit the church, child. She will be waiting for you.'

'Who?'

'The Mother Mary of Miracles of course,' the nun says as if it is the most natural thing in the world. 'Anyway, to tell you what I know, Sister Shanthi said you were a delight, loved by everyone. You brought laughter and happiness to the convent. Everyone had a spring to their step when you were around. But they knew you couldn't be there forever; the convent was not the place for a little girl. And one day a letter arrived, from your adoptive parents. They had heard about you. Who hadn't? Your fame had spread far and wide—the miracle child. Initially they wanted you for some sort of project, but when they saw you… they fell in love. They wanted to adopt you, take you to England. They promised to fix your cleft palate. Mother Superior Rose prayed and all the nuns prayed and your mother was consulted and in the end a decision was made. You would have a better life in England. And you said you've had one.' The nun's eyes settle briefly on the ridged skin above Nisha's upper lip. Nisha's hand goes there as if of its own accord, strokes the scar.

'Yes. Yes I have…' she says, softly. *A life based on dry facts, not blind faith. On miracles of the scientific kind. Numbers, not Catholicism, my religion.*

The nun looks at Nisha's plate, 'Not up to eating?'

'Not really. Um… you mentioned my mother. Do you know who she is, where she lives?' Once more she tries and fails to keep the hope from her voice. *Why is there no mention of my father?*

The nun sighs, wrings her hands. The cat mewls in complaint. 'Sister Shanthi couldn't remember her name. She said she'll call as soon as it came to her. None of us are getting any younger, child; our memory is not like it used to be.' A rueful smile directed at her.

Nisha swallows down the crushing disappointment with another handful of rice. 'Surely there must be some documentation somewhere?'

The nun sighs deeply once more. 'Documentation wasn't and still isn't the top priority here, child.'

The organised, methodical part of her is outraged. How can it not be? How can these nuns, this convent blithely rely on people's fallible memories?

'...Serving the Lord God's people is.' The nun continues. 'You will find your parents and sister, if that is the Lord's plan for you.'

She might be changing, becoming more open to things other than science and numbers, but she will still take the solid proof of documentation over God's plan any day. 'Is there anyone else who might know the whereabouts of my parents?' she asks.

'I asked Sister Shanthi that. She's promised to try and remember which sisters were here at the time and ask around.' She looks at Nisha's plate, 'Come, I'll take you to Sister Priya. Be warned, she's not always in the here and now.'

'Yes.'

'And she may not be precisely as you recall her.'

Nisha smiles at that, a watery smile, and the nun beams.

The room is small, dark, with a tiny window that looks out onto the garden at the back, billowing banana trees, overgrown grass and thorny bushes. The bimbli tree with its clusters of tart fruit is at the back right where she remembers but the guava tree is not there anymore. A banana-scented breeze drifts in every so often. Sister Priya lies on a little cot by the window, a wisp of a woman clad in the customary white habit, gaunt face, frail hands folded as if in prayer upon the tray of her chest. Her eyes flutter as they come in, as the nun beside her says cheerily, 'Sister Priya, look who's here to see you.'

Sister Priya's eyes fluster open, and her myopic gaze wanders and then settles softly on Nisha. Her gaunt face relaxes into a parody of a smile sending the lines on her face into a flap. 'You came,' she says and Nisha lets the tears fall as she kneels down beside this woman she adored, her childhood rescuer and friend. She puts her hand in Sister Priya's. She looks at the face, the eyes that are smiling at her, the thin lips, now blanched of colour, the mole on the side of the slightly too long nose with the two thick hairs growing out of it that she had tried to pluck once, startling Sister Priya out of slumber. This face so familiar and yet, lost to her until now. And it is as if she always knew this woman, as if she was waiting for this moment. 'I did.'

'The jasmine tree died,' Sister Priya says softly, each word a trial. 'Went to heaven. I will follow soon.' A hand reaches out, strokes Nisha's hair. 'Look at you, turned into a beauty. Did they look after you well?'

Nisha nods, unable to speak past the lump in her throat, the well of tears that are making their tortured way down her eyes. 'We all prayed, asked the Saviour's, the Mother Mary's direction on what to do. They were Hindus, see and you… a Catholic miracle even though you had been born a Hindu. But He spoke. Every time any of us prayed about you and referred to the Bible, it always opened to Luke 6:46 —"Why do you call me Lord, Lord and do not do what I say?"' Sister Priya's feeble hand flutters on Nisha's cheek. 'The Lord wanted you to go to them. It was

His wish...' A pause as she gathers breath. 'I missed you so after. Couldn't make the jasmine garlands, couldn't help out in church. But I knew you would be looked after, loved. You couldn't have stayed here forever.'

She pats Nisha's cheek, her touch like very soft paper, stroking, caressing. 'Your mother came often, asking after you.'

Nisha startles, looks up at the nun standing by the bed, wondering if she has heard what she just did. Yes, her eyes are as wide, as surprised as Nisha's.

That woman at the gate, eyes showering tears, face segmented by rusting bars, populating her dreams—her mother? Yes, her heart declares. That glimmer of recognition, the child she once was opening her mouth, she remembers now—with a clarity that tells that deep down she had known all along—what she was going to call out: 'Ma.' Not 'Mum' as she would later call a different woman, but 'Ma.' Her heart knew the word, but her memory had failed her... Even when she finally remembered the dream, she had suppressed the memory that she had recognised the woman, had been going to call her 'Ma'—it was only triggered just now. Why? Because the woman had disappeared before Nisha gave voice to the call of her heart, and hurt and bewilderment had settled like fog in Nisha's chest, had squeezed sobs of loss, of the pain of abandonment out of her.

If her mother had given her away, why had she come to see her—and then why had she disappeared when Nisha recognised her, was about to call out to her...?

'Do you know who she is?' Nisha asks, her voice a naked whisper.

'Shilpa. Her name is Shilpa. Lives in Sompur. Go find her, child. Make your peace.' Sister Priya's eyes flutter closed, her breath flapping like a distressed bird. Nisha places a kiss on the flimsy cheek which smells of mildew and Vicks, whispers in her ear, 'I will come back soon.' The lips lift upwards in a ghost of a smile. The eyes remain closed.

Chapter 20
Devi

Burst of Bougainvillea

Ma,

The horror you had to endure!

I sit here, rubbing my stomach where my baby nestles, jiggling and jumping, saying hello to me from within the safe harbour of my womb, and I think of you, trapped under the mango tree, having to choose between the husband you loved and the child you had waited for all your life. I think of the person my Da was, the person I am only just getting to know through your diary entries, of the mango tree slowly draining the life out of him, and I close my eyes. If I had been in your position, Ma, God forbid, if I had to choose between Rohan and this new life burgeoning within me, what would I have done? It doesn't bear thinking about and I cannot begin to imagine what you went through. But… it happened and you chose me, and for that I am grateful. You chose me and you tried to hold me close but I rebelled, I retaliated, I ran away. I went to England…

I understand fully now what you meant when you said, 'You are all I have, Devi.' Now that my baby is growing inside, I desperately want connections, family ties. I want you here, Ma, to partake in the joy of my child. But I have Rohan to share this with and, even if I can't stand them, his parents. You had no one except the madwoman and me. I realise now, Ma, why your love felt so heavy, like a burden almost too weighty to carry.

Ma, the doctors called me aside today. 'She is not getting better,' they said. 'She is in danger of slipping into a coma,' they murmured.

'She moves; she's come out of her unconscious state several times now,' I countered, indignant.

'It doesn't look good for her,' they said, clearly dismissing my words as delusions of a loved one. 'You must think about saying goodbye.'

Well, it was like waving a red flag in front of a raging bull. You know how I get, Ma; I was spoiling for a fight anyway. 'I am sorry you think that,' I snapped. 'I will have to get a second opinion and a third,' I barked. 'I have no intention of saying goodbye and I am not giving up on my mother!' I yelled. 'She is getting better, I have witnessed it!' I screamed.

I refuse to give up on you, Ma. I refuse to give the doctors the satisfaction of saying 'I told you so'. I am going to make you come back to me. We had some good times together, Ma, and I will jot them down here. And I will read them to you and convince you to come back, so we can make more memories, more good times: you, me and my child.

Here's what we'll do when you are better, Ma. First, we'll eat your favourite meal: boiled rice with the baby mango 'midi' pickle that you so adore. Picture it, Ma: that first bite of tart mango steeped in rock salt, seasoned with spices—the bitterness mixed in with crunchy saltiness exploding in sweetness at the very end. After, we'll lie side by side on a mat under the guava tree, breathing in the smell of mango leaves swirling in the breeze, sharp, tangy with a hint of the sugariness to come, revelling in the lethargy of the endless honey-tinted, sugarcane-scented afternoon, beneath the cloudless blue sky ringed with white just visible through a canopy of dappled green, guavas and cashews falling around us every once in a while with a thud and a squelch, the air syrupy, tasting of overripe fruit and composting leaves; a pitcher of freshly squeezed lime juice with extra sugar and disintegrating ice cubes—the power having not been on long enough for them to form fully in Sumitranna's freezer—beside us, shiny droplets of condensation twinkling silvery blue on the aluminium surface.

After, we'll go to the shops, Ma, admiring the burst of bougainvillea climbing up the compound of the crematorium, shocking pink against a backdrop of orange bricks velvet green with moss, graves nestling grey and forlorn amongst overgrown weeds the emerald hue of a placid sea just after a thunderstorm.

In the evening, as dusk tints the sky the ghostly grey of unrequited yearning, you will massage my hair with warm coconut oil and the nutty smell will inveigle into my dreams as I drowse on the stoop, Bobby a warm heft on my lap.

This season there have been so many mangoes, alphonso and thothapuri varieties, and I will save them all for you. When Jalajakka comes back from looking after her mother, she and I will pickle some in brine and store others in straw in the roof next to the coconut frond mats so you can feast on them when you come home.

Ma, do you remember how you always had a tumbler of tea ready when I came home from college, spiced with elaichi and cardamom and plenty of sugar and milk, and a snack with it—onion bhaji, aloo paratha? You would sit and watch me eat hungrily, waiting until I was full before eating yourself. You would have come from a full day's work cleaning other people's houses and then make this for me. You must have been so tired. Yet I never appreciated it, getting annoyed when you wanted to hear about my day, when you said, 'Talk to me, Devi.' Annoyed with that hangdog expression of need, of love writ large on your face.

Afterwards, after I had eaten my fill, you would say, 'So, what shall we cook today?' And we would stand side by side, chopping onions, tomatoes, chicken and once in a rare while, mutton—a smidgen of meat clinging to a profusion of bones, which you cooked with plenty of potatoes to bulk it up. 'The mutton infuses the curry with such flavour,' you'd say as you added chilli powder and chopped tomatoes to the bubbling concoction, emanating a potpourri of wonderful smells. I would watch over your shoulder as you cooked, and Bobby would dribble at the kitchen doorway, his tongue hanging out, drool pooling onto the steps leading down from the kitchen.

You would laugh, 'Look at the both of you, hungry for your dinner.'

Ma, remember those lazy Sunday afternoons, lying on the cool stone floor in the front room, door open, jasmine-infused breeze drifting in, Bobby fast asleep in the courtyard, the wind teasing the leaves on the trees, the fields draped in a summer haze, the smell of chicken curry mixed in with the phenyl used to mop the floor lingering? You would open the newspaper to read and in a couple of moments, you would be snoring, an arm flung across your eyes, hair and sari awry, cocooned in a newspaper blanket that flapped in the barley-scented air that wafted in, bringing various sounds with it: Sumitranna's cat screeching as she was chased by his dog for trying to steal the fish bones from his bowl; the neighbourhood children yelling hello as they walked past on their way to school after lunch, in between dissecting the previous day's India-Sri Lanka test cricket match; snatches of the song Somu hummed as he bathed his buffalo in the stream below and, very faintly, Nagappa's screams as his wife whipped him with a hibiscus branch for spending the previous day's earnings on arrack, sleeping in the gutter and staggering home in time for lunch. You would jolt awake, and I would smile, reaching across to pat your cheek crisscrossed with lines, shadowy imprints of the patterns gracing the worn cane mat you were lying on, and you would lay your hand on mine and smile right along with me.

Do you remember feast days, Ma—the excitement of guests arriving, the house full to bursting with people so we couldn't turn round without bumping into someone, you laughing for once without worry lines creasing your forehead, the rich smell of feast food, all the best dishes prepared for the guests: vegetable bhath and chicken sukka, kori kachpu and fish fry, kori roti and sambar and semige payasa for afters...?

Ma, the chickens peck busily at the cracked earth; frogs croak and crows caw as I write this. The air is perfumed with jasmine and the heady rich scent of mango, tinged with the spicy tang of tamarind and the sweet, milky whiff of paddy ripening in the sun. In the far field, a trio of birds perch on a cow as it grazes in the fields. Nagappa's wife gossips with Aarthiappa's, baskets filled to bursting with the ambades they had been picking off the tree balancing neatly on their hips, their bodies curved in the shape of the letter 'S'. Aarthiappa's son sits among the branches of the ambade tree, only his knobbly knees and sticklike hairy legs visible, dangling down like adventitious roots, his job being to give the branches a shake to dislodge any remaining ambades. He yells down to his mother, a disembodied voice coming from the bowels of the tree like God speaking: 'Is that enough?' She nods yes without looking up, hefting her basket from one hip to the other, her mouth busily working as she continues her discussion with Nagappa's wife.

The evening breeze blows fragrant on my face, twirling leaves on the trees and displacing mango- scented drops, carrying a whiff of rain and ripening pineapples. Twilight slowly saps the sky of colour and I sit here, letting the mosquitoes feast on me, not minding the flies that buzz, the crickets that chirp. Darkness descends slowly, an inky black curtain draining the sky of colour. On my lap, Bobby sleeps, nose twitching, waking up only when I stop scratching behind his ears, blinking up at me, a wounded expression in his caramel eyes.

Here, where I sit by the front door, all is quiet. Silence weighs down upon the house like clouds pregnant with condensation just before the heavens open. No Jalajakka sweeping her compound, her sari pallu tucked into her waist as she is wont to this time of day, no rhythmic thwack, thwack, thwack of broomstick hitting cement. No rustling of Sumitranna's *Udayavani*, as he sits on his veranda, slurping on sur, munching on chuda and squinting at the newspaper in the waning light.

Jalajakka, Sumitranna and their son have gone to Jalajakka's village, to care for her mother who is very ill. Ma, after I left for England, they looked after you, didn't they, making sure you ate on time, filling the silence with conversation, populating the lethargic hours that stretched endlessly before you with anecdotes, stories, the steady patter of their company? But once they left, you succumbed to loneliness, you forgot to eat, you fell ill... If Shali had not come looking for you when she did... I owe her a huge debt of gratitude.

The coconut trees silhouetted against a coffee sky whisper confidences in the conspiratorial breeze; lights twinkle in the darkness ahead, my baby jumps inside me and I miss you, Ma. I wish you were here, sharing this evening with me.

Come back to me, Ma, do. I will look after you and keep you company. I will not get irritated, impatient, angry with you. I will not yell at you and walk off in a huff. I will love you like you deserve to be loved. I will.

Yours,

Devi

Chapter 21
Shilpa

Semige Payasa and Goli Baje

Semige Payasa:

Ingredients:

1 cup semige/vermicelli
3 cups milk
1 cup granulated sugar
6 cardamom pods, peeled and seeds crushed to fine powder
2 tbsp ghee
12 cashew nuts
2 tbsp raisins

Method:

1. Heat the ghee in a pan and roast the cashew nuts in them until they are golden brown. Add raisins and fry until they plump up and take on a polished amber tinge. Take them out using a porous ladle and add vermicelli to the pan, roast till the vermicelli turns a warm honey colour.

2. Now add the milk.
3. Once cooked, add sugar and reduce the flame to low. Leave the mixture be until it simmers gently—around six minutes.
4. Switch off the flame and stir in powdered cardamom and the cashew nuts and raisins.
5. And there you have it—Semige Payasa, a treat fit for the kings.

❄ ❄ ❄

Dear Diary,

Semige Payasa is traditionally served at feasts, weddings and celebrations. And do I have something to celebrate! After years of waiting, wanting, yearning—I am a mother! Am writing this quickly, between chores—oh, if I thought I was busy before… not a moment to myself now and that is just how I want it. Any free moment and I ruminate; Manoj's face flashes before my eyes.

I have stolen moments from my other chores to put it all on paper, the fantastic miracle that is giving birth—lest I forget. My memory is not the best these days—too many things to do and not enough time, so tiny details escape into the recesses of my mind never to be retrieved again: the colour of Manoj's eyes when he wanted me, the expression on his face at the moment of waking—and I do not want to forget a thing, not a minuscule detail of the birth, not even the pain of labour. It will never happen again for me, this miracle of conception and birth. It is done now and I have such a fantastic reward to show for it.

So… one March morning, four weeks before I was due, my baby decided it wanted out. Later, the matrons would say it was the trauma of losing Manoj that caused the labour to start early. And I would agree.

But first: 01:00 a.m., March the twentieth announced its presence with a storm that thrashed the mango trees into frenzy and churned the fields into muddy slush. Thunder bellowed and lightning ducked behind clouds, scratching dazed 'V's and 'Z's on an ink-splattered canvas. The power was robbed by an ostentatious flash that targeted the electricity pole swaying in the fields. Rain drummed, flies sang and the dogs sleeping on verandas complained as they were sprayed with jets of water angling in on gusts of breeze.

I woke. Drenched in sweat, speechless with pain, mattress wet. My waters had broken. Another thunderstorm. Another crisis. Relentlessly pushing away memories of that other thunderstorm, sweeping the pain, the guilt that threatened to undo me to a corner of my mind, I shook Jalaja, who had taken to sleeping with me after what happened ('Only until the baby arrives,' she had said when I assured her I was fine, 'just in case'), awake. 'The baby…'

Jalaja ran next door in the blinding rain and Sumitranna arrived, hastily tying his lungi. He picked me up, despite the fact that I was doubly heavy with pregnancy, and carried me through the fields, his tread heavy and deliberate so as not to slip on the mud path which was disintegrating to slush beneath his feet. He carried me, my sari wet and sticking to a swollen body that jerked with convulsions every once in a while, tears of pain running down my cheeks and mingling with the rain, all the way to the road where Anthu was waiting with his rickshaw.

This is what Jalaja told me later: She had run to Anthu's house in the darkness without even waiting to light a candle, slipping once or twice in the sludge and almost drowning in the stream which was swollen to twice its size and was writhing in fury, the lightning that illuminated the sky every so often leading the way. She had banged on Anthu's door until he woke and stood in the doorway in his lungi and holey vest, bleary-eyed, staring at the muddy apparition stooped in front of him, dripping water and muck and shouting in Jalaja's voice to get a move on. I am sure Anthu was convinced he was having a nightmare, that Jalaja—whom he had always fancied and who had previously appeared in his dreams in a completely different guise—had transformed into this monster, this ghoulish apparition, to torment him, that God was teaching him a lesson for coveting what didn't belong to him. He clutched at his crotch for comfort, blubbering until Jalaja stepped forward, shook him vigorously and ordered him to take his hand away from his crotch and place it on the steering wheel of his auto straightaway because Shilpamma was having her baby.

Anthu was promised triple fare if he rushed all the way to the hospital, and he did. The nurse checked me and said I wasn't dilated enough. 'But the waters broke…' I said, willing my voice not to break too. 'Wait and see,' the nurse said curtly before moving on to the next patient. The contractions came and went, more painful each time. Jalaja sponged my forehead while Sumitranna went back to their boy.

Around midday, there was a loud din just outside the hospital. Women yelling and hitting their heads. Men huddled in groups, hitching up their lungis and talking busily, their expressions serious. The rain had cleared sometime during the morning and the sun, not taking lightly to being out-shadowed, was burning with a vengeance, in a mood to evaporate every stubborn drop clinging to the leaves.

I was in a long room, the general women's ward—beds on either side hosting women in various stages of agony. No door to the room, only a thin cloth curtain that lifted with what little breeze there was, on either end. One end led onto a corridor which connected with the men's ward, the toilets and the operating theatre. The other opened onto a balcony and if I craned my neck, I could see the entrance to the hospital and the mud road outside, even the little shop selling tea and vadai by the gate. This was where the men had congregated, sipping tea in hushed concentration, their expressions serious. Something had happened.

Jalaja walked in, averting her eyes from the sight of other women's distress, knowing they didn't want her to partake in it.

'What's happened?' I asked, between contractions.

'The Chief Minister of Karnataka is dead. Heart attack. They are closing the hospital. People are upset. Their relatives are suffering and need medical help.' She paused, wiped her forehead which was gleaming with droplets of sweat. 'I went to the nurse and fell at her feet, saying I would not leave until your baby was born safe and sound…'

'Oh,' I said, reaching out to squeeze my neighbour's hand, my eyes stinging with tears. 'Thank you.'

'But it didn't help, amma,' Jalaja said, grimacing. 'That stupid nurse asked me to stop the dramatics and free her leg, that you were not going anywhere, but the doctor was not coming in.' Jalaja sounded out of breath. 'I asked her, "What if something happens?" "Well, we'll see then, won't we," was that stupid, heartless nurse's reply. Pah!' She spat loudly and dramatically out the window and came back to perch at my bedside.

Several of the women had turned to watch Jalaja, transfixed. Now, they went back to moaning and groaning and sighing and complaining, while their husbands gossiped and discreetly partook of cashew feni outside, near the hospital gates.

Her narration finished, Jalaja lifted the aluminium jug on the table beside me and tipped its entire contents into her open mouth from a height, not missing a drop. Some of the women cheered. 'Don't worry, amma, I will stay here and look after you,' she said when she was able to take a breath.

'I know,' I managed before another wrenching contraction took possession of me again.

Something did happen. The baby was stuck. It was facing the wrong way and couldn't come out. I pushed and pushed to no avail. 'Where's the doctor?' I panted between contractions.

'No doctor, this hospital is supposed to be closed, the Chief Minister is dead, and I am left looking after twenty women all having their babies at once and not one of them straightforward,' muttered the nurse, taking out her frustration on me.

'Please… my baby.'

Jalaja fell at the nurse's feet again and was rewarded by a kick in the shins. 'Do you want me to help your amma or do you want to lie in the next bed? Because if you don't let go, I am going to kick you senseless.'

'Get me Devi,' I yelled amid contractions. 'Someone, please get me Devi.' Once she understood who I was talking about, Jalaja paid one of the jobless boys hanging by the little shop outside the gate of the hospital with her own money and asked him to fetch the madwoman who sat by the peepal tree. Jalaja told me later that as soon as he heard the word 'madwoman', the boy crossed himself, held out the money he had pocketed and refused to budge from his stance under the thatched roof of the shop.

'What are you crossing yourself for? You are not Christian,' Jalaja yelled.

'A Christian God will do as well as any,' the boy retorted.

'Look at you, cheeky; if your mother knew you were talking back like this, what would she say?' Jalaja yelled, and the boy had the grace to blush. 'And where are my other five rupees? I gave you ten and you are returning only five.'

The boy's face flushed even more and he held out the other five rupees.

'If my amma didn't need me by her side, I would go get that harmless old woman myself,' Jalaja grumbled. 'What do you think she will do to you?'

'Curse me, kill me, who knows? I can't read the mind of a madwoman!'

'No one's asking you to! Now, here's fifteen rupees. Go quickly—I need to get back to amma, sponge her head.'

'She'll curse me,' he repeated.

'Nonsense,' spat Jalaja, losing patience—never her best virtue—a mouthful of betel juice staining the boy's Bata chappals.

'Hey, watch out, they're new. Twenty rupees I paid for them,' he complained. And, 'She'll set the serpent which lives in the anthill beside her on me.'

'Nonsense.' Jalaja's palm itched to slap his insolent cheek, but for once she showed restraint, knowing that it would serve no purpose, that none of the other boys would agree to go fetch that old woman I had taken a fancy to (Why on earth couldn't I have liked someone more accepted by society? thought Jalaja, irritably), and she would have to abandon me in my moment of need and go herself. She settled for coaxing him instead, keeping her mounting fury in check—just— and consenting to pay him twice the original amount. And at last, just as she was losing her rag, he agreed.

And the madwoman, who, to everybody's knowledge, had never left the peepal tree except for when she disappeared weeks at a time no one knew where, came to the hospital at the boy's summons. The boy did not even go up to her, Jalaja told me later. He stood on the opposite side of the road, made a cone of his hands and yelled across, amid the blaring horns of the bus, the barks of the dogs and the mooing of the cows that Shilpamma needed her at the hospital. When Jalaja found this out, last week, from Shali the fisherwoman, she saw red. She hunted out the boy, who was lounging with his friends near the cycle repair shop, sitting on a pile of dusty rubber tubes and eyeing the girls sewing in the tailor shop opposite. She held him by the scruff of his neck and shook him, hard. 'Give me back my money. Thirty rupees I paid you—for what, to yell across the road?' She shook him once more, until she could hear his teeth chattering. 'You can keep five; give me back twenty-five,' she screamed, much to his friends' chagrin, as the girls in the tailor shop watched agog, giggling nervously. 'Or have you spent it already? What are you looking at?' She bellowed at his friends, who had identical horror-struck expressions on their faces. Her gaze then landed on the girls. 'Mr Prashant, what are you paying your girls for? To work or watch the show?' she shouted, and they bent their heads simultaneously and started working the sewing machines, wheels turning, needles clicking, feet tapping in unison.

Meanwhile, back at the hospital, I had lost my will to push, to do anything at all. I was so tired. Weighted lids dragged my eyes down towards blessed oblivion, free of pain. Just as I was giving in to that impulse, I glimpsed gnarled hands pushing the curtain aside and Devi the wise woman's long stride bridging the distance between the doorway and my bed, her weather-beaten face, the bushy grey hair and matching eyes oozing serenity. I relaxed. I knew then that my baby would be fine. Devi put both hands on my stomach and kneaded gently and I felt my baby shift. 'Push,' Devi urged, her steely gaze imbibing in me the strength I needed. I thrust with all my might and my baby popped out, blue in the face, floppy, limp. Devi held the baby in her arms very gently and then, to the fascinated horror of everyone present, Jalaja, the nurse and even me, who trusted her completely, dangled the baby upside down and shook her hard. 'No!' we all screamed in unison, and a tiny mewling cry joined our wails. Pink-faced, angry, the baby screamed at the top of her voice.

'She's so fair, a real beauty. Looking at all those foreign babies helped, amma,' said Jalaja, laughing through her tears.

'Wait, it's not over yet,' the wise woman said in her gravelly voice, handing my baby over to Jalaja, who cooed and gushed in a way I had rarely witnessed. 'Do you still feel the urge to push?' the wise woman asked of me, kneading my stomach.

I nodded, unable to speak. I wanted to hold my baby and yet my body was convulsing, the urge to push still strong.

'Go on,' the wise woman said, steel-grey eyes soft as they held my exhausted gaze. 'Push.'

I pushed, hard. There was a gushing sound, the feeling of something moving down and plopping out. I looked down, shocked. Another baby!

The room erupted. 'Twins, she has twins.' 'We didn't have a clue.' 'No doctor, that's why,' Jalaja's strident barb directed at the nurse.

I have two children, I thought, joy beginning to swell out of me in exalted waves.

More shouts. 'Another girl! What's the matter with her face?' And the nurse, her voice high-pitched, 'A monster, she has given birth to a monster.'

I am being punished, I thought, as my little girl's face came into view, *for what I did to Manoj*. The wise woman subjected this baby to the same treatment as my other, and she let out a plaintive mewl through the open wound that she had in lieu of a mouth. *Why punish my child for my mistakes, Lord?* I asked. *Why her face, Lord?* I knew the answer of course. For a girl, her face is her fortune. The best way to punish a mother is to give her a daughter who has no prospects, no groom asking for her hand in marriage.

I have two babies, I thought, before slipping into oblivion.

Dear Diary, I have to go; one of my babies has woken up—she needs me. I look at the words written down, 'she needs me', and my eyes fill up with tears. I am blessed twice over. I am a mother.

❄ ❄ ❄

Goli Baje:

Ingredients:

Maida flour–1 cup

Curds (yogurt)–½ cup

Curry leaves–12
Ginger–thumbnail-sized piece, chopped
Green chillies–2 chopped
Half of a fresh coconut, flesh chopped into bite-sized pieces
Baking powder–¼ tbsp
Salt to taste
Oil for frying

Method:

1) Mix maida flour, yogurt and salt to make a thick batter. Add water if required. Let it sit for three hours.

2) Add the rest of the ingredients to the batter and mix.

3) Heat oil in a frying pan and when it's hot, scoop a ping-pong-ball-sized helping of dough into the pan. Turn until both sides are a deep golden brown.

4) Scoop out using a porous ladle and serve with coconut chutney and sambar.

❄ ❄ ❄

Dear Diary,

My babies are sleeping now, my twin blessings. Right here in front of me. I watch them as I write. To me, they are both beautiful, but not so in the eyes of the village. Word spread like wildfire of course, and as soon as I was discharged from hospital, the matrons paid me a visit, 'Aiyyo Devare,' they sighed. 'What a calamity to befall a girl child,' they lamented, hitting their foreheads with the palms of their hands.

I bristled but said nothing.

'Did you eat only white foods, think only good thoughts?' they asked.

'Yes,' I muttered, wishing they would leave, holding the subject of their musings close, marvelling at her skin like milk, those inky black eyes like twin sparks charged with life squinting up at me, while the matrons passed my other daughter, my firstborn, around, oohing and aahing at her fair skin, her rosebud mouth, her blemish-less perfection.

'Were you guilty of praying only to Lord Ganapathy perhaps? It doesn't do to single out any one God, you know; the others get angry and cause mischief.'

Outside, the rain that had drummed a continuous lullaby when I got my girls home had stopped and the sun was peeking out from behind the clouds. The fields sparkled gold-green, and muddy brown water overflowed onto the paths. Crows squawked and the air smelled fresh, tangy.

'I prayed to all the gods equally,' I lied, hoping any gods listening and catching me out in my lie wouldn't smite me.

'Perhaps,' they said, chewing thoughtfully on the goli bajes I had made (the maida, coconut and all the ingredients in my kitchen supplied kindly, despite my token protests, by Sumitranna and Jalaja), helping themselves to more. My goli bajes, they all agree, are the best in the village.

My secret is chopping the coconut instead of grating it, so there's an unexpected crunch when you bite through the crisp outer layer and expect only soft flesh, and the coconut explodes in honey syrupiness in your mouth, the sweetness offset by the spiciness of the chilli. 'Perhaps, you are being punished because of some sin you committed in your previous life.' They eyed me thoughtfully, and I eyed them right back, refusing to give them the satisfaction of knowing how close to home they had struck.

Yes, I was being punished, but not for sins in my previous life. Manoj's face, his eyes full of pain. 'Stay,' he had pleaded. 'Please stay with me.'

'Why did the gods not punish me, then? Why my baby?' I asked, smiling at my beautiful girl. She tried to smile back, she did. All she could produce was a grotesque parody. I hugged her close. 'You are beautiful,' I whispered. 'You are.'

'Well, dear, the gods operate in strange ways. Perhaps they thought the best way to punish a mother was through her child.'

I had burst into tears then, despising myself for my weakness, and the matrons had descended on me like a pack of vultures on carrion, trying to soothe and console but only managing to scare the baby into ear-rending wails.

I look back to what I wrote not in my last entry but the one previous, the wise woman's last prediction. 'Your greatest test is yet to come. One to keep, one to lose.' Now it is perfectly clear what she meant by it. This is why I write everything down, so I can refer back, join the dots, make sense of what is happening. So, I have to lose one. Which one? And how can I? Why should I? This is the question I asked of the wise woman when I went to visit…

The doctors came back to work the day after my babies were delivered safely to me by the wise woman, well rested after their break thanks to the Chief Minister's timely demise. As soon as my babies and I were discharged, I took off along the well-worn path between the fields, my twin blessings wrapped in swaddling snug in my arms, fresh goli bajes that I had cooked slung in a basket at my side. Birds gossiped, the ears of paddy chattered, revelling in the sugarcane-scented haze of late summer, and my heart overflowed. In the dappled shadow cast by the peepal tree branches, I lay my babies down. The sun's rays filtered through the canopy of leaves, casting a burnished glow on the worn cane mat where my girls squirmed.

The wise woman's face softened when she touched the babies, one after the other, and she looked so much younger. She was the only one who could look at my poor wounded baby without flinching, apart from me. Even Jalaja winced, avoided looking at her, though she tried to hide it.

'Why?' I asked. 'Why did Lord Ganapathy punish my girl for what I did?'

And the wise woman looked at me and her eyes were soft, full of an emotion I later identified as affection, love even. Towards me. I am not worthy of love. I hurt those who love me, I leave them to die.

'Why do you think it is a punishment? Why can't it be a blessing?'

'That?' I asked, 'A disfigured face, for a girl. A blessing? How will I get her married? What prospects does she have in life?'

The wise woman smiled. 'You might be surprised,' was all she said.

'You said in your prophesy that I would have to lose one.' My heart in my throat.

The woman sighed deeply. 'You were not supposed to have children. You tricked fate. It wants repayment.'

'I have already repaid many times over.'

'Not yet,' she sighed. 'Not completely.'

'Destiny. Fate. Who says it's all decided for us? Who? Aren't we meant to create our own destiny?'

She didn't reply. She didn't have to. Just looked at me with those grey eyes full of love. She was the proof, right there in front of me, that our fate is decided for us. It's written in the stars long before we are born. We are given choices along the way, of a sort. This woman had known what I would choose. Pregnancy: my girls over my husband.

'You told me to protect them. And now you want me to stand by and lose one of them because fate decreed so? How is that possible?' I ranted, unmindful of the hot tears coursing down my cheeks. 'Why do I have to? I love them both. How can I bear to lose one of them now they are here?' I would not ask if by *lose* she meant one would die. I would not contemplate that possibility.

The wise woman said nothing, just patted my hand. My girls didn't cry, just wiggled their arms as the late afternoon light played hide and seek on their downy, fair skin and tinted it gold.

'Children. They are given to you for such a short while. You have to make the most of it. And they are never yours to keep, not really.' The wise woman sighed, a world of pain in her voice. 'I had a little boy once.'

I stared at my friend, tears collecting in my open mouth.

'Long ago. In another life. He died. Snake bite.' It was my turn to squeeze my friend's hand.

'The goat screamed. I went to tend to it. My husband was a drunkard. The goat was our livelihood. I used to sell its milk and feed the boy from the proceeds. So I tended to the goat and meanwhile the snake had free rein on my boy. The goat lived. My boy died. '

The bus gave a loud mournful horn as it trundled past. Someone giggled, the sound harsh. A mother yelled at her daughter as she dragged her along the road.

'My husband took up with another woman, kicked me out. For a while I was genuinely mad.' My friend took a deep, gasping breath. 'You've asked me many times why I pretend to be mad. It suits me to do so. It affords me freedom. I can do anything I want and nobody questions it, just chalks it down to my madness. After what happened, I lost myself, forgot who I was. I ended up at the temple at the confluence of the river and the sea, where your girls were conceived. I ranted and railed at Lord Ganapathy. I said,

"Why, Lord, why didn't you let me see into the future?" And then one evening just as the sun was dipping into the sea—the sky was a warm orangey red, I remember—He appeared before me. "I am giving you the gift," he said, "of being able to see into the future." I laughed. "Too late now, Lord," I said. But He was gone. The sky was black. The sun was nowhere to be seen…'

She stopped, spent. I put my arm around her. This friend of mine who had suffered so. At least my daughters were alive. My daughters were safe, wiggling their arms, resting peacefully right here in front of me.

'Your gift. It helped me. *You* helped me,' I said softly. And then, 'Aren't you going to ask me what I am going to name them?' The woman's intense gaze met mine. 'My firstborn is called Devi—named after the Goddess who eased her into this world.'

The woman's gaze did not falter, just became cloudy. I watched as one by one the tears brimmed over and traversed down the lined face. That was the only time I ever saw the wise woman—Devi—cry, that sun-kissed afternoon when she blessed my newborn baby girls.

'And this one,' holding the one whose face would mark her, the one I loved even more, if that was possible, close, 'I am going to call Nisha—the Goddess of Night.' My friend had said that I would be surprised, when I asked her what prospects this daughter would have. I hugged that assurance close.

Before I left, I asked one question: 'Which one? Please tell me which one, so I can prepare myself.'

'How?' the wise woman's eyes were soft. 'By loving her less or loving her more? Enjoy them, Shilpa. Enjoy them both for as long as you can.'

And I am. I am enjoying every moment.

Yesterday, I pulled the last of Manoj's savings out from under the mattress, the thought of him an arrow in the region of my left breast, swaddled my babies in my sari, tucked it around their tender heads so the sun wouldn't cause havoc on their delicate skin, and took the bus into town. My babies rested one on either side of my heart, snug, and in that moment, as they slept swaying to the rhythm of the bus struggling over potholes, secure in the warmth of my body, I was content. I went to Shankar's photo studio which nestles between the electronics shop and the sari emporium, huffing and out of breath by the time I had climbed the dark stairs smelling of mould and stale curry to the top. I laid my precious bundles down on the sheet and asked Shankar to take a picture, pressing the last of my money into his palm. He turned to them, smiling and I watched his smile freeze in place, be replaced by revulsion as he took my Nisha in.

I stood up very straight, looked right at him. 'I want a picture of the two of them.'

He hugged his camera close. 'She might put a curse on it,' he said, pointing at my innocent little girl, whose little fisted hands waved at me, and I was glad she wasn't old enough to understand a word of the exchange.

'She is just a baby. Don't you have children?' I asked.

I watched a flush darken his sooty skin. He lifted his camera, took a picture. Devi smiled, delighted at the flash. Nisha tried to. She did.

Once upon a time, I wished for a family, a husband, a bevy of children. I neglected to be specific. I did not ask that they all be with me at the same time. I got a husband, I lost him. I got two children—a miracle—and I will lose one. But for now, I watch them, I love them, hold them close, breathe them in, enjoy them. Some people do not even get this much. The privilege, the honour of calling themselves wife, mother. I have been given both. I thank you, Lord Ganapathy, many times over.

Chapter 22
Nisha

Yellow-Winged Rickshaws

The church is smaller than Nisha remembers, the ceiling not as high. And yet, everything else is the same as in her memories. The aroma of votive, incense, prayer. She feels peace settle inside her like a blessing. She looks at the pews, the dank wood smell, and wonders how she ever squeezed in under there. She lays her head down and looks up and, yes, she can see dust motes swirling, she can imagine why a four-year-old might think those were prayers swirling upwards towards God via chinks in the orange Mangalore tiles, which from down here look haloed and bright red, painted as they are with dappled light that dances from above. She walks up to the altar, and she can picture it: a little child hefted in the arms of the priest, the procession of nuns, a flock of white habits, following. She squats in front of the altar. The stone tiles are cool under her palms. She looks up. The statue of Jesus on the cross, his head haloed by the crown of thorns, his bloodied benevolent face looking down at her. Underneath that a gold curtain, which she knows if parted will reveal a tiny arched gold door which houses the consecrated Eucharist. To the left, a statue of the Holy Family. A boy Jesus flanked by his parents. Mary in her blue-and-white smock, Joseph in his brown one holding a cane, sporting a beard. And to her right, the Mother Mary of Miracles. A statue. The lips are closed, painted on. The eyes open and looking at her. She is neither smiling nor frowning. She looks peaceful. Nisha lies down on the cool floor where she assumes they must have laid her child self. A dove coos up in the rafters, a black shadow silhouetted against the orange speckled light. She looks towards the altar. Everything is as it was before, except for the Mother Mary of Miracles.

Nisha blinks, sits up. *Must have been my imagination making a reappearance after a hiatus of twenty years,* she thinks. *I can see why people think miracles happen. It is easily done.* This place, the soothing aura of peace, the words of the nun at the fore of her mind… *That's all,* she thinks, as she walks out into the blinding sunshine. *That must be why I could have sworn the statue smiled at me.*

❄ ❄ ❄

'I was a miracle child,' she says into the phone, which mercifully has managed to locate a weak signal. The sun beats down on her scalp, hot, insistent. Beads of perspiration stream down her face and collect around her lips depositing salty kisses.

'I knew that from the first moment I met you,' Matt says and she laughs, for the first time since she set foot in this strange country and embarked on a ride that feels headier than being on the highest rollercoaster.

Hot tears squeeze out from between closed, sun-baked lids as she tells him the story of her miraculous recovery. 'I think when they laid me down on the cool floor, my fever broke. I think that explains it. I was swaddled in garments, overheated. So when they laid me down…' The Mother Mary of Miracles' tranquil face, exuding contentment, the painted lips that she had imagined for a moment had lifted in a smile…

His voice is soft, very gentle as he says, 'I believe them totally. There is something special about you. I have always known.'

She tries on a laugh, the sound hollow. 'You are joking, right, Matt?'

'No, I am not. You don't have to find an explanation for everything, Nisha. Let go. Believe. There are some things out there greater than you and I…'

'But, Matt, you are a mathematician…'

'There are so many things science cannot explain. Open up your mind, Nisha. You might be surprised.'

'You will be surprised,' the nun had said… And the thought of the nun brings back the images of Sister Priya, beloved Sister Priya. 'I… I met Sister Priya. She recognised me, instantly, despite the years, despite the fact that when she last saw me I was a child. How could I have forgotten her, Matt, wiped out memories of her out so completely? I loved her. I love her so.'

'You were four, Nisha.' His voice is soft. 'Just a child. Lost and lonely. Torn between two different countries, straddling two lives—not wanting to be disloyal to the two strangers you were told were your new mum and dad. Your mind shut down, unable to cope. Trauma does that to a person. Try not to be too hard on yourself.'

How does he know her better than she knows herself?

Birds twitter among the branches of the banyan tree across the road. An auto filled to bursting with schoolchildren packed like Twiglets on top of each other, a few of them overflowing into the front sharing the seat meant for one person with the driver, creaks past, the chatter of excited conversations, the music of children's voices floating up to her. 'But…'

'You've found her now,' Matt says softly.

'She's dying.' One of the boys milling outside the building down the road whistles—a plaintive sound.

'You met her. She recognised you.' A burst of static. 'She knows you care, Nisha.'

When Sister Priya had smiled, her cataract-dimmed eyes shining bright and clear, Nisha had seen in the papery face crinkled like a mouldy onion the ghost of the woman she had been once, the woman who had populated her dreams. 'Yes. She does.'

A pause, then…'Matt.' She wants him here, with her, this man who understands her so, who makes her feel complete. She closes her eyes, pictures him. His sandy hair, the way the lock at his crown refuses to do his bidding no matter how much gel he uses, those twinkling aquamarine eyes that only have to look at her a certain way to turn her insides to liquid, the blond fuzz on his face in the mornings, the lemony musk smell of him, the way his arms can envelop her and make her feel she has come home. The depth of her feeling for him terrifies her because it leaves her without control, vulnerable, open to hurt. It is love. She knows this, has always known but has shied away from it, been afraid to accept it, because she cannot prove it, will never be able to prove it. But, she realises as she leans against the gates of the church, the smell of rust and iron with an undertone of something spicy making her want to gag, some things have to be taken on faith.

She takes a deep breath. Something has unfurled inside her, is blooming, slowly but surely, is pushing past the plug in her throat, is bursting out despite the clamped lips, 'I love you, Matt.'

She can hear his smile down the crackly, disturbed line populated by gremlins. 'Another miracle has occurred.' His joyous laughter bubbling down the static-infested line in infectious waves starts her off. And she stands there, the dust swirling around her, sweat drooling down her back, sandals biting into her feet, laughing until tears deposit briny caresses on her cheeks. It occurs to her that she hasn't laughed like this in ages. She feels unfettered, free. Despite the fact that she has yet to meet the woman who birthed her and then gave her away, despite the fact that her twin sister and father still elude her. She will find them, she knows, and the certainty fills her heart with the calm her calculations used to, once upon a time, in another world.

She does not know how and when but she knows she will. This is just the kind of thing her parents would have pooh-poohed, a conviction based not on fact, but on intuition.

'It is lovely to hear you laugh, albeit down a horribly poor line. I miss you so. Come back to me, Nisha,' Matt says.

'I will.' A motorbike starts with a rev and a whirr, the putter of the engine fading into the distance. Dirt swirls, making the air shimmer, assaulting her nose, stinging her eyes. Water sloshes from the pot of a woman effortlessly hefting a pail on her head, shiny drops glinting on her chocolate arms and standing out in relief against her red-and-gold-sequinned sari as she sways gracefully down the road, scarlet bangles clinking, silvery anklets teasing. 'Matt, I know who she is and where to find her. The woman who gave birth to me.' She cannot bring herself to say 'Mother'. 'I am…' The rest of her words are eaten by noise. Stomping, thundering noise as if a herd of elephants is bearing down on her. What is happening? A stampede?

In her ear, as if from a distance, she hears, 'Nisha? You there? What's that sound?' panic-laced.

'I don't know,' she yells, but her voice is drowned out.

A thousand voices buzzing busily. Marching feet. A man on a moped weaves unsteadily, brakes, and comes to a standstill next to her. A boy, looking to be about five, wearing a white robe with a red collar, walks past waving a round gold ball with holes, suspended on a chain, infusing the salty air with the distinct smell of camphor. He is followed by a couple of slightly older boys, wearing similar robes, marching with their hands wrapped around thick gold candlesticks, sprouting creamy candles topped with licking, dancing flames. A priest behind them, hands folded, expression serene, decked in gold and violet dress robes. Behind him, eight men bent heft a life-size statue of Christ on the cross replete with sainted expression and the halo of nails, red paint in lieu of blood dripping down his too-white face. Their vests and lungis are stained yellow with sweat and their faces strain with effort. A bevy of women in multi-hued saris follow, in two neat lines, prayer books in hand, mouths working busily. As they pass Nisha, they burst into song, a hymn that is at once familiar as it is alien. A group of bedraggled men, mostly old, bring up the rear. The man next to her executes the sign of the cross, his expression sombre, as the procession trundles slowly past, through the gate behind her and into the church. *That is why the church was so empty,* she thinks. A breeze caresses her face; where a minute ago it had smacked of incense, now it smells of churned earth and sweat with a faint undertone of cinnamon.

'Nisha? Helloooo?'

She turns away from the man who holds on to his moped with one hand and with the other whips from his pocket a blue-and-red-striped handkerchief the size of a dinner plate and wipes his gleaming face. 'Yes, I'm here. I forgot that it's Lent. They are doing Stations of the Cross.' Auto rickshaws honk. The traffic, what little there was, that had come to a standstill due to the procession, resumes.

'You were saying... that you know who your mother is,' his voice gentle.

Your mother came often, asking after you. Sister Priya's words, resounding in her head.

Why did you give me away? And once you did, why did you come back? And when I saw you, recognised you, was about to call out for you, why did you turn away, disappear like a fleeting mirage I had conjured up out of sheer longing? 'Her name is Shilpa. Sister Priya said she lives in Sompur. It must be somewhere near here. Can I rely on Sister Priya's failing memory, Matt?'

'She recognised you, Nisha.'

'Yes.' *And you have nothing else to go on. No other facts to follow up, no other clues…* 'I will make my way there now.'

'Nisha, when you find your mother, remember that it's okay to rave and rant. You are entitled.' His voice is gentle.

He knows exactly how she feels. And he said 'when', not 'if'. Bless this wonderful man she has the privilege of knowing and loving.

The man next to her pockets his handkerchief, climbs onto his moped, releasing a mini-avalanche of dust.

She sneezes.

'Sorry,' he says, kicking the throttle, and the moped springs to life with a phut phut phut.

Inspiration strikes. 'Hang on a minute, Matt,' she says into the phone, and to the man, 'Excuse me, Sir.'

The man looks up at her, his hands on the handlebars. 'Yes?'

She swallows. She might as well. Talking to Matt, knowing he's there, gives her courage. 'Do you know how to get to Sompur?'

The man smiles, the smile lighting up his whole face. 'I am going near there myself. Hop on.'

She stares at him, uncertain. This man is middle-aged, balding, except for his hirsute moustache. *How can you sprout hair above your lips while having none on your head?* she wonders, and then chides herself for thinking of this now.

The man senses her hesitation. 'Don't worry, Ma'am, I am not going to do anything to you. I have two children and a loving wife who's a great cook and I am going home to her cooking now.'

She looks at his earnest shiny face, the globules of sweat beading his moustache, the lines crowding his eyes. 'Matt,' she whispers into the phone, 'this man is offering to take me near Sompur where Shilpa lives.'

'I wish I could be there with you now.'

She knows that he understands exactly how she is feeling. Apprehension mixed in with wary expectation, warring with anger at the woman who birthed her and then gave her away—and hope. Hope of finding her sister hovering cautiously. *When I look at you, will I see myself? When I touch you, will I remember the nine months we spent together in the womb, jostling for space?*

'Good luck,' Matt says softly. 'Stay safe. Call me. I love you, Nisha.'

'Me too,' she whispers. 'I love you too.' This time round it's easier. It is as if there was a boulder in her chest that needed to be moved to allow her to say these things and even perhaps believe in miracles. *I am a miracle child.* Nonsense. And yet, isn't this nothing short of a miracle—she,

Nisha Kamath, pegging a lift on a stranger's moped in an alien country that nevertheless feels like home, to the village that supposedly houses the woman who conveyed her into this world and whose last name she doesn't know? The Nisha Kamath she was a few weeks ago would have blanched at the mere thought of this expedition, would have laughed at this foolhardy mission…

And there was that moment in church when she could have sworn the statue's lips had curved upwards at the sight of her…

And then she is sitting behind a complete stranger, holding on to him with all her might as the scooter trundles over the stones and bumps in the road of this extraordinary country which has populated her dreams this past week and is fast becoming familiar and, she thinks, much beloved, as they race past lorries which horn constantly, seemingly for pure sport, a grating sound fit to burst eardrums, as they squeeze in between two lurching buses with a temerity that terrifies her, the people hanging out of them almost falling on top of her. The wind, which carries the stench of fish and the tang of spices makes her hair dance and jig, the loose strands buoyantly trailing behind her.

'Are you Catholic?' she asks the man, shouting to be heard above the thrumming song of the wind.

'As Hindu as they come,' the man grins.

'You made the sign of the cross when the procession passed by us.'

He shrugs and the moped sways to the right. 'Oh, that. Catholic school upbringing. And you never know what works. Perhaps their God will help.' He flashes her a grin via the mirror.

We all need something to believe in, she muses. *I had the immutable solidity of numbers until recently. Now, I don't know what to believe.* And yet, this doesn't faze her as it would have a couple of weeks ago. She is happy to defer judgement, and that is an improvement. *I hated waiting, loose ends. I would have rushed to find answers. Now, I am relaxing into the languid pace of the inhabitants of this country, taking things as they come.*

They rush past fields twinkling gold green in the sunlight, past rows of women hawking baskets of jasmine and aboli garlands which they thrust boldly in their faces, past a little bridge with no barriers, the river winking silvery blue below. Nisha closes her eyes until she is sure they are safely past. When she opens them again, they are racing past a couple of small shops; women loaded with baskets and men chewing paan milling beside a bus shelter. A school ground, the red mud sprouting rows of children in uniform—light blue shirt, dark blue trousers and skirts, saluting a man in camouflage khaki the colour of vomit who stands in front of a post from which the Indian flag flutters: orange, white and green stripes, blue spoke eye winking from the centre.

They are approaching a town.

The man comes to a shuddering stop beside an auto rickshaw stand. The drivers in dirty beige uniforms stained red with mud are congregated in a huddle under a copse of bowing coconut trees, lounging possessively beside their yellow-winged rickshaws, smoking and gossiping. They look up as they see her hop off the moped, dusting the skirt of her dress, their keen eyes taking in her clothes and lighting up at the alluring prospect of a moneyed customer. They make a beeline for her as one, like a swarm of flies alighting on freshly slaughtered meat.

'You take an auto from here to Sompur, it's not far. It will cost ten rupees max,' the man says.

'Thank you so much,' she says squeezing his hand gratefully. Should she give him some money for his help? Will that insult him? While she stands there deliberating, one hand reaching for her purse, he grins, 'I don't want payment, Ma'am. Just include me and my family in your prayers, whichever God you favour.' And then, he starts up the moped and is gone and she is beset by rickshaw drivers, a flock of brown faces in brown uniform, all shouting at once, shouting each other down in a mixture of Kannada and broken English. 'I will only charge twenty rupees and take you where you want to go. Flat charge.' 'Don't listen to him; I will put the meter and charge accordingly.' 'Fifteen rupees and not one paisa more.'

She goes with the meter man, and the others mumble and fling their beedis into the street in disdain, reverting to leaning against the trunks of coconut trees, whistling at passing women and gossiping, no doubt, about the driver she chose, who is now looking at her expectantly to tell him where he is taking her.

'Sompur,' she says and after three tries he manages to understand her pronunciation.

'Where in Sompur?' he asks in Kannada.

Ah. She doesn't know. All she has is the name. Shilpa. 'Take me to Sompur,' she says, 'and then we'll see.' Blessedly, he understands, nodding vigorously and starting the rickshaw, or perhaps he doesn't but just wants to get away from the others who are pointing at him, shaking their heads and shouting, 'Lo...'

Dark purple hibiscus flowers nod from gardens and red, white and pink bougainvillea claim compound walls. A man drops a note on the floor and as he bends to pick it up, he kisses it, and touches it to each of his eyes before pocketing it. The air that whips her hair into frenzy and caresses her face smells of a nervous anticipation, tastes of earth and rain. She closes her eyes.

What will she find?

Chapter 23
Devi

Unresponsive Facade

Ma,

I am so angry at you, angrier than I have ever been. I rant and rave. I yell, scaring Bobby who hides among the aboli bushes. I throw your diary and it falls with a flop and a sigh. I loathe you, Ma. I cannot bear to look at you. If I came to the hospital now, I would shake you until I dislodged the truth out of you, an avalanche that finally purged a lifetime of lies, half-truths, aversions.

I am a twin? Me? Why didn't you tell me? Why did you keep it hidden? Who would have thought you were harbouring a secret of such colossal proportions?

I hate you, Ma—your betrayal, your keeping my sister from me. All these years I ached for a sibling to share the burden of your love, the burden I tottered under, the burden I shook off. And all this while I had one!

I called Rohan and he couldn't believe it either. Well, well, what else have you been hiding from me, Ma? If I read the rest of your diary will I find a brother I didn't know I had?

A sister. Mine. Where is she, Ma, this sister I have never known? What have you done with her? Did something happen to her? Did she die? Why do I have no recollection of her at all? How long were we together? Tell me, Ma. Oh, but you can't, can you? You are conveniently unconscious, opportunely escaping accountability.

Is it all there in your diary? The diary I cannot bear to look at right now, the diary I want to tear into a million pieces. You better have a good explanation for what happened, Ma. If you blame it once again on the madwoman, I don't know what I will do. I do not like to be made to look a fool, Ma, as you well know, and especially not by you. I thought I knew you, everything about you. But since I've started reading your diary, I have uncovered secret after secret… culminating in this.

So you were the one who had the twins. Why were you calling on Jalaja then? That is why you were so agitated, that is why… Hang on a minute—did you give my twin away? That is what you said when you came to. You gave her away to the wise woman perhaps? Because she lost her son? Did you? Was that her price for foretelling that you would have a child? The madwoman is long dead. So where is my sister then? Tell me. Speak. Stop hiding behind that unresponsive façade.

I cannot fathom this, cannot come to terms with this gargantuan deceit. The very thought of someone else who shares my genes living and going about their business somewhere gives me goosebumps. Does she know that she has a sister? I don't think so. If I didn't know, how would she?

How could you give her away, Ma, when you had ached and yearned for us, when you had chosen us over your husband, when you clearly loved us both so? Yes, I know I said I understood your need to believe in the wise woman, but not to the point that you give away your child at her say so! I always hated the wise woman but if I had known the whole story, her part in it, before, she would have foreseen her death that much earlier, let me tell you…

I am angry at you. So angry.

I say the name *Nisha* out loud. I roll the syllables round on my tongue. Nothing. Not a glimmer of recollection. I cannot remember her at all. Why? How could I forget such an integral part of me, the twin who shared your womb with me?

My baby grows inside of me and I am already so protective, so furiously in love with her. Just because a madwoman predicts that you will lose your child, how can you believe her, meekly accept it, prepare yourself? How can you let your child go? I am fuming right now; I do not have the wherewithal to read the rest of your blasted words. I would like to see the picture though, that photograph you had taken of the two of us with the last of your money. I want to see my sister. I have flipped through your diary—have ransacked the whole house. I cannot find it. Where is it?

I think of you, Ma, all that you went through, have gone through, the choices you made. I think of you running as fast as your pregnant belly could carry you to the hospital to ensure your babies were okay in the blinding rain, on feet swollen and bruised by being trapped under the mango tree, your hair wet and trailing behind you, while your husband lay desperately in pain, all alone as the mango tree squeezed the breaths out of him. I think of the madwoman telling you, 'This pregnancy will cost you dearly.' And you blindly believing her.

I understand now why I bore the brunt of your love, the love that was meant for the two of us. But was that fair? On me? On her?

On the subject of fairness, is it right that my baby would have been denied an aunt if I hadn't read your diary, found out about my sister? That, supposing Nisha has children, my child would have been denied knowledge of her cousins, like I was denied knowledge of my sister, my twin? Not that I have any idea how to go about finding her, but at least I know *about* her, *of* her now. It was my right and you denied me this joy, this comfort of having a sibling, someone else like me in the world.

This morning at the hospital, Ma, in that stuffy room populated with ghosts of past patients and the pain of more recent occupants, a miracle occurred. Reading all those memories to you worked. You stirred. But this time you were not agitated. This time you did not lash out. 'Manoj,' you called softly. 'Manoj.' And tears squeezed out of your closed eyes, they sparkled on your eyelids, they ran in marked grooves down your face. And then, your lips moved. They moved upwards in a smile. 'Devi,' you smiled. 'Devi.'

And I was blessed.

And then I came home and read your words, read of your deceit, your horrible betrayal.

You will come back to me, Ma. You will come back and tell me where she is so I can find her. My sister. My twin.

You better.

Chapter 24

Shilpa

Bitter Gourd Masala and Mango Pickle

Bitter Gourd Masala:

Ingredients:

Bitter gourd–4 big (approx 1kg)
Onions–3, sliced
Fennel seeds–1 tsp
Turmeric powder–1/2 tsp
Salt–to taste
Fennel seed powder–1 tbsp
Lime juice–2 tbsp
Sugar–to taste
Coconut Oil–1 tbsp

Method:

1. Wash, remove seeds and chop the bitter gourd into coin-sized concentric pieces.

2. Heat the coconut oil in a frying pan.

3. Add the fennel seeds and cook until brown and then add in turmeric powder and mix.

4. Add in the onions and salt and mix. Allow the onions to brown and get caramelised—this might take about 10-12 minutes. Stir frequently.

5. Add in the bitter gourd and a little more salt, just for the bitter gourd.

6. Cover and cook for 10-15 minutes, stirring in between.

7. Once the bitter gourd has cooked, add fennel seed powder, lime juice and sugar. Mix well.

8. Cook for another 5 minutes until all the flavours are mixed in well. Adjust seasoning if needed.

❄ ❄ ❄

Dear Diary,

Once upon a time, there was a girl who dreamed of having a husband to love her, a family all her own. She got it all, though not in the way she had imagined, hoped for. She got the husband. She lost him. She got the family, twin girls, and… lost one. Now all she has is one angry little girl, who will not do her mother's bidding, who misses her sister dreadfully.

Everything the wise woman predicted has happened. The prophesy has finally been fulfilled: I have paid in full. I mourn. I grieve. I rant. I rave.

Mostly, I regret—and it is like having the taste of bitter gourd in your mouth all the time. No matter how much sugar you eat, how many sweets, the acrimonious taste never really goes away.

And I remember. I remember. That fateful day, that monumental decision.

My babies are crying. My babies are crying and they won't stop, their cries getting weaker by the hour, resembling a kitten's pitiful mewls. My babies are hot, so hot, like holding live coals, one in each arm. I rock them, I sing to them, I cannot soothe them. They are inconsolable, they hurt, they look to me with eyes tired beyond their years, and I, who am meant to look after them, make them better, cannot. I have failed. Failed as a mother.

I longed and ached for children, and when the Lord Ganapathy finally blessed me with not one but two—nothing short of a miracle —I cannot afford to keep them, feed them, look after them. Bad mother, that's what I am.

Since Manoj… I have been living off Sumitranna and Jalaja's charity. While I desperately try and fail to relieve my precious babies of their suffering, doubts assail me, accusatory arrows find aim. *I did not feed them enough.* Did they fall ill due to malnutrition? I can't be sure. *Bad mother.*

There is no milk, so I give them drops of water through a pipette. They won't drink. They weep plaintively, hot slack tears squeezing out of barely conscious eyes, their breath like a furnace. Their little emaciated bodies, the ribs in danger of poking through fragile skin the colour of the inside of a watermelon, red and bruised. I put one to each breast, like I used to when they were younger, even though they're too big now, two and a half, even though their teeth will bruise my nipples. They won't latch on, they won't drink. The fever won't relinquish its grip, won't come down.

In desperation, I wrap both in my sari and carry them down the path, through the fields to the wise woman. I lay them down at her feet, on her feet. She doesn't flinch, though her eyes widen at the heat of my poor battered children.

I fall at the wise woman's feet. 'Do something,' I pray. 'Please do something.'

People stare, flinch away from the sight of Nisha's gaping face, her gash of a mouth. They turn away from the pitiful wails racking my daughters' ailing bodies.

'It is time,' the wise woman says.

I look up at her benevolent face crisscrossed with lines, her steel-grey hair, those matching eyes, soft as clouds at dusk.

'One to keep, one to lose,' she says.

'I cannot bear to lose either, I cannot.' I cry. 'Can't you heal them, intervene with Lord Ganapathy on my behalf?' I beg. 'Please.' I catch a hold of her bare feet, my tears washing the grime off them. 'Please.'

'You stole from fate, Shilpa,' she says, and her voice is gentle as twilight ushering out a perfumed summer's evening, soft as a mother's bosom. 'You were warned.'

I want to lash out, hit her, make her feel the hurt, the pain that is tearing me apart. I look at my babies, lying at her feet, mewling in agony. I pick them up; boiling, wailing, wrap them very carefully in my sari, heft them on either side of my heart. 'No,' I tell her, 'I will not lose them. I will not.'

I go to Jalaja. I link my hands as if in prayer, 'Please, I need to take them to hospital,' I say.

She covers my hands with her own rough, callused ones. 'You are shaming me by doing this, Shilpamma.' Her tears fall on our joined hands. 'You of all people do not have to beg. You, your girls, are family.' She takes care not to look at my Nisha as she says this; she still shies away from the sight of my poor girl with her wounded face.

At the hospital, my babies are whisked away from me, hooked on drips, tubes half their size feeding nutrients into their poor ravaged bodies.

'They are in safe hands now, they will be fine,' Jalaja chants, her words taking the form and rhythm of a prayer, and I try to relax, I do, but the madwoman's prophesy resounds in my head, her deep, melancholy sigh as I said no to her for the first time ever and left with my children, echoes in my ears. Doctors and nurses flit about the room, check on my children, the space around them a hive of activity, but they themselves lie unresponsive, quiet, pale, their little bodies lost under the machines doing the feeding, the beating, the living for them. They seem so distant and I ache to hold them in my arms, ache to hear their delighted laughter, their robust, healthy cries, not the mewls they have taken to emitting since this fever possessed them.

Once we put this behind us, my girls and I, I will go to work, I vow. It is my fault. My fault that Manoj…

I will not think of him. After he... I could not work, I was heavily pregnant. Then, after the babies... they needed me. Jalaja gave without me having to ask, but I hid how much I needed from her. She urged me to take them to hospital when they first fell ill, but I demurred because of the cost. And now... I hope it is not too late. I need the wise woman... But the wise woman, she's said... the prophesy... I cannot lose one, I cannot...

The main doctor, the one they all defer to, comes to me and I read in his eyes what he is going to say before he says it, echoes of the time Manoj and I went with folded hands to a doctor about my chances of having children reverberating from the past. Another hospital, another doctor. He had said I wouldn't have any kids, the chances were nil. Now I have two, and I listen to *this* doctor in *this* hospital say that it is too late, that nothing more can be done, that it is time to say goodbye to my precious girls. No. No, I cannot let that happen. I entrust my babies to Jalaja, who keeps watch at the hospital and I run through the fields, bare soles blistering on pebbles scorched white in the sun. I run to the wise woman, fall at her feet.

'Which one?' I ask like I did once before, when I've gathered my breath. 'Which one do I have to lose?'

'Your choice,' she says.

'What?' I blanch. 'How can Lord Ganapathy do this to me? How do I choose which one of my babies is going to die?'

The madwoman smiles, her face settling into familiar furrows, her grey eyes, like shadows dancing in the hearth of an evening, reflecting the turmoil I feel. 'Who said anything about dying?'

I stare at her as the meaning sinks in, lying prostrate in the mud, dust swirling around me, the peepal tree leaves swishing languidly in the leisurely breeze, unaware of the grit digging into my knees, unaware of my sore, scalded feet. And then I am smiling along with her, I am throwing my head back, revelling in the hot rays warming my face, feeling the sun for the first time in days, and I am laughing. 'They are not going to die; my babies are not going to die.'

'No,' she says, her voice soft as the gurgle of a faraway stream. 'But you have to lose one.'

In the market, life goes on. Aarthiappa's wife haggles about the price of fish with Shali, someone guffaws loudly and the bus trundles down, the driver tooting the horn relentlessly in an effort to chase the cows out of the road.

'Take her to the convent in Dhonikatte,' the wise woman says.

I do not ask why the convent, why not Lord Ganapathy. The gods work in strange ways; they work through this woman in front of me. I will do whatever she says if it means my babies will get better. I wearily pull myself to standing, make to leave.

'Wait,' her fingers on my arm. I turn. 'Once you give her to them, you can't take her back.'

❄ ❄ ❄

And once more, I have to choose. But this time, it is between my girls, both of whom I love more than life itself.

I look at them, lying there under the machines, barely breathing, their twin hearts barely beating. Jalaja is sobbing into her soggy pallu. The medical staff have given up on my girls. No activity around them now, no nurses hovering, no doctors with clip pads and devoted entourages.

I have to choose.

Devi? My first born? My perfect little girl?

Or Nisha? The one who arouses my protective instincts, on whose behalf I want to fight the world. Nisha whom I love so fiercely, the more because everyone else shuns her so.

How could I bear to lose either? But this way they both survive. Otherwise, as the wise woman has cautioned, as Lord Ganapathy has shown in no uncertain terms, if I go against the prophesy, I lose them both. I have to do this to save them.

A distressed whimper startles out of one of the girls, loud in the stark quiet of the room. Nisha.

Jalaja goes up to Devi, wipes her face with her pallu, whispers endearments into her ear. She carefully avoids looking at Nisha.

'It was Nisha who murmured, Nisha who needed comfort,' I want to yell. Instead, I go to Nisha, I wipe her face; I whisper endearments into her ear.

And that decides it for me.

❄ ❄ ❄

As I hand my precious little girl, her sickly little body so hot it feels like she is on fire, over to the nun, I watch the nun's face. She holds my daughter close, not recoiling from my child's gaping, ravaged face, and for that I am grateful. 'The Lord made us all in His likeness,' the nun says, her eyes tender as she plants a kiss on my baby girl's scorching forehead.

I have made the right choice, I think. *I have.* I dithered and dallied; surely Nisha needed me more because of her cleft? But if she stayed with me, in our village, without the security blanket of her sister beside her, shunned by even those closest to her, mocked and teased because of her disfigured face, would my love, my fierce protectiveness be enough? And the child who stayed with me would be in for a struggle—even though I vowed to find work, we wouldn't have much. I would barely be able to feed her. Nisha had already had a poor start in life; she deserved more than I could give her. So much more. Perhaps this was her chance; perhaps this was what the wise woman had meant when she said that Nisha's disfigured face could be a blessing rather than a punishment, a curse.

I fall at the nun's feet. 'Please,' is all I can think to say. 'Please.'

She hands my baby over to another nun, takes a hold of my shoulders, lifts me up. I collapse into her and I sob.

'The Lord has a plan for your child,' she says.

I have to believe her. I do. Blind belief is all I have left to fill the chasm that yawns between me and my precious little girl.

❄ ❄ ❄

Just as the wise woman predicted, as soon as I give Nisha away, Devi starts responding to the medicines and makes what the doctors term a 'fantastic' recovery. The fever drops, her colour returns and I take her home. But one thing, however, remains the same.

My girl cries and cries. She will not stop. She is crying for her sister. Not fevered mewls, no, thank the Lord Ganapathy; proper livid, furious sobs. 'Nini,' she moans. 'Nini.' This is what she calls her sister. She comes to me, her nose running, her face flushed and raging sobs escaping her. She grabs my sari with her little fists and urges me to search for her sister. I try to gather her in my arms and she pushes me away. 'Nini,' she moans. 'Nini.'

She waddles through the whole house looking for her Nini. Under the mattress, behind the door, even in the dog's bowl. She points to the empty space on the mattress next to her: 'Nini.' A question, a lament. She cries herself to sleep.

One day I spy her near the well, half her body dangling inside as she cries, 'Nini, Nini,' and my heart jumps to my throat. It is the monsoon season. The water is almost near the top and she had seen part of her reflection, mistaken it for her sister. I manage to pull her away just in time, thank the Lord Ganapathy.

She looks at her image in stainless-steel tumblers and smiles. She takes a tumbler to bed with her, hugging it close, talking to it, pushing me away—that is the only way she can get to sleep.

❄ ❄ ❄

My other daughter, however, is still ill, I hear, despite the nuns' prayers and the doctors' interventions. I worry,

I fret, I alternate between praying, desperately, frantically: 'What more do you want, Lord?' and doubting both Him, fate and the wise woman. I run to her, dragging a complaining Devi along. Devi takes one look at the wise woman and begins to yell, loud cries racking her body. I try to gather her in my arms but she pushes me away. 'Nini,' she yells, furiously ripping a peepal leaf to shreds, kicking up dust, making passersby sneeze. 'Nini…'

'Nisha needs me,' I cry to the wise woman. 'She is pining for me,' I sob. 'Perhaps if I had left her at the hospital…'

'Then you would have lost both of them; you heard what the doctors had to say,' the wise woman reminds me gently.

'If I had given Devi away perhaps…' I say softly, giving voice to the doubts that assail me every waking moment, that grip my chest in a vice-like fist, choking hot sobs out of me at night as I count out the hours till morning, second-guessing my decision, desperately missing my child, praying that she gets better, that my belief in the wise woman pays off, that this hurt, this pain of losing her, of giving her away was worth it. Guilt colours my voice the flaming scarlet of shame. 'Perhaps I made the wrong choice,' I mutter, while the precious daughter I chose to keep hits me with her palms, her fists, yelling 'Nini, Nini,' as if she knows the traitorous words I have just uttered, as if she wishes she could give *me* away, barter me for her sister.

'You made the choice,' the wise woman says, her voice stern, her eyes on my daughter, 'You have to live with it.' And then, more gently, as if she understands the constant war I wage with guilt and remorse, 'It will be alright, Shilpa, it will. Wait and see.'

But how can I wait when my daughter is ill, when the choice I had to make perpetually torments me? Have I done the right thing?

'Yes, you have,' the wise woman says as if reading my thoughts.

And I carry my daughter, who fights me all the way, home. And I wait.

I wait.

❄ ❄ ❄

A miracle occurs. My child is cured. This Catholic God, he is so powerful, dear Diary. He performs a wonder to top the one Lord Ganapathy did by consecrating my barren womb with twin blessings. Just as my daughter knocks on death's door, the Catholic God snatches her away, brings her back into the land of the living. That is what the Catholics specialise in, don't they? Resurrection?

I go often to see her, hiding out of sight, by the gates to the convent. A little girl skipping in a courtyard, the air fragranced with jasmine and a hint of lime—tangy, slightly bitter. The little snub of a nose. Eyes the colour of roasted groundnuts. A little girl, so close I could touch her, claim her. My little girl. Mine, and yet mine no longer.

I rage at the wise woman. I yell.

The rain arrives on a gust of wind, the drops smelling of mango and mud. Skittish, mango-scented, turmeric-tinged, bitter-tasting drops land on my face, my head, my arms, and gradually soak my sari. 'I miss her,' I lament. 'Devi misses her. How can you, how can Lord Ganapathy expect me to live without her, live knowing she's close by? So close.'

'She won't be for long,' the wise woman says in her gentle voice, and I am possessed of the urge to shake her, shake her as much as the leaves of the peepal tree trembling in the wind, shake her until her teeth chatter, until she tells me that my baby's rightful place is with me.

'What do you mean?' I ask instead. 'What do you mean?'

'She will be fine,' she says, laying a gnarled hand on mine. 'It is meant to happen. Everything that happens is meant to be.'

'Easy for you to say,' I yell, yanking my hand away.

'I lost a son too,' she says gently.

'He died!' I yell and for the first time I watch her cringe and I am pleased that I have at last pierced that calm countenance. 'My girl, she's so close, so close.' I give in to the tears that rock me. Devi is with Jalaja, she will not come to me. She is angry at me, blames me for her sister. As she should. And I blame this woman, even though a part of me knows that she is only a messenger. That she is as helpless as I am.

I ache for my child. I want her back.

'You gave her away,' the wise woman says softly. 'You could have kept her, disregarded my words. Why didn't you?'

I almost did. And I almost lost them both. Almost. I collapse into myself. She is right of course. If anyone is to blame, I am.

'Say you bring her back,' she says, and I look up at her, hopeful.

'How is it you will feed her, feed the both of them?' she says, her voice gentle, but it is as if she has slapped me, and the hope that bloomed within me moments before is displaced by wrath warring with guilt.

I glare at her and she looks right back, her eyes peaceful as the river at dawn. She is not mocking me, she is asking.

My secret shame, bitter as bitter gourd masala—that I cannot feed my own children, that I have to live off Sumitranna's charity. I am furious at the wise woman for bringing it up. If only Manoj were here. But whose fault is it that he isn't? His pain-filled eyes haunt me every single day, as does my daughter's face. When I am holding Devi, I ache for my other daughter. Devi searches for her sister. She looks behind me, beside me, up my skirts, in the hope her sister is hiding there. It breaks my heart.

'I will feed them, I will do it somehow,' I say through gritted teeth. 'Isn't it better for a child to be with its mother?'

'Not always,' she says, calm as the sea when the storm has passed.

'How dare you?' I shout. 'Are you saying I am not a good mother?' *She is only telling the truth,* a voice says inside my head; *they almost died because of your neglect.*

People stop what they are doing to stare. As if I care.

'I am not saying anything of the sort. I am just saying that she needs the kind of care you cannot afford to give.'

I could slap her. Right at this moment I could happily hit her until she was nothing but pulp, even though

I know what she is saying is the honest truth and only she is brave enough to tell me so.

'Can you fix her cleft palate? Get her married? Give her a face people will not flinch away from?'

And just like that, my anger deflates. 'No,' I say softly.

'Well then,' she says, and I look up at her, hope flaring once more.

'Is that what is in her future? Will her face be fixed? Will she be able to live a normal life, get married, have children?'

She doesn't say anything, just smiles. 'What will be, will be. You have made your decision. Learn to live with it, Shilpa.'

The rain has stopped; the world looks fresh, sparkling clean. Everything has a silvery sheen. The sun is setting. The sky is grey, tinged orangey pink, a rainbow peeking out from between clouds. The world is mellow. My heart rages. 'Was it the right one?' I ask. The question that has been tormenting me ever since I took Nisha away from the hospital bed and placed her in the nun's arms.

The wise woman does not speak, laying a gnarled hand on mine instead, letting it do the talking. And, sitting under the peepal tree, the smell of stale fish and fresh regret, the feel of the rough callused hand on mine, the soft breeze on my face tasting of tears, of guilt, the bitter aftertaste of loss, I feel something shift.

'Can't I get her back?' I whisper.

'Not if you don't want to lose everything,' she says.

I believe her, dear Diary. I do. Everything she has prophesied has come true so far, every single thing. If I bring Nisha back, I will lose everything, everyone. I don't dare.

And so, I sacrifice my girl for the greater good. The wise woman has said Nisha will be fine. She implied that her cleft palate would be fixed, that she would get married, have children, be beautiful. Didn't she? So I made the right choice, in the end. I have to believe that. I have to.

❄ ❄ ❄

There is no food. Nothing in the house. My mother taught me how to make something out of nothing. But I seem to have lost the ability to do anything at all since I lost my child. My Devi cries. And cries. Jalaja comes with milk and rice and curry. 'No,' I say. 'For the baby,' she says, pulling my daughter into her lap and feeding her. My daughter stuffs the food into her mouth, gasping in her rush to push it in. *She is starving,* I think, as I take in her concave stomach, the ribs poking out from the shelf of her chest. *If I am not careful, she will fall ill again,* I think. *I hope my other daughter is well fed, her stomach never reverberating with pangs of hunger.* I think, *please Lord; you owe me that much.* The next day I leave Devi with Jalaja and go to work, cleaning other people's houses while mine festers. That evening I come home with a chicken and my daughter's face lights up at the sight of me for the first time since I gave her sister away, only to crumple when I kill it for our supper.

❄ ❄ ❄

I visit the convent, devour my girl with my eyes and let her be, when what I really want to do is to snatch her away. Is it foolishness? I will never know. I want to take her home with me, but then I see her: happy, healthy, loved, a miracle—and I think of that limp girl hounded by fever whom I had conveyed here in my arms. She is happier without me. She is chubby, glowing with wellbeing. If I took her home, I would struggle to feed her. As it is, I can barely feed Devi. I am cursed. And so, even though it breaks my heart a little more each time, I let her be. I go home empty-handed to my other daughter's accusing eyes, her raging tantrums.

Nisha sees me only once. It is some months after I deposited her in the nuns' arms, begged them to heal her. She looks upset, worried, not her usual happy self. I cannot help it; I watch her for longer than I usually do. I stare through the bars, breathe her in for more than a fleeting second, wishing a smile upon her, wanting to hold her in my arms, to tenderly wipe the worry off her face. She looks up, sees me. I flatten myself against the wall. I watch her palms come up to the gates, rattle them, drink in her voice, low, musical as she calls for Sister Priya, watch her twig-like delicate hands waving as they snake through the bars, and resist, with difficulty, the urge to grab them, grab her and not let go. Then, everything is quiet. I think she's left. I count to ten softly in my head, wait one beat, two. When I peer inside, I see her. She is standing by the wall, diagonally opposite me, looking forlorn, lost. Before I have the chance to move, she spots me. Her eyes widen, then crinkle as she tries to smile, that ravaged mouth moving. She opens it and I know then that she has recognised me, despite the months that have elapsed since

I gave her away. She has recognised me, is going to call for me. I have to leave, I have to. I make myself move, walk away from my daughter, the torrent of tears blinding me as I collapse some distance away, in the mud by a tender coconut stall. The owner comes up to me, pats my arm, 'Do you need anything?' *Yes: my child. I need my child.* 'No,' I sob. He holds out a tender coconut. I shake my head, no. She recognised me, she remembered me, she was going to call for me. What am I doing? She is not mine anymore. I am harming her by doing this. I have to allow her to forget. And yet… I creep back just in time to see her disappear into a nun's waiting arms and I ache to be the one holding her, hugging her close, her arms encircling my neck, her face buried in my shoulder.

However much I want to, long to, I do not go back.

❄ ❄ ❄

A novice nun arrives with a letter from the convent. 'Some scientists from London who are in Mangalore at the moment heard about Nisha, about the miracle that cured her and have contacted us. They know that she is one of twin girls and they have enquired if she could be part of a project they are conducting. We have prayed about this and feel that it is what the Lord wants. If you are okay with it, could you send a picture of the twins, if you have one, with Sister Latha, please? The scientists would like it for their file, it seems.'

I give the novice some rice and sambar and ask her to wait while I run to the wise woman, the letter clutched to my chest. 'Everything happens for a reason,' she says, beaming.

And so I part with the picture taken that blissful morning in Shankar's studio, the only physical evidence I have of my twin blessings apart from what I have penned here within your pages, dear Diary, and the ache, the Nisha-sized hole in my heart. I kiss my baby's wounded face on the picture and hand it over to the nun.

❄ ❄ ❄

A few days later, the novice nun is back with another letter. 'The scientists, they came to see her and they fell in love with your daughter, Shilpa. They want to adopt her. It is all part of the Lord's grand plan for Nisha. They are good people; they genuinely love your child. They say they will fix her cleft palate. She will have a good life in England. She will want for nothing. Is that okay with you? Do you want to come and meet them, see what you think?'

I made the right choice that day, I think. *The wise woman was right,* I think. *My baby will have a good life,* I think. *Her face will be fixed, she will get married, have children,* I think.

'No, I don't want to meet them,' I pen with hands that tremble. How can I meet the people who will be to my child everything I long to be? How can I bear to watch my beloved little girl with them and not snatch her away, ignoring the wise woman's prophesies and everything that has gone before, not heeding what I know is right for Nisha, following blindly instead the yearning in my chest, the call of my heart?

'I trust you and your God,' I write with shaky fingers, in handwriting that I barely recognise as mine. *She will be so far away,* I think. *I will never see her again,* I think. 'Yes. It is okay with me.'

❄ ❄ ❄

Mango (Midi) Pickle:

Ingredients:

Tart, raw, baby mangoes–30

1/2 tsp mustard seeds

1 tsp coconut oil

1 tsp turmeric powder

Rock salt

20 fiery red chillies, arranged to dry on raffia mats in the courtyard. If your dog anticipates a forbidden treat, ventures to the chillies, sniffs them and sneezes in surprise, don't worry. Happened to my Bobby. The dog will be fine and so will the chillies.

Method:

Wash the baby mangoes, sharp and tangy, and steep them in rock salt. Leave for a couple of days and then take them out.

Grind the dry red chillies and mustard seeds to a coarse paste with a little water.

Fry oil in a pan. Add the paste and cook the salted mangoes in this paste along with the turmeric powder.

Once the mixture cools, steep into jars and let it rest to allow the flavours to mingle and settle a day or two.

❄ ❄ ❄

Dear Diary,

It's been years since I last wrote to you. My hands are pockmarked, my fingers tremble as I write. So much has happened in between. And now that my remaining girl, my Devi, has fled to that country which they say is so cold that your breath comes out as ice, that country that has now claimed both of my daughters, I have come back to you. Sorry, old friend, to have neglected you so. I have plenty of time on my hands now—I have nothing but time and I will make it up to you.

It is at times like these that I miss the wise woman the most. She is gone too, and I am bereft, lost without someone to look into my future, to look to that country, England, to keep an eye on my girls for me.

'Why do you set such store by some rubbish that mad-woman spouts, Ma?' Devi yelled countless times over the years. 'Why do you believe everything she says and make my life hell?'

Because she knows who I am inside, I wanted to say to her. *She has seen the worst I can be. And the best. Because she has such power over me. Because she can see into my future. If I keep her close, I believe nothing bad will happen, or at least that I will be warned before it does. Truth is, I am afraid to stop believing in her. If I stop, I am afraid something terrible will happen. But I am even more afraid of this: What if it doesn't? What if I have been following her every word blindly all this while, doing everything she's said, when perhaps if I hadn't, things would have been different?*

Perhaps if I hadn't, I would have both of my daughters with me.

I picture the wise woman as I saw her for the last time that aboli-scented, cerise-tinged evening, lying prone under the peepal tree, a white sheet covering her body, the lines on her face ironed out, peaceful in death. I miss those stark, grey-blue eyes, those eyes that could see so much. Why did she exit the world so suddenly, leaving me grieving, in the lurch, blind to the future…? Did she see her own death, a sigh and then nothing, the hand holding mine going slack?

I prepared the mango pickle (recipe above) and lime pickle, sambar and rasam powders to give to Devi when she left for England. I don't know why I write my recipes as if someone other than me will see them. My secret hope is that one day, my children—Devi or even Nisha perhaps (who knows, miracles happen; she is living proof), will keep a hold of you, diary, and read my words, follow my recipes.

And during the solitary nights after Devi got married and left home but before she left for England, when her absence beside me on the mattress ached like a physical wound, when sleep evaded me and ghosts from the past threatened, I wrote letters in flickering candlelight. Pages and pages of thoughts and musings. A sheaf of lined note paper torn from old school notebooks of Devi's that I had preserved, now busily populated with my spidery scrawl. All the things I had never told my daughter. Her story. Her father's story. Her sister's story, intertwined with hers. Missives of love, dotted with candle wax, briny with tears, to the daughter I chose to keep, the daughter I was also going to lose.

I wanted to tell her in person. I wanted to say, 'You are going to England—can you find your sister for me?' But I did not have the courage. She was going so far away and I did not want her to leave hating me for what I had done. I did not want to watch the rebellious, impatient expression that is the face she wears for me—in which, nevertheless, I see glimmers of the love she tries so hard to mask—replaced by hurt, mistrust, hate—all that I deserve but didn't have the strength to endure. And so I took the easy way out: gave her the letters.

When Devi was growing up, there was scarcely any money, never any food, and my mother's valuable tips and recipes on how to make something out of nothing came in handy. Each day heralded a new worry. The monsoons were late, the well was empty, my vegetable plants were not coping—droopy like children cooped up in school during that long drowsy hour after lunch and before home time. What to cook today? I wondered, every single day. These daily concerns, etched in the network of lines on my face, defined my life and Devi's life with me.

I hope my Nisha escaped them. I hope she never wanted for anything. The ache of missing her is a constant, like the sun rising every morning. I hope wherever she is, she is happy. I hope she is doing well. I hope her mouth is healed. I hope she finds a man who loves her. I hope she is blessed with many children. And I hope that one day, I get to see her. I don't deserve to, I know, but I desperately hope I could touch her. Just once.

I hope.

I gave her away—what right do I have to ask for her back? I console myself with the thought that if she had stayed with me, her face would never have been fixed; she would have always been an outcast, with people staring and pointing, flinching and turning away. I tell myself that I made the right decision, that I saved my daughter by giving her away.

When Devi was here, I used to see in her face, her voice, her laughter, her screams, the daughter I gave away. I measured Nisha's life by Devi's changing face, her growing body. I fed Devi and I was feeding them both. I held Devi close, kissed her forehead—she has not let me do that in a while now—and I was holding them both, kissing them both. Perhaps this is where I went wrong with Devi—I loved her too much, poured twice the love on one person and she reeled under the burden, ran away.

Because that is what she has done.

Devi's wedding ceremony was a success, everyone agrees. The Catholic ceremonies, prayers and hymns had been, strangely, as soothing as they were alien. As I watched my daughter being pledged to Rohan, the grief I felt was layered, buffeted by another dormant one. Longing. Like the dull ache of a rotting tooth. I wanted. And instead I was losing. Again.

This Catholic God, he is so powerful, dear Diary. He takes first one of my children, then another.

Devi, my girl, she took everything when she went to England—the pickle bottles, the powders, the letters, noise, laughter, bustle, life. Everything I see now is indistinct, lacking the definition, the colour my daughter's presence used to give it. The coconut trees, the crows sitting on telephone lines, the electricity pylons, the fields are blurred. A wavy not-quite-there sun descends wearily down a tangerine-spattered sky beyond the fuzzy jackfruit trees.

The letters I have written her, they tell her my story, the terrible choices I made. She hasn't read them yet. If she had, she would be yelling so hard down the telephone my eardrum would burst, never mind the distance. My Devi, she cannot keep anything inside; everything she feels is out there for everyone to see. She's so pure, so magnificent, so unlike me. She hides a beautiful, kind, loving heart behind an angry facade. Her defence against the world that stole her sister.

She took so very long to forget. And even though she was little, she somehow knew I was to blame. She never liked the wise woman either. She always called her 'madwoman' like the rest of the village. Slowly, very slowly, she let go. She still had dreams when she would wake up screaming, 'Nini!'

And that is why I didn't tell her. I couldn't invoke that suffering, that pain in her all over again.

I sit here on the veranda even though it's getting a bit too dark to see to write, dear Diary. Sorry about the messy handwriting. I do not want to go inside, do not want to face the night.

The nights are too long. I lie on the mattress that I shared with Devi, feeling bereft, forlorn, eyes wide open, staring up at the ceiling, at the lizards flitting between rotting wooden beams, happily going about their business, alighting on unsuspecting flies, their tongues darting out, teasing, tantalising, like the face of a North Indian bride glimpsed from underneath a pallu—there for a minute, then gone. Flies swallowed, kaput.

Outside, trees sigh as they revel in the wind's caress. Cats grumble and dogs howl. Stray cows moo dreamily. No Jalaja nearby (she had taken to sleeping here to keep me company after Devi left—'That old man can keep his hands to himself for once,' she'd said when I protested), her snores a welcome intrusion into my thoughts. She is tending to her mother who is very ill over in the next village; Sumitranna and their son have gone with her.

My neighbours are a blessing I feel keenly when they aren't around.

I gaze up at the ceiling and my eyes hurt with the effort it takes to stare in the dark. I am glad. I want to feel physical pain. I want Manoj. The ache to see my daughters is like a missing limb making its phantom presence felt. I want them here with me. I want my past back, so I can start over. But what else could I do different?

This is what I imagine, this is what I hope, this is what I pray for: That one day my girls will meet. That Devi will walk along a street and will see, walking towards her, someone who looks exactly like her. She will stop, she will stare and, knowing my Devi, she will shout, yell, rant. 'How dare you steal my face?' she will ask of the other girl. She will call me, she will be raging, 'Do you know, Ma, there's this girl who is the spitting image of me? How dare she?' And I will say, 'You still haven't read my letters, have you?' 'No, why?' she will ask, her bluster rising at the edges in a question. 'She's your sister,' I will say. 'Your little sister. You loved her so, were very protective of her.'

I imagine them meeting, talking, getting to know each other, and being as inseparable as they used to be once. And perhaps I will get to see Nisha. Perhaps I won't. But knowing that she has met her sister, known her, will be enough.

One day soon, I will gather the courage to tell Devi. 'Have you read the letters?' I ask during every phone call. 'Not yet,' she says, that familiar petulant tone creeping into her voice. If she doesn't read them soon, I will tell her. I have to. She cannot be so close to her sister and not know her.

I will.

Chapter 25
Nisha

Makeshift Steps

Sompur is a drowsy little village, a smattering of huts masquerading as shops littered beside the road, which seems to be mostly given over to a posse of cows and dogs who do not move away as the auto trundles up, so the driver, swearing profusely, is forced off the road and into the muddy ditch. The village seems to be an afterthought, an outpost between towns. A huge peepal tree takes up most of the space on the left, a fisherwoman squatting in the shade afforded by its overhanging branches hawking drooping sardines on a banana leaf tray hitched across the handles of her cane basket. There's a bus stop opposite, two tired-looking cement posts festooned with peeling posters holding up an awning. A group of teenage boys huddle around a hut sipping a pink-coloured liquid from tiny glass bottles shaped like a woman's body and look curiously at her as the auto navigates the ditch, gives a reluctant splutter, and dies.

'I can't go any further like this,' the auto driver grumbles in Kannada, lifting his hands up into the air in defeat. 'Lo,' he yells at the boys who come over and peek inside, staring right at her unashamedly. 'Is it always like this here? Those animals don't move?' His head jerks away from a cow which has come up to him and is sniffing the steering wheel.

'Except for the bus. They have respect for the bus.' The boys smirk.

The cow defecates right there, splattering the auto's rear wheels with dung, closing its eyes and mooing joyfully now that it has disposed of its burden. 'Now what am I to do?' the driver laments, head in his hands.

Nisha jumps off gingerly, trying to avoid getting stung by thorny bushes littering the ditch, picking her way through the various heaps of dung dotting the bushes. The air smells of earth and manure, an organic, earthy tang. Dust swirls in thick swishes around her eyes and she is temporarily blinded. She fishes in her bag for her sunglasses, puts them on. The boys melt away, back to the shop, and whistle softly from the safe distance. She presses fifty rupees into the auto driver's hands and he grins, yellow teeth flashing. 'Thank you, thank you, Ma'am,' he says, starting the auto with a flourish after only three tries, the wheels displacing dung helter-skelter as they navigate the ditch.

She cautiously makes her way onto the road. The dogs bark at this intruder and the cows lumber up to her and thrust their wet faces into her hips. She walks to the fisherwoman who is eyeing her inquisitively while fanning her face with one of the banana leaves. 'I am looking for Shilpa,' she says in Kannada, mentally thanking her parents once more.

The woman scrunches up her face in an effort to understand her accent. Nisha repeats her request, enunciating each syllable very clearly. 'Shilpa,' the woman shakes her head vigorously. She says something in rapid-fire Kannada, shaking her head back and forth, and Nisha struggles to make sense of what she is saying.

The tang of fish cooking in the relentless sun, the reek of sweat assaults her nose.

'Can you take me to her house?' She tries again.

The woman stares intently at her lips, trying to follow her speech.

Nisha points to one of the huts on the far side of the road. 'House. Shilpa's house.'

'Oh, yes, yes.' The woman nods enthusiastically. She stands, hitches the basket onto her hip and says in Kannada, but slowly this time, 'Come. I'll show you.'

And it is that easy. Her heart thudding vigorously in her chest, she follows the woman. She is lightheaded from her journey, the heat, the convent, meeting Sister Priya and now this. The air smells of dung and rotting fish, tastes of fear and a nervous excitement. The fisherwoman walks slightly ahead, her gait uneven, her pace languid.

Nisha wants her to hurry. She wants her to never get there.

The posse of dogs and cows follow at a regal distance. The fisherwoman turns off the main road onto a path which is little more than a strip of mud. A small pond on one side, mostly dry, the smidgen of water reddish yellow, silt overflowing the banks. A banyan tree on the other. A hut, roofed with yellowing hay, mud walls, big-eyed children with protruding bellies clothed in rags etching in the dust with twigs, stopping to stare curiously at them as they pass. A woman wearing a dirty brown sari cooking outside, earthen pot bubbling as it sits on a hearth of smoking twigs, the stinging tang of onion. Chickens squawking. A baby crying somewhere, a plaintive, keening sound. A dog's bark, sharp, staccato. And the entire posse behind them starts off, a cacophony of howls and yelps and barks and moos.

This may not be my mother. Sister Priya might have got it wrong. And if she hasn't, well, this might be a different Shilpa altogether. And then, *how many Shilpas can there be in this little ghost of a village?*

A cat sunning itself on a low wall, the bricks crumbling and riddled with moss: a glossy green carpet, the orange of the bricks peeking through in places. A well, an empty pail lying overturned and forlorn beside it, the coir rope hanging soullessly from the wheel pulley used to haul the pail upwards.

The woman comes to a stop at a little opening between thorny bushes. Nisha sees makeshift steps hewn from a couple of stones arranged on top of each other leading down to fields. The woman lays her basket down, wipes her face with her pallu. She points, gesticulates with her hands and Nisha follows her gaze.

'Down here,' she says. 'Not the big house but the little one after, that is Shilpa's.'

Nisha nods, presses twenty rupees into the woman's hands. 'No, no,' the woman protests. 'Yes, yes.' Nisha insists.

The woman touches the notes to her forehead, kisses them and then deftly ties them into a knot at the end of her pallu. And then she turns and walks away, swallowed up by the haze of yellow dust swirling in her wake, her red sari shimmering in the sun, the mob of dogs and cows following. Nisha stands there for a minute eyeing the makeshift path and then, slowly, she makes her way down.

Fields stretch out on both sides of her, a profusion of twinkling emerald basking in sunlight. A stream tinkles nearby—she can hear it, the gurgle and splash of water play-fighting with the rocks, but she cannot see it. She walks on like the woman asked her to. The path is precarious, requires all her concentration, only wide enough for a foot at a time, the mud slippery, giving way beneath her feet.

The path widens with no warning at all and suddenly she is at a clearing. A dog barks. A house looms up ahead. Hibiscus and aboli flowers wave. Orange tiles, red pillars, veranda. Deserted. A dog bounds up, quickly followed by another. They dance around her legs, and she squats down, pats them, scratches behind their ears. They lick her hands happily, obviously glad of the company. The veranda is cool, the house looks abandoned. The washing line is empty, no clothes billowing on it, the washing stone bereft. The front door, ornate, wooden, carved with impressions of the gods, is shut. 'Hello?' She calls.

No response. No noise from within. She walks round the back and sees the little house, huddled in the big one's shadow. Its front faces the fields. There's a tamarind tree, knobbly brown fruit dancing on every branch. Chickens peck in the mud. The dogs are still boogying around her legs. There's a veranda running the length of the house, which isn't saying much. Two doors, both open. A banana tree rocking in the breeze. Her heart thuds loudly in her chest. A crows cries mournfully from its perch among the coconut trees.

'Hello?' She calls. From somewhere within she hears a sound. She peers inside the first door. A kitchen, dark. There are a couple of broken flip-flops, the straps held together with safety pins, sitting forlorn on the stoop. She slips off her sandals and leaves them there beside the flip-flops to give them company. They smile up at her, pleased, safety pins twinkling. *Get a grip, Nisha.*

The floor is cool beneath her bare, blistered feet. The kitchen smells stale of food gone bad: old rice, congealed curry. Her head brushes the rotting beams of the ceiling. She bends, ducks inside. There's only one other room. It houses a worn wooden bench and a book lying on a fraying mat beside the open front door, sheaves of loose, lined paper splayed on top, a pen and an aluminium jug keeping company. The dogs who came bounding up to her sprawl across the stoop beside the front door, side by side, tongues hanging out.

A noise behind her. 'Who are you and what are you doing here?' A woman's voice, strident.

She whips round, colour flooding her cheeks, trying to come up with an excuse for entering this house without permission. What has gotten into her? This is not the Nisha she knows; this is a stranger who has inhabited her body, taken her over, ever since the letter. She wants to say all this, she wants to explain, but the words die on her lips as she takes in the woman facing her, her legs set apart in an argumentative stance, her hair obscured by a towel masquerading as turban, her body sporting a loose nightie, her hand brandishing a coconut tree frond. Nisha takes in the woman's eyes, leaf-shaped, the colour of coffee with just a dash of milk, her straight nose curving slightly at the end, her perfect voluptuous lips. She stares shamelessly, breathing in the sight of her twin, her doppelganger, standing right there in front of her so close she could touch her if she stretched her arm, and the winter that has taken residence in her chest since her parents died relinquishes its icy hold, allows spring access to her heart.

Chapter 26
Devi

Ebony Waterfall

Ma,

My sister is in England? I flipped through your diary searching for an address, contact details—nothing. No more entries. This is it… All that you have written. Your story.

Weren't you curious about the couple who adopted Nisha, Ma? Didn't you want to know where in England they were from, where they were taking your daughter? Why didn't you find out, ask the nuns? Or did you? But if you did, surely there would be a mention in your diary? Or was there a letter from the nuns somewhere in the house, replete with information about my sister? Once more, I ransacked the house, searched it top to bottom. Once more, I did not find what I was looking for.

I think I know why you didn't find out, why you let things be, Ma. The temptation to find Nisha, look her up somehow, would have been too much. And you knew only sorrow would come of it, even if you could afford by some miracle the airfare to England, even if you found her, contacted her. What would you say? 'I am sorry I decided to give you away and keep your sister?'

Ma, the choices you had to make—no mother should have to.

In your diary you say that your hope is that one day my twin and I meet. I will find Nisha, Ma. That is a promise. I will find her and she will be amazed at our likeness. I will open my mouth to speak and my voice will be an echo of hers. I will smile and she will smile right back; the joy that I feel will be mirrored in her face, the face that is a reflection of mine. I hope, Ma, that my sister has had a wonderful life. That your sacrifice paid off. That she is happy, that she is loved.

I have a confession to make, Ma. The letters you wrote to me, that you pressed into my hands at the airport as I was leaving—I can picture them, untouched, smelling of lime pickle, waiting in the suitcase on top of the wardrobe in the flat in England. I didn't read them. And then, as is my wont, I blamed you for not telling me the truth. You tried, Ma, perhaps later rather than sooner, but you did try.

Ma, I understand so many things now.

The answer to the question—What mother gives her child away at the behest of a madwoman? A desperate one. Your children are comatose with fever; the doctors have given up hope. If someone told you they would both live if you gave one of them to the convent, wouldn't you do it? Wouldn't you try anything, anything at all?

I understand why I forgot Nisha—it was my way of coping with the trauma of losing her, much as I fought to remember.

I understand why you didn't tell me about her.

I understand why I am so angry all the time, why my default emotion is rage, aggression. It is a reaction against a world that bequeathed me a sister I loved and then took her away so capriciously.

I understand fully now why you are the way you are with me. You had to make a choice no mother should have to—choose between her children. And you chose me. I don't know whether to be grateful or angry. I don't know what I would have done in your place, if, God forbid, I had to face that decision.

Ma, you wanted me to read your diary; you hoped I would and that Nisha will, one day. When I find her, I will give it to her, Ma, this gift of your words.

In the end, though, despite everything, what comes at me is this: I have a sibling, my twin.

❄ ❄ ❄

Ma, a miracle has occurred! It has… a real, live, miracle. A Catholic miracle, a Hindu miracle, A You-Name-It miracle, but a miracle all the same.

I read your entry. I wrote to you. I resolved to find Nisha. And then I went to have a wash.

As I was pouring lukewarm water on my body, I thought I heard a sound. I paused. Bobby barked in that sharp staccato way of his that signals visitors. A few seconds later, I heard him pant the way he does when he's trying to please whoever's deigned to pet him. You used to say that the dog was useless as a guard, that he was so friendly all a burglar had to do was scratch him behind his ear.

I knew there was someone at the door, Ma. I was scared, I'll tell you that. I was all alone, no Jalaja, no Sumitranna, nobody about in the fields. I hurriedly pulled a nightie over my head, wrapped my dripping hair in a towel, picked up one of those coconut tree fronds lying in the bathroom and tiptoed outside, inching along the veranda and into the house. Bobby was nowhere to be seen. On the kitchen stoop lay the gaudiest pair of sandals I ever had the misfortune of setting eyes on, the sequins dotting them no longer shiny, dulled as they were by a coating of brown dust.

My thudding heart relaxed a tiny bit. This was no burglar, I decided. A burglar would not take care to remove their sandals before entering the house they meant to ransack, and, judging from the style and cut of the footwear, the intruder was a woman.

I crept inside, still holding on to the coconut frond, just in case. A woman, endless legs unravelling from beneath a dress so short it could have passed for a T-shirt, bending over the cane mat by the front door, Ma, snooping at my things, making to touch your diary and my letter. The temerity of the woman! First of all she barges into the house uninvited and then attempts to pry into my private musings. Bobby was lying on the front steps, Jalajakka's mongrel beside him, both of them looking up at this woman, this intruder who seemed to have won them over, with adoring eyes, tongues hanging out.

'Who are you and what are you doing here?' I snapped, just as the woman reached out to pick up my letter—my private correspondence with you.

The woman's hand fell to her side. She straightened, turned around.

The endless legs lived up to the promise. She was tall, dark and stunning. Her hair cascaded down her back, an ebony waterfall, her mouth curved up naturally, as if it was made for smiling. It was slightly lopsided but that added to her charm. She was wearing sunglasses. I knew that when she took the glasses off, her eyes would be almond-shaped, the colour of milk chocolate melting in the sun, framed by long eyelashes. My eyes.

She took a tentative step forward. 'I'm sorry.' Her voice was soft, hesitant, musical. Like hearing an echo. 'I…'

And a name erupted from within the depths of me, rolled out my tongue like a cherished sweet, 'Nini,' I whispered. 'Nini.'

She leaned forward, and shyly put her arm out to touch me. I took her hand, pulled her into my arms. She smelled of sandalwood and vanilla. 'It's like looking into a mirror and seeing a more perfect version of me,' she said softly, and I looked up at her and kissed her cheek and tasted the memories that had bound us together once, sweet, salty, smacking of love.

And in her embrace, Ma, that part of me that was always searching, always wanting, always restless, always torn, relaxed. It had found, finally, what it was searching for. Without even knowing I was incomplete, I felt whole again.

Like how I only realised just how much I loved you when I arrived in England and started missing you, Ma. Like how I realised I had taken the sun for granted when I faced the English winter. I only realised I was missing my sister when she walked into my arms and I felt complete.

She sleeps now, beside me on the mattress that I used to share with you. Soft sighs escape from between half-open lips. I keep watch, just in case she disappears again like she did once before.

I watch her and I write, Ma, the joy blooming out of me in the form of words, settling onto this paper, seasoned with tears, like the first soft snow of winter.

She showed me her notebook. All those many jottings in her methodical, organised, mathematician's scrawl. My sister the statistical consultant. I read about her upbringing, how she was loved and yet denied physical affection, the affection I had in droves but pushed away. I read about Matt, who loves her like she deserves to be loved. I read about her turmoil when she found out she was adopted. I read about how she found the picture of us, the picture I ransacked this house for. I read about her quest to find me. I read all her many questions, neatly noted down in her book: Why did my mother give me away but keep my sister? Where is my father? Why is there no mention of him?

I gave her your diary and my letters. She can speak, read and write Kannada, Ma; her adoptive parents made sure she learned it.

Tears rolled down her cheeks as she read your words, Ma, and I reached out, caught one, and it shimmered iridescent on my fingers. My sister's tears, like precious jewels. And I thought: Three women. A mother, two daughters. Finding succour in words. You with your diary, Ma. Me with my letters to you, and my sister with her lists. Words that brought us all together in the end.

Ma, the irony of it! She went to parents who provided her with the best of everything but who could not show their love even though they loved her. And I grew up here, in this little house, with none of the material things, the expensive education that Nisha took for granted. But, I was loved too much… Two girls, created by a single egg splitting in two, sharing a womb for nine months. Two very different upbringings, two very different lives…

If you had made a different decision that day, kept her, given me away, where would we be now?

Afterwards, she whispered, softly, her face glistening, 'I was wanted. I was loved.'

I cupped her face in my palms. 'Nini,' I said. 'You *are* loved.'

And then I asked the question that had been hovering on my lips as she read the diary: 'Do you resent the fact that she kept me, and gave you away?'

A shadow flitted across her face and I resisted the urge to reach across, wipe it away. 'I understand why she did it,' she said softly, her eyes brimming, overflowing.

I took her hand and placed it on my stomach. My baby tumbled happily in my womb, and in my sister's eyes, widening with awe, I saw the reflection of what I felt.

'She likes you,' I said as my baby jiggled and wobbled, as she kicked and jumped.

And, 'Yes,' she said, smiling with wonder, with delight. 'Yes, I think she does.'

'She's a girl, I just know it,' I said.

'I have a family,' she said softly. 'A sister, a mother, a niece.'

And then, my sister laughed, she threw back her head and laughed. And then we were both laughing and the dogs were barking and the crickets were singing and it was the sound of happiness, the sound of family, the sound of coming home after years of being lost. We laughed together—a wet splatter of a sound—and I couldn't make out if the laughter I was hearing was hers or mine, just that our joyous voices met somewhere in the middle and mingled and that they were one and the same sound.

Ma, I regret the lost years but we have the future together. We have the future.

Ma, this is it, the last page in the last of my letters. We have been through such a journey together, you and I. And, Ma, finally, this is what I want to say: you are the bravest woman I know. What you did, having to choose between your daughters, give one away to save both, allow her to go far away so she could have a better life—I couldn't do that. I was angry with you, but now, having met Nisha, my Nini, I think you made the right decision. I have lived in Sompur and I know how narrow-minded, how closed the people can be. My sister, she is so accomplished, so clever, so quietly confident, so beautiful. Her life would have been very different here. I salute you, Ma.

I love you.

Devi.

Chapter 27
Shilpa

Whirlwind

Dear Diary,
I have lost interest in cooking. I am not concocting recipes anymore. No new recipes to add and I can't seem to remember the old ones. I… I am not able to summon the energy to move from here, my bed. It is dark I think. When I get up, I will write in you. Until then, I will just talk to you if that's okay. I know you won't mind, old friend.

I have this dream. In it, Devi is beside me, sharing the lumpy mattress, just the same as always. The smell of the evening's curry lingers, mixed in with the phenyl used to mop the floor before laying the mat ready for bed, and the residual charred smoky scent from the fire used to heat the urn in the cramped bathroom. Devi is talking, her mouth working busily as she recounts news of her day, long chats punctuated with laughter. My daughter smells of the sandalwood talcum powder she smothers herself in before bed, her shiny oiled hair is fanned out on the pillow, long strands staining the yellow pillow the dark black of the hour right before dawn. 'I can't sleep, Ma,' Devi complains. 'It's too hot.' The front door is open, Bobby sprawled across the stoop. Every so often, a reluctant breeze whispers in, dispensing secrets, reeking of intrigue. 'Listen to this joke, Ma,' Devi says, and I watch my daughter's beautiful face with awe, seeing in it, as I always do, the presence of my other daughter, who is loved and looked after by someone else, who calls someone else 'Ma'. I marvel, as I always do, at how Manoj and I have managed to create such beautiful girls, twin miracles. I breathe in those liquid eyes the colour and texture of coconut oil warm from the hearth, fish-shaped and lilting upward at the corners, voluptuous lips the shape and hue of sprouting buds, the expressions flitting Devi's face like shadows on the forest floor, as she hoards punch lines like long-anticipated, hard-earned treats. 'Ma, you were snoring. You stopped for a bit then started up again, sputtering like Mr Rano's scooter. Am I that boring?' Devi is giggling. Her giggle like a waterfall, twinkling silvery bright among the bright green hills, falling from a height. Devi giggling…

I am hot, so hot. 'Devi,' I call. 'Hey, Devi, are you there? Listen to me. Remember how you loved it when I lifted you up and twirled you around in circles? "Higher, Ma, higher," you would say. "I am a butterfly, a ballerina," you would say, and throw your head back and laugh. "The sky is spinning, there's a whirlwind," you would say. And I would hold you close and kiss your sweet cheek and whisper, "The whirlwind is you."'

It is cold suddenly; do you feel cold, dear Diary? Of course you don't. I think of you as a person, as the wise woman, my friend, my nemesis. In my head, I seem to have interchanged you both; I don't know if I am speaking to the one or the other. I can't seem to get warm, despite pulling the old sari I use as a blanket tight around me. Why is it so cold?

I am so thirsty, my throat parched. I am too tired to reach for the tumbler I know is beside my bed, next to the book. Next to you, dear Diary. Where are you? I scramble about, blindly, too weary to open my eyes. You must be near. I picture your rough edges, your worn binding, your dog-eared pages bearing witness to my story. I root around my too-dry mouth for saliva, swallow. I want to talk to Devi again. 'I love the way you look at things, Devi, did I ever tell you that? You make the world new for me again. I have missed you so. Come back, Devi. We have so much to do yet.'

Why am I asking Devi to come back? Has Devi left? Do you know, dear Diary? Isn't she beside me on the mattress? 'Devi? Where are you? Where have you gone?' I am so tired. I want to sleep, but my eyes feel too heavy, my body too warm and then too cold.

Jalaja, oh Jalaja. Where is Jalaja when I want her? Has she gone to the market? She is taking a long time getting back, chatting as usual I think. She will know where Devi is, why she is not there beside me. I am so tired. My eyelids are weighted down, figures dancing across them. Ghosts from my past pay visits, tell stories. You are one of them, aren't you? What do you see in my future, my friend? Once upon a time I trusted you; I called you wise woman when everyone else termed you mad. You were my beacon, my guiding lamp. I did everything you said. Then how have I arrived at this point, where all I see is darkness? Is the light coming? If so, when, my friend, tell me. Please tell me. What do you see now?

I can hear a dog howling somewhere, mournfully. Why are you so sad, dog? Why do you sound like a funeral dirge? At Manoj's cremation, I did not shed a tear. Everyone pointed, said I was cold. 'I have forfeited that right,' I wanted to shout. 'He doesn't deserve my tears. I am not worthy.' And so I stood, dry-eyed, even though my eyes were stinging and my babies danced within me, though I didn't know then that there were two.

A crow calls, the sound like a sob breaking.

I was blessed with two daughters, twins. Now both are gone from me.

I was blessed with a husband who loved me. And I killed him. I did.

I am boiling. So hot. So hot. I want… I want. Manoj. Manoj? Where are you?

My throat is parched. Too dry. Why? Is there a drought again? Has the well dried up? I do not have the energy to get water from Sumitranna's well. Perhaps Devi will. Devi? Where is she?

❄ ❄ ❄

Dear Diary,

Am I speaking to you? Or to you, Oh, Wise Woman? Manoj, could I dare to hope it is you?

There is a girl. Devi? She sponges me, cool fingers ministering when my head feels too hot. She is real, this girl. Unlike you, whoever you are. The ghost of a feeling. A shadow from my past.

When she is here, I am able to sleep. This girl makes me feel calm, restful, looked after. I do not worry now she is here. Not about the past, the decisions I had to make. She has a soothing aura about her, this girl. Is she an angel?

It is dark but not silent. The hum of machines. The soft murmur of voices. Where am I? It takes such effort to open my eyes; I much prefer to be with you, populate this shadowy world of dreams. The beep beep sound of a monitor. Machines crooning. A tube leading from my body to a gurgling pipette. The girl. Slender. Fair. Vulnerable. Her tall body folded into a chair beside my bed. Fast asleep. Her head dropping sideways, curtain of hair obscuring her face, casting it in dappled shadow. I want to reach out and hold her, let her rest her head on my shoulder, but I cannot move. I am strapped in place. What is it about this girl that arouses the protective instinct in me? Tugs at my heart strings. Makes me want to wrap my arms around her and hold her there forever. Something in the curve of her face, something familiar. Who is she?

Soft words muttering endearments, gentle fingers, smelling of something floral, on my face, wiping away my tears. 'I do not deserve this,' I say. 'I am a horrible woman, a cursed woman, I do not deserve kindness.' I open my eyes, look at that face. The curve of her chin. Those eyes, the colour and texture of warm sunflower oil.

The complexion like burnished sandalwood. Hair the colour of ripe tamarind, cascading down her back in glossy waves. The face I have watched take shape, grow into its contours. The face whose every expression I can predict, I know by heart. So familiar, so desperately loved. She's here. My daughter is here. The only thing marring her perfection is the ridge of bumpy skin above her upper lip. I reach to touch it.

'What's happened there, Devi? When did it happen?' My heart sings with joy. She's here.

'I'm not Devi,' the girl says.

I must not have heard right above the hum of the machines. 'When did you come, Devi?' Every word is a trial. Every blink drags me back into that restful state, blessedly free of pain.

'I'm not Devi,' the voice soft, her eyes gentle. 'I'm Nisha.' The lips curved up in a soft, hesitant smile.

Nisha? 'Am I dreaming?' I don't realise I have spoken aloud until my daughter, *my daughter*, the one I chose to lose, smiles at me. That smile, the miracle of which I had never expected to see. The mouth, whole again. Even pearly white teeth.

'My girl.' I am touching her, unable to believe it. She is perfect. She is here. She has found me. 'I prayed and prayed for you. And here you are. A miracle. An angel. My girl.'

Chapter 28
Nisha

Home

The woman is tiny, barely taking up any room on the bed, lost under a shell of machines, tubes poking out from various parts of her. Threadbare blue sari bunched up around a slip of a body, wispy hair, flesh the colour of coconuts. She is looking at Nisha like she cannot believe her eyes. Nisha watches as the wonder in her eyes overflows, spills down her cheeks, pools under her chin. Her mother lifts one hand to cup her face and with a finger, traces her features—her eyes, her hair, her cheek, the ridged skin above her upper lip. She whispers something, her lips barely moving, her eyelids fluttering. She whispers again, the dust motes beside her mouth fluttering like trapped moths, and Nisha bends down to catch what she is saying.

'I am sorry,' the woman whispers, every word uttered with great effort. 'So sorry. I…' Her mother's gaze settles on her upper lip, the ridged skin marking it. 'It was the hardest thing I had to do in my life.'

Nisha bends down beside her mother, brushes her hair away from her eyes. 'I know,' she says softly, holding her mother's gaze.

'Nisha.' Her name a hymn of longing on her mother's lips.

She cups the scorching face, mapped with busy lines, 'I am here now,' she says.

And holding her mother in her arms, in that hospital room smelling of phenyl and very faintly of urine, mosquitoes buzzing and feasting on flesh, the ceiling fan droning, the breeze wafting in from the open windows, smelling of overripe fruit, Nisha realises she feels whole, like she belongs, that rootless feeling gone. She was loved. She was wanted, so very much. She was longed for and missed. She bends down, pushes her mother's grey hair gently from her eyes and places a soft kiss on her papery cheek and it feels right. She has come home.

Chapter 29
Shilpa

Kaleidoscope

Dearest Manoj,
It is you. Here beside me. Keeping me company. I don't deserve you, Manoj. I wasn't there for you when you needed me the most, and yet, here you are. Beside me.

Nisha. Our daughter. I had to give her away, Manoj. But you know that. You know everything. And despite that, you are here with me. I am lucky. I am blessed.

Isn't she beautiful? Aren't they both? Didn't she turn out well? I did the right thing by her. Though it hurt. It did. It hurt like hell.

I can feel your presence, Manoj. I know you are there. Why can't I see you? Talk to me, Manoj. Please. Talk to me. Do. I'll listen. I'll do anything you ask. This time round I will not let you down. I am so pleased, so honoured you are here. I am.

I want to see her. I cannot get enough of seeing her. Nisha. Our daughter. Her perfect face. So like Devi's.

I want to stay here with you, Manoj. But I want to see her too. Just once more. I want to breathe her in. Lethargy weights down my eyelids, dragging them closed. I won't let them. I won't. Here we go.

Oh. I am alone. The room silent except for the regular beep and hum of the machines keeping tab on me. The bitter tang of medicine, of illness and fear. Has my new-found daughter—Nisha—left already?

The wise woman had not predicted this, any of this. Had she known? Seen it in the future and kept mum? But surely, if she had, she would have told me, not directly perhaps but via prophesy. Perhaps I set too much store by Destiny, like our Devi said countless times. Perhaps I believed too much and shaped my life to concur with the prophesy. Perhaps I would have had Devi and Nisha anyway, wise woman or not, praying at that temple in Manil or not. And perhaps our girls would have been fine if I had stayed with you, Manoj, that terrible evening instead of abandoning you like I did. And perhaps they would have recovered that fateful day even if I hadn't given Nisha away to the convent like the wise woman dictated. But how could I have taken the chance, prophesy or not?

Regrets—they keep me company; hound me here in this strange state I find myself in. So many mistakes. Committed in the name of Destiny, blaming the inevitability of Fate.

Where are our daughters?

I am tired, Manoj, tired to the bone. Everything hurts, despite the medicines, despite the joy of seeing Nisha, meeting with her. And Devi. My feisty girl. How I've missed her. Devi's back from England. And she's pregnant, Manoj. She is. We are going to be grandparents! Is it possible to be too happy, Manoj? Is there such a thing?

Nisha came looking for me, for her sister. She has turned into a fine girl, the scar above her upper lip adding somehow to the air of vulnerability, of fragile beauty. And she has a man who loves her, she tells me. A man she's going to marry. Her face lights up when she speaks of him. The dreams I had for her when I gave her away—they've realised, Manoj. They have. All that pain, the hurt, was worth it. It was.

I hope both our children are blessed with many children. I hope neither of them has to live with the loss of losing a husband, the ache of missing a child, have it grow up without them by its side, have it call someone else 'Ma'.

Emotionally I am rejoicing, Manoj, but physically I am spent. Weary. I ache. Everywhere. Intensely, immensely. My body is giving up on me. Is that why you are here, Manoj? To help me into the next world? I do not deserve it. I do not deserve you.

I cannot keep my eyes open any longer.

Pictures float in front of my closed lids—a kaleidoscope of images. Can you see them? Our daughters being born, first Devi, then a miracle. Another baby. Caramel eyes the exact shade of yours, Manoj. A gash for a mouth. Someone yelling, 'A monster. You've produced a monster.'

Your eyes, Manoj, full of pain. Your laboured whisper, 'Stay with me. Please.'

The wise woman lying under the peepal tree, those constantly moving hands finally at rest. 'Come back, Devi, my friend, come back to me,' I had begged, that jasmine-scented, cerise-tinged evening, shaking my friend, unable to let her go, unequipped to face the future alone.

Jalaja sitting on the veranda beside me, munching on paan, her mouth working busily as she updates me on the latest gossip, her expressive face working overtime.

Devi, my beautiful, beloved Devi, laughing at something, her whole face lighting up with joy, transforming from beautiful to stunning. Devi scraping dregs of the burnt mixture congealing in the kadai on the rare occasions I made biryani off the pan, her face puckered in concentration. Devi putting her little hand in mine and tugging me along, unable to contain her excitement when we visited the sea for the very first time. Waves undulating gently, the expanse of blue and frothy white. Leading her to the edge of the sea so the waves kissed our bare legs, depositing gentle caresses. The awe on her face. The sheer delight. Looking at her and fantasising she was Nisha, that I was doing this with both my girls. 'Ma, look.' The sun a tangerine orb, sliding towards the sea across a rain-splattered sky. Devi bending down and grabbing fistfuls of water, spluttering as the salt assaulted her tongue. The look of utter surprise on her face, replaced by disgust. 'It tastes horrible, Ma; how can something that looks so inviting taste so horrible?' I had thrown my head back and laughed.

And Nisha, my youngest, my miracle, my long-lost girl come to find me. Her soft voice, that delicate neck, that dimpled smile the pleasure of which I never thought I would experience, precious, like bestowing a gift.

Voices, soft, familiar.

Much beloved voices, rising and falling. Fingers on my face, soothing.

'Mum?' A hesitant voice.

And, 'Ma, come back to me.' Petulant. Tearful. Devi.

Oh I am so tired; my eyes do not want to open, they will not do my bidding.

'Mum? It's Nisha.'

I have to see them one more time. I can't not.

'Please, Ma. I want you here for me, for my baby. I miss you, Ma. I need you. My baby needs you.'

Something hot lands on my hands. I battle the urge to ignore it, ignore everything and open my eyes, slowly, fighting against the exquisite pull of weighted eyelids. A face swims into view. Devi. She is clasping my hands and on it her tears fall unchecked.

'I am so sorry. So sorry I was so horrible to you so many times.' My daughter's familiar, much loved voice. The voice I have missed desperately while she's been away.

I try to smile. I try. I do not know if my lips obey. Everything is so hard. 'The book. The diary. It will explain. Read it. Both of you,' I say and a barely audible hoarse whisper is all I can manage. I hope they have heard. 'Please.'

'We have,' I hear from either side of me, in unison. 'We have.'

They learned to talk almost simultaneously. Their first word was, 'Ma.' I would hear one 'Ma' and then another, and they would keep repeating and laugh, and I would think how blessed I was. How blessed.

'I love you, Ma, very much.' Devi says.

'And I… I love you,' an echo in a voice with an English accent.

I am blessed. Right now. To hear their simultaneous declarations of love. I am blessed.

My daughters, both of them, on either side of me, my daughters beside me, holding my hands, anchoring me. I am so lucky to be blessed with such beautiful children, twin miracles. I am so lucky.

And then, in the distance, a bright light, and in the midst of it, you, Manoj. Smiling your gentle smile, beckoning to me. 'Come, Shilpa.'

I can see you, hear you now, Manoj. I didn't before.

'It is time, Shilpa.' Your smile gentle, filled with so much love.

'Have you forgiven me, Manoj?'

'What is there to forgive, Shilpa?' Your face benevolent. 'I would have done the same, for them.' Looking towards your daughters. The pride in your face is reward enough.

'I did not, do not, deserve you, Manoj.'

'I loved you, Shilpa. Still do. Only you. Come to me.'

I want to go. I am ready to go.

I smile at my daughters, both of them. They have each other.

'I love you,' I manage, my voice a laboured whisper. Their faces swim before my eyes. 'I love you both. Look after each other.'

And I come to you, Manoj. I come to you.

Letter from Renita

First of all, I want to say a huge thank you for choosing *The Forgotten Daughter*, I hope you enjoyed reading Nisha, Devi and Shilpa's story just as much as I loved writing it.

If you did enjoy it, I would be forever grateful if you'd **write a review on Amazon**. I'd love to hear what you think, and it can also help other readers discover one of my books for the first time.

Also, if you'd like to **keep up-to-date with all my latest releases**, just sign up here:

www.renitadsilva.com/e-mail-sign-up

Finally, if you liked *The Forgotten Daughter*, I'm sure that you will love my debut novel ***Monsoon Memories*** – you can read an excerpt on the following pages.

Thank you so much for your support – until next time.
Renita.

Monsoon Memories

It was when she was visiting her grandmother on a rain-drenched, gloomy afternoon in September and there was nothing better to do than go over old photographs, musty and yellowed with age, that Reena found it. It was tucked away behind one of the other photos in the album. She would never have discovered it if it hadn't been for Chinnu the cat, who squeezed in through the bars of the open window, landed on the album and then proceeded to shake vigorously to rid herself of the raindrops in her coat. Reena squealed. She had been lying on her stomach, legs bent at the knees, feet swinging merrily in the air, on the cool cement floor. Madhu had warned her repeatedly not to do so. 'You're a city girl and not used to these floors. You'll catch a cold. It will seep straight into your chest from the cement. Then how will you travel back home in the overnight bus, tell me?' Madhu had yelled just that morning when she found Reena sprawled on the naked floor.

Reena smiled as she remembered asking her dad once, when she was little: 'Is Madhu your aunt?' Her dad had picked her up and twirled her around, so her dress bloomed in patterned swirls like a Bharatanatyam dancer's, and, laughing, had said, 'No, darling. She's more like a second mum.'

She had scrunched up her nose, puzzled. 'Another mum?' From up in the air, suspended in her dad's strong arms, his face had looked different, wider somehow.

'She came to stay when your Mai was about to give birth to me, to help with the housework. She's never left. She's part of the family now.'

'Why don't I have a second mum?' Reena had asked and her dad had laughed. She had watched, fascinated, as his face became wider as it got closer, until she was so close she could see the tiny hairs curling just inside his nostrils.

'Your mum's a superwoman, that's why. She says she manages quite well on her own.' Reena had wrapped her arms around her dad's neck, had laid her head in that warm safe space just above his left shoulder and breathed in the familiar smell of his sweat.

'Yes,' she had said, voice muffled, 'she does.'

Reena jumped up and pulled the album out from under Chinnu. That was when she saw something peek out from behind the picture she had been looking at.

Wonder what that is, thought Reena excitedly, imagination in overdrive. *Perhaps something of great value that someone wanted to conceal… What better hiding place than an old, woodlice-ridden album of photographs!*

She had just started reading *Nancy Drew* and wanted so much to be a sleuth like her. She knew her mother hoped she would be a doctor, and her father wanted nothing more than for his only daughter to follow in his footsteps and become a computer programmer. But ever since Reena had laid her hands on the first *Famous Five* book at the age of nine, she had wanted to be a detective. Solving mysteries seemed such fun. And there was a dearth of Indian detectives, which was a shame really considering there was so much crime in India, so many unsolved murders.

She had listened enough to her parents' laments after they watched the news or read the paper. Her mother would shake her head sadly and say to Mrs. Gupta next door, 'Did you hear about the poor woman being attacked and left for dead in her flat for hours? Everything taken, even the dog's bowl it seems.'

'Arre Baap re,' Mrs. Gupta would moan, 'I am sure it was the servants. You have to be very careful, Preeti. They are very sly, these lower-class people. Once they know where you keep your keys, God help you...' One of Mrs. Gupta's hands would be clutching her right breast dramatically, checking to see that the keys she kept tucked inside her bra were safe. Reena was sure Mrs. Gupta was aiming for the 'tragic heroine' look, but with her long pointy nose and evil face, she was anything but.

Murli, Mrs. Gupta's cook and Reena's friend, regaled her with horror stories about crimes that went unchecked in his village. In Murli's version, it was the rich people, the employers, who were the villains.

All this only served to make Reena more determined to be a detective. It would have helped if she had a book starring an Indian detective as a guide. The India she knew didn't have moors, gorse, secret islands and open spaces like the England of the *Famous Five* books, except maybe at her grandmother's house. But the open spaces in Taipur were populated with mud, mosquitoes and snakes. She couldn't find a single book, fiction or otherwise, with an Indian girl, boy or adult detective. She had even braved asking the Scrooge of a librarian at her school, who had looked down her nose at Reena with her ogre-like eyes and pinched-together face and asked, 'Who wants to know?' Reena was a tiny bit ashamed of the fact she had fled. But, she reasoned, detectives needed to keep a low profile. They couldn't afford to blow their cover...

In the beginning she had been all for forming a club like in the *Famous Five* or the *Secret Seven* and had spent ages concocting names and passwords. She had given up when she realised that she had names aplenty but a scarcity of friends or siblings who could be coerced to join. Then she started reading *Nancy Drew* and bingo, she realised that she could go it alone. She spent hours practising her signature in her notebook, adding flourishes and titles. She personally liked 'Reena Diaz, Super Sleuth' best. It had a nice ring to it. She decided she would be the first Indian girl detective. All that remained was to find a mystery. The only problem was that once Reena decided to become a detective, there were no mysteries to be found. No murders or burglaries were reported in the local newspapers or on the TV channels. Even Murli didn't have any more horror stories of unsolved crimes to impart. Her life, Reena was fast coming to the conclusion, was extremely mundane. Nothing thrilling ever happened in it.

And now, thanks to Chinnu, she seemed to have stumbled on something exciting, even if it wasn't the murder she'd been hoping for as her debut case.

Before proceeding any further with the discovery, and wanting to prolong the sense of mystery as much as possible, Reena glanced furtively around her, as she imagined Nancy Drew would. Chinnu was sitting under the wooden bench in the corner cleaning her whiskers busily with her paw.

Her grandmother, Mai, was having her afternoon siesta. She lay on the mat by the front door. Her mouth was open and little snores escaped it from time to time. Her sari was slightly askew, the pink skirt she wore underneath showing. The steady hum of rain relentlessly beating down on the tiles and the steps leading down from the front door served as a familiar lullaby.

Outside, the coconut trees stood out in relief against the blanket of rain which muddied the courtyard that Madhu had diligently swept and tidied just that morning. Dirty little puddles had formed everywhere.

Her parents were out visiting with her father's old school friends. They had tried to get Reena to go but these friends of her dad's did not have any children and nothing could persuade her to venture out into the blinding rain, get wet and muddy only to sit in their house, stare at their walls and listen to her father reminisce about the good old days. Looking at yellowing photographs of people she didn't know to the accompaniment of Mai's snores, while eating hot golibhajis dipped in coconut chutney and sipping cardamom tea was much better.

At least she was dry.

She went to the kitchen, ostensibly to get a tumbler of water, but in reality to check on Madhu. Madhu was sitting beside the hand grinder which she used to pound spices into thick masala for her curries, preferring it to the new electric grinder, which she insisted didn't make a smooth enough paste. Her knees were drawn up, and she was resting her head on them. Strands of grey escaped her bun and obscured her lined face. She was wearing the stained, old apron that she was never without around her sari. She was fast asleep. The kitchen door was wide open and sprawled across the entrance was Gypsy. She was fast asleep as well.

Reena hurried back into the living room. Luck was on her side. Her parents were not due back for a while yet. And it was as if an epidemic of sleep had struck the rest of the household. Even Chinnu was asleep now, lying on her side under the wooden bench, paws stretched out.

Slowly, Reena pulled out whatever it was that was peeking out from beneath the picture she had been looking at—and sighed in disappointment. Just her luck! It wasn't a mystery at all but another black-and-white photograph. It must have slipped behind the other one by mistake. Like the others, this one too was yellowed with age. And, like the others, rot had begun to eat away at it.

She pulled it closer for a better look—and noticed something different. Unlike the other pictures she had spent the afternoon flicking through, this one was creased and worn, as though someone had run their fingers across it many times and then folded it and tucked it away. It was a picture of three children, all of them smiling what were obviously false smiles for the camera. The youngest—the little girl sitting cross-legged on the floor, hair in bunches, flashing dimples—Reena recognised as Aunt Anita, from the countless pictures she had seen of her as a baby and toddler. The boy in the photograph, tummy sticking out, adorable gap-toothed grin, awkward stance, was her father, Deepak, as a child.

It was the other girl in the picture who captured Reena's attention. She was chubby and dark-complexioned. She wore seventies-style churidars and her long thick hair was in pigtails and tied neatly with matching ribbons behind her ears. She had a kind face and an open smile. And she looked very much like Reena herself...

❄ ❄ ❄

Madhu was washing clothes on the little granite stone by the well, in the shade of the tamarind and banana trees. The heavy thud of clothes hitting stone guided Reena there.

Deepak had tried countless times to get Madhu to use the new washing machine he had had installed in the bathroom. But Madhu was having none of it: 'I wash the clothes, rinse them and then scrub them again. Will that square little box do that? I am not using any fancy machines when my hands will do.' Since then, the washing machine had sat forlorn in the bathroom gathering dust and chicken droppings where the hens perched on it when being chased by Gypsy, the gleaming white exterior fading slowly to dull grey.

Reena sat on the cement rim surround of the well and watched Madhu. Her sari was tied up, the pallu tucked tightly into her waist. Her worn apron was wet and hair escaped the confines of her bun and collected in greying tendrils around her face. Every once in a while she used her arm to push it away, leaving wet soapy smudges on her face. She had finished scrubbing the clothes and was wringing the water out of them by rolling them into a tight cylinder and then bashing them very hard against the stone. The bar of Rin soap that she had used lay on the stone beside her, bleeding dark blue water onto the streaky granite surface. Gypsy, who followed Madhu wherever she went, lay curled beside her feet. She looked lost to the world, except for the deep growl that escaped her every once in a while and the little twitch her nose gave when a fly landed on it. *Do dogs dream?* Reena wondered.

Every so often the spicy, scented breeze stirred the tamarind and banana trees, releasing a little flood of raindrops that had adhered to the leaves. The garden in the front courtyard which Madhu diligently tended was in full bloom, and Reena breathed in the sweet honey aroma of the hibiscus and jasmine flowers mixed in with the earthy smell of rain-washed mud. Bees buzzed, butterflies flitted and a fat frog stirred in the grass next to the well. Reena sighed, for just a moment loath to disrupt the peace and stir up old secrets. The moment didn't last long, however.

'Madhu,' she said, 'I've got something to show you.'

Madhu jumped, startled. Gypsy barked. 'Gypsy, shush. Rinu, you gave me a fright. How long have you been sitting there?'

'Not long. I like sitting here, watching you. It's peaceful.'

'What's that?' Madhu rubbed soapy hands down the sides of her apron and extended wet fingers to receive the photograph Reena was holding out to her. Reena watched as she squinted at the picture, as her smile stilled and her face lost colour.

'Where did you find this?' Madhu asked.

'Oh, you know...' said Reena vaguely, deliberately nonchalant, even though her heart was pounding.

Up until now, though she had wanted to find out more about her lookalike, wanted to get to the bottom of the mystery, a part of her had thought that it was all in her head. The adults would pooh-pooh her wild theories as just that. There would be a perfectly simple and straightforward explanation.

Although she'd hoped to have stumbled on something, now, as she looked at the myriad emotions flitting across Madhu's lined face, as her breath came out in long sighs, as the smile fled her face to be replaced by grief, Reena wished she had never found the photograph. She wished it had remained hidden in that old woodlice-ridden album. For the first time, she considered the fact that the girl might be dead. But that didn't make much sense either. Why hide her photographs? Why forget her? In Reena's experience, the dead were revered and remembered all the time, even more than the living, she sometimes thought.

There was a seven-day mass after the funeral, a thirty-day mass, a yearly mass, framed photographs adorned with garlands taking pride of place next to the altar...

Again she found herself asking the same questions. Why the secrecy, the conspiracy of silence?

Madhu used the pallu of her sari to wipe away the tears streaming down her face.

Reena was horrified. She had never seen Madhu cry. She didn't know what to do. Guilt, sharp and painful bound her to her perch on the rim of the well. Try as she might, she couldn't seem to move to comfort Madhu.

The frog hopped away in wet sticky plonks, drawing arches in the air. Gypsy stirred and ambled up to Madhu, licking away the salty tears which kept on coming.

'Shoo, Gypsy,' Madhu murmured, patting the dog's flank. 'I saved it in a safe place, but couldn't remember where I had put it. I looked everywhere, but in the end had to accept it was lost. And now...'

So the photograph had been Madhu's.

Madhu ran her fingers gently over the girl's face, her hair.

And Reena understood why the picture was worn.

'She had lovely hair, thick and long. I used to plait it for her in two long braids, and tie it up behind her ears. She always made sure I used matching ribbons.' Madhu smiled. 'She sat so still while I oiled it and combed it, no matter how knotty it was, no matter how much it hurt. And I talked to her the whole time. She was my favourite, you know. It was a secret—hers and mine.' Madhu's voice broke.

Reena waited until Madhu had composed herself somewhat.

She hated herself for doing so but she had to ask. 'Did she die?'

Madhu blanched. Years of living in a Catholic household had rubbed off on her and she made the sign of the cross, her puffy, red-rimmed eyes sprouting fresh tears. She spoke so softly that Reena had to strain to hear. 'No. Thank God, thank Jesus, no.'

❄ ❄ ❄

Find out the secrets behind the old photograph in *Monsoon Memories.*

OUT NOW.

Praise for Monsoon Memories:

'D'Silva weaves a tale so rich and complex in detail and history that I found it quite impossible to put the book down. The characters really came to life for me and I grew attached and invested in them and what was going to happen. The details are rich, vivid and so well described that I truly felt at times that I was there or at least was hearing the story first hand from the main character... **from start to finish I loved this book and couldn't recommend it more.' 5/5.** *NovelEscapes.com*

'**It mesmerized me** with its poignant narration and heart-warming story and kept me hooked until the last page. 9/10. *ChickLitClub.com*

'**A wonderfully dramatic and poignant debut novel** from Renita D'Silva. I was captivated by the characters and their plight. I was intrigued by what deep secret could have torn the family apart... I simply could not put this book down and although I figured out the secret about half way through, I had to know what would happen and if the family could resolve their issues.' *Momssmallvictories.com*

'**a really moving and poignant story**.' *Novelicious.com*

'Full of gorgeously crafted settings and descriptions, you'll be pulled into this lush novel. Renita paints the most beautiful images with a few, perfectly chosen words. **Monsoon Memories is a book to fall in love with**.' *KimTalksBooks.com*